T0285273

The

WITCHFINDER'S
SERPENT

The Witches of Windsor: *Book 1*

The WITCHFINDER'S SERPENT

RANDE GOODWIN

GREENLEAF
BOOK GROUP PRESS

Published by Greenleaf Book Group Press
Austin, Texas
www.gbgpress.com

Distributed by Greenleaf Book Group

For ordering information or special discounts for bulk purchases, please contact Greenleaf Book Group at PO Box 91869, Austin, TX 78709, 512.891.6100.

Design and composition by Greenleaf Book Group and Mimi Bark
Cover design by Greenleaf Book Group and Mimi Bark
Cover image used under license from ©Shutterstock.com/Superstar

Publisher's Cataloging-in-Publication data is available.

Print ISBN: 979-8-88645-090-3

eBook ISBN: 979-8-88645-091-0

To offset the number of trees consumed in the printing of our books, Greenleaf donates a portion of the proceeds from each printing to the Arbor Day Foundation. Greenleaf Book Group has replaced over 50,000 trees since 2007.

Printed in the United States of America on acid-free paper

23 24 25 26 27 28 29 30   10 9 8 7 6 5 4 3 2 1

First Edition

For my girls:
Beth, Sarah, and Emily

The devil is precise; the marks
of his presence are definite as stone.

—Reverend John Hale, Arthur Miller's *The Crucible*

CONTENTS

THE WITCH OF IPSWICH

Rushmere Heath on the Eastern Outskirts of Ipswich,
Suffolk, England, September 1645

Matthew Hopkins, the well-respected and highly sought-after Witchfinder General, sat atop his horse, making his way slowly toward the gathering of spectators. It was unusually chilly for early September. In addition to the tall capotain hat, with its flat top and narrow brim, he wore his woolen cape to the proceedings—and though he suspected he wouldn't need it much longer, for the time being at least, he was thankful to have brought it along.

Taking a deep breath, he scanned the area, excitedly taking in the view. Open grassland sprawled in all directions, its greenery baked brown by weeks of summer sun. Patches of cheerful pink and purple heather broke through the drab landscape, flouting the onset of autumn. Off in the distance, a platform had been constructed, a heavy, wooden pole erected at its center. It was this structure that filled him with exhilaration—this and the impressive throng of people surrounding it.

They were all here because of him. He was the one to extract the

confession from old Mary Lakeland. No one else had been able to do so—
the crone had proven to be a tough nut to crack.

"Nice job, Hopkins," said Justice John Brandling as he rode past. The
man was one of the judges who had prosecuted the Lakeland case. Bailiff
Richard Pupplet rode alongside him.

Hopkins nodded to each of the men in turn as they hurried on ahead.
Brandling was one of the officials set to preside over the execution—and
no normal execution it would be. Due to the charges to which she had
been found guilty, Mary Lakeland was to be burned at the stake—not
hanged in the manner of most witches. This was a first for Hopkins—of all
the women he had dealt with in East Anglia, no others had been set ablaze
for their crimes.

His success in this case would only bolster his reputation, he knew.
He would be even more highly sought after—and he and his partner,
John Stearne, would be able to charge top rates for their services. Mary
Lakeland had certainly made him work for the confession, however. For
a time, he had wondered if she would outlast him, if she would be the
first subject to endure all his interrogation techniques without breaking.

They had stripped the old woman naked and used a witch-pricker to
hunt for a witch's mark. There had been no confession, even though her
seventy-year-old skin was awash with discolorations and blemishes—any
of which could have been placed there by the devil himself. They had
beaten and starved and deprived her of sleep, to no avail. They had bound
her cross-legged and left her that way for more than a day. Not even the
cramping and discomfort of that experience had broken her. Finally, they
had forced her to march naked, back and forth, hour after hour, until her
strength had waned, and her bare feet had bloodied a path on the hard
stone floor of her cell.

Eventually, she had collapsed. The thin skin of her knees tore as they
struck the rough surface, and her bruised body came to rest in an ungrace-
ful heap at the witch hunter's feet.

"Mother Lakeland," he had said. "You are a stubborn one—are you
finally ready to confess?"

He had taken the low moan, emanating from deep within her throat, as the affirmation he sought.

"Do you admit to being a witch? Did you in fact use witchcraft to murder your own husband?"

He was rewarded with another moan. The old woman's eyelids fluttered weakly in her semiconscious state.

The interrogation continued in this manner—and before long, Mary Lakeland had confessed to each and every one of her sins to the complete satisfaction of Hopkins and the two witnesses he had arranged to have present. In the end, the court had found her guilty, and she had been sentenced to death. It had been the crime of murdering her husband that had escalated the severity of her charges from felony to petty treason, thus warranting the uncommon execution by fire.

And soon, he thought excitedly as he approached the milling crowd on this cool September morning, *old Mother Lakeland, the evil witch of Ipswich, will be burned at the stake.*

The men were hoisting the unconscious woman's body by the time he had arrived, securing it firmly to the stake with heavy chains. Dressed in a simple white gown, Mary Lakeland's wrists and ankles had been bound with rope. A noose had also been tightened about her throat—an indication that she had already been choked into unconsciousness as a gesture of mercy. In all likelihood, the noose, with the aid of the smoke and hot gasses from the pyre, would bring death by suffocation before the worst of the flames reached the woman's flesh.

Bundles of sticks and brush had been piled high around the small platform, intermingled with heavier pieces of dried timber and branches. Hopkins noticed that other items of scrap had been stacked around the base of the construction as well—weathered sections of wooden fencing, fragments of broken furniture, and other flammable objects that had no doubt been added by enthusiastic onlookers.

Shortly, Justice Brandling appeared. After giving a summary of Mary Lakeland's crimes, he signaled for the execution to begin. Four men with torches approached, each one choosing a different cardinal point around the pyre. As one, they touched fire to kindling, and the towering heap of wood began to burn.

In moments, Hopkins could feel heat radiating from the bonfire. The blaze spread far more quickly than the witchfinder had expected, stoked, perhaps, by the cool morning breeze. Mary Lakeland's limp body hung unmoving, partially suspended above it all, the flames dancing about her legs.

Suddenly, her gown caught fire and it, too, began to burn. The glowing hot conflagration traveled swiftly up her body, leaving scorched and blistering skin in its wake. It reached her hair. The long gray locks burst into flame, fluttering loosely about her shoulders.

It was then that Hopkins heard the collective moan from the crowd. He watched in horror as Mary Lakeland's burning head shifted, her now-open eyes widening in terror, a silent scream issuing from her swollen, useless windpipe. Her body began to twitch as she struggled weakly, uselessly against her bonds.

Several members of the crowd turned and fled in that moment, having seen enough. The witch fell still as the flames grew taller, and before long, the smell of cooked flesh permeated the air. Soon, Hopkins decided that he, too, had seen enough. Although the pyre and witch's body would burn for some time, there was no doubt in the witchfinder's mind that Mary Lakeland was dead. His job here was done. It was time for him to move on. The war against witches had only just begun, after all. Other towns were in desperate need of his services. They needed him—and it would be wrong to keep them waiting . . .

Chapter 1

A New Home

Windsor, Connecticut, May 2019

"Where's Aunt Celia off to so early this morning?" asked Nate Watson as he and his brother sat finishing their breakfast. The hum of a vehicle could be heard outside, getting softer by the moment. Partially eaten bowls of Lucky Charms cereal sat on the table before them. It was Marc's morning to make breakfast, and Nate's younger brother knew how to prepare exactly one meal.

"No idea," replied Marc, brushing a strand of unruly hair from his eyes. He smiled and hopped to his feet with far too much energy for a Wednesday morning. Collecting his dishes, he carried them to the sink. "I haven't seen her yet today. I'll wash these dishes after school."

"Sure thing," said Nate. He watched his brother, dressed in Gryffindor pajamas that seemed to be growing shorter by the day, head up the back stairs to get ready for school.

People frequently told Nate how much he looked like his brother. They shared the same shade of light brown hair and blue eyes, traits inherited from their father. Nate had a couple of pounds and inches on his brother, but Marc was catching up fast.

Nate eyed the brown cardboard box that sat on the counter. This morning he brought it up from the basement where it had been sitting since the day he and his brother arrived. It was all that remained of their father's life, and the idea of rummaging through it threatened to unearth emotions that he fought so hard to keep buried. He had to remain strong for his brother's sake—but he didn't want to postpone it any longer. Doing so, he felt, would be insulting to his father's memory. The idea that a man's life could be reduced to the contents of one musty box seemed so unfair.

Kenneth Watson raised his boys alone after the death of his wife, Lynne, who had been struck by a bus just five years after the young couple had married. For the ten years that followed, it was just the three of them. Then last summer, after a long battle with lung cancer, he too died. Nate and his brother found their lives turned upside down. They were passed from home to home for several weeks as family acquaintances pitched in to put roofs over their heads until permanent arrangements could be made. Their father's lawyer arranged the sale of their Upper West Side New York City apartment and all its contents, except for the brothers' clothing and the one medium-size box of items some unknown person had determined to be their dad's most important personal effects.

It was a difficult and sobering period for the two of them. Nate was fourteen, and he was suddenly forced into the role of protector and counselor for his brother, who was two years younger. Nate felt a huge responsibility. They were powerless as they watched their father's health decline, and Nate wasn't sure he had it in him to properly care for Marc.

He wouldn't have to do it alone, fortunately. He remembered that moment in the lawyer's office, nine months ago, when he and Marc first met their Aunt Celia.

"We're going *where?*" Marc asked.

"You're going to live with your father's sister in Connecticut. Her name is . . . Celia," said the lawyer, glancing at a sheet of paper in front of him.

"Your father made his wishes clear in the will. It took me some time to iron out the details."

"But our father never mentioned anyone named Celia—are you sure?" asked Nate.

"Quite sure," he said before lifting the telephone receiver and pressing a button. "It all checks out—Ms. Feldman, please send her in."

"But we've never met her. What if we don't want to go with her?" asked Marc, glancing at his brother.

"I'm sorry," said the lawyer. "It's all been arranged. I'm sure you'll get along just fine."

A well-dressed woman entered the office. She seemed old to Nate—not grandmother old, but older than their father, at least. She wore her blond hair in a tight bun. A pair of glasses with black frames—the kind that came to funny points at the temples like you saw in old TV shows—sat perched on her nose. A large red stone hung suspended from a gold chain around her neck.

"Hello, boys," she said. "You can call me Aunt Celia. Please gather your things. We have a bit of a drive ahead of us."

And that was that. Nate and his brother followed Aunt Celia out of the lawyer's office to the car that was parked out front on East 42nd Street. The car was light blue and old-fashioned. Nate found out later it was a 1957 Chevy Bel Air, which despite its age looked brand-new and was spotless inside. Someone had loaded their suitcases into the car, placing the box of their father's possessions in the front passenger seat.

The boys climbed into the back, and soon they were on their way. As they drove through the city, Nate watched the familiar buildings and landmarks pass by on either side. He felt sad not knowing when (or even if) he would ever see them again. Leaving Manhattan, they passed through the Bronx before entering Interstate 95, heading north. The exciting hustle and bustle of the city behind them, the brothers settled in for the trip ahead.

"Your father cared very much for you two," said Aunt Celia after about an hour of silence. "I'm pleased to be able to offer you a home."

Nate and Marc exchanged glances.

"He, um—he never told us about you," said Nate, unsure of what else to say.

Aunt Celia chuckled in response, an unexpected yet nonthreatening laugh. She said nothing further.

Marc smacked Nate's leg with the back of his hand and discreetly raised both palms in a what-was-*that* gesture.

Nate just shrugged. He wasn't sure what to make of the brief exchange.

A while later, they passed through the city of Hartford. The highway wound past the cluster of office buildings downtown. It may have been the capital of Connecticut, Nate thought, but compared to New York City, it didn't seem like much.

"We're nearly there, boys," said Aunt Celia.

Ten minutes later, they arrived in Windsor, an old New England town on the Connecticut River. Nate gazed out the window as they left the highway. They passed houses of varying ages, shapes, and sizes. Many of them were set far back from the road, nestled in the trees. He was surprised at how spread out everything was and how well tended the lawns were. It occurred to him that he had never seen this much greenery in his life. He also noticed the lack of traffic and noise. It was nothing like the Big Apple. Nate wondered how he would be able to sleep without all the familiar sounds of the city.

They soon pulled up in front of a large, old house that looked to Nate to be at least ten times the size of their apartment in New York. It was three stories tall and made of brick, with a big wraparound porch in front. Aunt Celia got out of the car, turning around to face them as they struggled to take in their new surroundings.

"You boys collect your things and come inside," she said. "I'll show you to your rooms and you can unpack. Dinner is at five o'clock. We'll discuss the rules of the house at that time." Aunt Celia climbed the wide wooden front steps onto the porch and unlocked the massive oak door. She disappeared inside.

"Is it me, or is she strange?" asked Marc, wrinkling his forehead.

"It isn't you."

The brothers hopped out of the car and studied their surroundings in awe. The spacious, neatly manicured lawn stretched from the driveway, past the front of the house, and around the far side. Colorful flower beds surrounded the porch, its overhanging roof set atop thick, round, white pillars.

"This place is gigantic!" said Marc, eyes wide.

Nate nodded. *It sure is*, he thought.

They gathered their suitcases from the trunk and headed for the house. As they mounted the steps, Nate realized they had left his father's box in the car. Setting his suitcase on the porch, he turned to his brother.

"Hey, you go on ahead," he said. "I forgot the box—I'll get it and be right in."

"OK," said Marc, grabbing Nate's suitcase with his free hand. "I'm going to take this with me so you aren't tempted to run off and leave me here." He smiled.

"That would never happen," said Nate, mussing his brother's hair with one hand. He watched for a moment as Marc went inside the house.

Nate got the box from the front passenger seat and headed back toward the house. This time, he saw an African American boy sitting on the steps. He hadn't been there before. The newcomer wore a simple button-down shirt and gray trousers that Nate assumed to be work clothes. They were a bit worn and stained in places.

"Hello, I'm Nate," he said.

"Oh—hi, the name's Noah," the boy replied, a smile brightened his face. "You must be Ms. Watson's nephew. Welcome to the neighborhood."

"Thanks," said Nate. "You know my aunt?"

"Sometimes I run errands for her," Noah told him. "I live nearby."

"Sweet. Hey, it was nice to meet you. I've gotta run—suitcases don't unpack themselves." Nate hefted the box, grinning. "See you at school?"

"Um, no, actually—I'm, uh, homeschooled."

"Ah," said Nate. Turning, he climbed the steps. "I'll talk to you later, then—" Glancing back, he was startled to see that the boy was no longer there. He quickly scanned the surroundings, but Noah was nowhere to be found.

Strange, he thought.

A little thrown by the encounter, he pushed opened the door and found himself inside a large foyer. His brother sat on the steps of a grand staircase that stretched up toward the second floor, the two suitcases resting on the floor beside him. Intricate oak woodwork stained a dark brown stretched in all directions—from the baseboards to the crown molding. The ceilings were made of suspended canvas, painted an off-white. Intricate sliding doors that retracted into the walls separated the foyer from an immense living room. Through the partially opened doors he saw large windows, bordered on top by panes of stained glass.

The doors opened wider, and Aunt Celia stepped into the foyer.

"There you are," she said. "Please follow me. You boys will have the third floor to yourselves." She led them up the stairs to the second floor and down a long hallway. They passed several rooms along the way, most with fireplaces. A second, smaller staircase led down to another part of the house. At the end of the hall was a staircase leading to the third floor. This one was narrower than the others, and much steeper. They followed Aunt Celia up the stairs, which creaked in certain places. At the top was a small landing with doors to the left and right.

"Do you live here alone?" asked Nate.

"Not anymore," replied Aunt Celia, with a warm, cheerful smile. Other than the brief, odd conversation in the car, it was the first time he noticed a break in her severe demeanor. "You boys may use this level as you like."

They examined their surroundings. The door on the left opened into a large bedroom with a hardwood floor, furnished with several pieces of sturdy but well-worn furniture: a double bed, a chest of drawers, and a table with two upholstered chairs on either side. The room was much larger than the one they shared in New York. Opening a door on the far wall revealed a walk-in closet that branched off to the left. Hooks for hanging clothing sprouted from the walls at regular intervals. Entering the closet,

Nate was surprised to find that it was more of a passageway. At the far end was another door that opened into a small bathroom with old-fashioned fixtures. A pedestal sink stood beside a porcelain tub that rested on legs with clawed animal-like feet.

"There's only the one bathroom," said Aunt Celia, following along behind them. "You boys will have to share."

"Not a problem," said Marc. "We've shared much smaller spaces."

"Shall I show you the rest?" asked Aunt Celia.

"There's more?" asked Nate.

Aunt Celia laughed. She led them back to the landing at the top of the stairs and opened the door opposite the bedroom.

They found themselves in an enormous clutter-free attic. Bare wooden rafters stretched inward on all sides until they met at a point a dozen feet above their heads. If Nate thought the bedroom was large, this area was *gargantuan*.

A door stood open along one wall. The small room beyond was paneled in oak with a window that faced the street. A twin bed rested against one wall opposite a small dresser and writing desk.

"Now we're talking," said Marc, with a grin. "This one's mine!"

Aunt Celia laughed again. It was an infectious, heartwarming laugh that made Nate smile. *Maybe things are going to be all right after all,* he thought, feeling himself relax for the first time in what seemed ages.

"Be careful if you explore the widow's walk," said Aunt Celia, pointing to a hatch in the high attic ceiling. In the center of the large space a flight of stairs led to a hatchway, allowing access to the roof.

"The widow's walk?" asked Nate.

"It's a railed area at the top of the roof," Aunt Celia explained. "It was a common feature in early New England houses. It was said to be used by the wives of mariners to watch for the return of their husbands' ships. Sadly, sometimes their ships would never return."

"Huh," said Marc, a horrified look on his face.

That was their introduction to Aunt Celia and their new home.

That evening at precisely five, they met in the formal dining room. Though it was still light outside, the room was lined with lit candles that gave it an otherworldly atmosphere.

"I've prepared a special welcome dinner for our first meal together," said Aunt Celia, as the boys made themselves comfortable at one end of the table where fancy place settings were laid out. The table was large enough to seat twelve. Aunt Celia's chair was at the head of the table between the two boys.

Their aunt served them a meal unlike any they had previously experienced. From soup to nuts—literally—they were presented with all sorts of delicious foods. Nate couldn't believe how much of it there was. Their aunt left the table in between each course to retrieve new trays and platters from the kitchen. For starters, they ate rolls with butter, French onion soup topped with gooey melted cheese, and a Caesar salad. The main courses came next, and there were three of them: mouthwatering prime rib with a garlic herb crust and baked potatoes, chicken cordon bleu in a buttery cream sauce with asparagus tips, and lasagna.

"Did you make all this yourself?" Nate asked around a mouthful of potato.

"Yes, more or less," she replied.

"Why so much food?" asked Marc, stabbing a piece of prime rib with his fork. "I mean—I'm not complaining."

"I wasn't sure what you boys liked. And there's nothing wrong with leftovers."

"Especially leftovers like these," said Nate, enthusiastically.

After the main courses, Aunt Celia produced a cheese platter with several varieties of crackers, candied nuts, and strawberries. Finally, for dessert they were served a rich black forest cake with vanilla ice cream and two types of fruit pies, apple and blueberry. Marc and Nate tried some of everything but finished nothing, and by the time they were done eating, Nate wasn't sure he would be able to walk.

"I'm glad you enjoyed the meal," said Aunt Celia. "And now, let's get down to business—the house rules." She stood, glancing at each of them. Her seriousness had returned.

This ominous topic had concerned Nate since his aunt first mentioned it upon their arrival, so he was surprised when the house rules amounted to them having unlimited freedom. As long as they picked up after themselves, completed a couple of minor weekly chores, and performed well at school, Aunt Celia told them, they had free run of the house and could come and go as they pleased.

With one exception.

"On the second floor," she said, "there's a single room that shall remain locked at all times. Under no circumstances shall that room be entered. *Under no circumstances.* Do you understand?"

The brothers exchanged a quick glance. "Understood," they replied in unison.

They spent the next several weeks adjusting to their new home. When not at school, they spent much of their time on the third floor of the house. They got comfortable around Aunt Celia as well. She made dinner for them each night, although nothing as elaborate as their first meal together. They would sit together at the dining room table at suppertime and share the day's events. Although Aunt Celia never went into much detail as to how she spent her free time, it was clear that she didn't hold a job outside of the home. Nate assumed she spent her days taking care of the house and preparing their next delicious evening meal. Although she still remained very much a mystery, she was kind to them and saw to all their basic needs. Often, he wondered why their father had never introduced—or even mentioned—her while he and Marc were growing up, but he hadn't yet found the right opportunity to ask her.

They explored the house from top to bottom. They discovered four and a half bathrooms and eight or nine bedrooms, each one decorated in intricate woodwork, wallpaper, and rugs. Eclectic antique furniture tastefully filled each room, and fireplaces with finely detailed mantlepieces were spread throughout. According to Aunt Celia, the house was well over a hundred years old, but even so, it appeared very well maintained.

It didn't take them long to find the door Aunt Celia warned them about—it was the only locked door in the entire house. It was also the only door that was retrofitted with a modern lock. Most of the doors in the house had old-fashioned locks with a keyhole that could be peered through and an old-style key—the kind consisting of a circular shaft with a handle on one end and a bit for turning tumblers on the other.

The brothers imagined various usages for the room, and it became a running joke between them.

"It's a torture chamber," offered Marc on one occasion. "She brings unsuspecting children there and feeds them lollipops as she cuts off their toes."

"No, it's a bank vault containing the sacks of money and jewelry she collected during her career as a cat burglar," said Nate.

"You're probably right," laughed Marc. "How else could she afford to live in a place like this?"

The boys passed by the forbidden room regularly, and it never ceased to pique their curiosity. *What was Aunt Celia hiding behind the locked door on the second floor*, Nate asked himself, *and why was she so intent on keeping it a secret? Was it something embarrassing? Something valuable? Something dangerous?* Nate wondered if he would ever find out.

Nate removed a knife from the kitchen utensil drawer and sliced through the tape that held his father's box closed. He glanced at his watch. It was later than he thought—Marc would be ready soon, and they would have to head off to school. Lifting the flaps, he found a framed photograph sitting on top. It was his parents' wedding photo, which had hung on the wall of the apartment living room. The photo showed an attractive couple on what had been one of the most joyous days of their lives. Nate felt a twinge of sadness knowing that he would never see either one of them again.

The next item he pulled from the box was an old photo album he didn't recognize. *Dad must have kept it buried somewhere in his old bedroom*, Nate thought. He sat down and began flipping through the pages. The photos were all from his father's early years. There were photos of him as a toddler with Nate's grandparents—he recognized them from other pictures he had seen over the years. Birthdays, Christmases, and other family events were all documented. The final photos in the book were of his father, wearing cap and gown at his high school graduation. Why hadn't he ever shared the album with them?

He flipped back to a page near the beginning of the book, where there was a photo of a cake with the inscription "Happy Birthday Kenny!" Five candles were clustered together along one edge. The next photo showed a very young version of his father attempting to blow out those candles, a cone-shaped party hat perched on his head. In each photograph his smile was bigger than in the last.

Nate's eyes were drawn to a particular photograph from that day. His father stood in profile as a woman knelt to face him, a small, wrapped present in her hands. The woman looked oddly familiar. *No—it couldn't be*, thought Nate.

His five-year-old father stood face-to-face with their Aunt Celia—and the Aunt Celia in the old photo looked no different than the Aunt Celia of today. But that was impossible, Nate told himself. It *had* to be someone else—a close relative perhaps?

The woman had long blond hair and wore a pair of glasses remarkably similar to those worn by Aunt Celia. She also wore a necklace resembling the one that always hung from his aunt's neck. The woman could have been her twin. He wondered if there were any other photos of her in the book. He began flipping through the album, this time closely examining each photograph.

Before Nate could get past the first few pages, he heard his brother moving hurriedly down the back stairs. He burst into the kitchen fully dressed and holding something in his hand.

"Look what I found!" he said, a mischievous grin on his face.

Nate knew that look—his brother had been up to something.

"What is it?" asked Nate, closing the album, his concentration broken.

"I found the key—to Aunt Celia's sex palace!" said Marc, laughing, holding the key between two fingers.

Nate chuckled, but something told him to be cautious.

"It was hanging on a hook behind the door in her bedroom," said Marc.

"You searched her bedroom?" asked Nate. "And the key was just hanging there out in the open?"

"Yeah, it's almost like she *wanted* us to find it," said Marc.

Nate rolled his eyes.

"You know the locked room is off limits—go put that back before you get us in trouble."

Just then they heard Aunt Celia's car pull into the driveway.

Marc's eyes widened. Suddenly panicked, he turned and ran out of the kitchen and up the back stairs.

Nate quickly reopened the album, pretending to study it. He did his best to look innocent as his aunt stepped through the back door, a bag of groceries in her arms. With a widening smile, he glanced at her.

"Good morning, Aunt Celia," he said.

Chapter 2

THE INDICTMENT

Windsor, Colony of Connecticut, May 1647

This is it, thought Alse Young as she stood before the town assembly, her arm held firmly in the constable's grip. The meetinghouse was overcrowded and unusually stuffy on this warm spring afternoon. The rows of hard wooden benches were at capacity. Everyone came to see her accused: the settlement's leaders and business owners, former friends, and family. Even Reverend Thomas Hooker, founder of the Connecticut Colony, traveled from nearby Hartford to preside over the arraignment of America's first witch.

A wave of nausea flowed through Alse's body as Reverend Hooker stepped forward to announce the committee's ruling. His voice carried through the chamber, the silent crowd hanging intently upon his every word: "Alse Young, through the power of this committee, you are hereby indicted and at the earliest opportunity shall stand trial in Hartford for the crimes of murder and the practicing of witchcraft!"

A flurry of gasps and mumbled voices spread through the gathering, putting an end to any sense of order. Alse's vision blurred, and for a moment, she thought she might faint. Only the hand clamped tightly on her arm prevented her from tumbling to the floor. Even though she foresaw this ruling, she found herself utterly unprepared for the feeling of hopelessness washing over her.

She felt a hand lock down upon her free arm, and before she knew it, she was being yanked down the center aisle toward the exit, rows of agitated onlookers staring and jeering at her from either side.

"Witch!" cried a voice.

"God help us all!" cried another.

As the constable and his assistant dragged her to the door, her eyes locked upon the newcomer, Malleus Hodge. A vocal proponent of her indictment, he was a man she had come to despise. He stood leaning against the rear wall, staring back at her from beneath his tall, brimmed hat, an ugly smirk plastered across his face.

Her captors pushed her out the door and onto the village green. The sun shone brightly in the afternoon sky as they led her toward the tiny shack that served as her prison over the last several days. It sat where a section of the settlement's stockade once stood, the tall wooden fence that once surrounded the Windsor Green to protect the settlement against attacks from native Indians. It had long since been taken down, and though the town had expanded beyond the once fenced-in area since its founding fourteen years earlier, it remained the center of life, commerce, and worship for the New England town.

Reaching the shack, her captors yanked open the single door and tossed Alse to the ground inside, slamming it shut behind her. She pulled herself to a seated position against one wall, her tattered and filthy dress tearing even more than it already was. She listened as their voices faded away, and she knew she was once again alone—both in her prison and in the world.

Except that wasn't quite true—she thought of her daughter, Allie, quite possibly the only person left who hadn't abandoned her. At eight years old, Allie was blond like her mother, smart and funny, caring and curious. Alse named her after herself, in the family tradition. Her daughter was the only light that shone through her sadness and despair.

Her daughter would miss her when she was gone, Alse thought. She hoped she would be well cared for. That was the one thing that concerned her—her daughter's safety and happiness. She did not doubt that her own days were limited. The court in Hartford would convict her, and she would be hanged. She *had* confessed, after all—confessed to every charge they had weighed against her. They had really given her no choice.

The afternoon slowly turned to night, leaving her cell in ever-deepening darkness, the only light coming in through the cracks between the shack's rough planks. Alse didn't mind the darkness. It meant that her captors wouldn't be back to harass her for several hours. The same cracks that let in light during the day also brought in the chill at night, and she felt a cool breeze hit her, raising goosebumps and stirring up the dank air enough to carry the stench of the bucket to her nostrils. The bucket was the only thing they had given her to relieve herself in, and it was emptied far too infrequently.

Her hopelessness made Alse think of the time she moved from the Massachusetts Bay Colony to Windsor with her husband, John Young, and Allie, then two. Their prospects for a long and happy life seemed endless. The newer settlement had plenty of land for farming and many of the townsfolk were familiar to her, having relocated from the Bay Colony themselves.

She and John purchased a small cottage on Backer Row, just to the north of the green. The house was big enough for the three of them, with just enough room out back for a vegetable garden and a barn to house their horse and a single milking cow.

Those early years were difficult but fulfilling for Alse and John. John worked the land and performed carpentry jobs to make enough money to support them. Alse cared for Allie and tended to their modest house as the community continued to expand and tame the surrounding Connecticut wilderness.

In Windsor, as elsewhere in New England, life focused heavily on the church. Attending services on the Sabbath was expected, and each member of the community was required to demonstrate true devotion and reverence to the Lord. Those who didn't follow God's path were considered servants of the devil or under the influence of demons, witches, or other evil forces.

Alse had always considered herself a good, godly human being, and she did her best to fit in and live life following the guidelines of her congregation and community. But as time went by, she found herself feeling impatient with the strict rules, especially having to dress in such drab clothing. Hadn't they left that behind in Massachusetts Bay?

She also found herself drifting away from John. Now, sitting in her dark cell, she realized that that was perhaps the beginning of her demise. While she never openly defied her husband and was courteous and compliant in public, she didn't always agree with him or abide by his wishes as a good Puritan wife was expected to do. She spent whatever free time she had with her daughter. Whenever possible, she would take Allie for walks in the wilderness, introducing her to the various woodland creatures, collecting herbs and other edibles, and sharing her love of nature.

"Alse, you know it's not safe!" John once said to her. "Our relationship with the savages is uneasy, not to mention the wolves and bears that live in these woods."

"John, what I know is that you worry too much," she replied. "I can safely be in the forest for short periods of time. I don't stray from the well-worn paths or remain after dark. Besides, all the natives I've met have been helpful and kind." John stomped off in frustration.

Other members of the community were aware of Alse's journeys away from the settlement. They came to appreciate her skills in mixing tonics and salves from the ingredients she collected and rely upon her healing abilities. They called on her when their children fell ill or when Jane Fyler, the town's midwife, needed assistance with a delivery. The neighborhood children would run to her upon sight for a quick hug, frequently to be rewarded with a sweet from her basket. All of Windsor loved Alse Young—or so she thought.

How quickly things would change . . .

The previous winter had been a rough one in the village—extremely rough. A great fever passed through Windsor and left many casualties in its wake. Try as she might to aid the sick, Alse's herbal remedies did little to heal or comfort them. Her own family survived unscathed, but many others lost loved ones, most of them children. Once the fever left the community, neighbors consoled neighbors, helping where they could. The congregation prayed together for their loved ones to ensure them a safe journey into God's kingdom. As soon as the ground began to soften, the bodies would be laid permanently to rest in the earth. In the meantime, the men of Windsor gently placed their loved ones for safekeeping in the very same shack on the green in which Alse now found herself imprisoned.

The horrors of winter were soon overshadowed by the horrors of spring.

It began slowly at first—a question here, a comment there.

"Why would God punish us in this manner?"

"This was not God's doing."

"There are those among us who never succumbed to the fever."

"Has evil entered into our midst?"

The gossip and accusations gathered momentum, growing as the village desperately sought answers where none existed—and Alse became their target.

To their thinking, Alse's nature walks became dark rendezvous with the forces of evil. Her herbal remedies were poisons with which she brought death. She spared her own family while bringing illness and destruction to the innocent. Clearly Satan had waged war on their town, and Alse was his commander-in-chief.

And that was how she ended up here, shivering and unable to sleep.

But why had they focused their attention on her? Had she angered someone? Could they really believe her responsible for the death of the settlement's children? Even John abandoned her as the paranoia and hysteria gained a life of its own. Did he believe the rumors? Had he tired of her and her independent ways? It was more likely, she felt, that John and some of the other townsfolk distanced themselves from her in an attempt at self-preservation. Showing sympathy for an accused witch would cast suspicion on them as well.

And then there was the newcomer, Malleus Hodge. He was pleasant at first, dropping by their house and introducing himself to her small family. He even gave Allie a doll he brought from England. It had been intended for the child of a business partner, but upon arrival in America, he discovered the child had died during the harsh winter. As soon as the man left, Allie expressed dislike for him. Alse was surprised but hadn't thought much of it. Over time, Goodman Hodge's attitude toward her changed, and he became one of the most vocal proponents for her indictment. Had he merely been influenced by the village gossip? Or had he, for some unknown reason, helped stoke the flames of suspicion and hatred toward her?

As she sat staring into the darkness, she pictured the man in her mind—the fancy, well-made clothing he wore, the long greasy brown hair that hung from beneath his hat, the disconcerting, self-satisfied, and ever-present grin on his face. What made him hate her so?

The frustration and anger Alse felt toward the newcomer evolved into a hopeless sadness. She closed her eyes, allowing herself a moment to grieve the loss of the life she held dear. In that moment she longed for companionship, for a distraction from her dreadful predicament, however brief. With all her energy, Alse prayed for a momentary reprieve.

A flutter against her cheek broke her concentration. She opened her eyes to see a lone firefly. Its greenish light flashed on and off as it floated silently in front of her. She raised her palm and smiled as it settled in her hand.

"Hello, my friend," she said. The fireflies were out early this year.

She looked up to see another fly toward her through a gap in the shed's wall. And then another. In moments, the room was aglow with dozens of shimmering insects. Their abdomens twinkled in shades of yellow, orange, and green, illuminating the small shed in bright, wondrous color.

Alse leaned back in amazement, awed by the sight. Her plea for company had been answered. She sat mesmerized by the playful dance of the fireflies until her eyelids grew heavy, and at last, she fell deeply asleep.

When she woke, the insects were gone, replaced by morning sunshine and the dread of things to come. Rubbing sleep from her eyes, she got to her feet and peered through a crack in the door, watching as the town came alive. Men, dressed in jerkins and knee-length breeches, chopped wood and fed their horses, readying themselves for the day ahead. Women and children soon appeared. The women wore long skirts in subdued colors, their hair tucked neatly beneath close-fitting coifs. The children ran and played in the grass as their mothers chatted in groups.

Soon, a group of men came through the meetinghouse doors, heading in her direction. It was the constable, along with Reverend Hooker and several other men she recognized, including the newcomer, Hodge. Sliding her hand across the wood of the door, she adjusted her position to get a better view. Pain blossomed across her palm, and Alse realized she cut it on a protruding nail. She lifted the jagged cut to her mouth to stanch the blood.

The men reached the door and, unlocking it, threw it wide.

"Alse Young, it's time," said Reverend Hooker as the men led her outside. The townsfolk paused their activities to watch as the constable tied her hands behind her back with a rough cord. A crowd gathered. Alse looked at the villagers, hoping to catch one last sight of her daughter, but Allie was nowhere to be seen. She had done so much for these people—and she had harmed no one, even though they had forced her to confess. Why couldn't they see that? With a heavy heart, Alse turned her back to the community she had been part of and, surrounded by her escort, started off in the direction of the river and the boat that waited to take her to Hartford.

Chapter 3

ANGRY DUCKS

Windsor, Connecticut, May 2019

"Are you going to the Shad Derby Festival this weekend?" asked Jennifer Quigley as she secured her bicycle to the old rack with a locking cable. Freeing her backpack from the bike's rear cargo area, she hiked it over one shoulder and turned to face her friend, Zach, who was fiddling with his own bike and chain. The large brick structure of Windsor High School stood in the background. A quick glance at her watch confirmed that they had arrived early for school.

"I wouldn't miss it," Zach replied, standing upright and securing his shoulder-length black hair behind his head with an elastic hair tie. He wore a small hoop earring in his left ear and a polo shirt embroidered with the red, black, blue, and white Mohegan tribal symbol, a nod to his ancestry. "Although I heard Courtney was selected as Shad Derby queen—she'll be more insufferable than ever."

"She's not so bad," said Jenn. She adjusted her glasses and tucked a strand of dark brown curls behind an ear.

"To you maybe," said Zach. "But that's because you help her with her homework—which is amazing since she's two grades ahead of us. I don't know how you manage that."

Jenn shrugged. Unlike the popular Courtney, she and Zach were self-proclaimed nerds who had been best friends since kindergarten. Jenn had always been a quick study at school, and everyone knew it.

"Speak of the devil and she doth appear," he continued, giving a sideways glance.

"Doth?" said Jenn, amused by Zach's use of the archaic word. Following his gaze, she saw Courtney Stevens and her two underlings, Katsumi Tanaka and Kamala Singh, heading in their direction. All three girls wore ponytails with matching pink scrunchies. They were virtually identical in height and posture. There was no question however, as to which one was in charge. Courtney gesticulated dramatically to the others as they chatted, her blond ponytail bobbing this way and that. Kat and Kam listened intently to her every word, speaking rarely and only when spoken to.

"I'll show you. Watch this," Zach whispered as Courtney came near. "Hi Courtney, congrats on y—"

"Hi Jenn," she said and walked on past as if Zach were invisible, her two dark-haired followers trailing close behind.

"Yeah? You see?" said Zach with a smirk.

Jenn smiled. Maybe Zach had a point. Courtney could be condescending and dismissive at times.

"Being nice is optional when you're fabulous," said Zach.

Jenn preferred to avoid the politics of popularity—and she succeeded for the most part, due to her academic reputation and her willingness to tutor anyone in need. Zach had nothing similar to elevate him past nerd status in Courtney's eyes, a fact over which he lost little sleep.

Jenn glanced around at the assembling students. Groups of various sizes were forming: the freshmen, awkward and uneasy, and the seniors with their more confident swagger, the rugged, outgoing jocks, and the quirky, more reserved video gamers, the popular kids, and those who were ignored. Somehow, they all formed a singular functioning society. But with no rule book, each student was on their own to figure out how to best fit in. It was a challenging endeavor that sometimes felt like survival of the fittest—a juvenile *Game of Thrones*.

"Whoa, that's not good," said Zach suddenly, glancing over her shoulder.

Turning her head, Jenn gazed across the schoolyard to see a trio of familiar figures standing menacingly over a fourth. Her heart began to race. The three tough guys laughed as the heavyset kid before them struggled to pick himself up off the ground. She recognized the boy—and there was no way this was going to end well for him.

"Douglas is in trouble," said Zach. "Poor kid's a bully magnet."

Douglas didn't stand a chance against one of them, let alone three. Shy and overweight, the boy was frequently picked on. Jenn scanned the crowd of students, quickly determining that no one else was likely to go to his aid. She had to do something, and she had to do it now—but what? She doubted reasoning with them would do the trick. Still, she had to try. More afraid than she cared to admit, she shrugged off her book-laden backpack, dropping it to the ground. Taking a deep breath, she headed with determined steps toward the bullies and their struggling victim.

Zach followed closely behind.

The high school and the middle school were a ten-minute walk from Aunt Celia's house. The schools were visible from one another, each set back from the single road that ran between them. Nate walked his brother to the front doors of the middle school—a practice that started when they first arrived in town. Initially, it was meant to comfort Marc, who had been nervous about starting at a new school. Now it was more habit than anything, but Nate felt comfortable knowing his brother was safely delivered to the building without incident.

After his aunt's reappearance that morning, Marc successfully and discreetly returned the pilfered key to her bedroom. Nate chose that moment to ask her about the photographs in his father's album.

"Oh, that's my Aunt Lacie," she said. Without missing a beat, Aunt Celia explained that her doppelganger—the woman with whom she shared the resemblance—was a distant relative.

"She looks just like you," said Nate.

"Amazing, isn't it? We were very close at one time. I got glasses to match the ones she wore. She left the necklace to me when she died." Aunt Celia clutched the pendant as she spoke. "I never take it off."

The explanation satisfied Nate. *Of course it wasn't Aunt Celia in the photo,* he thought as he crossed the lawn between the road and the high school.

He soon became aware of the commotion taking place in his path. He was too far away to make out faces—but he didn't have to. It would surely be the two Jones brothers and their friend causing trouble again. So far, Nate had stayed off their radar. He remembered when Zach and Jenn first pointed them out. Zach called them the Ducks—a ridiculous nickname, but it was one they apparently came up with themselves.

"The Ducks?" Nate asked.

"Yeah, that's what everyone calls them—stay away from them. They're trouble."

"Why do they call them Ducks?"

"Well, the two goons are named Huey and Louie," continued Zach. "And the big, mean one's name is—"

"You can't be serious . . . Dewey?" guessed Nate.

"Nope, it's Donald," said Zach. "He's Huey's brother, and he's the worst—a true nightmare."

As Nate got closer, a group of spectators began forming a circle around the bullies and their latest victim. A girl with long, dark curly hair approached—it was Jenn. She removed her glasses, slipping them into the pocket of her jeans. Nate's heart sank as she stepped into the fray to get the bullies' attention.

She's gonna get herself killed, he thought.

"Leave him alone," Jenn cried, as the boy was again shoved to the ground. Nate recognized Douglas Ramirez, the heavy, quiet kid with braces who usually kept to himself.

"Get lost. You're embarrassing yourself," Donald said to her. He was the biggest, the obvious instigator. He pointed a dirty fingernail at her as he spoke. The shoelaces of his worn sneakers, as usual, were untied.

"I swear, if you lay another finger on him . . ." she began.

"And your gonna do what?" he replied, roughly grabbing her arm and twisting it behind her back, his greasy forehead glistening in the morning sun. With a forceful shove, he threw her to the ground beside Douglas.

Nate wasn't a fighter, but adrenaline and concern for his friend got the better of him. With a running start, he rushed into their midst, plowing into Donald at full speed.

It was like running face first into a wall.

Taken unaware, the bully gasped as the breath was knocked out of him. He fell backward ungracefully, landing on his rear end, his momentum sending his legs sprawling over his head. Adding to the indignity, one grungy shoe came off and sailed into the crowd of onlookers behind him.

Instantly, Nate regretted his decision. The side of his face and his shoulder ached—and he knew that the worst was yet to come.

A cheer went through the assembled mob. Donald's companions wore shocked expressions. The muscular, better-groomed pair stared at Donald for a moment before rushing to their leader's side. They tried to help Donald to his feet, but they were batted away by Donald's angry fists.

"The bigger they are . . ." whispered Zach, suddenly beside Nate. He reached a hand down to Jenn, pulling her to her feet.

The cheers died quickly as Donald pushed himself up off the ground. His face was red, his hair disheveled.

"Who the *hell* are *you*?" he spat out, with venom.

"Nate . . . er—Nate Watson," he replied nervously. *And why did I just tell him that?*

"Well, Nate Watson," said Donald, approaching quickly and standing closely enough for Nate to smell his sour breath. "You're going to regret what you just did. From *this* moment on, consider me your *biggest nightmare*." Donald pulled back a meaty fist and jammed it into Nate's stomach. Nate dropped to his knees, struggling for breath. He felt like he had been hit by a truck. Several of the onlookers booed. Others watched intently, waiting to see what happened next.

To the crowd's disappointment, the school bell chose that moment to ring. With a collective moan, the students scurried like ants toward the now-open building.

"Consider yourself lucky, asshole," Donald continued. "This isn't the end of this."

Donald then turned to Huey and Louie. "Find my shoe," he muttered under his breath. Without speaking another word, Donald turned and headed toward the building, as swiftly as his uneven gait allowed.

Fighting back nausea, Nate watched him go.

"Dude, that was *epic*!" cried Zach. "No one's ever hit Donald without ending up in the hos—"

"*Zach*," said Jenn, silencing him with a look.

Nate, feeling slightly better, rose slowly to his feet.

"Have you met Douglas?" asked Zach.

"Douglas," said the boy, reaching out a hand. "Thanks—I owe you one. You too, Jenn."

"You're welcome," said Nate, accepting the handshake.

At that moment, a second bell rang. Nate looked toward the school to see the last of the students filing into the building. If they didn't hurry, they would be late.

"Guys, we better get inside," he said.

As they moved toward the doors, Nate saw something in Zach's hand.

"Hey, what's that?" he asked.

"It's nothing," said Zach with a mischievous grin. "Some poor fool lost a shoe." He tossed it into a bush.

Nate smiled, shaking his head. He was relieved that for now at least, the confrontation was over. He surprised himself by his actions. His fear for Jenn had overridden his sense of self-preservation. He was glad he had been there to help. Aches and pains aside, he felt pretty good—until he remembered he just made an enemy, quite possibly the worst one he had ever had.

"Good morning, class," said Mr. Foster. "Who can tell me the name of the first permanent British settlement in America?"

Jenn loved her history period—in large part because Mr. Foster was one of her favorite teachers. He was younger than a lot of the other faculty members, with short brown hair and a neatly trimmed beard. She would be lying to herself if she didn't admit to having a bit of a crush on him.

Another reason she enjoyed history class was because she shared it with both Zach and Nate. Douglas was also in the class, and today he sat with them rather than taking his customary seat in the back.

The morning's altercation was still fresh in her mind—she had never seen anyone get the better of Donald Jones. The expression on his brother Huey's face had been priceless. Louis Bellamy, whom everyone called Louie, was the third member of their group. He was probably the smartest of the three, but for whatever reason, he always took a back seat to the other two. Why he would want to hang out with the Jones brothers, she couldn't guess.

"Anyone?" asked Mr. Foster again after receiving no response. Zach raised his hand. "Yes, Mr. Greenwood?"

"The first settlement was . . . Bedrock?" asked Zach.

Jenn suppressed a smile as several students chuckled. She and Zach sat next to each other in the second row, with Nate and Douglas seated behind them.

"Good guess, but the Flintstones weren't British colonists," Mr. Foster said with a grin. "Ms. Quigley?"

"Jamestown, Virginia in 1607, I believe?"

"Very good, Ms. Quigley. You win the prize," he said, tossing her a Hershey's Kiss.

Jenn smiled as she caught the chocolate and placed it on the desk in front of her.

"Now who can tell me the name of the first permanent British settlement in *New England*?" asked Mr. Foster. He was met with silence.

"Ms. Quigley?" prompted Mr. Foster. "Do you know?"

"Wasn't it the Plymouth Colony? Plymouth, Massachusetts?" Jenn replied.

"That's absolutely correct," said Mr. Foster. "Everyone's heard of the Pilgrims, right? Plymouth was the second British settlement in America, and also the first one here in New England. And you'll all be happy to know that for the remaining weeks of the school year, we'll be focusing our studies on those early New England settlers."

Mr. Foster spent some time discussing the Puritans—Christian Protestants who came to New England shortly after the Pilgrims, looking to escape the Roman Catholic influences of the Church of England. Although they held similar beliefs, the Pilgrims desired separation from the church entirely while the Puritans sought simply to purify the Church of England. They believed religion should be based entirely on the Bible and chose to reject any elements of worship not specifically from it. They desired a simple, understated existence and believed they could commune directly with God, without the flashy ceremonies and practices of the Roman Catholic Church. A number of Puritan settlements, including the Massachusetts Bay Colony and the Connecticut Colony, were established within the two decades that followed the arrival of the Pilgrims at Plymouth in 1620.

"Religion was extremely significant to the Puritans," explained Mr. Foster. "They were a superstitious and fearful people. They believed the devil was an ever-present and malicious threat that sought to undermine them at every turn. This fostered a strong belief in witches and demons and other malevolent agents of evil.

"Interestingly enough," continued Mr. Foster, "our town of Windsor, founded in 1634, was the first settlement in Connecticut. The congregation established here by the Puritans, the First Church in Windsor, still exists to this day. The current church stands not far from the original meetinghouse built by the first settlers."

The school bell rang. Jenn had lost all track of time, fascinated by all this information.

"Thank you, class," said Mr. Foster. "We'll continue this discussion next time. No homework for tomorrow." A few departing students cheered.

Jenn gathered her belongings, including the pile of Hershey's Kisses she had collected. She tossed one to each of her friends as they made their way out of the classroom.

"Witches and demons and devils—oh my," said Zach with a grin. "The settlers considered Native Americans to be heathens and devil worshippers because they didn't worship the One True God. My ancestors would *not* have been welcomed."

"Their loss," she replied.

What Mr. Foster said about Windsor was particularly interesting, thought Jenn. Her family had lived in town for several generations, and her grandmother was still a member of First Church. She wondered what else her grandmother might be able to share on the subject.

When the final bell sounded, signaling the end of the school day, Nate left his biology class and retrieved several books from his locker. His biology teacher, Mr. Black, was an interesting man—immaculately dressed, he spoke with an accent that Nate couldn't quite place. He was strict but fair—and he loved his animals. The biology laboratory contained cages and tanks with frogs, turtles, a pair of birds, and quite a few mice. Mr. Black spent his free time between classes feeding and caring for his pets.

As Nate walked down the corridor, he kept an eye out for Donald and his gang. He had been able to avoid them so far that day, but he knew his luck would run out eventually. His stomach felt better, but he wasn't looking to repeat the encounter. As he approached the exit—and saw the door was propped open—he stopped short. He recognized Donald's voice, deeply engaged in conversation.

Nate flattened himself against the wall just inside and took a quick peek around the door frame. Donald stood there, an irritated look on his face, exchanging sharp remarks with the other two Ducks.

"That can't be right," Donald was saying in a loud voice.

"I'm pretty sure," replied Louie.

"What do you think, Hue?" asked Donald.

"He's right," replied Huey.

"No, you're wrong," began Donald, shaking his head. "Hamburgers are made from cows. You're telling me that hamburger patties and cow patties are *not* the same thing? No—I just don't buy it."

"But—" started Louie.

"Oh, forget it," snapped Donald. "As soon as that Watson kid comes out, you two hold him down and I'll handle the rest."

Nate didn't wait to hear more. Retracing his steps, he slipped out a side door and made his way past the tennis courts. Then he took off at a run toward the middle school. As soon as he had put some distance between himself and the school he glanced over his shoulder and saw that the Ducks hadn't moved. They still stood around the main entrance, engaged in what appeared to be another important debate, totally unaware that their quarry had escaped.

"So the woman in the photo looks like Aunt Celia?" asked Marc as he and Nate walked home from school. Nate first told him about Donald, his new enemy, but then the photo popped back into his mind.

"Yeah, I'll show you when we get home."

As they approached the house, they saw Aunt Celia's car in the driveway, but there was no sign of their aunt when they went inside. In the kitchen, the box was where Nate had left it on the counter. He opened it and removed the album, flipping through the pages until he got to the photos of the birthday party.

"Right there," said Nate, pointing at the photograph of their father and the woman.

"Wow, you're right—it looks just like her. Is she in any other photos?"

"Not that I've found so far. I'm going to take a closer look. Weird, huh?"

Marc shrugged. "I dunno, maybe." He turned to do the breakfast dishes, which he had left in the sink.

"I'm going upstairs," said Nate, putting the album back in the box.

"OK," said Marc. "I'll be up in a bit."

Nate hefted the box and climbed the stairs to the second floor. Marc had been so proud that morning to have found the key to the locked room. He chuckled to himself. It was certainly tempting, he thought, to borrow that key, enter the forbidden room, and satisfy their curiosity once and for all.

Walking down the second-floor hallway on his way to the third-floor stairs, he came upon the mysterious locked door. He glanced at it and did a double take. Underneath the door he saw a streak of light.

Someone's in there, he thought. Did Aunt Celia notice that the key had been moved?

Stepping quietly, Nate stopped and listened. He heard the murmuring of a voice from within—no, it was two voices. He recognized the voice of his aunt, but he also heard a deeper voice—a man's voice. The words were unintelligible, but there was most definitely a conversation going on.

Nate raised his fist to knock on the door, but quickly thought better of it. He wasn't sure what to do. He didn't want to invade his aunt's privacy, but the mystery of the locked room had fueled his imagination for months.

"We must stay the course," she said, in response to the muffled sounds of a disagreement. Nate pressed his ear against the door and struggled to make out more of the conversation. "No, I've managed to keep them in the dark this long," said Aunt Celia, her hushed tones suddenly sounding closer than before.

Nate realized his aunt was just on the other side of the door. He watched the doorknob as it began turning in front of him.

Still clutching the cardboard box, Nate ducked into the doorway of the closest room, one of several unused bedrooms nearby. He placed the box on the floor and slid quietly behind the door, where he was able to peer through the crack into the hallway. The door to the room opened and Aunt Celia emerged. She quickly turned and locked the door, before moving hurriedly in the direction of her bedroom. He waited, holding his breath, until she was gone. His heart beating a mile a minute, Nate stepped back into the hallway and climbed the third-floor stairs, choosing his footsteps carefully to avoid the squeaky stair treads.

Only after he made it safely to his bedroom and shut the door did he realize that no light was visible beneath the locked door as he passed—and that only his aunt emerged from the room.

Later that evening, Nate and Marc sat on Nate's bed with their father's album between them.

"What did she say again?" asked Marc.

"That she had 'managed to keep them in the dark,'" said Nate.

"And you think she was talking about us?"

"I mean, who else?" Nate said. "Between the photos, the locked room, and that conversation I overheard—what do we really know about her?"

As it turned out, Aunt Celia's look-alike appeared in no less than five different photos, the last of which was a photo from their dad's high school graduation—twelve years after the birthday party. In all of them, the woman looked *exactly* like the Aunt Celia of today. Also, Nate wondered, shouldn't there be *some* younger photos of their aunt—at a birthday party, a holiday gathering, the graduation, *somewhere*? But there were none—not a single photo of Aunt Celia in her youth.

"But I don't get it," Marc said. "How could the woman in the photos be Aunt Celia?"

"I don't see how," replied Nate. "It's a physical impossibility—but nothing makes sense here."

"And you couldn't tell who she was talking to?"

"No—it sounded like a man, but I couldn't make out any of the words."

"Maybe she was on speaker. Or maybe FaceTime or Skype," Marc offered.

That would be a logical explanation, Nate thought. And after all, Aunt

Celia came out of the room *alone*. "It really sounded as though he was in the room—but you must be right." Nothing else made sense.

"So, what are we going to do?" asked Marc.

"I'm not sure," said Nate. "I'll think of something."

They heard a car door shut outside, followed by the revving of an engine. It was Aunt Celia's car. Marc ran over to the window just as both of their cell phones chirped.

"She just drove off down the street," said Marc.

Nate glanced at the text that just arrived:

Boys, you're on your own for dinner. I'll be back late.

"Are we in danger?" asked Marc, suddenly looking very concerned. He walked slowly back to the bed and lowered himself onto the edge of the mattress.

That was the question that had been eating at Nate for the last hour. Yes, Aunt Celia was good to them, but his gut was telling him that something was very wrong.

And what had his father known of Aunt Celia? Clearly, she had been a presence in his life—he specified her as their guardian in his will, after all. But did he truly know her? Could she somehow actually be the woman in the photographs? How was that possible? Why had their father never once mentioned her when they were growing up?

It became clear to Nate that he must do something, and he must do it immediately.

"Marc—go get that key." Nate jumped to his feet. "We need answers, and we need them now—and that room is the place to start looking for them."

Chapter 4

THE EXECUTION

Hartford, Colony of Connecticut, May 1647

"Goodwife Young, I'm afraid I cannot help you," said Josiah, the young attendant hired by William Ruscoe, the administrator of the Hartford Gaol.

"But you must, I'm truly desperate," Alse pleaded. "I just need a pen and ink and a parchment—I beg of you." She had been in the jail for several days now, since her arrival from Windsor, allowed to leave only for the duration of her trial two days earlier.

"You ask too much. Goodman Ruscoe would never allow it," replied Josiah.

"Please, it's my only chance to leave a final note to my daughter." Surely he knew that she wouldn't survive the day, she thought.

Josiah's firm features softened a bit. "Ah, I'll see what I can do."

As he turned and left the building, Alse felt a glimmer of relief. She hadn't been allowed to see her daughter since the day she was taken from her home by the people of Windsor. Here was her chance to tell her one last time how much she loved her.

On that final day, she and Allie had gone for a walk in the woods. The return of spring provided a welcomed opportunity to restock the supply of herbs exhausted during the difficult winter, not to mention a respite from the recent murmurings of the townsfolk. They spent a wonderful morning together, talking and running and laughing. As late morning arrived, they began their journey home with a heaping basket.

Nearing the settlement, Allie spied something laying on the ground. "Look, Momma, a baby bird."

"It's a baby crow, with a broken wing," Alse replied.

"Can we take it home and make it better?"

"Yes, we may. We should care for nature as nature cares for us."

Alse gently scooped up the bird and carried it home. Allie followed close behind. As soon as they arrived, Allie collected some cloth and fashioned a bed. Alse showed her how to use a water-dipped stick to carry drops to the bird's beak.

"After it's had time to rest, we'll reset its wing," said Alse, gently tapping her daughter's nose with a finger to draw out a smile.

The townsfolk chose that moment to throw open the door. "Goody Young, we've come to arrest you for sins against God!" They took her into custody immediately. As they dragged her away, Alse saw the terrified look on Allie's face.

The following hours were a blur. At the meetinghouse the women, led by Jane Fyler, stripped her naked and placed her on a cold hard table. Inch by inch they searched her body for the devil's mark—the permanent branding that signified eternal allegiance to the devil, placed by Satan himself with a flick of the tongue. To Alse's humiliation, not one part of her body was bypassed. They also searched for the witch's teat—that spare nipple they claimed was used to suckle a familiar or other dark creature of hell.

They found what they sought, or so they said—though Alse knew this to be untrue. She was no agent of Satan and never had been.

Then came the interrogations and the accusations and the pressure to confess. She remained strong and defiant through all of it—until they threatened her daughter. If she didn't succumb, they told her, then Allie would be searched and interrogated as well. And for final confirmation they would take both of them to the river and toss them in—if they were witches, they would float. If they were not, they would drown.

So Alse confessed. After that, the town hearing was but a formality. She was indicted and would most likely be executed—but her daughter would live.

The jail in which she now sat was made of wood, built within the last six or seven years. She guessed it to be eighteen by twenty-four feet, and she would have considered it an improvement over the shack on the Windsor Green if not for the heavy iron gyve she wore around her ankle. It was attached to the floor with an equally heavy iron chain. Similar shackles, currently empty, sprouted from other sections of the floor at regular intervals. High, narrow windows provided the room's only light.

A tiny squeak announced the presence of a mouse, her lone companion since her arrival. She smiled at the sight of it.

"Good morning to you too, sir," she said, tossing a crumb of bread into the middle of the room. The mouse grabbed the crumb and scurried out of sight.

The trial itself took place on May 24 at the Hartford Particular Court, moderated by a Roger Ludlow with Henry Wolcott acting as magistrate. John Haynes, serving his fifth term as governor of the Connecticut Colony (formed of the towns of Hartford, Windsor, and Wethersfield) was in attendance as was Reverend Hooker. Haynes, a colonial magistrate, had come from the Massachusetts Bay Colony, where he once served a term as governor, to establish Hartford with Reverend Hooker.

A jury of twelve men heard the evidence against Alse. They listened to the witnesses and accusers from Windsor and were shown the incriminating portions of Alse's body. Alse saw no point in retracting her confession at this point. They would never believe her, and she had no desire to put Allie at risk. She was hardly surprised when she was found guilty and sentenced.

She remembered the reading of the verdict clearly. The magistrate, Henry Wolcott, loudly announced: "Alse Young, not having the fear of God before your eyes nor in your heart, you've entertained familiarity with Satan, the great enemy of God and mankind, and with his help you've done unnatural works which both according to the law of God and the established law of this Common Wealth you deserve to die by hanging."

Her husband visited Alse in the prison shortly after her conviction.

"If you can see it in your heart, please take me back to our home afterward and give me a decent godly burial," Alse said to her husband. "Please see that our daughter is safe and cared for. And please, above all else, promise me Allie will be nowhere near Hartford on the day of my hanging."

"I promise you these things, and please forgive me for my actions and inability to save you," replied John, as a tear rolled down his cheek. He looked broken and defeated.

Alse didn't envy him. Life would not be easy for the husband of the witch.

Two days later, resigned to her fate and feeling mostly numb, Alse now waited to die.

Eventually, Josiah returned with her meager midday meal of stale bread and water. "I've brought what you asked for," he said, handing her the writing supplies he had collected. "I can do no more. Good luck to you, Alse Young."

Having no interest in food, Alse sat down to compose a final letter to her daughter, praying that somehow, some way, she would be able to get it to her.

The ink was nearly dry when she heard men approaching. She slid the pen and the inkwell into the darkest corner of the cell she could reach and folded the letter several times, clutching it within her closed fist as the men opened the door.

It was time to go.

Her wrists were secured behind her back and Governor Haynes, Reverend Hooker, and jailor William Ruscoe led Alse the short distance from the jail to the Hartford Meetinghouse and the gallows. The ominous structure loomed ahead as they passed the stocks and the pillory, where the guilty were punished for lesser crimes. A sense of dread filled Alse—not the dread of imminent death but of the fact that she wouldn't have a chance to arrange for the delivery of the letter to her daughter. She hoped perhaps to see John one last time and give it to him—to make him promise not to read it. She still clutched it, hidden in her fist behind her back—she could not allow her captors to discover it for fear of the harm it could cause.

And she was running out of time. They led her up the stairs to the gallows and the stool that waited there. Strong hands on either side of her lifted her forcefully by the arms to the top of the stool. The noose was then looped around her neck—she knew what would happen next. The stool would be kicked out from under her, and she would drop the short distance allowed by the tightening noose. There wouldn't be enough slack for her feet to touch the ground, nor enough of a drop to snap her neck. She would hang by the neck, slowly suffocating, the noose cutting deeper and deeper into her skin as she struggled. Eventually she would lose consciousness. It would take ten to twenty minutes for her to die.

"Alse Young, do you have any last words?" She was unsure who spoke. Her thoughts were wandering.

The murmuring of the gathered spectators—those people from Hartford, Windsor, and other settlements who longed to see the death of America's first witch—roared in Alse's ears as her panic set in. The letter . . .

And suddenly her panic and despair quadrupled as she saw the small figure separate from the crowd in front of her.

"Momma—"

Alse gasped. No—not Allie! She couldn't see this.

"May God have mercy on your soul," someone said.

The stool was kicked out from under Alse, and the noose snapped taut. She struggled uselessly against her bindings for several moments, fighting to focus her thoughts one last, desperate time. A final urgent plea formed in her mind just as oblivion overtook her, putting a permanent end to her suffering.

No one noticed the letter as it fell from her limp grasp and fluttered to the ground, or the small brown mouse—Alse's faithful familiar—that scurried off with it.

Chapter 5

THE FORBIDDEN ROOM

Windsor, Connecticut, May 2019

"Are we really going to do this?" asked Marc.

Nate and Marc stood before the forbidden room on the second floor. Marc clutched the key, retrieved from the hook in Aunt Celia's room, in his hand. Nate glanced at his brother and the key before nodding slightly.

"I don't think we have a choice," said Nate. He lifted the key toward the lock, almost hoping it wouldn't fit. It slid in smoothly. He felt the slight resistance of the locking mechanism as he turned the key and the bolt inside slid open with a gentle click.

"Now, remember," said Nate, "we're just gonna take a quick look around. Don't touch *anything*." Nate hoped that the room would turn out to be a storage closet, just as Aunt Celia described. If that turned out to be the case, their actions would be a betrayal of trust. Whether he would confess to the betrayal, he wasn't sure—but if Aunt Celia noticed anything out of place, it would force the issue and bring about the uncomfortable conversation before he was ready.

On the other hand, if they found anything incriminating, he realized there was a good chance Aunt Celia posed a threat to their safety. Either way, they couldn't afford to leave behind evidence of their trespassing.

"Ready?" asked Nate.

"Let's do this," said Marc.

Nate held his breath as he turned the doorknob and pushed open the door. It glided open without a sound, revealing the darkness within. A thin beam of moonlight filtered in through a window on the far side, providing the only illumination. Feeling along the inner wall, Nate found the old-fashioned, two-button light switch common to the rest of the house. He firmly pressed the on button until it retracted with a sharp click. The overhead light came on, bathing the area in light.

"Doesn't look like a love dungeon to me," said Marc. "I mean, does it? I've never seen one before."

Nate wasn't sure *what* they were looking at. The room was full of bookcases, display cases, and an array of strange objects he didn't recognize. His eyes were drawn to a small metal device that sat on a nearby shelf—it had a round opening lined with sharp metal teeth. A large screw protruded from its center. Next to it he saw what appeared to be a branding iron, with a long metal handle with the letter *H* on its end. An old wooden stick with a split down one end sat next to it.

"What's *that* for?" asked Marc.

Nate shook his head, confused and creeped out. Maybe this room *was* a torture chamber.

Along one wall there was a large empty birdcage, sitting alone on a table. Next to another wall was a workbench cluttered with flasks and tubes of various shapes and sizes. There was a mortar and pestle on the table, too—maybe, Nate thought, to grind the assortment of dried herbs and flowers that hung suspended from the ceiling.

"What *is* all this?" Nate muttered. He continued looking at the shelves. He saw a pentagram, enclosed in a circle, painted on one wall.

"Day-mon-ollo-gee," Marc pronounced from the other side of the room, where he was peering at a brittle old book on a pedestal. "What does that mean?"

Nate walked over to his brother. Brows furrowed, he leaned over to examine the strange script.

"*Daemonologie, In Forme of a Dialogue*," read Nate. "Divided into three Books: Written by the High and Mighty Prince James, by the grace of God, King of England, Scotland, France and Ireland, Defender of the Faith. Well, that's a mouthful."

"What does it mean?" asked Marc.

"I'm not sure," replied Nate, trying not to show too much concern on his face. "But it looks like a book about demons—written by a king." Nate pulled out his phone and snapped a photo of the page. He would ask Jenn tomorrow if she could help research the book. He snapped a few more photos of the room and its contents from a variety of angles. Maybe Jenn and Zach would have some thoughts on what exactly he and his brother had found.

Nate felt a cool breeze and saw that the window was halfway open. He resisted the temptation to close it—he didn't want to disturb anything. Marc moved on to a display case, which contained shelves of crystals and other assorted items kept behind glass.

As he glanced around the room taking in more of the objects around him, it also occurred to Nate that for all the strange items in the room, everything was orderly and tidy. Even if many of the items were peculiar, there was nothing there to indicate that Aunt Celia had any evil intentions toward him and his brother. Maybe she just had a strange interest in the occult and was uncomfortable sharing it with them.

"So is Aunt Celia a witch?" asked Marc.

"What?" asked Nate. To his horror, he saw that Marc had opened the glass display case and pulled out something from inside.

Nate rushed over to him. "What are you doing? I said *don't touch anything!*"

"It's OK, I'm being careful. Do you think Aunt Celia is a witch?"

"Why do you keep asking that?"

"I found this." He showed Nate the old book in his hand. On the cover it read "*The Discovery of Witches* by Matthew Hopkins, Witch-finder."

"Where *exactly* did you get that?" asked Nate, studying the glass cabinet before them. They had to make sure they left everything as they had found it.

"It was next to *that*." Marc pointed to an old earthenware bottle sitting on one of the shelves. The bottle had a stopper held in place by a covering of melted wax.

"And check this out," Marc continued. Tucking the book under one arm, he reached back into the case and picked up another object from the same shelf. It was an intricate representation of a serpent, two feet long when outstretched, and made from a dark metal. It appeared pure black in the light of the room. The segments of its body moved as his brother handled it, gravity causing the head and tail portions to shift as if alive. It had two red crystals for eyes that glittered in the light of the overhead lamp.

"Wow," said Nate. "That's—something. Listen, let's put it back and get out of here. Aunt Celia has an interesting collection of items, but we haven't found answers to any of our questions—if anything, we've just found more questions. I'll talk to Jenn and Zach tomorrow and see if they can help make sense of any of this."

"OK," said Marc, as he handed Nate the snake. "So, you don't think Aunt Celia is a witch?" He sounded disappointed.

"There's no such thing," said Nate. He lifted the serpent to return it to its place within the cabinet. There was a glow within the eye crystals— more than just the reflection of the overhead light.

Suddenly the serpent twisted within his grasp, wrapping itself around his right forearm. Mechanically, it shifted before his eyes, the head of the snake coming to rest just above Nate's wrist, its body coiling around the thicker part of his lower arm. As it settled furiously into place, he felt it tighten.

The constriction was painful and unlike anything he had ever experienced. A wave of fear and nausea washed through him. He stumbled against the cabinet, knocking it back against the wall. The old bottle teetered for a moment before falling on its side with the sound of glass hitting glass.

"Nate!" Marc yelled, grabbing his brother's arm to steady him.

The serpent's ruby-red eyes grew brighter as Nate grasped the serpentine head in his left hand and began to pull. He yanked hard—and the serpent clamped down even harder. Nate's vision darkened as the pain worsened until he could no longer take it.

He released the serpent's head and immediately, its eyes began to dull. Relief flooded through him as the serpent began to relax its grip.

"Are you OK?" Marc asked frantically.

"I—I think so," Nate gasped. He felt dizzy, but the pain was becoming manageable. He ran his fingers over one of the snake's dark, metal coils. "It's not as flexible as it used to be. It's like it's locked into place."

"What do we do?" asked Marc, eyes wide.

"Let's get out of here before anything else happens," gasped Nate. "I have to figure out how to get this thing off!"

Marc quickly righted the old bottle in the cabinet before shutting the glass door. Nate knew they would have to come back with the serpent once they removed it from his arm. Hopefully Aunt Celia wouldn't notice it missing in the meantime.

But as the brothers started for the door, it became clear to Nate that his ordeal was far from over. The serpent's eyes flashed once more as metallic fangs erupted from its mouth. He cried out in pain as the icy barbs penetrated his skin. Blood began to seep from beneath the horrific bracelet's head.

"Oh my God!" cried Marc as he helped Nate to the door. "Should I call 911?"

"No!" said Nate. "If we do then Aunt Celia will know we were in here. Let's try to get it off first." A trickle of blood began dripping down his arm.

Great, thought Nate, clenching his teeth through the worst of the pain. *The last thing we need is to leave a path of blood behind us like a gruesome trail of bread crumbs.*

He hurriedly mashed down the light switch's off button, plunging the room into darkness before the brothers burst into the hallway, slamming the door closed and locking it behind them. The serpent's steel embrace continued as they raced for the third floor.

"What have we done?" Nate mumbled under his breath. What was happening to him, and what were they going to do about it? Nate hated to admit it, but he was afraid.

Very afraid.

In the third-floor bathroom, Nate carefully washed the blood from his hands and arm. He balled up the T-shirt he had been wearing—he would have to hide it. He had no idea how to get the bloodstains out. The serpent's fangs were still stuck in his skin, but the trickle of blood was tapering off and the pain diminishing to a dull throb.

Marc left to return the key to Aunt Celia's bedroom while Nate tried various things to remove the serpent bracelet, all of them unsuccessful. There was no way to slide the serpent off his arm since its fangs were embedded in his skin. He tried prying it off with a flathead screwdriver, but that failed as well. The once-articulated snake locked itself into position and couldn't be moved or flexed in any manner.

The glow he had seen in the serpent's eyes indicated to Nate that there was an electrical component to the bracelet. Something he had done triggered the device. He searched for an off button or some other mechanism that would cause the bracelet to release its grip. He tried depressing the eyes of the serpent, first one at a time, and then together. Nothing did the trick.

Nate heard his brother moving in the outer room.

"Success," said Marc, slipping back in through the bathroom door. "I put the key right back where I found it."

"Thanks, bro," replied Nate.

Marc nodded. "Any luck?"

"None." Nate picked up a clean towel. "It's getting late. Let's get some sleep. We'll figure this out tomorrow."

"Are you going to wear it to school then?" There was concern in Marc's voice.

"I don't think I have much choice." He glanced at the serpent. "My sleeve should cover it, at least."

In its coiled state, the bracelet measured maybe six inches in length from its first coil to its last. It had relaxed slightly, and the pain was subsiding. Nate flexed his wrist and then his elbow. He could still move his arm normally. If the serpent remained still, the discomfort was tolerable, and it wouldn't affect his normal routine. Carefully, he wrapped the clean towel around his arm. Even though the bleeding had stopped, he didn't want to risk bloodying his sheets.

Nate said good night to Marc, changed for bed, and settled in for the night. Alone in his room, he closed his eyes, but sleep didn't come. For a while he stared at the ceiling, replaying the evening's events in his mind.

Eventually Aunt Celia returned home. Nate was tempted to go to her, confess everything, and ask for her assistance—but he wasn't sure that was the right thing to do. For now, he didn't want to risk making things worse.

Tomorrow, he thought. They would come up with a plan.

Later that night, in the cabinet, in the darkened room—illuminated only by the soft light of the moon that made its way in through the window—the old bottle shook.

It was just a slight vibration, and it occurred just the once—but it was enough to turn the small chip in the bottle, formed when it had fallen over, into a crack.

The crack widened slowly over the next several hours as the ancient magicks within sought to be free. They had been imprisoned for far too long. As the witching hour approached—that time of night when mystical energies were at their most powerful—they felt a change in the balance of power. It wouldn't be long now. As the crack in their prison widened, they felt a weakening in its magicks. As the hour progressed, there was a natural boost to their own.

Suddenly they were free. The dark magicks emerged as a single black cloud from the crack in the compromised bottle. The cloud gathered for a moment inside the cabinet before pushing with just enough force to pop open the glass door of its outer prison. The swirling cloud of darkness recognized that the item it needed—its prized possession—had been taken. It would have to get it back. But for now, it would rest for a time and regain its strength.

The dark cloud flowed silently out of the cabinet and across to the window, escaping into the night. Not even the large crow that sat dozing in its cage noticed its departure.

Celia bolted upright in bed. She looked at the clock, which read 3:00. She glanced around the darkened room, unsure what had awoken her. The room was empty, and everything was in order. If she had been dreaming, she retained no memory of it.

It's nothing, she thought before turning over, pulling the blanket over her head and settling back down to sleep.

Chapter 6

THE SERPENT AND THE GIRL

Nate was up early. He had barely slept, between the ache in his arm and the certainty that Aunt Celia would burst into his room at any moment in a furious tirade, having found evidence of their trespassing.

He texted Jenn and Zach:

Important. Need to see you right away.

Nate and Marc left the house without breakfast. As far as Nate knew, Aunt Celia hadn't noticed the missing serpent yet, and he still planned to return it before she did. Hopefully his friends would be able to help. Four minds were better than two.

At the sight of Jenn and Zach seated on the steps of the middle school, Nate breathed a sigh of relief.

"So what's the big urgency?" Jenn asked cheerfully. She stood to greet them.

Nate pulled back his right sleeve, exposing the metallic serpent coiled around his forearm. Its eyes were dark. Dried blood flaked from around the serpent's fangs.

"Wow," said Zach. "That looks—*really badass!*"

"Except it won't come off," said Marc.

"Wait, what?" Jenn's eyes went wide.

Nate explained about their discovery of the locked room, and what happened when they opened the mysterious cabinet. He told them about the photos of the woman who looked like Aunt Celia but couldn't be.

"And now you can't get it off," Jenn mused. She stepped up to examine the bracelet, probing the serpent's head and feeling carefully along the length of its body.

"I haven't been able to figure out how," said Nate, "and I need to get it back in the cabinet before Aunt Celia notices it's missing."

"Does it hurt?" asked Zach.

"Stings a bit," said Nate, pointing at the puncture marks. "It isn't bad at the moment." The contractions had stopped. He hoped it would stay that way. He wondered if he was making a mistake by not involving Aunt Celia. He could still change his mind and ask for help later—but for now, he would ride it out and see what the day brought. Removing the bracelet and returning it to the cabinet before Aunt Celia noticed was still the best possible outcome.

Jenn snapped a photo of the bracelet with her phone.

"I'll see if I can find anything like it online," she said. "Who knows, we might get lucky."

"Dude, have you tried cutting it off?" Zach, hands in his pockets, bent to take a closer look.

"No," replied Nate, with a shake of the head. "I was hoping not to have to. It may come to that."

"Well, keep an eye on it," said Jenn, a look of concern on her face. "If it punctured the skin, it could get infected."

Nate nodded. "I will."

"Hey, let them see the other stuff," said Marc, excitedly.

"Oh yeah, there are these, too," said Nate, showing Jenn and Zach the photos he had taken of the other things in the room.

"That's some strange shit right there," said Zach, as Nate flipped through the photos. Zach had a grimace on his face.

"Hmm," said Jenn with a frown. "Send them to me. I'll see what I can find."

"Sure," said Nate. He had no idea if any of them would prove useful in answering his questions concerning his aunt, but it was a place to start—and maybe they would learn something to help with the serpent.

"Oh, and then there's this," said Marc pulling out the copy of *The Discovery of Witches* from his backpack.

Nate couldn't believe his eyes.

"Um, yeah—about that," explained Marc after seeing the glare on Nate's face. "There was a lot happening. I forgot to put it back with all the—you know—blood and screaming and stuff."

"Can I borrow that?" asked Jenn. "I'll give it back before the end of the day."

"Fine with me," said Marc, handing her the old book.

"Go ahead," replied Nate. At this point, he didn't see what additional harm it could cause. Jenn flipped through the pages for a moment before stashing it in her backpack.

Nate, Jenn, and Zach said their goodbyes to Marc. With a wave, he disappeared inside the building.

"So, about your Aunt Celia . . ." began Zach, once the three of them were alone. "If she isn't your aunt, then who is she? And who is the woman in your father's album?"

"Good questions," replied Nate. "And that's exactly what I'm hoping to find out."

Nate headed off toward the high school with Jenn and Zach. He felt a little better now, just knowing that his friends knew what was going on. Hopefully Jenn would be able to find something with her research. If anyone could help, he knew she could.

They hadn't gotten far when they saw a rusty old pickup truck coming down the road they were about to cross.

"Nate, get down!" exclaimed Zach, turning around. They ducked behind a parked car. The truck passed by them. A little farther down the road, it turned into the high school entrance.

"Donald Jones," said Jenn.

"Yeah, the Ugly Ducklings' ugly truck," said Zach as he helped Nate back to his feet.

"Thanks," he said, brushing off his jeans.

Not caring for another encounter with the bullies, Nate kept an eye out for them as they approached the school. By the time they reached the entrance, the last of the students were trickling in.

"Excuse me," said a voice Nate didn't recognize. At that moment, something collided with the backpack that was slung over his shoulder. He struggled to maintain his grip as its straps began sliding off his arm.

"Oh, sorry!" said the voice. Delicate fingers closed about the pack, stopping its downward momentum.

He looked up to see the most beautiful girl he had ever laid eyes on. She was fair skinned and slight of build, with a mane of flaming red hair that flowed down her back. Soulful green eyes stared back at him.

"Uhhh . . ." Nate muttered.

A grin brightened her features as she released the backpack. Nate noticed a small scar on her left cheek. The imperfection made her all the more perfect. She turned and walked past them through the doors of the school, her hair floating behind her with each step.

"Who was that?" asked Nate.

"I don't know," replied Zach, "but close your mouth before something builds a nest."

Jenn was smiling at him, too.

"What?" said Nate, grinning in response. For the moment he forgot all about Ducks and serpents and aunts and forbidden rooms.

Later that day, Nate sat in Mr. Adams's shop class fussing with the lopsided birdhouse he had been working on for the last couple weeks. He had come to the sad conclusion that he had no skills in carpentry. He was tempted to toss the whole thing in the trash, but then he would be certain to get an *F*.

Not that it really mattered—he had bigger concerns at the moment. The serpent had begun squeezing his arm again. It would ease up for a while and then he would feel another contraction. It was a nuisance mostly, but what if it got worse? At least no one could see it. It was hidden beneath his sleeve, and it would stay that way until he could remove it.

What was the bracelet's purpose? It surely wasn't meant to be ornamental—was it? *Yeah*, he thought. *Made for that person who loses everything. Guaranteed not to fall off! Buy one for your loved one now. A gift to be cherished forever—like it or not.*

What if the serpent had something more in store? The thought sent his mind tumbling through all sorts of horrific scenarios. What if it started squeezing his arm like it had initially? If it cut off the blood flow, he could lose the arm. Could it be on a timer and set to explode? What if the fangs that had penetrated his skin were injecting some sort of poison?

"Excuse me, class," said a voice behind him, the words thankfully breaking Nate's train of thought. It was Mr. Adams.

"We have a new student starting today," Mr. Adams continued. "Please welcome Ms. Alexandra Bradley to the class."

Nate turned to see the girl with the red hair and great smile. The girl Zach and Jenn had teased him about.

"Alexandra," said Mr. Adams, "please find a seat."

"It's Alex," she said as she started off in Nate's direction.

For a moment, he thought she would sit at the station next to his. But to his disappointment (or maybe relief?), she walked on past to the back of the class. She sat next to the football player, Stephen Ross. Steve was as muscular and fit as Nate was not. The jock helped Alex select wood for her project and showed her around the room. Nate couldn't help noticing the beautiful birdhouse sitting at Steve's station.

Damn, he thought with a sigh.

The serpent chose that moment to contract. Nate almost cried out in pain. It felt like the snake was punishing him for his momentary distraction. Nate decided he had to do something. His eyes wandered to the open tool cabinet, where an assortment of metalworking tools hung. He walked over and grabbed a handheld bolt cutter.

Everyone in the room was preoccupied with their projects. Nate turned away from the class so he was facing the cabinet. Its open doors helped to block the view. He didn't want anyone to see what he was about to do.

He lifted his sleeve and slid a blade of the cutter beneath the serpent. It was a snug fit, but there was enough give to his arm to make that possible. He squeezed the cutters awkwardly with his left hand, using all the force he could manage—but it wasn't enough. The snake held its shape.

He tried again, this time rocking the cutters back and forth as he squeezed. He soon felt and heard the wonderful *pop* of snapping metal followed by the metallic ding of something hitting the floor. *Oh, thank God!*

But Nate's relief was short-lived: he withdrew the cutters to find just one blade where there had been two. The bracelet was still intact. The cutters were made of steel and shouldn't have snapped—especially with the force he had managed with his weaker left hand. *They must be defective*, he thought.

Slipping the broken bolt cutters under one arm, he grabbed another pair from the cabinet. He would try again—and this time it would work. Nate repeated the process, carefully watching as the cutters rocked back and forth. He squeezed as hard as he could, his hand trembling with the exertion.

Twang! The steel gave way from the pressure. In a fraction of a second, the blade broke free. He felt the sting as it bounced off his cheek and fell to the floor. Raising his fingers to his face, he pulled them back to find blood.

The serpent once again contracted tightly—if Nate didn't know better, he would have thought it was angry.

What should he do? He had broken two bolt cutters and there wasn't even a scratch on the bracelet. There were larger cutters in the cabinet—the long-handled variety that would supply more leverage—but there was no way to use those without someone noticing, and he wasn't sure he could even manage it.

Suddenly he had an idea. Taking a quick look around the room and satisfied that no one was watching, he returned the damaged bolt cutters to the cabinet, kicking the two broken blades beneath it. He wasn't sure what else to do with them, and he couldn't afford any extra attention at the moment.

Nate grabbed a long screwdriver from the cabinet and walked over to the scrap bin, where he took out a piece of wood. Any piece would do. On the far side of the room was a band saw, with a new metal-cutting blade. Mr. Adams had demonstrated it in preparation for their next project. It would do the trick.

He flipped the power switch on the saw, watching as it revved up. Holding the piece of wood, he slid it forward into the blade—and the blade sliced through it like butter. It would do the same on metal.

Nate took one last look around the room. It was time. Soon he would be free. He grabbed a pair of nearby goggles to protect his eyes, lifted his sleeve, and slid the screwdriver between the serpent and his skin. It would offer some protection from the saw. He took a deep breath, holding it as he pushed his arm forward into the blade.

The moment it touched the dark metal, the blade gave off a blood-curdling screech. It snapped, burning out the motor. Nate would have been horrified if it had ended there, but he wasn't so lucky. The entire band saw burst into flames that grew faster and larger than he would have ever thought possible. Chaos erupted. The fire alarm shrieked as Mr. Adams shouted for everyone to make for the exits. Nate jumped back from the flames, but rather than flee, he just stood there staring at his arm in the midst of the pandemonium. It wasn't the flames that scared him. The most horrific thing of all was that the serpent bracelet still encircled his arm, fully intact and damage-free—and its eyes were now glowing an angry, burning red.

Chapter 7

ALSE YOUNG AND *THE DISCOVERY OF WITCHES*

Jenn walked into the school library—her favorite place, a large open room in the middle of the school, lined with what seemed to Jenn to be miles of bookshelves. In the center was the librarian's station, behind which stood Ms. Brooks, the school librarian, in her natural habitat.

"Good morning, Jenn," said Ms. Brooks. "How are you?"

"Good, thanks. Do you have anything for me today?"

Jenn had been coming to the library during her lunch period since the beginning of her freshman year. She wasn't fond of the cafeteria or its food, and she enjoyed being able to get away for some quiet time during the school day. She found herself frequently assisting Ms. Brooks with random projects—returning books to their shelves, watering the plants, straightening magazines. Ms. Brooks was easy to talk to and full of good advice—an unofficial guidance counselor of sorts.

"As a matter of fact, I do," said Ms. Brooks. "We have a number of new books in the donation box—if you'd like to take them in the back and go through them, we can see if we have anything worth shelving. Anything we don't want, we can regift to the Windsor Public Library's book sale."

"Sounds great," Jenn replied, hefting the large box.

Jenn wasn't about to go into the details of her morning with anyone—including Ms. Brooks—just yet. She had spent a good portion of it on her laptop googling various topics. She knew she shouldn't be surfing the web during class, but she hadn't gotten caught. And anyhow, she was far enough ahead in her classes that her teachers usually cut her some slack.

She hadn't found anything that would be of use to Nate in removing the serpent. There seemed to be a million different pieces of jewelry that featured a snake in its design. Rings, necklaces, earrings, and bracelets—but nothing remotely similar to the thing that had wrapped itself around Nate's arm and wouldn't let go.

She *had* been able to identify some of the items from Nate's photos, however. Among them was a set of thumbscrews—a torture device used to crush a person's thumbs, fingers, or toes, either as punishment or as a means to obtain a confession. She suspected anyone would confess to anything if subjected to them. What would Nate's aunt be doing with those? Hopefully she was just a collector and had no plans to use them.

There was also the branding iron. The letter *H* most likely stood for *heretic*, Jenn learned. The brand would be used to burn the letter into the skin of a person as a form of public shaming—similar to the infamous scarlet letter, which she had read about just last year in English class. But the *H* would be much more painful and permanent.

The cleft stick was another shaming device, to be placed on a person's tongue as a punishment for verbal infractions such as lying and swearing. Both the brand and the cleft stick were known to have been used by the Puritans as punishment.

Jenn set the box of donated books on a table in the back of the library. She pulled a sandwich out of her bag and ate as she removed books from the box with her free hand. It was an odd assortment of things. She pulled out two copies of *Harry Potter and the Half-Blood Prince*, a tattered copy of Michael Crichton's *Jurassic Park*, an Indian cookbook, and a copy of *The Book of Mormon*.

Jenn chuckled to herself. Had a single individual donated all these books? *If so, I'd like to meet that person*, she thought.

At the bottom of the box there was an old leather-bound book. Flipping it over, she was shocked to see that the title was *The Discovery of Witches*—the same book Nate and Marc had given to her before school. She pulled Nate's copy out of her bag and set it next to the other. They were virtually identical.

Well that's odd, she thought. It was a small book—more of a pamphlet, written by a man named Matthew Hopkins. The title page read:

The Discovery of Witches:

In

Answer to severall

QUERIES,

LATELY

Delivered to the Judges of Assize for the

County of Norfolk.

And now published

By MATTHEW HOPKINS,

Witch-finder

FOR

The Benefit of the whole

KINGDOME.

M.DC. XLVII

Witch-finder? she thought. The date at the bottom translated to the year 1647. Jenn scanned through the pages. The book was written as a series of questions and answers that seemed to describe the methods Matthew Hopkins used for identifying witches and obtaining confessions from them—while at the same time justifying those methods.

But who was Matthew Hopkins? And why were there now suddenly two copies of this strange book in her hands on the very same day?

Jenn put Nate's copy back into her bag and carried the other copy back to the main desk.

"Ms. Brooks, take a look at this," said Jenn. "It was in the donation box."

The librarian picked up the book and flipped through it.

"Hmm, I really don't know what to make of this, hon." She lifted the book to her nose and sniffed the pages. Her face wrinkled in response. "Why would anyone donate this to a school library?"

"It seems to be a book on witch hunting, by a seventeenth-century English witch hunter named Matthew Hopkins. Have you ever heard of him?"

"I can't say that I have," replied Ms. Brooks. "But did you know the very first person hanged for witchcraft in the American colonies was from right here in Windsor? That was some time before the Salem witch trials—but it all started right here in this town."

"No kidding," said Jenn. She was hearing far too much about witches lately.

"She was innocent, of course—but back in those days the Puritan settlers were paranoid about the influence of Satan and his minions over their lives."

"Wow," said Jenn. They had all heard about the Salem witch trials in school, but now she was realizing there was a lot she *didn't* know. "I had no idea. Would you mind if I hang on to this?" She didn't know why, but somehow Matthew Hopkins and his book were of some significance to Nate's Aunt Celia. The fact that it had turned up twice within the last day was just too much of a coincidence.

"Be my guest," said Ms. Brooks.

Courtney strutted into the school cafeteria, Kat and Kam in tow. It was lunchtime, and she was still upset that Mr. Johnson had assigned homework that morning. *Who needs algebra anyway?*, she thought. *And who ever*

thought it would be a good idea to add letters and numbers together? It made no sense whatsoever. She didn't have time for homework. She had to prepare for the Shad Derby parade—but did anyone care? She was the star of the show! It amazed her how selfish other people could be.

"Go and find us a seat," Courtney instructed her companions. Without waiting for a response, she grabbed a tray and jumped on the food line. She had recently submitted a list of acceptable menu items to the suggestion box and was eager to see if they had listened to her recommendations. Sadly, they had not. Meatloaf and Brussels sprouts again? *Puh-lease.* These cafeteria workers would just never get it. One day, she would open a restaurant of her own just to show them what edible food looked like.

Grabbing a salad and a bottle of water, Courtney headed off to locate her friends. The room was full of students, chewing and chatting. People waved to her as she passed, but she ignored them—they were either people she didn't know or didn't care to know. She saw Nate Watson, sitting with Zach Greenwood and Douglas Ramirez. She had never noticed Nate before his confrontation with the Jones gang the day before. He was kind of cute—and heroic. She wouldn't have risked her neck for Douglas or Jenn Quigley, but she had to respect his bravery. What was he doing sitting with those losers? Didn't he realize he was committing social suicide? She decided to step in and help save his reputation before it was too late.

"Hi—Nate, right?" she said as she reached his table. "I'm Courtney. I was wondering if you'd like to leave this nerd table and sit with my friends and me."

Nate looked up and grinned at her.

Zach rolled his eyes. "We're in the middle of a conversation—"

"I'm sorry, did I make you think I was talking to you?" Courtney snapped. "I can assure you, I wasn't." Some people were so rude.

"Excuse me, Your Highness," said Zach under his breath.

"I heard that," Courtney said. "Did you say that because I'm the Shad Derby queen? Or have you just come to understand your social standing around here?"

"I said it because I've come to understand that you're a royal b—" Zach began.

"I'm sorry," interrupted Nate. "Thanks for the offer. Some other time maybe?"

"Um, yeah—no," said Courtney. *Why do I bother?* she thought as she turned and walked briskly away, off toward the table where Kat and Kam sat waiting for her.

"Was she serious?" asked Nate as Courtney walked off in a huff.

"I'm afraid so," said Zach. "She tends to be pretty direct and to the point."

"Good to know."

Nate had filled Zach in on the morning's attempts to remove the bracelet before Douglas had joined them. For the most part, the bracelet had stopped giving him trouble, so long as he didn't try to remove it.

"Do you know that lunch lady, Mrs. King?" asked Douglas, changing the subject while popping a french fry into his mouth. "The older one with a mustache?"

"Yeah, what about her?" asked Nate.

"I don't think she likes me," said Douglas. "She always shorts me on the fries."

"She gives me the creeps," said Zach. "I caught her nose-mining one time—and she smells like wet dog and cigarettes."

Yuck, thought Nate. It was nice to have a regular conversation with friends—one that didn't involve his aunt in any way.

"You noticed that, too?"

Nate looked up to see none other than Alex, standing there with a tray and a smile.

"Mind if I join you, Saw Boy?" she asked Nate.

Nate found himself at a loss for words.

"Er, yeah, sure," he managed. He wasn't sure how he felt about the new nickname—but it meant she must have seen him in shop class after all. He was amazed that she remembered him.

"Saw Boy?" asked Douglas.

"Yeah," said Alex. "Our boy here blew up a band saw in shop class this morning. You remember the fire alarm?"

Mr. Adams had put out the fire with an extinguisher, but the entire school had had to evacuate until the Windsor Fire Department had given the all-clear to re-enter the building.

"That was you?" said Douglas, clearly impressed.

"Yeah, never saw anything like it," said Alex. She placed her hand lightly on Nate's shoulder for a moment.

"I have a knack with heavy machinery," said Nate. Her touch, though brief, had put him at ease.

Before Nate knew what was happening, the four of them were laughing and joking like they had all been friends for a long time. Nate couldn't believe how quickly and easily he and Alex were hitting it off. She was so easy to talk to.

"Same time tomorrow?" asked Alex, as they were leaving the lunchroom.

"It's a date," said Nate. He was disappointed that the lunch period wasn't longer. He had forgotten about the bracelet entirely. He couldn't remember feeling this happy since his parents were alive.

"Hello class," said Greg Foster. "Does anyone have any questions on what we covered last time before we get started on our next topic?" The history teacher slid open a desk drawer and pulled out an open bag of Hershey's Kisses.

"Mr. Foster?" asked Jenn, raising her hand. Nate, Zach, and Douglas sat nearby.

"Yes, Ms. Quigley, go ahead."

"You said the Puritans believed in witches. I heard the first woman hanged for witchcraft in America was from Windsor. Do you know any-thing about that?"

"Ah yes, Alice Young," replied Mr. Foster. He wrote it on the board as "Alse Young." "Little is known about her or why she was accused of witch-craft. In fact, it was only about a hundred years ago—approximately two hundred and fifty years after her death—that her name became generally known."

"Why?" asked Zach.

"Well, recordkeeping back then wasn't what it is today—and of course they didn't have Facebook to preserve every minute detail of the times." Mr. Foster grinned. "The first known record of the hanging was found in the journal of John Winthrop, the Governor of the Massachusetts Bay Colony. It said something to the effect of 'On May 26, 1647, one woman of Windsor was arraigned and executed in Hartford for witchcraft.' And then much later, a note was found written on the inside front cover of a journal written by Matthew Grant, the second town clerk of Windsor. It showed the same date followed by the note 'Alse Young was hanged.'"

Jenn immediately picked up on the date—1647. It was the same year Matthew Hopkins published *The Discovery of Witches*. Was it just a coinci-dence? What were the odds?

"Didn't they burn witches at the stake?" asked Douglas. Jenn was sur-prised—Douglas never asked questions.

"No, not in America—hanging was the standard means of execution." Douglas nodded his head in response.

"Is that how they spelled 'Alice' back then, A-L-S-E?" asked Nate.

"That was apparently one way. Unfortunately, they frequently didn't have standard spellings for first or even last names at the time—which makes it even more difficult to research the facts. Records show Alse Young's name written in a number of different ways: Alse, Alice, Achsah, Young, Youngs, Younges." Mr. Foster wrote all the variations on the board.

"Must have made it hard to google someone," said Zach.

Several students snickered. Mr. Foster smiled.

"Was anything else known about her?" asked Jenn.

"Not a lot. There was a John Young, who most people believe to have been her husband. And she had a daughter, also named Alice. Unfortunately, much of the recorded information from that time was focused on heads of household, most of whom would have been the men of the families."

Mr. Foster went on to explain how Alse Young's hanging sparked the beginning of the Connecticut witch hysteria during which another ten people were convicted and hanged over the span of fifteen years, including a second resident of Windsor.

"The American witch hysteria that began right here in Windsor in 1647 eventually peaked with the Salem witch trials of 1692 to 1693," explained Mr. Foster. "The Salem witch trials are more well-known due to the sheer volume of accusations and executions that occurred during that sixteen-month period. There were over two hundred accusations and more than twenty deaths."

Jenn had visited Salem, Massachusetts, one summer with her family and the Salem witch trials had always fascinated her. Why hadn't she ever heard of the *Connecticut* witch trials? She glanced around the room as other students raised their hands and asked questions of their own. Normally by this time, some members of the class would have begun fidgeting, but Mr. Foster had managed to hold everyone's attention.

"You mentioned a second resident of Windsor was also hanged?" asked Jenn when her turn came.

"Yes, a Ms. Lydia Gilbert. Convicted and executed in 1654, I believe— seven years after Alse Young."

"Did they know each other?" asked Nate.

"I can't say for sure, but it's likely," replied Mr. Foster. "Windsor was a much smaller town back then."

Jenn glanced at Nate. "Crazy, huh?" she whispered to him.

"Batshit crazy," added Zach under his breath.

Nate glanced at each of them, nodding his agreement.

Mr. Foster soon moved on to other topics. Jenn was intrigued by everything she had heard. She hadn't been aware of any of this town history before—and somehow it seemed especially important now.

After class, Zach and Douglas headed to their lockers. Nate took Jenn aside and filled her in on his attempts to remove the serpent bracelet.

"So *that's* what the fire alarm was about," Jenn said, laughing. "As a matter of fact, I have something to show you, too." She handed him the Hopkins book she had taken from Marc that morning—along with the second copy she had found in the library.

"OK, that's a strange coincidence," said Nate. "*Two* copies? And now we hear that two women from Windsor were executed for witchcraft."

"And the first woman, this Alse Young," added Jenn, "was hanged in 1647—the same year the book was published."

"What are you thinking?" asked Nate. They stood silently for a moment as Jenn reconsidered the information they had learned.

"I really don't know," she said, shaking her head. "I mean, we know that Matthew Hopkins lived in England and the executions took place here in Connecticut. So common sense tells me they aren't related."

"True," he replied with a frown. "And yet . . ."

Nate handed the library copy of the book back to Jenn. Wincing suddenly, he glanced at his arm.

"Are you OK?" Jenn asked.

"I think so," said Nate. "I don't know. It seemed like it was tightening again for a second." Glancing around to make sure no one was nearby, Nate pulled back his sleeve. They both looked at the bracelet, still tightly affixed to his arm.

"Have you decided what to do about it?"

Nate shook his head. "Not yet. I have a few more hours before I have to go home and face Aunt Celia. I hope something will come to me before then."

"Good luck." She said goodbye to Nate and headed off to her next class. *Matthew Hopkins*, she thought, *who are you?*

Jenn was determined to find out.

Celia stood before the glass cabinet in the locked room, the neighbor boy, Noah, at her side. "You were right," she said, glancing at him, a nervous frown on her face. "I sensed it last night, too."

"I'm sorry," he replied, looking up at her, his brown eyes open wide. "I was hoping to be wrong. Corvin didn't notice anything unusual?" He pointed at the crow perched on the windowsill.

The bird squawked and ruffled his feathers.

"No," she replied, quietly. She leaned forward and removed the piece of duct tape she had placed across the cabinet's doors. One end of it had been pulled away by whoever had opened the cabinet. She turned it over and examined the powdery remains of the secondary containment spell. It had been added as a safety measure, a backup should the bottle fail.

And it had failed. She reached into the case, pulled out the ancient container and ran her finger down its prominent crack.

"This is very bad," she said softly.

"Is there anything I can do to help?" asked Noah.

"No," she replied, glancing fondly back at him. "Not just yet. Thank you, though."

Noah nodded. A sad smile adorned his face. The smile, along with the worn clothing he habitually wore made him look like a waif, a stray—which, it occurred to Celia, was exactly what he was. Or what he used to be, at least. She glanced from him to Corvin and thought of the boys. The notion that came to her made her smile—she was a collector of orphans, it would seem.

But she had work to do. The boys would be home before long—she would have to talk to them. She assumed they were somehow involved. She had to protect them, of course. She had to protect them all.

As she gazed back at Noah, his form grew fuzzy, opaque. And in moments he was gone entirely. It didn't faze her—she was used to it.

Such was the nature of ghosts.

"Five times around the track," said Mr. Mitchell, the PE teacher. "You can hit the showers when you've finished." It was a nice sunny afternoon and not too hot, so the class had come outside to exercise. Across the street from Windsor High was a running track that was shared with the middle school. Nate took off jogging down the track. He was conscious of being the only one in a long-sleeved T-shirt, but he had to keep his arm covered. He didn't want anyone else noticing the strange bracelet on his arm, or asking questions.

He was still trying to make sense of everything—the photo album with the pictures of Aunt Celia, the room full of her crazy items, the damned serpent coiled around his arm, Matthew Hopkins, and the witches of Windsor. And on top of that, he might have met the girl of his dreams and she seemed to like him, too! What more could happen today?

He saw Douglas running laps ahead of him, struggling. He had slowed so much that Nate had almost gotten a full lap on him.

"Hang in there, Doug," he said as he passed him by. His friend was covered in sweat and huffing and puffing.

Poor kid, thought Nate. Unfortunately, he knew there was nothing he could do to help. Picking up speed, he ran on ahead.

Douglas was dying. Or so he thought. He was only on his fourth lap around the track, and he felt like he was going to throw up. Everyone else had already finished and left. He had tried to sneak away when Nate was leaving, but Mr. Mitchell wasn't about to let that happen.

"Ramirez! Where do you think you're going—two more laps! Get to it!"

At least if I pass out, they'll have to carry me back, thought Douglas.

Douglas had been heavy all his life. "You're big boned," his mother would say, or "It's the family genes." And whenever someone made fun of him or made him feel bad, she would always be there to make it better by feeding him cookies or ice cream or some other treat. Food wasn't just for the bad times, either. His family celebrated with food. They socialized around food—food, food, food.

He realized it wasn't his mother's fault. She had been brought up that way herself. He had tried dozens of times to cut back—but he just couldn't kill that urge to eat.

Maybe I should just run every day until I almost pass out, he thought. *I sure don't feel like eating right now.*

And people could be so mean—it wasn't just people like Courtney Stevens or that horrible Donald Jones. Other people made comments or judged him in one way or another—not just the kids his age but the adults, too.

He was a good person—he knew that much. Why wouldn't people give him a chance? At least he had his friends, Zach and Jenn. And now Nate, which surprised him at first. Nate could be one of the cool kids if he wanted to be. Even Courtney had tried to invite him to have lunch with her.

Douglas always held back. He wished he could be more outgoing and funny like Zach or more well-spoken like Jenn—even though she wasn't popular, she was still respected for her brains.

Maybe he would try the diet thing again, he thought. If he kept exercising like this, it would get easier over time. *Yeah, I'll definitely do that, if I survive this.*

Douglas returned to the locker room after finishing the last lap. He was exhausted and soaked with sweat, but he also felt a sense of accomplishment and some new bit of hope. He felt good about committing to making a change.

The locker room was empty. Everyone had showered and left. He considered skipping the shower, but he could smell himself so he knew others would be able to, too—and he wasn't going to be made fun of for something he could control.

Douglas undressed, wrapping a towel around his waist. Since no one was around, he could shower without feeling self-conscious. He hung his towel on the hook outside the shower room and turned on the closest faucet. He looked around as he waited for the water to warm. There were half a dozen shower faucets on either side of the room, and he was once again glad he was alone. He had never had the courage to shower with others before, and fortunately he had never needed to this badly.

It was after he had soaped up that his heart nearly stopped.

"Well, what do we have here guys?" he heard someone say. "It's the little pudge nugget." To Douglas's horror, he realized Donald and his two thugs had come into the locker room—and they were headed his way. He was alone, naked, and defenseless. *This can't be happening*, he thought— but it was. The Ducks surrounded him in the shower. Donald shut off the water before Douglas had a chance to rinse off the soap.

"You and your hero caused me a lot of trouble yesterday," began Donald. "You made me look bad in front of the school, and I had to walk around all day with just one shoe. I haven't been able to catch up with your buddy yet, but you'll do for a start."

Douglas made a break for it, making it past Donald and into the main locker area before he felt the foot smash into his back. He fell hard, hitting the floor in a soapy heap, his chin cracking on the tile. His vision blurred for a moment, and when he was able to refocus, he realized the Ducks had once again surrounded him.

"Nice try," said Huey, giving him a firm kick to the rear. He saw Louie, pulling his towel from the hook and tossing it into the puddle that had formed just inside the doorway to the showers.

Terrified, Douglas closed his eyes and covered his head with his arms. He was in trouble, and he knew it. *Don't cry . . .* , he thought, knowing for sure that this time he was about to die. *Please, just don't cry.*

And that was when the three bullies closed in on him.

Nate was kicking himself. He had gotten all the way to the other side of the building before realizing he had left his cell phone back in the locker room after PE. *What an idiot*, he thought as he turned to retrace his steps. Walking as quickly as he could, he made his way back to the gym. As he burst through the locker room door, he suddenly found himself in the middle of the craziest scene imaginable.

What the hell?

The Ducks were towering over a wet, naked Douglas, taking turns snapping wet towels at him. Douglas just lay there on the floor, hands covering his head, his body reacting to every blow.

Nate jumped into action. Without thinking twice, he took a running lunge at the nearest Duck—which once again happened to be Donald. With a heavy thud, Nate landed on Donald, sending the two of them crashing into a wall of lockers. Both of them landed in a heap on the hard tile. Untangling himself, Nate hopped quickly back to his feet. Huey and Louie, seemingly in shock at how the tables had turned, stepped away from Douglas and began approaching Nate and their fallen leader. Nate felt the serpent tighten about his arm.

Douglas started picking himself up from the floor. Nate grabbed a towel from a nearby bench, tossing it his way. By then Huey and Louie had closed the gap, coming within two feet of Nate. Nate pulled back a fist and swung it at Louie, missing as Louie ducked out of the way. His sleeve shifted as he moved, briefly exposing the head of the serpent. Its eyes were glowing an angry red. He pushed the sleeve back into place, hoping that no one had noticed. Hearing a sound behind him, Nate quickly turned and met Donald's fist with his face. Pain shot through his nose and into his skull as he struggled to maintain his balance.

Nate realized he had run out of luck and time. The bullies were about to attack, and he had no chance against all three—but then two things happened.

There was a ferocious yell, and Nate saw a large pinkish shape charging in his direction. It was Douglas—a wet, soapy, still-naked Douglas. His friend stepped onto a nearby bench and jumped off onto Huey's back, looping a towel over Huey's head and around his neck. It looked to Nate like a bull riding a cowboy, an image he would have found funny under different circumstances.

And then came the shout from the other end of the locker room.

"Ramirez, is that you? What on earth is going on?" It was Mr. Mitchell, who had apparently heard the fight and was now heading their way.

Donald immediately shoved Louie—who was in his escape path—through the exit door and into the hallway. Tumbling after him, Donald yanked the door closed behind himself. By this time, Huey had buckled under the weight on his back and both he and Douglas sprawled to the floor.

Mr. Mitchell arrived a moment later to see Huey Jones and a naked Douglas Ramirez, rising to their feet, both damp and covered with traces of soap, while an out-of-breath Nate stood nearby, hands on knees, blood dripping from his nose and onto the tiled floor.

The serpent, still hidden beneath his sleeve, had once again gone still.

Huey was furious. His brother and his pal Lou had left him behind to take the blame for the locker room incident. He hadn't even wanted to pick a fight with the fat kid—but what Donald said to do, they always did. He was getting tired of it. And then Donald just took off, leaving him with that naked kid riding him like a horse.

"What's the explanation for all this?" Mr. Mitchell had demanded.

Fortunately, Watson and the fat kid kept their mouths shut, so Huey didn't have to worry about Donald getting into trouble and blaming him for it. Mr. Mitchell insisted they head to Principal Wright's office as soon as the fat kid had gotten dressed. He escorted them there himself to make sure they didn't "get lost" along the way.

They then had to sit for twenty-five minutes before Principal Wright called them into her office. It was uncomfortable sitting there with the two of them, no one saying a word and everyone avoiding each other's eyes. In her office, the principal tried to get the three of them to snitch on each other. He had to admit that Watson and the fat kid were good at keeping silent. Unfortunately, before dismissing them, she said she would be immediately calling their parents for a conference.

And now, as Huey approached his house, he felt a building anxiety. His father was going to be angry—and Donald wasn't even there to witness it. His brother always found ways to avoid difficult situations at home. Hopefully Principal Wright hadn't yet made the call.

The Joneses lived in a run-down three-bedroom house in the south end of town. It needed a new roof and a coat of paint, but Huey knew that wasn't likely to happen anytime soon. His mother worked two jobs to keep things afloat, while his father spent his days on the couch watching TV and downing his beers. His mother had long ago stopped trying to suggest he get a job. A belt in the mouth had shown her she was better off not trying to get his father to do anything.

The lawn was in bad need of mowing—he would do that later so his mother wouldn't have to. He quietly climbed the steps to the porch and opened the door, trying to make as little sound as possible. If he could get to his room without his father noticing—

"Hubert, is that you?! Get your ass in here—this instant!" yelled his father from the living room.

Great, here it comes, he thought. He went into the living room, accidentally sending an empty beer bottle spinning across the floor. Fortunately, it looked like his father had been at the beer for some time—he probably didn't have to worry about him standing and getting physical with him.

"I just got a call from your school. What were you thinking, you little piece of shit?!" his father began. "Now I have to get up early for a conference with your principal."

Huey said nothing, keeping his sarcastic retorts to himself.

"You can't make it through a day of school without causing me trouble, you worthless—"

And so the conversation went for several more minutes. Huey tuned out most of it. It was always the same. His father made everything about himself. He never took responsibility for anything and contributed nothing. One of these days, Huey knew he was going to snap—and when he did, his father wouldn't even know what hit him.

"I'm going to do this alone," said Nate to Marc as the brothers arrived back at the house after school. "I want you to go straight to your room and stay there."

Nate had decided the time had come to tell Aunt Celia about the serpent—and to ask for her help. He had made no progress in trying to remove it. All his attempts had failed miserably, and its unpredictable contractions and unknown purpose were beginning to really unnerve him.

"But—" Marc said excitedly, his eyes wide.

"Listen, I'm going to tell her that I broke into the room myself. I don't know how she's going to react. I have no choice at this point. I need her help to remove this thing. And I don't want you involved."

"What if she's dangerous?" asked Marc.

"She's been good to us for the last nine months," Nate said. He hoped he sounded convincing. "I've been thinking a lot about this, and I'm sure it'll be fine. You have to trust me."

"Are you sure? What if something happens to you? I—" Marc sounded scared.

"If something does happen, text Jenn and Zach—you can trust them. They'll help you."

The brothers climbed the porch steps. As Nate opened the door to the foyer, they heard Aunt Celia's voice.

"Boys, are you there?" she said from the living room. She sounded irritated. Had she noticed the missing bracelet?

Nate made eye contact with his brother and mouthed the word *go*. To his relief, Marc quietly climbed the stairs and disappeared in the direction of their rooms. Nate headed through the open doors of the living room.

Here we go, he thought.

Marc tiptoed carefully back down the front stairs, careful not to make a sound. There was no way he was going to hide in his bedroom while his brother faced Aunt Celia. He'd found the key, after all, and he had been the one who removed that horrible serpent from the cabinet. All of this was his fault.

He quietly made his way to the open doors of the living room and crouched low, peeking around the door frame. His brother and aunt were already deep in conversation. Aunt Celia held the old bottle from the cabinet in both hands. It appeared to have a crack down its length that hadn't been there when he had last seen it. They stood before the large fireplace at the far end of the room. Aunt Celia began pacing.

"I specifically told you not to enter that room," she was saying, an angry tone in her voice. "You have no idea what you've done." Her brows were furrowed. She set the bottle on a table and continued pacing.

"I'm sorry, but I didn't break your bottle—it wasn't like that when I left."

"But you did open the cabinet?" She turned to face Nate. Her eyes bore into him.

"Well, yes—but you really didn't give me a choice!" Marc heard an edge in his brother's voice that Nate had never used with Aunt Celia before.

Marc braced himself for the scolding he was sure was coming. Instead, Aunt Celia said, "Your father would be disappointed, Nate." Her comment was brief and nonthreatening, but it triggered a transformation in his brother.

Nate's posture changed. He stood taller and appeared more self-assured. He took a step toward her and responded in a voice that told Marc that his brother had had enough.

"Don't you ever bring up my father again," Nate spat. "I know you're not really his sister—you show up mysteriously for the first time after his death when we've never even heard of you. Where were you all our lives? Where were you during our father's life? I didn't see one picture of you in our father's family photos—just the woman who looks like you.

The woman who doesn't age throughout his entire childhood—or do you expect me to believe that our family is full of identical cousins that I've never met?"

Aunt Celia's features suddenly softened. Her anger vanished.

"You're right," she said.

"And then I overhear you," continued Nate, "in your secret little room, explaining to some man—wait, what?"

Marc felt as confused as his brother seemed.

Aunt Celia continued. "You're absolutely right—I've been careless. I should have seen this coming."

Marc wasn't sure what was happening. He certainly hadn't expected Aunt Celia to agree with his brother. She looked concerned now.

"Tell me," said Aunt Celia, "did you happen to see a metallic bracelet, in the shape of—"

"I'll say!" said Nate, cutting off Aunt Celia midsentence and pulling back his sleeve to reveal the serpent encircling his forearm. The serpent's eyes were again glowing a deep red, visible from Marc's position.

There was an audible inhalation from Aunt Celia and her eyes went wide. She exhaled slowly, and Marc couldn't tell if her expression was one of relief or fear—or possibly both.

"We're in grave danger, Nate," she said. "You, me, your brother—and most likely many others as well. We need to talk—and there's something I need to show you. We have no time to waste."

Aunt Celia locked her arm around Nate's and pulled him toward the foyer. Marc scurried backward and flattened himself against the wall just as Aunt Celia led his brother through the foyer and out of the house. He considered revealing himself for a moment, but he knew Nate would be angry if he attempted to accompany them.

Marc dashed to the window in time to see the closing doors of the Bel Air. A moment later, Aunt Celia's vehicle pulled out into the street and drove off into the afternoon sun.

Chapter 8

CROW, WOLF, AND FAWN

Windsor to Hartford, Colony of Connecticut, May 1647

E ight-year-old Allie Young lay in a large wooden box. She didn't know its purpose, or why it was headed to Hartford. She just knew it was hard and uncomfortable and that she didn't dare leave it. She desperately needed to find her mother and knew that every second spent hidden in that box brought her a little bit closer to her.

Several days ago, the men had come without notice and burst into her home. Full of anger, they had accused her mother of terrible things—things that Allie knew to be untrue. Her mother wasn't a sinner and would never hurt anyone. She was nothing but good, kind, and caring. Why had they said such things?

"Don't worry," her mother had said, as the men surrounded her. "Everything will be fine."

But nothing had been fine. The men were scary and mean. And that horrible man had been there—that man Goodman Hodge. He hadn't said a word during the confrontation. He just stood there behind the others, watching and listening. Allie had caught him staring at her as they led her mother from the house—and he had smiled in a way she had found frightening. She didn't like him. He had made her uncomfortable from the start, but no one would listen to her. Could he have done something to cause this?

Her father had kept her in the house since that day. She wasn't allowed to leave, and she didn't know why. He answered none of her questions. The family's neighbor, Anne Thornton, stayed with her when her father was gone from the house. Anne told her stories and played games to pass the time, but she, too, explained nothing and left as soon as her father returned. With so much free time and very little to do, she spent hours thinking of her mother and how much she missed her.

Allie distracted herself by caring for the bird that she had found in the forest. Allie had had to set the bird's wing herself. The bird was alone now—a feeling Allie understood well. She had to help it since no one else would. Gripping the bird's body, she tugged firmly on its wing with her small hand. The bird's screeches were horrific, but Allie knew it was necessary. It took two attempts, but eventually the bone popped into place. She placed a short stick against the wing, wrapping it carefully in a strip of cloth as her mother had described. The baby crow was going to be all right.

As the days passed, she continued to wonder—where was her mother and why hadn't she returned?

Then last night in bed, she had heard a knock at the door—and the sounds of a visitor in the outer area. Hopping quietly out of bed, she moved as close as she dared to the great room and listened to the conversation taking place nearby.

"Tomorrow I shall travel to Hartford by wagon to see Alse for the last time," said her father. "Can you come early? She'll still be asleep."

"Yes, I'll come," Anne Thornton replied.

And that was how Allie knew her mother was in Hartford. She immediately formed a plan.

The following morning as the first rooster crowed, Allie dressed and gathered some bread and cheese, placing them in a sack. It would be a long day, and she would be on her own. When she heard her father stirring, she jumped back into bed, pulling the quilt up to her chin. She closed her eyes and pretended to sleep. Before long, her father entered her sleeping area. She felt a light kiss on her forehead and then he was gone.

Knowing she had to act quickly, Allie hopped out of bed and arranged the quilt and pillows in just the right way. No one would realize she had gone until it was too late. She moved to the window and carefully pushed open the casement. Climbing over the sill, she dropped softly to the ground and swung the window closed behind her.

At the edge of the house, she peeked around the corner, seeing no one in sight. She spotted the wagon her father would take to Hartford. She expected to see the large canvas tarpaulin in back, but not the object beneath it. *What could that be?* she wondered, hoping it wouldn't affect her plan.

Allie jumped onto the back of the wagon and slid under the tarp next to the long, rectangular, wooden object. She didn't think her father would notice the extra bump in the fabric. Her plan was to stay hidden for the ride to Hartford and then somehow locate her mother once there. But for now, she would just wait.

Soon she heard her father approach. He spent several minutes hitching and watering the horse. Not long after that she heard voices she recognized—Anne and her husband, Reverend Thomas Thornton. She knew Anne was there to keep watch over her, but why Reverend Thornton? She had no idea.

"John, my apologies, but you know Reverend Warham and the other leaders won't allow you to bring her back to the settlement," said Reverend Thornton. "I suggest you take Alse to the nearby forest to rest."

"I understand, Reverend," said her father.

"Allow me to aid you in getting the supplies you'll need," said Reverend Thornton.

Allie didn't understand the meaning of what was said, but she realized they would likely bring the supplies to the wagon—and then she would be discovered. As soon as the voices faded, Allie sat up. *I need to hide!* Feeling the top of the crate, she found a lid. Pushing it aside with all her strength, she created an opening just big enough to slip through. Once inside she used her hands and feet to slide it back into place.

As soon as she had finished, the men returned. She heard movement of the tarpaulin followed by the loud heavy clatter of items being tossed next to the crate—in the exact spot where she had hidden just moments before.

"Good luck to you, John Young," she heard Reverend Thornton say.

"Thank you, Reverend."

A large crater in the road brought Allie back to the present. They had left an hour or so before, and her back was already sore from all the bumping and shaking. She would be glad when this journey was over. She was getting closer to her mother with every second, but she still had no idea why they had taken her mother so far from home.

She thought again of the wounded bird and how she and her mother had rescued it. Her mother had taught her much about the local plants and wildlife. She cared deeply for nature and all God's creations. Her mother had also warned her that nature could be as dangerous as it was wondrous.

Allie remembered that day two years ago when she had first understood her mother's connection to the earth and its creatures. She and her mother had gone to the forest on one of their regular outings. They had wandered for some time when they came upon a lone fawn grazing on the leaves of a bush. The fawn was startled at first, but then her mother spoke.

"Hello, little one," she said, reaching toward the small deer. "Why are you out in these woods all alone?"

The fawn approached her and nuzzled her hand.

"Her mother was killed by wolves. The poor thing's all alone," said her mother.

"How do you know, Momma?" asked Allie.

"I can just tell," she replied, without further explanation.

Allie petted the fawn for some time as her mother picked herbs nearby.

"What will happen with the fawn, with no mother to care for her?" she asked.

"I don't know," said her mother. "I hope God will watch over her and keep her safe."

Just then Allie heard a low growl off in the bushes. Turning her head, she located its source—there, not three yards away, stood a large wolf, its mouth dripping saliva.

"Momma!" cried Allie, just as the fawn, recognizing danger, fled into the woods.

The wolf moved forward, still growling, its teeth now visible. Allie was terrified. Would it attack her or her mother? Would it chase after the fawn? They had nothing to fight it off with. Allie saw no good ending to this situation.

Her mother, now at her side, raised her palm toward the beast.

"Stop," she said loudly, her hand forming into a fist.

And to Allie's amazement, the wolf did in fact stop—but not of its own volition. Green tendrils erupted from the forest floor beneath the wolf, spreading quickly, first around its legs and then its entire body. The vines held it firmly in place.

Her mother then approached the creature, raising her hand to its head. The animal gave a soft yelp.

"Rest easy, my new friend," she said, gently caressing its fur. "There is nothing to fear."

Slowly the vines released their grip, gently retracting into the earth. The wolf approached her and sat by her feet, licking her hand with its tongue.

"I must ask a favor, friend wolf," said her mother.

A moment later, Allie heard a rustling in the trees. She turned in time to see the fawn leap gracefully from the foliage and bound happily to the beast's side, expressing no further fear.

"Please protect our little friend," her mother continued. "She's all alone in the world."

With a feeling of wonder, Allie smiled.

Chapter 9

WITCHES AND WARLOCKS

Windsor, Connecticut, May 2019

"A public park? You didn't tell me you were taking me on a picnic," Nate joked, as Aunt Celia pulled the Bel Air into a parking space and stepped out of the vehicle. He hopped out of the passenger side and shut the door.

Northwest Park was located in the Poquonock section of town, a part of Windsor Nate didn't know at all. Several cars were scattered about the parking lot. A couple headed toward the main entrance, their small children running happily along behind them. The trees were green and flush with new spring leaves, the weather perfect for an afternoon stroll—and for the life of him, Nate couldn't imagine why Aunt Celia had brought him here.

They followed the young family into the park, passing over a small, wooden bridge. Aunt Celia's expression remained serious, her voice low and purposeful as they walked.

"This land was originally purchased from the Podunk Indians after the settlers arrived from Europe," she explained. "It remained mostly untouched until the 1800s, when portions of it were industrialized and cultivated. A number of iron ore blast furnaces and paper mills were built, and other areas were used for farming tobacco."

"Um, OK," said Nate. His brows were furrowed. He wore a perplexed expression. He wasn't sure why she was telling him this.

"In 1936," she continued, "a flood uncovered a series of dinosaur tracks that created a lot of excitement in the area, and later, in 1953, the town of Windsor began reacquiring the land in an attempt to preserve it. They eventually turned it into a public park."

"All this is interesting," said Nate, as he quickened his pace to keep up with Aunt Celia. "But what does this have to do—"

Aunt Celia cut him off. "There are certain areas in this park, Nate, that have not been disturbed since the first Puritans settled Connecticut."

The revelation threw him. He wasn't sure how to respond, so he said nothing. Where was she taking him? Were they about to see something from the time of the first settlers?

The park opened up and they came upon several wooden, barn-like buildings. Children played with balls on the grass, their parents chatting nearby. Picnic tables could be seen in all directions, nestled in the trees. Off to the right were several pens of farm animals. Nate saw a young boy standing with his mother, feeding carrots to a brown-and-white cow through a tall wire fence. They walked hurriedly past the nature center, heading directly to one of the many walking trails that wound through the forest.

Although it was daylight, the heavy tree cover blocked much of the direct sunlight.

"This would be really creepy at night," he said, relieved that sundown wouldn't arrive for several hours.

Aunt Celia nodded. "It can be—but don't worry, we won't be here long."

Nate continued walking with his aunt in silence. They soon turned off the path and into an untraveled section of woods. Nate looked warily behind him, worried that he wouldn't remember the way back.

He pulled up his sleeve and glanced at the serpent. Its black surface glistened when light hit it through the trees, but its eyes remained dark. It hadn't contracted in some time. He wished he knew what triggered it. For the time being, at least it was dormant and leaving him alone.

Aunt Celia didn't slow. She walked with extreme purpose, seeming to know exactly where she was headed. Nate stepped carefully through the brush and debris, trying to keep up.

Other than the history lesson, she hadn't shared any information. After all the months of secrecy, Nate was surprised that she had finally agreed to talk. But the deeper they got into the forest, the more worried he became that maybe that wasn't her intention at all. This untraveled section of the park would make a fine place to leave a body, if one so desired.

He pulled out his phone, thinking to text Marc or Jenn or Zach—only to find no cell reception. *What have I gotten myself into?* he thought.

Eventually they came to a small break in the trees. Wildflowers dotted the area, and to Nate's surprise, there was a rather healthy patch of green grass covering the ground. He wouldn't have expected it to grow in such limited sunlight.

Aunt Celia walked to the center of the small clearing where a cluster of purple and white flowers grew.

"Come here, please, Nate," she said.

Nate walked over to her side.

"Do me a favor," she said. "Clear away that patch of flowers if you would."

Nate kneeled to obey, common sense arguing against it. In this position it would be easy for Aunt Celia to hit him in the head with a rock or harm him in some way, but he needed whatever information she could provide, and he wanted to trust her. The flowers came free with a gentle tug, revealing a flat gray stone. A gravestone. He brushed away the dirt and read the inscription:

Alse Young
B. 1617 D. 1647

It was the name he had heard earlier in the day in Mr. Foster's class!

"I don't understand," said Nate. "Why are you showing me this?"

"This, Nate Watson, is your eleventh-great-grandmother on your father's side."

"Really? Are you sure?" asked Nate. "Wasn't she hanged as a witch?" He didn't know what to make of this information.

"I'm sure—and yes, sadly she was."

"But what does it mean?" he asked, confused. He looked up at Aunt Celia and saw that her expression was sorrowful.

"I'll tell you why this is important," said Aunt Celia, "but the reason I'm so certain about this is because—she was also *my mother*."

"Wait, *what*?" said Nate. What she was saying made no sense. He stood. Brushing the dirt from his hands, he waited for her to continue.

"Alse Young was my mother. My true name is also Alice—Alice Young Beamon."

"But that would make you . . . over 350 years old," said Nate. He looked at her, askance. *How could that be?*

"Yes. That is correct." Aunt Celia seemed sincere.

He believed that she believed what she was telling him. Was she delusional? She wasn't generally the joking type. He decided to play along for the moment.

"So, the photos in my father's album—that really *was* you?"

"Yes, I'm sorry for the deception," she said. "The truth would have complicated matters, and I knew you would find it hard to believe."

He thought about it for a minute. "It actually makes more sense than the army of clones I had imagined," he said.

Aunt Celia laughed. Her expression relaxed. "You're taking this much better than I expected," she said.

"Well," said Nate, "it's been a strange couple of days, and not much has made sense. How is it that you haven't aged?"

"We can talk about that later—but first, we need to talk about the damaged bottle and the serpent." Celia gestured toward his right forearm. Nate pulled back his sleeve.

"This part you may find hard to believe—" said Aunt Celia.

This part? Nate just nodded—the thoughts and emotions he had been experiencing had left him somewhat numb, and he now just wanted to hear what she had to say.

"Magick and sorcery are very real things. True mystical powers are extremely rare, but there are individuals with the ability to make use of such powers."

"Magickal powers?" asked Nate. Where was she going with this?

"Yes. Let me explain. There are three types of magick, and although it's rare, a select group of people are able to tap into one or more of them. The first type is *innate* magick. For some, these powers are innately part of their being, given to them at birth through genetics—some even say they're gifts of God."

Nate nodded, letting her continue.

"The second type is *learned* magick. Other individuals, although they may have no natural magick of their own, are able to make use of the magick that exists naturally in the world through the use of spells, charms, and potions. These methods of channeling and manipulating external powers are more difficult and less predictable, but there are some who are able to do so quite masterfully.

"And finally, the third type is *borrowed* magick. There are yet others who obtain their abilities through darker means. These individuals are rare, and usually very dangerous as they've taken steps to gain power through bargains with dark entities."

"Dark entities?" he said with a look of disbelief.

"Yes," she replied. "Through bargains with demons and other dark creatures—and occasionally even with Satan himself."

Demons? Satan? thought Nate. *Oh my God—this poor woman is cracked.* He had been taking in her explanations until this point, but he was starting to wonder if he should try to make a run for it.

But then he thought of the serpent and the album and all the other strange and impossible things that he had encountered. It was important for him to listen to the rest of Aunt Celia's story.

"So, what are you saying?" he asked.

"The first point I'm trying to get to is that my mother, Alse Young—your ancestor—had certain magickal abilities—of the innate variety."

"So she really was a witch?"

"I personally despise that word. For me, it's had such negative connotations. But to answer your question—yes. At the time my mother was hanged, the common belief was that all people with magickal abilities obtained them through direct ties to Satan, and they used those abilities exclusively to further his evil agendas. My mother was a caring, loving person who did everything she could to help people. She would never ally herself with Satan. Ironically, the majority of the people executed for witchcraft in America and in other parts of the world were not witches in any sense of the word."

He nodded. He had always assumed as much—but then again, he had grown up believing that witches were imaginary.

"The fact of the matter is that if the Puritans had ever actually captured and tried to execute a witch of the type they sought—one with evil intentions and ties to Satan—they'd have been promptly met with fire and brimstone. Everything they knew and loved would have been burned out of existence. That type of witch is one you just don't mess with."

Aunt Celia's voice was gradually rising in volume and a scowl had taken over her features. She continued, "The only actual witches that were executed were ones like my mother, who sacrificed themselves to protect those they loved. The biggest irony of all is that in their paranoia to eliminate Satan's agents of evil, the Puritans were themselves actually doing Satan's work by killing scores of innocents—both here and in Europe."

"Wow," said Nate, unsure what else to say and surprised by her sudden intensity.

Aunt Celia paused, taking in a couple of deep breaths. Her body began to relax, and her features softened. Nate waited a moment for her to continue.

"I'm sorry," she said, "this topic is difficult for me. After witnessing my mother's hanging, I broke with Puritan beliefs—although I had to live among the Puritans for many years. They even accused me of being a witch myself once, but thanks to my son, Simon—he was my staunchest defender—it didn't make it to the courts."

"Um, well—are you?" Nate studied her face, waiting for a reaction.

"Am I a witch?" Aunt Celia laughed. "Well, I did inherit some magick from my mother, so yes—but again, I don't like that word."

Well, Marc will be thrilled, thought Nate.

"About the bottle and the serpent," he prompted. The more he was hearing, the more anxious he was to get the bracelet off his arm.

"Yes," said Aunt Celia. "Once, a long time ago, I encountered a man by the name of Malleus Hodge. He was a selfish man, an opportunist who sought money and social standing at the expense of others. He was partly responsible for the execution of my mother. I made an enemy of him early on—I was but a child at the time, but I was able to evade him and live my life in peace. I married, had children—it was a good life.

"To make a long story short, one day he returned. But he was a man no longer—he was something more, something evil. Through a pact with a demon, he'd gained incredible powers—the powers of blood magick and necromancy, among other things. And though the idea terrified me, I knew I had to do something to protect myself and my family. I knew one day he'd find me and then it would be too late. So I sought him out, and with the help of a woman greatly skilled in magick, I was able to trap his essence in a bottle where it would be able to do no harm."

"The old bottle in the cabinet?"

"The very same," said Aunt Celia. "Through magick, I was able to extend my life so that I could guard it and keep it safe." Her hand went to the amulet she always wore around her neck.

"But it's broken—"

"Yes, and he's free," she said. "We're in great danger. It'll take him some time to regain his strength—I'm not sure how long we have, but not long."

With horror, Nate realized the implications of his actions, if what she was saying was true. He kept trying to tell himself it was unlikely, but he had to admit she was very convincing.

"But what does he want?" asked Nate, his face showing some concern in spite of his doubts.

She pointed once again to his forearm.

"Well first and foremost, he's going to want that bracelet—it's the source of much of his power. We're lucky he doesn't have it, but it also makes you a target."

Could he afford *not* to believe Aunt Celia? She herself clearly believed, and if there was the slightest chance that she spoke the truth, he was in serious danger. If there was a centuries-old evil sorcerer—witch? warlock?—with the powers of hell after him, then he had better do whatever she suggested. As much as he had wanted to deny it, the serpent did seem to have a mind of its own, and the idea that it was magickal didn't seem so far-fetched.

"Can we destroy the serpent?" asked Nate. "Or hide it? How do I take it off?"

"A friend and I did extensive research after obtaining it. My understanding is that it chooses its owner, and it appears to have chosen you," said Aunt Celia. "It fell free when Hodge was first trapped in the witch's bottle. There may be a way to remove it, but the only person I know of that may have that information—"

"Is Hodge himself?" Nate frowned. The realization felt like a kick to the stomach.

"Yes, and there's a good chance he'll be able to detect the serpent's location simply by the amount of power it gives off."

"Like a GPS from hell," Nate said. His aunt smiled kindly at him, but then her expression became serious again.

"I'm afraid we haven't much time," she told him.

"So what do we do?"

"We should get back to the house. There are some things we need to do to prepare."

Suddenly, Nate had the feeling that something was off. From the corner of his eye, he sensed an encroaching darkness. Turning, he saw the healthy green grass begin to turn black in a wave that radiated out from a point near the tree line.

As if on cue, the serpent clamped down on his arm. It began to pulse, and he was certain he could feel its fangs digging deeper into his skin.

"Um, Aunt Celia . . ." he said, pointing frantically to the ground. The grass was turning black beneath their feet.

"Nate, stay close to me," she said. Nate sensed from the look on her face that something bad was about to happen.

From the wave's point of origin, he became aware of a small dark creature. It blended in with the blackened grass but became clearer as his eyes adjusted. It resembled a furless, horned monkey with wings—and the face of an old man.

"What the hell *is* that thing?!" cried Nate, equally repulsed and frightened.

"That is an imp," said Aunt Celia, excitedly. "Stay behind me, and don't let it touch you. It would seem that I've grossly misjudged the amount of time we have. If it's here, its master can't be far behind."

"*Its master?*" The complete and utter realization that everything his aunt had told him was true hit him like a ton of bricks. There was no doubt left in him.

They stood there in the center of the clearing waiting for the creature to make a move. It stared at them, its furless arms dragging on the ground. Every so often it hopped several inches into the air and released a hideous chittering sound before coming to rest and continuing its still and silent observation of them. Nate had never been so terrified in his life.

"It's waiting for something," said Aunt Celia.

"What are we gonna do?" asked Nate. They had no weapons or means of defense. Nate thought of Marc—who would take care of his brother if they didn't make it out of these woods?

The serpent began to convulse furiously, the sudden, increased pain causing Nate to cry out.

The entire clearing suddenly darkened as if the moon had chosen that moment to eclipse the sun. Within the forest a flame appeared. It was moving closer by the moment.

"Stay behind me," Aunt Celia repeated.

"You got it."

As the burning light source got closer, Nate realized it was a torch—or maybe a staff, topped with fire. The man who held it wore clothing from another century: a long-sleeved, button-down jacket with thick cuffs over a pair of baggy shorts, cinched at the knees. On his calves he wore dark socks that disappeared into high-tongued leather shoes. On his head sat a tall brimmed hat. A long, dark cloak billowed out behind him as he moved. He stopped at the edge of the clearing and smiled at Aunt Celia. Nate didn't like the look of the smile one bit.

"Alice, my dear. So good to see you," the man said. The imp loped over to its master.

"Hodge, stay back," Aunt Celia commanded. She raised a palm in his direction.

"Not likely," Hodge said. "You have something of mine. And I want it. *Now.*"

"You're still weak—this will not turn out as you hope."

Nate prayed that Aunt Celia wasn't just bluffing. Here in front of them was the evil being he had freed—and they were totally unprepared. He desperately looked around for a weapon of any kind, but the clearing was free of rocks and loose branches. Nate felt his pockets. He had his phone and his house key. Neither would do any good.

"We can do this the easy way," began Hodge, "or the hard way. Your choice." The creature chittered again at his feet.

"Begone, Hodge!" said Aunt Celia sharply in response.

Out of the darkness appeared two large shapes that loped toward them. They looked like oversized house cats. In the light from Hodge's staff, Nate saw that they were spotted, with bobbed tails. *Bobcats?*

Oh God, what now?

The cats came to a stop on either side of Nate and Aunt Celia. To Nate's utter shock, they turned to face Hodge and his creature and began to hiss.

Nate had expected to be mauled—but the cats stood *with* him and Aunt Celia. They were the *good guys*.

"The hard way it is," said Malleus Hodge, in a tired, disappointed voice. He beat the heel of his staff against the ground, and the ball of flame doubled in size and intensity. "Go find it, boy."

The imp, as if set free from a leash, bolted in their direction. It was after the bracelet, and Nate could tell it sensed its location. Its horrible cry broke the silence, and as it neared, it leaped directly at Aunt Celia, who stood between it and the bracelet on Nate's arm.

One of the bobcats leaped to intercept the imp, while the second cat hissed loudly and launched itself at Hodge. Nate watched in frozen horror.

The first bobcat took down the imp, rolling with it on the ground as it attacked the hell beast with both tooth and claw. The bobcat's fur started to smolder before suddenly bursting into flames. With a pain-filled shriek, the cat dropped its prey and began rolling around on the ground to put out the blaze. Had the imp's simple touch caused the animal to catch fire?

The second bobcat fared even worse. As it leaped for Hodge, it was met with the flaming end of the staff, and the cat's smoldering husk fell to the ground, incinerated before even reaching him. Nate saw, however, that Hodge's staff had dimmed—the huge fiery ball was now a simple flame. Did this mean he was weakening, as Aunt Celia had suggested?

Aunt Celia had taken advantage of the brief distraction to grab a branch from the tree line. Nate wondered why he hadn't thought of that—or why he hadn't just run like hell. But then again, he was probably better off with Aunt Celia. The imp had recovered and was heading his way. Without the light from Hodge's fireball, the creature was difficult to see, so Nate pulled out his phone and shined its flashlight straight at it.

The creature let out a squeal and backed away, momentarily startled. By the time it recovered, Aunt Celia was back at his side. She swung the large stick with all her might, making contact with the imp and sending it flying back several feet. Unfortunately, her momentum got the better of her, and she fell to the ground, the branch tumbling from her grasp.

"Come on, Alice," said Hodge. "You're embarrassing yourself!"

Nate was reminded of his encounter with the Ducks, after Donald had shoved Jenn to the ground. *Bullies are all alike*, thought Nate. He felt an anger rising. *Why can't they all just leave us alone?*

Out of the corner of his eye, he saw the imp. It was heading toward him again, with Aunt Celia—still on the ground—in its path. Nate thought of the blazing bobcat, still writhing on the scorched grass. He couldn't let that happen to his aunt. He couldn't let the monster touch her.

Nate quickly picked up the fallen branch and, with all his might, brought it down, barely missing the creature's head. The imp dodged at the last moment, and as soon as the business end of the branch hit the ground, the creature jumped onto it, climbing quickly toward Nate. It leaped onto his arm—the arm with the serpent bracelet—and held on tightly with both arms and legs. Nate dropped the branch and fought to shake the hideous beast loose, to no avail.

"Nate!" he heard Aunt Celia cry out as she struggled to her feet.

Nate held out his arm, lifting the creature as best he could, trying to keep it away from his body. And then the inevitable happened—his sleeve burst into flames. He heard the roaring of the blaze as it grew higher and higher, and he was terrified.

But then Nate realized he felt no heat.

"*No!*" he heard another cry. This time it was Hodge. Nate could see the fury on his face as his precious imp burned.

With a loud screech, the creature fell to the ground, scampering unsteadily off toward its master, the flames dying away as it got farther from Nate and the bracelet. Had the serpent protected him? It was the only thing that made sense.

The snake on Nate's arm glowed orange with flame, its eyes an even brighter red. If Hodge hadn't known Nate had his hell bracelet before, he certainly knew now.

"Are you OK?" asked Aunt Celia.

"I think so," said Nate.

"Get ready to run," she said.

Just then a huge black bear rose behind Malleus Hodge. With a thunderous growl, it knocked him to the ground with its huge claws, sending his staff flying. Hodge was pinned beneath the weight of the bear. The remaining bobcat, somewhat recovered, leaped at him as well, its teeth clamping down on Hodge's shoulder as the sorcerer struggled in pain and frustration to get free. The darkness that had blanketed the area lifted suddenly and was replaced with the afternoon sun. For another shocking moment, Nate watched the surreal struggle between witch and wildlife.

"Let's get out of here," Aunt Celia said. "Now!"

Nate didn't have to be told twice. His heart thumping in his chest, he turned immediately and ran for the trees. His Aunt Celia—the witch—followed closely behind.

Chapter 10

THE PROTECTION SPELL

"The bear just came out of nowhere?" asked Marc, later that night. "And Aunt Celia was controlling it?" The boys were in the living room. Aunt Celia had gone upstairs to begin preparations for dealing with Malleus Hodge.

"I don't think she controls them," said Nate. "I think she communicates with them mentally somehow and asks for their help."

"Like Aquaman?" asked Marc, excitedly. "Can she talk to fish?"

"I have no idea," said Nate.

"Did she show you her broom?" asked Marc. "Does she have one of those big black soup pots that witches stir?"

"I don't think witches really have those things," said Nate. "But listen, we need to keep this to ourselves and listen to what Aunt Celia tells us. We're in danger from this Hodge person, and we need to do whatever she says." Nate wanted to make Marc understand that they were facing real danger, without scaring him too much.

"We can't even tell Zach and Jenn?" Nate saw the disappointment in his brother's eyes.

"Not just yet. We need to wait."

Just then, they heard a voice from upstairs.

"Boys," called Aunt Celia, "come up here, please."

Nate and Marc climbed the stairs to the second floor. They were surprised to see the door to the forbidden room standing wide open for the first time. Aunt Celia was inside, arranging chairs around a table in the center of the room. The table hadn't been there before.

Aunt Celia gave Marc an affectionate look and ruffled his hair. "I assume Nate's had time to fill you in?" she asked.

"Yeah, I'm good—is that a bird?" asked Marc, noticing the large crow sitting in the birdcage. He walked over to it and peered inside. The cage door was wide open. "Where did it come from?"

"Yes, I call him Corvin," said Aunt Celia. "He comes and goes as he pleases. We've known each other for some time."

Nate saw that the window was still open. The crow really could come and go as it pleased.

"First off, I want to apologize for my earlier deception," said Aunt Celia. "If I'd told you the truth about my situation to begin with, we wouldn't be in this predicament. There's generally nothing good that comes from sharing the existence of abilities such as mine. In my younger days, it would have resulted in a death sentence, as it did for my mother. I should have told you sooner. I'm sorry that I didn't.

"Furthermore, you're now free to enter this room as you please. We'll use it as our base of operations for our new project. I just ask that you be careful with all the items in here. We can't have any more accidents."

At this Nate squirmed with embarrassment, but when he looked up, he saw that Aunt Celia didn't look angry. Still, it *was* his fault that they were in such a terrible predicament.

"There isn't anything truly dangerous in here now that Hodge has escaped," she went on. "But some of the items are very old and quite rare. Do you have any questions?"

"Did our father know our family history?" asked Marc. He returned to the table and took a seat. "Was he a witch, too?"

"Yes, he knew," said Aunt Celia with a smile. "But he had no skills in magick. It's extremely rare and tends to surface primarily in females. But your grandmother had some magickal talents. She and I were quite close, and I know she encouraged him not to talk about it. When people know you're different, they tend to fear and mistrust you."

"Funny," said Nate, choosing a chair beside his brother, "I hadn't thought about it, but our grandmother's name was Alice, just like yours and your mother's."

"Yes, that's not a coincidence," said Aunt Celia. "My mother was named Alice, although it was spelled differently, as was her mother before her, back many generations. I myself had twelve children, and in only one did I sense magickal potential—I named her Alice as well. And you're a descendant of hers. That tradition continued through to your grandmother."

"And they were all witches?" asked Marc, eyes wide. His mouth fell open.

When Nate saw his brother's expression, he had to suppress a laugh.

"They all had some level of magickal ability," said Aunt Celia. "But most of them lived just ordinary lives."

"You had twelve children?" asked Nate. "You must have hundreds of descendants."

"Yes, you're correct," said Aunt Celia, somberly. "Sadly, there soon became too many to keep track of, but I made sure to stay in touch with the Alices. I was able to share with them the reason for my longevity."

"Are any of the other Alices still alive?" asked Marc.

Aunt Celia grasped the stone around her neck.

"No, they had no reason to extend their lives. They preferred to grow old with their husbands. It's difficult to live so long, watching as the world changes and friends and loved ones grow old and pass on. I had to move around periodically, changing my name and starting over so no one would realize my age. It hasn't been easy. But I had an important responsibility—to watch over that bottle and make sure Hodge didn't escape to hurt anyone."

"And then we came along . . ." said Nate with a frown.

"That's water under the bridge," said Aunt Celia. "Let's focus on fixing this. Together we can find a solution."

"So, what's the plan?" asked Nate.

"Well, first of all," said Aunt Celia, "we need to protect this house so Hodge cannot enter it. Marc, can you get that mortar and pestle from the table over there?" She pulled a couple of crystals out of the cabinet that had contained the witch's bottle.

"It's the stone bowl with the crusher thing," said Nate to his brother, pretty sure Marc didn't know what Aunt Celia was referring to. Marc went to the table and picked up the mortar and pestle. He carried it over to her.

"Crush these for me, please," she said to Marc, handing him the two crystals. One was pink and one was white. Marc went to work grinding them into a powder while Aunt Celia pulled a large ceramic bowl out of another cabinet.

"We're going to cast a spell that will prevent Hodge from entering the house," she said. "I'll need your help to complete it." She wandered around the room grabbing various herbs and other items. Finally, she approached the cage with the crow.

"I'm sorry, old friend," she said as she reached into the cage and plucked a couple of the crow's feathers. He squawked once but made no further sound.

"So, who exactly is this Hodge guy?" asked Nate as he watched Aunt Celia mix various items together in the bowl.

"Malleus Hodge was the name he was using when I first met him," said Aunt Celia. "He'd just come over from England, I found out later, to escape prosecution for some horrible crimes he'd committed there. Apparently, he faked his death and changed his name, coming here to America where no one was likely to recognize him. Unfortunately for my mother, he decided to set up residence here in Windsor, where we were living at the time."

"What did he do in England?" asked Marc.

"Well, the year was 1647—there was great political and religious unrest in England at the time. The country was in the midst of civil war while a struggle was taking place between Protestantism and Catholicism. Hodge took advantage of the chaos to benefit himself at the expense of others.

"Similar to what later occurred in America, there was a witch hysteria that went through the country at the time. Hodge proclaimed himself

Witchfinder General and became quite wealthy by charging towns a fee for identifying witches in their midst and getting them to confess. Hundreds of innocent people were hanged directly as a result of his actions."

"Wait a minute," said Nate. "You said 1647. That book—*The Discovery of Witches*. It was written by someone named Matthew Hopkins. Was that actually Hodge?"

Aunt Celia stopped what she was doing and raised an eyebrow. "You know of that book? Yes, that's the name Hodge used when he was in England."

"Sorry," said Nate. "I meant to tell you—we have the copy of the book that was in the cabinet with the bottle. And then our friend Jenn came across a second copy yesterday at school—it was donated to the school library."

"I see," said Aunt Celia. "I'd assumed Hodge had taken the book from the case—it was his own personal copy. He'll likely be wanting it back. It's odd that the book would also show up at the school. I doubt it's a coincidence."

Aunt Celia took the crystal powder from Marc and stirred it into her mixture.

"What happened next?" asked Marc.

"Well, Matthew Hopkins, a.k.a. Malleus Hodge, faked his death and came to America where he found something he'd never seen before—a person with true magick. I found out later that he witnessed my mother on one of the rare occasions she used her abilities. He'd caused the deaths of so many innocent people in England—and here for the first time he found an opportunity to eliminate an actual witch. He was careful about how he went about it this time, influencing the people of Windsor just enough to make them think it was their own idea to accuse and prosecute Alse Young.

"I think he hoped that her execution would start a fear of witches here in America that he could profit from like he did in England—and he'd be able to justify his methods and actions more easily if America's witches were actually the real deal."

Corvin squawked in his cage. Aunt Celia glanced in his direction and nodded. *The crow just spoke to her*, Nate realized with amazement. Aunt Celia continued stirring.

"Ironically, in the end, I think he regretted his involvement in my mother's execution. He'd developed a fascination for magick and had been responsible for eliminating the only person he'd ever met with magickal abilities. He soon became interested in me, hoping I might have inherited some of her talents. I believe he hoped to make use of my magick to further his own goals. Fortunately, I was able to disrupt his plans and evade him. He traveled around Connecticut for some time stirring up trouble as he went, until one day I learned that he'd obtained magick of his own. In pursuing his obsession for magick, he'd performed a ritual and summoned an agent of Satan. He made a bargain with that demonic entity—his soul for magick power of his own. And that's how he became a witch. He was given power along with the serpent to significantly enhance it."

"Did he stop witch hunting when he became a witch himself?" asked Nate.

"No, unfortunately he didn't. He was never able to build a reputation as a witchfinder in America as he had in England. He continued his efforts to create hysteria here, but his motives seemed to have changed. I think he was able to gain power directly from the emotional turmoil he caused. Power seemed to be what he sought most by then. And it was much easier for him to stir up trouble—blaming others for performing witchcraft is certainly easier when you have magick of your own to frame them with. My last interaction with him was in Salem at the height of the hysteria, and he was very powerful at the time."

"Did he cause the Salem witch trials?" asked Marc, eagerly.

"Well, he certainly contributed to them," Aunt Celia replied. "Marc, please bring me those candles. I think we're ready to begin." She pointed to a cluster of candles on a shelf that were well-used and covered in drips of wax.

"Nate, please shut off the lights," she said as soon as Marc had placed the candles on the table. Nate did as he was asked, feeling a bit of excitement as he returned to the table—never in his life had he expected to participate in the casting of an actual magick spell. It had gotten dark outside, and he moved carefully back to his spot next to the others.

"OK, please remain quiet until I'm finished," said Aunt Celia.

"*Adolebitque*," she said, beginning her incantation. The flames on the candles lit, bringing a soft glow to the room. She continued, carefully pronouncing the remaining words of the spell:

Tuebor,
Ab intra,
Hic et nunc,
Concilio et labore,
Bono malum superate,
Dona nobis pacem,
Luceo non uro,
Protecto maxima,
Consummatum est.

As soon as she uttered the final word, a pink flame erupted from the bowl, the color of one of the crystals Marc had ground to powder. It was gone as quickly as it appeared.

"Well, that should do it," said Aunt Celia. "Nate, can you please get the lights?"

That was a bit anticlimactic, thought Nate as he obeyed.

"Are we done?" asked Marc as the lights came back on. Aunt Celia blew out the candles on the table.

"No, not quite," she said. She walked over to a drawer and pulled out three black Sharpie markers. "This part of the spell is complete. Next, we need to go to each room in the house and draw one of those on the floor," she said pointing to the encircled pentagram on the wall. "We'll then place a small amount of the ash from the bowl on each pentacle."

"Isn't that a satanic symbol?" Nate asked.

"No, not at all," said Aunt Celia. "The five-pointed star is a pentagram, but with the circle around it, it's called a pentacle. The symbol has many meanings, but it's frequently used as a symbol of protection."

The three spent the next two hours going from room to room, drawing the pentacles on the floor and sprinkling a bit of ash on top. The lines of each pentacle glowed momentarily to indicate the spell's completion. Aunt Celia then placed a strip of packing tape over the ash to make sure it stayed in place.

"It isn't pretty," she said, "but it'll do the trick."

When they were finished, they went down to the kitchen for a glass of homemade lemonade.

"Thanks for your assistance tonight. We work well together," she said with a smile as they sat around the kitchen table. "Hodge won't be able to bother us here in the house. Do either of you have any more questions?"

"Is Hodge a witch or a warlock?" asked Nate.

"They really mean the same thing," said Aunt Celia. "Witches can be male or female, but the term warlock is frequently used to distinguish a male witch. There are a lot of other words that can be used, but you generally only see them in fantasy novels. They're all roughly the same: mage, sorcerer, enchanter, and so on. I prefer not to use such labels."

"So, what happens next?" asked Marc.

"Next, we go to bed," said Aunt Celia. She smiled. "You two have school tomorrow. Just be sure not to go anywhere alone and be back in the house by dark. I'll work on planning our next course of action."

"We don't have to worry about Hodge coming after us tomorrow?" asked Nate.

"I didn't say that," said Aunt Celia. "You need to remain vigilant. He'll be back, but he'll not likely confront any of us in public. It's in his best interest to be discreet. Have you ever heard of an actual witch in the real world?"

"No," said Nate and Marc in unison.

"There's a reason for that. They need to act with care, using their powers creatively to avoid public scrutiny. A single person witnessing magick isn't taken seriously. A hundred people crying 'Witch!' aren't as easily dismissed. Most evil witches scheme and use their magick with subtlety—they take the longer, safer path to power, becoming politicians, dictators, and presidents. Hodge has been out of circulation for some time, but I'm certain he'll see there's nothing to be gained by public displays of death and destruction.

"Hodge will need to rebuild his strength and come up with a plan to retrieve the serpent. We'll just need to stay one step ahead of him. He'll be looking for substitute power sources to supplement his own until he can get the bracelet back. I just need to determine how he'll go about that. But for now—let's get some sleep."

As they got up to head off to bed, Nate remembered something he had forgotten in all the excitement.

"Um, Aunt Celia?" he said. "Something happened at school today." He filled her in on the fight with the Ducks and the meeting with the principal in the morning. He was relieved when she brushed the whole thing off.

"Don't worry about it," she said. "You did the right thing. I'll take you to school tomorrow, and we'll deal with it."

As the three of them climbed the stairs to the second floor, Nate thought about how things had changed with Aunt Celia. He had woken that morning not knowing what to make of her, thinking she was mysterious, deceitful, and potentially dangerous. And since then, he had learned how strong and courageous a person she was and how much she did care about him and his brother. He also came to realize he really liked her—how many people had a person like her in the family? He shook his head as he considered the craziness of the whole thing.

Nate went on ahead, but Marc stopped at the bottom of the stairs.

"I've been meaning to ask," Nate overheard his brother say to Aunt Celia. "Can you talk to fish?"

The imp followed the scent of magick to the large Victorian on Windsor Avenue. Its master would be pleased that his prized possession had been located—and even more pleased if the creature could find a way to return it to him. The imp would have to be careful, though. It still remembered the burning pain it had experienced earlier when trying to take the artifact from the boy in the forest. As a denizen of hell, the imp was usually immune to heat and flame. It was far more used to causing pain than receiving it.

The beast chittered as it circled the building, looking for a way to enter, its hands and feet moving quickly along the ground. Eventually it found the open window on the second floor and using all of its limbs, it gingerly climbed the brick wall below it. As it approached the sill, it leaped, propelling itself through the open window. It was met with an invisible barrier that tossed it back out into the darkness.

The crow, perched on the table within the darkened room, watched intently as the creature attempted entry again and was again expelled by the barrier. Corvin never once doubted the reliability of his mistress's spell. The crow continued to watch as the creature attempted this several more times before giving up in frustration and loping off into the night.

Chapter 11

THE WINDSOR WITCH

Hartford, Colony of Connecticut, May 1647

Allie wandered through the crowd of people assembling outside the Hartford Meetinghouse. She had never before seen this many people gathered in one place. Small groups of men stood talking to each other. Groups of women chatted as their children ran around playing tag and rolling hoops through the throngs of people. Some families sat, finishing the lunches that had been carefully prepared for their journey into the Hartford settlement.

During the long ride from Windsor, Allie had finished the bread and cheese she had taken with her. She ate more from boredom and anxiety than out of hunger. She didn't know what she would find upon her arrival in Hartford, but it certainly hadn't been a community celebration or whatever this was that was going on around her.

As soon as her father stopped the wagon, he again watered the horse before heading off—she assumed—toward Meetinghouse Square. As soon as she was confident he had left the area, she climbed out of the long crate, careful not to step on the pile of shovels and rakes that Reverend Thomas and her father had tossed into the wagon. Was her father planning to do some gardening after the trip into Hartford? It seemed a strange thing to do after a long day of travel, but Allie didn't give it much thought. Her top priority was finding her mother.

Hopping off the back of the wagon, she saw that a number of other wagons had been left in the area, too. She had only been to Hartford a couple times with her parents, and they had traveled by boat. The majority of the grass in the area was healthy and untrampled, and it didn't appear this was a regular stopping point for visitors.

Off in the distance she saw a horse and rider heading in her direction on the road from Windsor. Fearing someone might recognize her, she quickly hid behind the wagon. She had gotten this far, and she had no intention of getting caught now. As Allie waited, it occurred to her that Anne Thornton had probably already realized she was missing and was at this moment frantically searching for her. She felt bad about that. But no one had been willing to tell her why her mother had been taken, and so she had done what she felt was necessary to find her.

Allie flattened herself against the wagon as the rider approached. She peered cautiously around the corner as he passed. The man wore a dark cloak and the popular capotain hat that many men wore around Windsor. It wasn't until the man passed close by the wagon that Allie was able to get a good view of his face. She inhaled quickly, holding her breath and flattening herself even more tightly against the wagon. It was Malleus Hodge—one of the last people she wanted to see at this moment.

What is he doing here? she thought. Could he have followed them to Hartford?

Allie waited until he was a good distance away before heading into the settlement, trying to remain out of sight as much as possible. She saw no further sign of Hodge or her father and found herself in the midst of the gathering townsfolk. She recognized several other people from Windsor in the town square and tried her best to avoid them.

Why were all these people here?

Unsure what to do, and feeling overwhelmed by the press of the crowd,

Allie headed toward an edge of the square to gather her thoughts and come up with a plan. She thought it best to stay away from the crowd as much as possible for the moment, worried that someone would recognize her or ask where her parents were. She sat beneath a tree, wondering if she might locate her mother somewhere in that mass of people. The Hartford Meetinghouse stood amid the gathering. She also saw a large wooden structure standing erect near the building. From her position she couldn't tell what it was or recognize its purpose.

An old woman sat several yards away against a fence. She wore a simple, if soiled, dress with a bonnet on top of her head, its ribbons blowing loosely in the breeze. She was all alone, and yet she appeared to be animatedly talking to someone. Her behavior was odd, but she seemed harmless—at least from a distance. Allie wondered if she should talk to her. Maybe she knew where her mother was? The woman looked feeble. Allie could always run away before the woman could even stand up.

Suddenly Allie was struck and knocked to the ground. An enormous tongue coated her face in spittle, and she found herself laughing at the funny-looking dog that towered over her, its tail wagging furiously.

"Hello boy," she said as she struggled to a seated position against the tree, wiping the moisture from her face with her sleeve. "What are you doing here?" The dog's fur was matted but it appeared healthy enough. She petted it for a few moments, pulling out several burs.

"I don't suppose you've seen my mother, have you?" she asked, not expecting an answer. The dog looked at her for a moment before lying beside her. It rested its head in her lap. She glanced at the old woman, still engaged in her private conversation.

For the second time in several minutes, she was startled by an incoming object. A large hoop crashed into and over the dog before bouncing off the tree and back toward the girl who had lost control of it. With a yelp, the dog took off at a run.

"Sorry," the girl said. She held the hoop stick in one hand. She wore a gray dress and bonnet and had dark brown braids sprouting from beneath the cap. "Who are you?" she asked.

"I'm from Windsor," Allie said. She didn't want to tell the girl her name since she wasn't supposed to be there.

"Oh, do you know the Windsor Witch then?" the girl asked, her eyes lighting up with excitement.

"The Windsor Witch?" Allie asked. She had no idea what the girl was talking about.

"Everyone is here to see her," the girl said.

Allie shook her head. "No, I don't know her." The conversation made her uneasy. If there was a witch in Windsor, why hadn't she heard of her? She glanced at the old woman by the fence and saw that the dog had made its way over and had become the woman's partner in conversation.

"Say," said Allie, "do you know who that old woman is?" She pointed toward the fence.

"Oh, that's Goody Davies," said the girl. "She's always there. My mother brings her food sometimes. Not everyone wants her here. Some say the devil has been speaking to her since her husband died. My mother says she's harmless."

Had the woman seen her mother? If she always sat in the square, she might know something. The girl's mother believed her harmless—and the dog seemed to like her, so she couldn't be all bad.

"I'd better go," the girl said suddenly. "They're supposed to bring out the witch soon."

"Thanks," said Allie. The girl ran off, rolling her hoop with the stick back toward the meetinghouse. It occurred to her after she had left that she should have asked if the girl knew anything about her mother, but the conversation about the witch had spooked her.

Allie stood, determined to talk to Goody Davies—if she could break into her conversation with the dog. She started off toward the fence.

Before she reached the old woman, two older boys ran out of the crowd, heading right toward her. They pulled tomatoes from behind their backs and threw them at Goody Davies. One hit the dog, sending him scurrying off with a yelp. The second tomato hit the old woman in the chest, scattering seeds and juice over her dress before coming to rest in her lap. Allie listened as the boys laughed and recited a rhyme:

Momma cat, momma cat
Steer clear of Old Goody Davies
She'll swallow you whole with all the fur on
As soon as she's eaten your babies

The boys ran off and were gone as quickly as they had arrived. Oddly, Goody Davies didn't even react to the incident. Could it be that such an occurrence was so commonplace that the woman thought nothing of it?

"Pardon, ma'am," said Allie, as Goody Davies began to eat one of the tomatoes. "I'm trying to find my mother." Allie wasn't sure how the woman would react, but it wasn't with the clear-minded, focused attention she now received.

"Yes, my child," said the old woman, turning her head and looking directly into her eyes. "What's your mother's name?"

"Her name is Alse Young, ma'am," said Allie.

"Ah, yes, I know of her. She's in that building there," said Goody Davies, pointing to a wooden structure to the north. "But you must hurry, child—you haven't much time. And beware the hunter. He's more evil and dangerous than the ones he hunts." Goody Davies turned away.

The hunter? What did she mean by that? *She must be confused*, Allie thought. Already, the woman was back to conversing with her invisible companion. Allie just hoped that Goody Davies had been correct when she had identified her mother's location. She set off toward the building. If all went well, she could be on her way home with her mother within the hour.

As she wandered through the crowd, she kept an eye out for her father and anyone else who might know her. Now that she was so close to finding her mother, it was important not to get caught. Fortunately, no one paid attention to her.

The sign on the front of the building read Hartford Gaol. This couldn't be right. Why would her mother be visiting a jail? Allie tried the latch, but the door was locked. She tried knocking on the door with her small fist, but there was no response. As she was about to knock a second time, a gruff voice called out to her.

"You there—girl," said an older man as he quickly approached. "This is no place for you."

"I'm looking for Alse Young," said Allie. "I was told I could find her here?"

"Aye," said the man. "Everyone is wanting a glimpse of the witch. Get back to your parents. They'll be bringing her around to the meetinghouse shortly." The man walked off, turning at the corner of the building and disappearing from view.

Allie was confused and becoming afraid. These people couldn't truly believe that her mother was the Windsor Witch, could they? Witches were evil followers of Satan. Her mother would never harm anyone. But they *had* called her a sinner and accused her of horrible acts on the day they had taken her. Had her mother been in jail this entire time? Tears welled in Allie's eyes. They were wrong! She had to set them straight. Why had her father kept this from her?

Her father—she had to find him right away and make him explain. How could he have let this happen? He had to help her fix this. They had to get her mother and take her back home where she belonged.

Allie ran as fast as she could into the throng of people, searching for her father. She wound her way through the gathered mob until she was out of breath, but her father was nowhere to be seen. She stopped for a moment to catch her breath, scanning the crowd around her. There was no sign of her father. Her eye traveled to the tall wooden structure in front of the meetinghouse. She headed toward it, weaving through people until she broke through the front line of townsfolk.

There stood the gallows, and for the first time Allie recognized it for what it was. She gasped, hit by the horror of what was happening. Her tears started flowing in earnest. The gallows, the crowd of people, the digging tools, and the box on the back of her father's wagon—she knew what it all meant now. The noose hung empty, but it wouldn't stay that way. Her mother was the Windsor Witch, and everyone was there to watch her die.

It was then Allie saw her father near the gallows platform, talking to Malleus Hodge. What was left of Allie's heart crumbled at the sight. Her father was here with the man who was responsible for her mother's plight. Had her father helped him? Was he partly to blame?

Allie couldn't stand it anymore. She turned and ran from the gallows, from her father and Hodge, through the assembled throng and past it. She ran until she could run no more, collapsing against the side of a building. And there she sat, the tears flowing down her cheeks and onto her dress. She closed her eyes, praying she would wake to find herself in the comfort of her bed, to learn that all of this had been a dream.

Once again, she felt a wet tongue on her cheek. She opened her eyes to see the stray dog standing beside her. Immediately wrapping her arms around its neck, she hugged it for some time, crying into its fur until she had exhausted her tears. The familiar, furry face had lightened her despair, and after a few moments she was again able to think. What was she going to do? How could she save her mother from this horrible nightmare?

At that moment she heard the meetinghouse bell sound twice, and she knew she had run out of time. She had wasted the last few minutes she had.

Running back to the assembled people, she fought her way toward the front of the crowd, pushing and shoving with all the strength she could muster. It was more difficult this time, as everyone had packed together to get a good view.

Allie broke through, bursting past the line of jeering people and into the area in front of the gallows.

"Momma—" she cried out. She saw the look of horror on her mother's face as their eyes made contact.

"May God have mercy on your soul," someone said.

The stool was kicked away, and the noose snapped taut. Her mother struggled at the end of the rope as Allie made a last desperate run toward her. By this time, everyone had noticed her attempts to reach the gallows. She ran toward the steps leading to the platform, slipping past hands that reached for her from every direction.

"It's the daughter," she heard someone say. "It's the witch's daughter."

Then she saw her father. He was directly in her path.

"Allie!" he cried, reaching for her as she approached. At the last second, however, she dodged past him and up the steps.

But it was too late. Allie saw that her mother had stopped struggling and was now swinging gently back and forth at the end of the rope, her feet inches above the wooden surface.

"Momma!" Allie cried once again as she ran to her, throwing her arms around her legs. "Please don't go." Fresh tears flowed as she held her, feeling the warmth of her mother's body for the last time. She stayed that way, holding on tightly, until rough hands tore her away.

"Calm yourself, young Alice," said a voice she recognized. She craned her neck to look at the man who towered over her and caught sight of that terrible grin on his face.

It was Malleus Hodge.

Chapter 12

THE WITCHFINDER GENERAL

Windsor, Connecticut, May 2019

"We take fighting and bullying seriously here at Windsor High," said Principal Wright. The principal was an imposing woman whose mere presence commanded respect. Her light brown skin was flawless, her delicate features framed by long, slender braids that cascaded over her shoulders and down her back. "Since no one will elaborate on exactly what occurred and it's clear that something *did* occur, I have no choice but to impose three days of after-school detention for each of the boys involved in the altercation."

Nate and Douglas sat in Principal Wright's office, along with Aunt Celia and Douglas's parents. Huey sat off to the side. Nate was surprised that neither of Huey's parents had shown up for the meeting.

"But Ms. Wright, surely you don't think Nate was responsible for this," said Aunt Celia. "He's never been in trouble before, as his records attest."

In the chair next to her, Douglas's mother mumbled "*Dios mio,* my baby," in between quiet sobs, as Mr. Ramirez patted his wife's folded hands gently with his own.

"Ms. Watson, if that's the case, then I'd again encourage the boys to explain exactly what did happen," the principal responded, leaning forward in her chair. "I have my suspicions," she said, glancing quickly at Huey before continuing. "But without any additional explanation, I have no choice but to punish everyone involved."

Aunt Celia glanced at Nate, and he could tell she wanted him to say something—but he couldn't. Doing so would only make life at school much worse for both him and Douglas. Couldn't she understand that?

"The boys should consider themselves lucky," said Ms. Wright. "If I had confirmation of what did occur, any guilty parties would be subject to immediate suspension from school."

Mrs. Ramirez mumbled again and shook her head, still sniffling.

"Do you have anything to add, Huey, since your parents failed to show up?" asked the principal.

"No ma'am," said Huey. "My dad was—um, no ma'am." He shrank back into his seat.

"Very well," Ms. Wright sighed. "Then I'm afraid it's after-school detention for all of you boys, starting on Monday."

Nate, Douglas, and Huey got up and left the room as the adults remained for a few more words with Ms. Wright. Huey gave them a nod before heading down the corridor and off to class. A nod of respect? Was that even possible?

"Thanks Nate," said Douglas. "I owe you another one."

"No problem," Nate told him.

Douglas glanced at the floor and asked, "Nate, why did you do it? Help me, I mean. You didn't have to."

"Well, because you needed it—and you're my friend," said Nate, surprised to see tears in Douglas's eyes. Before he realized what was happening, Douglas embraced him in a full bear hug. Nate awkwardly patted him on the shoulder, unsure of what to do next.

"Besides, I think naked Duck riding may catch on as a sport," said Nate.

A burst of laughter came from Douglas as he broke the embrace.

Just then, the adults emerged from the principal's office. Douglas's mother was still dabbing at her eyes with a wrinkled tissue. Aunt Celia walked over to Nate.

"Are you OK?" she asked.

"Yeah," said Nate. "I'm sorry—I just couldn't say—"

"I understand," said Aunt Celia. "Listen, I'll see you later at home. There's someone I have to talk to."

"Sure—and thanks," said Nate as Aunt Celia headed down a corridor. Mr. Black, his biology teacher, emerged from a classroom and exchanged a hug with Aunt Celia. How did they know each other?

"Ready for class?" Douglas asked, and Nate saw that his parents had already left the building.

"Yeah, sure," said Nate. He took one last look at Aunt Celia and Mr. Black, now intensely engaged in conversation, as he and Douglas headed down a different hallway to class.

"Hi, Ms. Brooks," said Jenn, as she came into the library. Mr. Foster was chatting with the librarian by the checkout stand. "Mr. Foster—thanks for meeting me here."

"There's a lot of interest in witches this week," said Mr. Foster with a grin.

"Well, that's probably my fault," said Ms. Brooks. "Someone placed the Hopkins book in my donation box, and then I put Jenn onto the topic of Alse Young." Ms. Brooks picked up a book from the counter, placing it on a nearby cart.

"Ah, so now we know—what kind of info were you looking for?" Mr. Foster asked.

"What can you tell me about Matthew Hopkins?" asked Jenn. She had done some online research of her own, but she hoped that Mr. Foster could help to fill in some of the gaps. She was still hoping to help Nate in some way. He had texted that morning that he still hadn't been able to remove the serpent from his arm.

"He's quite an interesting historical figure," said Mr. Foster. "Surprisingly, most Americans have never heard of him. I understand, however, that in Britain, he's quite infamous."

"What do you mean?" asked Ms. Brooks, removing her glasses.

"Well, here in America," he continued, "when we think of witch hysteria we think of the Salem witch trials, which took place over a sixteen-month period and resulted in over twenty deaths of accused witches. In England, Matthew Hopkins and his colleague John Stearne were estimated to have been responsible for the execution of over three hundred."

"That's . . . *fifteen times* the number of hangings in Salem," said Jenn, astonished.

"Yes," said Mr. Foster with a nod. "And over a shorter period of time, too—just a little over a year, between 1644 and 1646, mostly in East Anglia. That's northeast of today's Greater London. Hopkins claimed to be officially commissioned by the English Parliament, calling himself the Witchfinder General—although he was never truly sanctioned by the government."

"Wow," said Jenn. "So why did he stop after such a short period of time?"

"Eventually," said Mr. Foster, "the methods and motives of Hopkins and Stearne were questioned by the law, after which they both retired rather quickly. Also, it's possible that Hopkins retired in part due to illness. After publication of his book in 1647, he died suddenly—some say of tuberculosis. He was probably not much older than twenty-five at the time."

"He died in 1647?" asked Jenn. *Hmm, that year again,* she thought. *The year Alse Young was hanged.*

"Records show he died in August of that year and was buried in the graveyard at the Church of St. Mary in Mistley Heath, a town just east of his home in Manningtree. Although one popular legend says he was subjected to one of his own tests and executed as a witch."

"How did he go about hunting witches?" asked Ms. Brooks, as she continued tidying up her workspace. She tapped a pile of papers against the counter to line up their edges.

"Well, he certainly took advantage of the instability and fear of the times. England was in the midst of a civil war, and Charles I was an unpopular king. He believed in the divine right of kings, which meant he felt his power was absolute and that he wasn't subject to any earthly authority—including the Parliament of England. He was also married to a Roman Catholic, Henrietta Maria of France, and his subjects felt his views were too Catholic—one of the reasons the English Puritans began coming to America. Eventually, the Parliamentarians won the civil war and Charles was executed for high treason, putting an end to the monarchy in England."

"Wait," said Jenn, with a tilt of the head, "but they have a queen now, right?"

"Oh, yes," said Mr. Foster. "Parliament ended up deciding that the monarchy wasn't so bad after all, and they eventually restored King Charles I's son, Charles II, to the throne. That's the period known as the Restoration.

"But anyway, during this time of upheaval Matthew Hopkins traveled from town to town, claiming to be Parliament's official witchfinder. Few people questioned his authority. In their paranoia, the towns would offer up people to test. Torture was unlawful in England, but Hopkins's methods really pushed the boundaries. He used sleep deprivation and forced marching to obtain confessions. It was believed that witches had a devil's mark on their body, signifying their allegiance to Satan, or an extra nipple that was used to suckle their familiars. So accused witches would be stripped and sometimes shaved of all body hair before being thoroughly searched."

Jenn's mouth dropped open. She glanced at Ms. Brooks, who turned toward Mr. Foster with a look of distaste.

"Even if no marks were found on an accused witch, they were thought to have invisible devil's marks—areas of skin that were dead to all feeling and would not bleed if pricked. Hopkins would use 'witch-prickers' to find these spots, probing the accused with knives and needles." Mr. Foster frowned.

"That's definitely torture," said Jenn with a grimace.

"I agree," said Mr. Foster. "One of his most controversial methods was the swimming test. Since witches had renounced baptism, people believed that water would reject their bodies. So the accused would be tied in a way that prevented swimming, or they'd simply be tied to a chair—and then tossed into a river or pond. If they floated, they were considered a witch. If they sank—well, if they were lucky, they'd be fished out before they drowned."

"Who wouldn't confess to avoid these things?" asked Ms. Brooks, raising her palm for emphasis.

"Exactly—Hopkins could get a confession from just about anyone he wished. Eventually he stopped using the swimming test—he was warned it was unlawful without first obtaining the permission of the accused. My guess is it drew quite a bit of attention, whereas his other methods could be performed more privately."

"What about thumbscrews?" Jenn asked, furrowing her brows. She remembered the device Nate had found in his aunt's room.

"I haven't read any mention of them and Hopkins," said Mr. Foster, "but there's record of thumbscrews being used at other times for obtaining confessions from accused witches."

"So what ended up happening with Hopkins?" asked Ms. Brooks. She had stopped her tidying to give her full attention to the conversation.

"Well eventually, Hopkins and Stearne became notorious enough to draw the attention of the authorities," Mr. Foster said. "They were interviewed and asked if their methods of investigation didn't make them witches themselves. Their motives were also questioned, as they'd made quite a fortune charging the towns and villages they visited for their services."

Jenn rolled her eyes. "Of course—they did it for money!"

"Hopkins claimed that he asked for only enough payment to cover his expenses. This did not correspond at all with the records kept by the towns that hired him, however."

"Figures," Jenn said, shaking her head.

"Do you have his book with you?" asked Mr. Foster.

"Sure do," replied Jenn. She unzipped her backpack and pulled out *The Discovery of Witches*.

"Take a look at the dedication," said Mr. Foster, pointing toward the old tome.

"It says 'Delivered to the judges of assize for the county of Norfolk.'" Jenn looked up at Mr. Foster. "'Judges of assize'? Who were they?"

"Traveling judges," Mr. Foster replied. "They came from the higher courts to the smaller counties and towns. Hopkins probably dedicated the book to them to get them off his back. If you look, you can see that it was written as a series of fourteen questions and answers—some of the questions are quite accusatory, as if they were posed to him by the judges of the assize themselves. He explained his methods and attempted to justify them."

"Huh," Jenn said. She set the book on the counter and flipped through the pages. Mr. Foster and Ms. Brooks scanned the pages with her.

"How did Hopkins come up with this knowledge of witchcraft?" asked Ms. Brooks.

"He claimed he learned it from his own personal experiences," Mr. Foster replied. "But he also refers to *Daemonologie*, which he used as justification for his use of the unlawful swimming tests. So clearly, he'd done some reading on the subject."

"Did you say *Daemonologie*?" asked Jenn, looking up from the book. That was the other book Nate had found in Aunt Celia's room.

"Yes," said Mr. Foster. "A book written by King James VI of Scotland—who also later became King James I of England, after the death of Queen Elizabeth I. He was in fact the father of Charles I, the king executed during the civil war. King James was considered a scholarly king—you've heard of the King James Bible?"

Jenn nodded.

"King James also had a personal interest in witchcraft and demonology, so he wrote *Daemonologie* in 1597. And it's not just about witches and demons—he also mentions vampires, werewolves, and magick. He fully believed in the influence of Satan and endorsed the practice of witch hunting, although some people believe he wrote the book not to cause hysteria, but so that people would identify and deal with witches in a rational, responsible manner."

Jenn thought for a moment. "Are we sure that Matthew Hopkins died in 1647?" she asked.

"As far as we know," said Mr. Foster, with a shrug. "There's a record of his burial in the parish registry of the Church of St. Mary at Mistley Heath in 1647. He apparently died in October."

Jenn thought about the timeline—Matthew Hopkins had published his book in early 1647, Alse Young was hanged in May of 1647. And Hopkins himself died in October, five months later. So if those dates were accurate, it was only an interesting coincidence.

"One more thing to note," continued Mr. Foster. "A last will and testament belonging to James Hopkins—Matthew's father—was found, dated 1634, in which there was mention of a decision to send Matthew's brother Thomas to 'friends in New England.' This would mean the family had ties to America. We know that Hopkins's book made it over here and likely influenced the witch hysteria that occurred—but it's possible, if not likely, that the book could have made its way here to Connecticut by the time of Alse Young's trial."

Hmm, thought Jenn. With the help of friends or family in England and in America, Matthew Hopkins could have conceivably faked his death to avoid prosecution in England and made his way here to the colonies.

"So, does that answer your questions?" asked Mr. Foster. He stood up straight and stretched, and Jenn realized how long they had been talking.

"It only makes me have *more* questions, honestly," Jenn said. "But it's all super interesting, that's for sure." She thanked Mr. Foster and Ms. Brooks and headed off to her next class.

Now she had a *lot* of information to process—and she couldn't wait to share what she had learned with Nate and Zach. She didn't know what relationship there could be between Matthew Hopkins and Nate's Aunt Celia, or if either of them had anything to do with Alse Young, but hopefully they would be able to figure it out together.

"Isn't a shad a type of fish?" asked Alex as she and Nate sat behind empty trays at a table in the cafeteria. It had been another amazing conversation with Alex, and the lunch period had flown by for Nate. Zach had also invited them to the Shad Derby Festival, which was taking place on the following day.

"Yes, shad are fish," said Zach.

"Then what the heck is a Shad Derby?" she asked, turning to Nate. "I'm imagining fish with tiny hats perched on their heads."

"Don't look at me," said Nate with a grin. "I've never been to it, either."

"It's a lot of fun—the whole town goes," said Zach. "It's a big party on the town green with food and a parade. Jenn and I will be there. The only downside is that Courtney's been selected as this year's Shad Derby queen—and she'll be in the parade."

"The blond with all the attitude?" asked Alex.

"Ah, so you've met," said Nate.

"Sort of—she told me the eighties called and they want their hair back." She rolled her eyes, obviously unfazed.

Nate and Zach both laughed.

Just then Douglas walked by with his tray.

"Hi guys," he said. "Going to the Shad Derby tomorrow?"

"I don't know," said Nate looking at Alex with a hopeful expression. "Are we?"

"Sure," she said. "Why not?"

Yes! thought Nate.

Chapter 13

PET SEMATARY

Alexandra Bradley walked down the corridor toward her locker, stopping to refill her water bottle at the fountain along the way. *Might as well make the most of that five-cent deposit*, she thought. She had moved around several times in her life and each time it had been more difficult for her to make friends and fit in. She had a tendency to be a bit assertive and rough around the edges, and that had turned people off in the past. She couldn't believe how quickly she had made new friends here or how much she was enjoying their company. They seemed to like her as well, which was a plus.

She remembered her time in Boston, where the girls had been a bit too proper and reserved for her tastes. She had always been the one to get in trouble and be sent home from school. Her father had been furious with her every time.

"Can't you even try to fit in?" he would say. Her father could be harsh sometimes, especially since her mother had died. He had never been the same after that. Alex's mother made her father happy and relaxed—most of the time, at least. She longed to see him that way again.

She reached her locker and set the bottle on the floor so that she could open the door. As she reached to grab a book off the top shelf, her sleeve slid down, exposing the cut marks on her forearm—reminders of her difficult childhood. Many of those cuts had been made while living at her previous address.

She chided herself for dwelling on the past. It was important that she put the bad history behind her so that she could finally move on. She felt a bit happier now, just thinking of going to the Shad Derby Festival tomorrow with Nate. *It'll be fun*, she told herself. Finding the books she needed, she shut the door to her locker and bent to pick up the water bottle.

Before she could stand up again someone ran into her and she lost her balance, flopping ungracefully to the floor. Looking up, she saw it was Courtney Stevens, her phone open in front of her. Clearly, she hadn't been paying attention to where she was going.

"Hey, watch it!" said Courtney, indignantly. She turned and gave Alex an icy stare.

"Um, you ran into *me*," said Alex, picking up the water bottle and regaining her feet. "Don't worry, I'll be fine."

"I'm just saying you need to be more careful," Courtney said condescendingly.

"As I said, *you* ran into *me*," said Alex a little more loudly. Every instinct was telling her to let it go—but who did this girl think she was talking to?

"Look," said Courtney, crossing her arms. "I know you're new around here but—"

"Listen, Fish Queen," began Alex, unhappy that that was the best she could come up with and getting angrier by the moment.

Courtney raised her arm toward Alex, her palm inches from Alex's face. "Just stop," she said. "I don't have time for this." She turned on her heel and began moving down the hallway.

Oh, I'm going to regret this, Alex thought—as she pulled the cap off her water bottle and squeezed it, shooting water all over Courtney's back.

"You bitch!" Courtney cried as she spun around. She was met with a second blast of water to the face. It dripped from her nose and chin, dampening the front of her outfit.

Alex laughed. Then she noticed Principal Wright coming down the corridor and her mind immediately went to her father.

Damn, she thought, *he's definitely not going to be happy about this.*

As Principal Wright closed in on her, Alex glanced at the empty water bottle in her hand and back up at Courtney, who was soaked and seething. Her dripping hair was plastered to her forehead. A couple of passing students chuckled, further increasing Courtney's ire. Alex had lost control of her temper, and she had done it in front of the principal. Now, as a result, she would have to pay the price.

And it was totally worth it.

Jenn and Nate sat at a table in the chemistry lab. Mr. Sullivan was at the front of the class, droning on about various elements of the periodic table and their melting points. He was a frumpy, middle-aged man with a receding hairline who seemed a bit too clumsy to be working with test tubes and flasks for a living. Nate was pretty sure he always wore the same black suit with the same dusting of dandruff on the shoulders.

"So she told you you're a descendant of Alse Young?" Jenn asked.

"Yeah," said Nate. "That's what she said." He was tempted to tell her the full story of Aunt Celia and Malleus Hodge, a.k.a. Matthew Hopkins, but at this point he felt he needed his aunt's permission before discussing anything more. He would talk to her as soon as he got home from school. He felt terrible keeping Jenn in the dark, even for a short time, and it was making the current conversation awkward.

"Well, that could explain her interest in witches and witchcraft," said Jenn. "And she didn't know how to remove the serpent?"

"Unfortunately, no," said Nate. "It hasn't been bothering me today. I've hardly noticed it's there."

"Still," said Jenn. "Aren't you going to get it checked by a doctor? Its fangs are embedded in your skin."

The conversation was making Nate anxious. He didn't want to lie, but there were things he just couldn't talk about. Fortunately, Mr. Sullivan chose that moment to drop a beaker. It shattered as it hit the ground, sending glass flying across the floor. He scurried off in search of a broom.

"That's the second thing he's dropped this week," said Jenn.

Just then the bell rang, and students headed for the door, walking carefully to avoid the glass. Jenn looked Nate in the eyes.

"Hey, you sure you're all right?" she asked.

"Yes," said Nate. "I promise—we'll talk more tomorrow."

Mr. Sullivan ran back into the room as they were leaving, broom and dustpan in hand. Jenn offered to help with the glass. She told Nate to go on without her.

Now that school was over, Nate would meet his brother before heading home to talk with Aunt Celia. It was important to be able to include his friends in the events that were unfolding in his life—he just hoped he would be able to convince her to share her secrets with them.

"I haven't seen her in a while," said Zach, as they climbed the front steps of Jenn's grandmother's house. "Is she really that different?"

"Not really," Jenn replied. She hoped that was still the case. She hadn't seen her grandmother in a few days. "Mostly, her memory's getting bad. You'll hear her repeating herself."

Jenn and Zach hadn't talked much during the short walk from school. Jenn's grandmother, Martha, was in the early stages of dementia. It had come on quickly, and her parents were still trying to figure out how to handle it. Martha, at eighty-nine, had been an active and independent woman—until recently. A longtime widow, she lived alone in a small house near the center of town. She refused to leave her home.

"Mom and Dad are planning to have another discussion with Gran this weekend," Jenn went on. "She really shouldn't be by herself now. They're worried she'll leave the stove on or something like that."

"What're they going to do?"

"They want her to come live in our guest room. For now, they've been calling her regularly and visiting every day."

"That's too bad," Zach told his friend. "She's so nice. And a great cook."

Zach rang the doorbell as Jenn inserted a key in the doorknob and pulled open the door.

"Hi, Gran, we're here—Jenn and Zach," Jenn called out as they stepped into the house and looked around, closing the door behind them. The house seemed in order. Everything looked as it had the last time she had visited. "Gran, are you here?"

A door opened, and Jenn's grandmother walked out of the kitchen, drying her hands on a towel. The smell of freshly baked cookies followed her into the living room. Jenn smiled. Maybe it was one of her good days.

"How *are* you?" she said, giving each of them a hug. "It is so nice to see you."

"Hello, Mrs. Gregory," said Zach.

"Call me Martha—how many times have I told you that, Zach?"

Jenn was relieved. Her grandmother really did seem her old self. Maybe she wasn't as bad as her parents had said.

"We just dropped in to say hi."

"Well, it is wonderful to see you," said Martha. "And you can tell your parents I'm just fine. They worry too much. I'm perfectly able to take care of myself," she said with a knowing wink.

"That's good to hear, Gran," said Jenn. "Can we do anything for you while we're here?"

"As a matter of fact, you can," she said. "I just baked some chocolate chip cookies, and you can help me eat them."

Jenn watched Zach's expression brighten visibly. They followed Martha into the kitchen. Zach took a seat at the table while Jenn helped her grandmother pour three glasses of milk.

"Did I tell you Mr. Flufferton came home?" Martha asked, handing them each a cookie. "That naughty kitty."

"That's great," said Jenn. Her mother had stopped by the day before to find the back door left open, the cat nowhere to be seen.

They ate several more cookies. Jenn was feeling better by the moment—her grandmother was as clear minded as ever; she had been worried for nothing. She was doing just fine. When they were finished, Jenn washed the dishes and put them away as Zach and Martha continued to chat.

"We should be going," she said when she finished tidying up.

"OK, my dear," said Martha. She and Zach stood and followed Jenn back into the living room.

"Can I offer you kids some cookies?" asked Martha. "I just baked them." Jenn and Zach exchanged glances. The relief Jenn had been experiencing suddenly vanished.

"Gran, we just finished eating cookies," said Jenn after a moment.

"Oh, you're right. Silly me," said Martha. "Look, here comes Mr. Flufferton. Did I tell you he came home? He's such a good boy."

A nauseating smell assailed Jenn's nostrils: it smelled of earth and something else she couldn't quite place. Sensing movement from what she knew to be the bedroom, Jenn turned her head in time to see the cat heading their way. With tail twitching, it crossed the room to sit at Martha's feet. The animal was matted with dirt and some other greasy substance.

"Gran, he's filthy—I think he rolled in something," said Jenn, raising her hand to her nose. Cats were normally such well-groomed animals, she thought. What was wrong with Mr. Flufferton?

Martha bent, stroking the cat's head. "Oh dear," she said, "you may be right." Leaning down, she lifted Mr. Flufferton into her arms. Purring, he rubbed his head against her chin, leaving behind a dark smear. "I'll give him a bath right now."

"Good idea, Gran," said Jenn. "We have to head home. Are you going to be OK?"

"Oh, sure—don't you worry about me. I'm fine."

"It was nice visiting with you, Mrs.—Martha," said Zach.

"Good to see you Zach. You two come back soon," she said as she headed off into the bedroom, carrying the cat.

"Dude, did you see that!?" Zach exclaimed once they were out of the house. "That cat was full-on *Pet Sematary*."

"Fluff just needed a bath," said Jenn defensively. "He's been running loose in the neighborhood. It's a bit weird that she didn't notice his condition before we pointed it out though—not that anything's normal with her these days, apparently."

No, her grandmother didn't seem to be doing well at all. Jenn wasn't looking forward to the conversation she would be having with her parents when she got home.

"My dear Mr. Flufferton, what did you get yourself into?" asked Martha Gregory, as she set the cat into the bathtub she had filled with shallow warm water. "Don't worry, we'll get you nice and clean again." Mr. Flufferton purred in response.

She removed the cat's collar, placing it on the sink.

"I'll take care of you," she said, unfolding a small hand towel and dipping it into the water. She thought about the last conversation she'd had with her daughter and son-in-law. She didn't understand their concern about her living alone. She was fully capable of taking care of herself. Hadn't she raised two children and been an independent woman for the majority of her life?

Squirting a dab of No More Tears shampoo onto the cloth, she gently worked it into a lather. She would give her pet a nice bath and he would be good as new. She wasn't going to leave her home of over fifty years. So much of her life had taken place within these walls. And who would care for her darling pet if she were to leave?

"No need to fear, Mr. Flufferton, I'm not going anywhere," she said as she gently rubbed the soaped cloth against the fur of his scalp.

Little by little and ever so gently, she rubbed away the dirt and the grime, not noticing the clumps of hair and then skin she was taking off with it. Slowly and gently, she continued, taking her time, chatting sweetly with her beloved pet as she worked. She dipped the cloth once more into the tub not noticing the ear that floated from it, bobbing gently in the water.

"I have an idea, let's bake some nice chocolate chip cookies when we're done," she said lovingly. "Would you like that?"

She didn't notice the electric blue glint that appeared in the cat's eyes before vanishing just as quickly, or the soft, brief crackling sound that went with it.

With a sudden churning intensity, Mr. Flufferton leaped from the water and dug his front claws into the sides of Martha's head, sinking his fangs into the soft, loose flesh of her face. With a furious motion he tore repeatedly at the skin of her chin and neck with his back claws, like a kitten playing with a ball of yarn. Strips of flesh and blood flew, staining the bright white of the bathroom tile.

With a gasp, Martha reached up to remove the cat from her face. Her fingers found purchase and with all the strength she could muster, she attempted to push the cat away. Rotten, greasy skin and fur sloughed off in her hands, falling with a splash into the tub.

"*Oh my*," Martha whispered softly as she lost her balance and fell back, cracking her skull against the porcelain sink—mercifully losing consciousness as the rest of her lifeblood drained from her body.

As death claimed Jenn's grandmother, the dark crystal attached to her pet's collar—the crystal she had neither noticed nor placed there—glowed brightly before vanishing from sight.

Chapter 14

THE SHAD DERBY

At 8:43 a.m., Police Officer Samantha Foster pulled up to the house on Kellogg Street and verified the street address against the display in her vehicle. *This is the place*, she thought. *Mrs. Martha Gregory*. Concerned relatives had called in requesting a wellness check on their elderly family member after not being able to reach her by phone.

It was a typical type of call for the Windsor Police Department. There wasn't a lot of crime in the town, which Sam found nice, if sometimes a bit boring. She and her husband had relocated here from Philadelphia three years ago after Greg had been offered a position teaching history at Windsor High. While she had enjoyed living in Philly, she appreciated the hometown feel of Windsor and had come to love it pretty quickly. She spent much of her day patrolling the neighborhoods, performing wellness checks, responding to home security alarms   most of which were set off by the homeowners themselves—and making the occasional traffic stop.

She stepped out of the patrol car, gently closing the door with a click, and approached the small house. Well-maintained flower beds lined the sidewalk leading to the front door. It appeared that Mrs. Gregory was an avid gardener. Nothing seemed unusual as she knocked on the front door, ringing the doorbell for good measure.

"Mrs. Gregory," she called after several moments, knocking a little more firmly. There was no sign of movement from within the house, so Sam tried the doorknob. The door was locked.

Retracing her steps, Sam made her way around to the side of the house and into the backyard. Again, nothing seemed amiss. A well-maintained white fence enclosed the area, more beds of brightly colored flowers running the length of each section.

"Hello, Mrs. Gregory!" she called once more as she knocked firmly on the back door. Turning the knob, she discovered the door unlocked.

"Martha? This is Officer Foster of the Windsor Police—are you OK?" she said loudly as she pulled the baton from her belt and stepped inside, leaving the door open behind her. Using the baton to flip on a light switch, she found herself in a small but tidy kitchen. Noting nothing out of place, she continued through the doorway and into the living room, again flipping on a light with her baton. *Why do older people love those heavy curtains that block out so much light?* she wondered.

Hearing a sound to her right, Sam passed into the master bedroom, for the first time sensing something was wrong. By the soft light of a bedside lamp, she noticed a strange pattern of dark marks dotting the floor, running from beneath the perfectly made double bed to the open door to the right. A rancid smell hit her nostrils—a smell she recognized but hadn't encountered since her days in Philly. It was the scent of death.

Hefting the baton, she took two more steps into the room, moving toward the open door, and what she saw there horrified her more than anything she had ever seen. Inside the brightly lit bathroom she saw the body of Martha Gregory, her lifeless eyes staring at her from a ruined face. Streaks of blood marred the glistening white walls, flowing into the monstrous pool that covered the floor. And sitting at the edge of that pool was a creature, purring softly as it lapped at the sticky red liquid.

Sam backed up with a startled gasp that alerted the creature to her presence. With a loud hiss, the gore-covered beast bounded out of the bathroom and straight toward her, leaving small, bloody paw prints on the floor behind it.

The thing leaped into the air as it neared her, claws extended. By pure reflex, Sam swung the baton with both hands, making contact with its body. With a loud crack, the creature was thrown to the side by the force of her swing, striking the wall and dropping to the floor with a thud. It lay with its back bent at an unnatural angle.

What the hell is that? she wondered, peering at the broken mass of fur, skin, bone, and claw.

Before she could register what was happening, the creature's misaligned back popped back into place, and with an unnatural sounding *mrawww*, it righted itself and half-ran, half-crawled at terrific speed out of the bedroom, through the living room, and into the kitchen.

It was at that moment, with a mix of relief and horror, that Officer Samantha Foster remembered she had left the back door wide open.

"Your grandmother didn't notice the condition of the cat?" asked Nate as he walked with Jenn, Zach, and Marc along the town green. The Shad Derby Festival was in full swing. There were people and tents containing food, crafts, and games everywhere.

"It was disgusting!" exclaimed Zach. "Dude, it looked and smelled like *roadkill*!"

"Come on, you're exaggerating," said Jenn. "But I really think my parents need to do something," she continued. "Gran just doesn't seem all there anymore. It's really sad and frightening."

"Sorry, Jenn—that sucks," said Nate. He scanned the crowd looking for Alex. She had promised to meet him here, and he was looking forward to seeing her—but he wanted to talk to Jenn and Zach first. Aunt Celia had said he could fill them in on everything he knew about her history, and on the situation with Malleus Hodge, a.k.a. Matthew Hopkins. Unfortunately, he hadn't yet figured out how to broach the subject—and the topic was so crazy that he wasn't sure Jenn and Zach would take him seriously.

"Hey guys," it was Douglas, who held a stick of cotton candy in one hand.

Shoot, he thought. He'd missed his opportunity to talk with Jenn and Zach for now. He liked Douglas, but he didn't know if he could share this with him, too.

"What do you have there, Doug?" asked Zach, pointing to a piece of paper in his hand.

Douglas shrugged. "Not sure. There's a man handing them out in front of the town hall," he said, showing them the paper. It read:

They're already
among us

"What are among us?" asked Nate.

"The aliens have landed," said Zach with a grin, wriggling two fingers behind his head like antennae.

"It's probably some sort of advertisement," said Jenn, "or part of a political campaign." She smirked.

"Or the guy is just a raving kook," said Alex. Nate hadn't seen her approach. She held a similar flyer in her hand. He smiled at her, and she smiled back.

"There you are," said Nate. He put his arm around her back, pulling her into the group. "This is Jenn—and my brother, Marc." Nate pointed to each of them as he spoke. They smiled and nodded.

"Hi guys," she said, glancing at each of them in turn. "So *this* is a Shad Derby! I'm still not sure what it has to do with fish, but I like it." She crumpled the flyer and tossed it into a nearby trash can.

"It used to be a fishing tournament," Jenn explained. "For helping the pollution problem in the Connecticut River. Now it's much bigger."

"Jenn knows all," said Zach. "You'll come to appreciate that."

"We'll get along perfectly then," said Alex with a laugh. "I've been accused of knowing very little." The two girls shared a friendly glance.

"We have about an hour before the parade—and Queen Courtney," said Zach, which elicited a groan from Alex. They looked at her quizzically.

"So I'm not a fan," Alex said. "I got myself into a little trouble yesterday." She told them about the incident with the water bottle.

"You soaked her front *and* back?" asked Zach. "I wish I had been there to see that." Even Jenn, who usually took the high road in such matters, seemed to find it amusing.

"Yeah, I admit it," said Alex. "I lost my cool—not my finest hour."

Nate was thrilled that Alex and his friends were getting along so well together—but he had also been looking forward to talking to her alone. When Zach suggested getting an early snack and claiming a spot to watch the parade, Nate saw an opening and took it.

"You guys go on ahead," he said. "I want to talk to Alex for a minute— we'll catch up in a bit." He looked at her, and she nodded in agreement.

"But—" began Marc.

"It's OK, Marc," said Jenn. "Come with us—we'll get some burgers and hang out."

Nate mouthed a *thank you*, to which Jenn responded with a wink. As the larger group headed off in search of food, Nate and Alex walked slowly off in the other direction.

"My friends really like you," said Nate.

"And I like them," said Alex. "They're a lot of fun—I mean it. I really feel like I fit in."

"You do," said Nate with a smile. They walked along the edge of the green where the parade would be passing later. Across the street was a string of brick storefronts, including a hardware store and an old movie theater that had been closed for ages. Its marquee was blank. Aunt Celia had told him that years ago she would go to see movies there for just ninety-nine cents.

"Tell me," said Nate, "did you get in trouble for the Courtney thing?"

"Ms. Wright said there'd be a punishment, but she didn't say what. My father was pretty angry though—that can be punishment enough."

"How'd your mother take it?" asked Nate.

"It's just me and my father—my mother died a long time ago." Alex glanced at Nate.

"Oh, I'm sorry—I didn't know," said Nate. "My mother died when I was young, too."

"We have something in common," she said. She grabbed his hand and squeezed it. "I think my father expects me to screw up sooner or later." Alex laughed. "It wouldn't be right to disappoint him."

"You don't seem like a troublemaker," said Nate.

"Well, let's just say the other day when you blew up the band saw," she said, "I knew we were destined to be friends. That is totally the type of thing that would happen to me."

Nate stopped walking for a moment.

"Oh yeah?" asked Nate with a grin. "How many things have you blown up?"

"Oh, one or two." Alex smiled. They began moving again. "So, what about you? Is it just you and your brother and your dad?"

They paused at a tent selling flowers and potted plants. Alex picked up a small flat of purple violets and held it to her nose.

"No, actually Dad died not long ago," said Nate as he watched her studying the other seedlings. "Marc and I live with our aunt."

"Wow," said Alex, glancing at him. "I'm sorry—that must be rough."

"It was in the beginning," said Nate. "It's gotten easier, though I think Marc needs me more than ever now."

"I know what you mean," said Alex. "I felt like I had to care for my dad when my mom died. It's like I suddenly had to grow up fast."

"Yes!" said Nate. "That's it exactly."

Nate and Alex walked around the perimeter of the green where the tents began to thin out. They continued past the public library and back toward the festivities as they continued their conversation. Alex really seemed to understand him, he thought. And he was understanding everything she told him about herself, too.

They soon approached a sign mounted next to a bench that read:

WINDSOR
THE FIRST PERMANENT ENGLISH
SETTLEMENT IN CONNECTICUT

On September 26, 1633, a company of men under Lieutenant William Holmes arrived by ship from the Plymouth Colony in Massachusetts, on invitation of the local Indians, and established a trading post near the junction of the Farmington and Connecticut Rivers. In 1635 these first settlers were joined by a larger group which came overland from Dorchester in the Massachusetts Bay Colony. Windsor, with Hartford and Wethersfield, formed the Colony of Connecticut in 1636.

"This place has been here a long time," said Alex.

"Yes," said Nate. "It certainly has." Nate realized Aunt Celia would already have been born and living here within ten years of those dates—definitely not something he planned to share with a girl on the first date.

They sat on the bench for a while, chatting. When they ran out of things to say, they sat silently holding hands as they watched the people pass by. It felt natural to Nate—a perfect moment on a perfect day at the end of a truly insane week.

"We should probably get back to the others," said Alex.

Sadly, Nate knew she was right.

And suddenly, his perfect day became a little less perfect.

"*Witches*? Seriously?" someone said as they stood to leave. "What a nut job!"

It was Stephen Ross from their shop class, speaking to an older woman pushing a stroller. "What are you talking about?" Alex asked as he approached.

"Oh, hi," he said. "That guy over there is going on about the dangers of witches and telling everyone they're running around town." He pointed to a man standing in front of the town hall. "What a freak—I wonder where he escaped from."

"That's the guy who was handing out the flyers," said Alex.

"Yeah, he's also handing out these pamphlets," said Stephen, holding out a small, blue stack of pages held together with staples. "Take it if you want—I was gonna toss it." Alex took the booklet.

"Huh," she said.

"What is it?" asked Nate.

Alex shrugged. "No clue," she said. "Any idea?"

Nate felt his stomach tighten as she showed him the cover. It read *The Discovery of Witches*. Nate took the pamphlet from her.

He read the cover again, not wanting to believe what he was seeing. It was a cheaply constructed copy of the book—something one would have made at an office supply store, rather than the nicer leather-bound copies from Aunt Celia's case and the library.

Nate glanced at the man standing in front of the town hall, no more than ten yards across the green from where they stood. He held a stack of flyers under one arm, and several piles of pamphlets lay by his feet. Nate's first thoughts were of Hodge. But the man wore jeans and a T-shirt and was clean-shaven. Could it be him? It certainly didn't look like the man Nate had seen in the forest. Hodge had been wearing seventeenth-century clothing and sporting a full beard. But it had all happened so quickly, and he couldn't say for sure that it *wasn't* the same man. Maybe he was in disguise.

If it *was* Hodge, then what on earth was he trying to accomplish? Aunt Celia had said he wouldn't call attention to himself—but this man was doing just that. If it *wasn't* Hodge, then who was he and why was he handing out that particular book? Nate was starting to feel a bit sick.

"Earth to Nate," said Alex, breaking his concentration. He saw that Stephen had already left.

"Sorry," said Nate. "One sec." Nate pulled out his phone and shot off a text to Aunt Celia. She had to know about this ASAP. "Listen, I have to find Marc and the others."

"Sure," she said. "Everything OK?"

"Oh, yeah," he lied, forcing a smile. "Of course."

"Sounds like the parade is starting anyway," she said. Sure enough, the sounds of a marching band could be heard in the distance. "I could use a snack if you don't mind stopping on the way."

"Yeah, sure," said Nate. His mind was all over the place. He really wanted to tell Jenn that Hopkins's book had surfaced again, but he hadn't yet had a chance to tell her its real significance, and it didn't look like he was going to have that opportunity anytime soon. Hopefully Aunt Celia would get there quickly—the house wasn't far away, but they had blocked off many of the roads into the center of town to accommodate the parade.

Nate's phone chirped:

Be right there. Keep your distance from him.

He felt a huge relief knowing Aunt Celia was on her way. He felt powerless and in over his head when it came to all this witchy stuff. What could he really do if Hodge were to confront him at this moment? Well, that was an easy one—die.

After grabbing a fried dough and a caramel-covered apple, Nate and Alex found the rest of the group sitting along a curb, the parade already passing by in front of them. Nate was relieved to see his brother happily sitting there with the others, blissfully unaware of the mental turmoil he was experiencing. Nate had no appetite at the moment, but he took the piece of dough Alex handed him and absentmindedly chewed as he actively watched the crowd around him, hoping to see Aunt Celia and hoping *not* to see Malleus Hodge.

If Alex hadn't elbowed him, he would have totally missed Courtney. She sat there on the float as it came down the street, looking exactly in her element. She wore a yellow gown with a sash that read "Shad Derby Queen" in shiny letters. Her freshly curled hair tumbled about her shoulders, and she wore thin white gloves on her hands. The crown on her head glistened as she made queenly waves to the crowd. Kat and Kam sat on either side of her, tossing pink rose petals into the air.

"Oh yuck," said Zach. "I'm going to be sick."

Alex groaned.

Before Nate knew it, the parade was over. Courtney's float had been one of the last to pass by. The gathered crowd started to disperse back across the green to the various tents.

"Look, it's Aunt Celia!" said Marc. "I didn't think she was coming."

Thank God, thought Nate.

"I'll be back in a minute," he whispered to Alex. She nodded. He told the rest of the gang that he needed to talk to Aunt Celia for a moment and quickly ran off to meet her.

He filled her in quickly, showing her the copy of *The Discovery of Witches*.

"This is troubling," said Aunt Celia. "Show me where he is."

Nate led Aunt Celia across the green, wandering between groups of people and tents. Every so often he saw one of the flyers or a pamphlet laying on the grass where someone had dropped it, or on a table, abandoned— or even stranger to Nate, grasped in someone's hand. What were people thinking? Did they consider the whole thing a joke? Could anyone be taking it seriously? No, he didn't think that was possible—people didn't believe in witchcraft anymore. It had taken seeing that imp creature for Nate to truly believe any of it himself.

When they reached the steps of the town hall, the man was no longer there. Where could he have gone? Could someone have asked him to leave the festival?

"He was right there," said Nate, pointing to the place where the man had been handing out his propaganda.

"Well, he's not here now," said Aunt Celia. "Did he see you?"

"I'm not sure, but I don't think so."

They continued to scan the crowd.

"And you aren't sure it was him?"

"Sorry, I really couldn't tell," said Nate. "This guy's clothing was more modern. What do you think it means? Why would anyone intentionally spread rumors about witches? It's the twenty-first century—no one's likely to believe it."

"I don't know," said Aunt Celia. "But Hodge must be involved somehow—he must be. If the man you saw wasn't Hodge himself, then it was surely someone he sent."

Just then, the doors to the town hall opened, and out walked a middle-aged man in a suit. Nate recognized him as the mayor, Kevin Kinkaid. He walked up to a microphone that had been set up outside the building.

"Hello, everyone," said Mayor Kinkaid. "Can I have your attention please?"

A crowd started forming around the steps of the town hall. Nate felt a hand on his shoulder. It was Alex, with the rest of the gang. She was cutting pieces off the caramel apple with a plastic knife. She offered Nate a piece, but he declined.

"I'd like to thank everyone for coming," said Mayor Kinkaid. "I hope you're enjoying this year's festivities. The parade was lovely, I'm sure everyone will agree."

Alex pulled out her phone, which was vibrating. She typed a few words and sent off a text.

"I'm supposed to be doing something for my father right now," she whispered. "He's not amused." She smiled at Nate and winked. She went back to eating the apple.

"Before I let you continue your day," said Kinkaid, "I'd like to present this year's Shad Derby queen one last time. As I'm sure you'll agree, she brightened this year's parade—Miss Courtney Stevens!"

The crowd clapped as Courtney came out of the town hall doors, still dressed in her gown and crown, a bouquet of roses in her hands. At that moment Nate saw the man who might be Hodge standing next to a group of onlookers. He touched Aunt Celia's arm and glanced in the man's direction as soon as he had her attention.

That's him, she mouthed. *Stay here.* Nate nodded in response. Aunt Celia headed off in the direction of Hodge.

"Courtney, would you like to say a few words?" asked Mayor Kinkaid. She approached the microphone.

"I'd love to," she beamed. "I would like to thank everyone who voted for me this year. It's a true honor, and I'll do my best to fulfill my duties as your queen." She extended her arms wide as if to embrace the audience.

"What kind of duties could she possibly have?" whispered Alex. Nate smiled, although his attention was on Aunt Celia. He wasn't at all sure what she was about to do.

"And I'd like all my loyal subjects to know I love each and every one of you—even if you didn't vote for me," said Courtney.

The serpent chose that moment to contract against his skin. It had remained still since the incident with Hodge in the forest—long periods of time had passed when Nate had even forgotten it was there. The snake was making its presence known now, however, which likely meant something unpleasant was about to happen.

"Thank you, Courtney," said Mayor Kinkaid.

"And I want to assure you," she continued, "that you couldn't have chosen a more deserving—"

Something big and wet and alive hit the concrete at Courtney's feet. It was a large fish, flopping powerfully against the hard surface. Courtney's eyes widened but she remained still. The crowd gasped and Nate saw Aunt Celia pause, turning to see what had elicited the reaction from the crowd.

"What the frig!" said Zach.

"Who threw that?" yelled Mayor Kinkaid. Nate glanced quickly at his companions. All of them were as shocked as he was.

A second fish hit Courtney directly on the head, taking the crown with it as it bounced off her shoulder and landed on the ground with a juicy splat. It too was alive and struggling for its life, flopping against the hard ground. This time, she screamed.

And that was when chaos erupted.

The heavens opened, raining dozens and dozens of shad all over the spectators gathered before the town hall. People ran for cover, cramming together beneath nearby tents. Nate and his friends took shelter beneath a canvas canopy where homemade jams and preserves were being sold. Others followed, pushing and shoving the people who had gotten there first, sending jars of canned goods tumbling. The saleswoman screamed uselessly for everyone to leave the tent before all her merchandise was destroyed.

Nate quickly verified that Marc and his friends had made it safely to the tent with him. Alex still held the apple and knife, but the apple no longer appeared edible. It was covered in blood from the open gash on Alex's hand. She must have sliced it open in the rush to get under cover. Blood dripped from the wound.

"Are you OK?" he asked.

"Yeah," she said. "I'm an idiot. I'll be fine."

Nate looked out to see Courtney, still standing in front of the microphone, seemingly in shock, while fish rained down around her. There was nothing Nate could do to help, however. The crush of the crowd prevented any movement. Mayor Kinkaid emerged from the town hall and hurriedly pulled Courtney to safety.

Then Nate saw Aunt Celia. She stood unmoving in the midst of everything, still several yards from the warlock. She looked about in confusion, her eyes moving rapidly between scattering onlookers and Hodge. Even from where he stood, Nate could see the look of smug satisfaction on Hodge's face.

What's he up to? thought Nate. *And why is she just standing there?!* She and Hodge were the only people who hadn't run for cover. As the downpour of fish slowed to a stop, Nate saw that the area around Aunt Celia was entirely clear of the struggling shad. It was a perfect fish-free circle, two or three yards in diameter, with Aunt Celia directly at its center.

"What have you done, Hodge?" he heard Aunt Celia say. By this time, the sounds of the crowd had died away. Everyone stood silently within their shelters, watching the two people outside and trying to make sense of what was happening.

Hodge climbed the stairs of the town hall and picked up the micro-phone. Aunt Celia hadn't moved, and Nate wondered if he should try to get to her, but the crowd was still preventing him from going anywhere. The shad littered the green and the front of the town hall, silently suffocat-ing in the sun. Hodge raised the microphone to his mouth and spoke. His voice carried loudly and clearly across the green.

"Can I please have your attention—it's urgent you listen to what I have to say. We are all in great danger. What you've just witnessed should attest to that. There's great evil in this town, sent here by Satan himself. His minions have been here for some time, working their way into your businesses and homes. They've infiltrated your friends and families. No one is safe. You must seek out and destroy these agents of evil before it's too late."

Hodge raised his arm, pointing his finger directly at Aunt Celia.

"I put myself at great risk by bringing you this warning—heed my words. The woman who stands here before us is extremely dangerous. Don't let her—or others like her—bring Satan's destruction down upon us. You must . . ."

Nate gasped in pain as the bracelet tightly squeezed his arm. He knew he had to get to Aunt Celia immediately. He shoved the table penning him in, knocking it over along with dozens of jars of preserves. The sound of smashing glass broke the silence as Nate leaped over the table and ran in Aunt Celia's direction.

But before he reached her, she raised her arms toward Hodge. Blue fire erupted from her fingers, bathing him in a beam of azure flame. Onlookers gasped in horror as Hodge's clothing and skin melted from his body, accom-panied by hideous screams of agony. Aunt Celia's assault continued in this manner for seemingly endless seconds as Nate watched in disgusted awe. When the flame finally died away, there was nothing left of Malleus Hodge.

Chapter 15

THE DROWNING

Hartford, Colony of Connecticut, May 1647

Allie was drowning. She had never been much of a swimmer, and even without a strong current, she struggled to keep her head above water. It was a small river—the town referred to it as the rivulet to differentiate it from the larger body into which it emptied—but to Allie it made no difference. The water was deep, and she was going to die.

The panic set in quickly. She kicked her feet as she fought to breathe, her hands and arms moving forcefully but inefficiently. Her mother's desperate cries carried across the river, only to be muffled each time her head bobbed beneath the surface. She wouldn't be able to continue this for long. She was using oxygen faster than she could replenish it, and the fatigue and lack of air were taking a toll. Agonizing moments passed before her arms and legs grew heavy, her vision darkened, and her thrashing slowed. As she sank beneath the surface, she fought the urge to inhale, but eventually that irresistible compulsion took over and her struggling ceased. Allie felt the water flood her lungs as complete darkness overtook her.

Allie came awake with a gasp. She had had the dream again, forcing her to recall the horror she had felt the day she had experienced it. It took her a moment to remember where she was. She looked around the empty room, once again seeing the iron chains that sprouted from the floor around its perimeter. She was in the Hartford Gaol, where her mother had been kept—and where Malleus Hodge had taken her after ripping her away from her mother's dying body.

He had tossed her to the ground before slamming the door closed behind her—and there she had remained, her face pressed against the cold floor as she cried herself to sleep, the emotional and physical exhaustion too much to bear.

Allie rose to her feet, wondering how long she had been there. Where was her father, and why had he let Hodge take her? What was Hodge planning? She hoped not to be here to find out. She ran to the door and pulled as hard as she could, but it was locked and wouldn't budge. She stood on her tiptoes to peer through the barred window in the door's center. On the other side was a small room with a table and two chairs—no doubt the guard's room. It was empty. Her mother had been the jail's only prisoner and now she was gone.

There were no other doors. Several small windows, the room's only source of light, were positioned high upon the walls. They too were barred and far too high to reach. There would be no escape. It was a jail cell after all—it had been built to keep people inside.

"Help!" she cried. "Somebody help me!" She doubted anyone would hear—there had been no one near the jail when she had arrived. Everyone had been gathered around the meetinghouse, and even they would have most likely dispersed by now. As she had expected, no one responded to her cries. She would have to wait for Hodge to return.

Allie sat down, her back against the wall. She needed her mother. She regretted ever leaving her bed that morning. She wished she had never come to Hartford, and most of all, she wished she hadn't seen her mother swinging from the end of that rope. But if she had stayed in her bed, she wouldn't have learned what had happened to her mother—at least now she knew.

Allie thought again about the day she had come close to drowning. She had nearly died that day—and she would have, if not for her mother and her special talents. She and her mother had left the meetinghouse that morning after church service, heading south from the village green. They had followed the well-worn path to the rivulet that flowed through the woods on that side of the settlement. Her father had chosen not to join them, preferring to stay and socialize with the townsfolk on the green.

The rivulet was only a few minutes away, and as they approached, a couple of old friends came running from between the trees. It was the wolf and the deer. Allie and her mother had seen them on occasion, but never this far south and never this close to the green. The fawn had grown into a beautiful doe in the two years since they had met, and soon she would be having fawns of her own.

Growing bored of the wordless communication taking place between her mother and the two animals, Allie wandered to the bank of the rivulet. She picked up a flat stone, skipping it across the surface of the water. She gathered more, skipping several before hearing a low growl behind her. Turning, she saw the wolf, now facing toward the settlement. It was growling at something in the forest.

"What is it, Momma?" she asked.

"I'm not sure," her mother replied.

The wolf bolted into the trees.

Allie turned to skip the last two stones in her hand. She assumed they would leave in a moment to investigate the wolf's sudden departure. Several loud yelps echoed through the forest. She spun around quickly, her concern for the wolf overriding her judgment. She slipped on a wet pile of dirt and leaves and lost her balance, tumbling into the dark, chilly water.

Sometime later, she awoke, coughing and gagging. Water spewed from her lungs, all over the forest floor, and all over her already soaked dress.

"Easy—just breathe," said her mother. "You're going to be fine." Allie felt anything but fine—but it didn't take long for her to start feeling better. Her strength slowly returned and eventually she was able to rise to a seated position.

It was then she noticed the huge tree that had fallen across the rivulet. It hadn't been there before.

"Momma?"

"Yes, I did that—it was necessary to reach you."

Allie knew her mother would never use her abilities in such a manner unless she had no choice. Doing so put everything at risk. The townsfolk would never understand. Her mother had said her powers had been given to her by God—she referred to it as her numen, a divine power instilled in her by the Lord himself.

"But if God's given you these powers," Allie had asked on one occasion, "why does He make it so difficult for you to use them?"

"I don't know," her mother had replied. "But He has His reasons."

Allie's mother walked to the base of the large oak. Its roots, still intact, hung over the crater they had once occupied. She placed her hand on the tree for a moment, before stepping back several feet and raising her arms.

The ball of roots suddenly took on a life of its own. Like a writhing mass of snakes, the roots thrashed, straightening before Allie's eyes and lengthening until they could once again reach the ground inside the hole. With a series of ominous creaks, the roots tightened, thickening as they burrowed deep into the earth.

The creaking grew louder as the roots fought to right the tree by brute force. The tree slowly rose from the rivulet, water pouring from its branches as it was slowly lifted into the sky. It took a full minute to return the tons of hardwood to an upright position, and when it was done, her mother dropped to the ground in exhaustion. Water continued to rain down from the tree's branches and flow down its trunk to puddle on the ground beneath it.

By the time they were ready to head back toward the green and their home to the north, Allie and her mother were both cold and damp and covered in mud.

"Momma, what happened to the wolf?" Allie asked.

"I don't know," she replied.

In a matter of moments, they found the wolf, lying dead and bloodied by the side of the path. With a deep sadness, Allie knelt next to her mother who had stopped to examine the animal's body.

"It's been killed with a knife," she said, pointing to several deep puncture marks visible on the wolf's fur. Blood covered the creature's mouth. Whoever killed it hadn't left the encounter unscathed. Allie saw the deep look of concern on her mother's face.

It wasn't until sometime later, as she sat alone in the Hartford Gaol at the edge of Meetinghouse Square, that she understood the true reason for her mother's worry. They hadn't been alone in the woods that day—and there was a good chance someone had witnessed her mother using her powers to save her life. And Allie had a strong suspicion that that someone had been Malleus Hodge.

Chapter 16

THE ABDUCTION

Windsor, Connecticut, May 2019

"It seemed as real as the three of us standing here," said Nate. He and Marc had hurried with Aunt Celia to her car and driven straight back to the house. "First the fish fell from the sky, then everyone went psycho and finally, you killed Hodge—burned him alive with blue fire that shot out of your fingers."

"Well, I assure you I can do no such thing—and I didn't kill Hodge," said Aunt Celia. The three of them went upstairs to the special room and chose seats around the table. Nate felt anxious, horrified, and confused, and he hoped that Aunt Celia would be able to explain what they had just witnessed.

"My mother taught me that magick should never be used against humans—she died believing that," Aunt Celia said, with a frown. Nate could tell that recent events were weighing as heavily on his aunt as they were on him—if not more so. "But Hodge isn't entirely human anymore, and I can't say I wouldn't kill him if I had the opportunity—he's evil and needs to be stopped." She thumped her palm on the table, showing her frustration. "But I certainly wouldn't do it in front of the entire town."

"So where'd he go?" asked Marc.

"I'm not sure—he was there one moment and gone the next," she said.

"How did he do it?" asked Nate. "Are you saying none of it was real? The fish?" Surprisingly, Nate was having a harder time believing the whole thing had *not* happened—he had seen it with his own eyes, and it had seemed so real.

"It's called a glamour—a specific type of spell that tricks the senses," she said. "It can make you see, hear, or feel things that aren't there. Or it can make you *not* see things that *are* there—I'm assuming that was how he made his quick exit."

"But I saw a shad knock Courtney's crown right off her head," said Nate.

"That could have been part of the illusion—but I saw the crown fall myself. Most likely it was a small touch of kinetic magick to make the overall illusion more believable."

"Kinetic magick?" asked Marc.

"Yes, magick that involves the movement of an object," she said. "Telekinetic magick, for example, is the ability to move objects with the mind."

"Can he do that?" asked Nate. "Move objects with his mind?"

"I'm not sure," she said. "In this case, it could have been just a simple spell—or even a carefully thrown stone—it's hard to say."

"Well, the whole thing was pretty convincing," said Nate. "He made you look like a witch and a murderer."

"Yes . . ." said Aunt Celia, with a look of concern. "Although, if I'm correct and the whole thing was an illusion, there'll be no lasting evidence of any of it—just the memories of the witnesses. So, at least the worst of the damage will be contained to those people right there at the fair. Hopefully, over time the memories will fade, and they'll start to doubt what they saw."

"Won't they share what happened with other people?" added Nate.

"I'm sure they will," she said. "There will be talk and rumors for a while, but without the evidence to back them up . . ."

"But what about all the people with cell phones?" asked Marc.

"Fortunately, glamours affect only the mind. None of it would show up in photos or on video—so there will actually be evidence out there proving that the whole thing did *not* happen. The best we can hope for is for the madness to die down quickly."

A flurry of feathers appeared at the open window as the crow landed momentarily on the sill before hopping onto the table in front of Aunt Celia. She stroked its back for a moment before speaking again.

"Thanks, my friend," she said. "Apparently, the glamour faded soon after we made our exit. If anyone returns to the green, there will be nothing to see."

"Was he there?" asked Marc, pointing to the crow.

Aunt Celia nodded.

"Yes, there was a lot of confusion after we left, especially once the fish started vanishing."

"That's a good thing, right?" asked Nate.

"Anything that makes them doubt what they saw is a good thing," said Aunt Celia. "But the fact that any of this happened at all is very bad."

"Well, what's he trying to do?" asked Nate. "You said he wouldn't use magick in public."

"Well, I was wrong—I didn't expect this," she said, thoughtfully. "Although I probably should have. He's always used fear, doubt, and paranoia to his advantage. I have an idea what he's trying to do—the flyers and pamphlets, the public display of magick—"

"What is it, Aunt Celia?" asked Marc, concern in his eyes. Aunt Celia remained quiet for a moment. Nate and Marc waited silently for her to continue.

"I pray I'm wrong," she said finally, "but he might be able to make people believe that magick is real and that there's a strong reason to distrust neighbors, friends, and even family—that anyone you know could be dangerous, that anyone could have unchecked supernatural powers at their disposal."

"Are you suggesting," began Nate, "that he's trying to stir up a modern-day witch hunt? It's the twenty-first century. Is that even possible?"

"You tell me," she said. "With everything you've seen in the last few days, and knowing that this morning was just the first step in a bigger plan?"

Nate and Marc shared a glance.

"Damn," said Nate. "We're screwed." He thought about how hard it had all been to believe—until he started seeing magick with his own eyes.

"And he's singled me out as the town's first witch," Aunt Celia said. The irony of the same thing happening to her mother so long ago wasn't lost on Nate.

"So what're we going to do?" asked Marc.

"I've been thinking about it and have done a bit of research," said Aunt Celia. "I think the only option we have is to trap him in another witch's bottle. I was hoping to find something more permanent, but we don't have any more time to waste."

"While you're working on that, can I have Jenn and Zach come over?" asked Nate. "I never had the chance to fill them in."

"I'll tell you what—have them come over first thing in the morning," she said. "We'll tell them everything then. We can use their help."

Nate was relieved. He was still trying to figure out what he would say to Alex—he hadn't even given a reason for their quick departure this morning. No doubt she was confused and maybe scared by what she had seen. And he had just gotten up and left her there in the center of town. He would have to find some way to make it up to her once everything settled down.

As the three of them stood to leave the room, Nate's cell phone chirped. Maybe it was Alex. If so, he could begin smoothing things over with her. He opened his phone, however, to find a message from Zach:

Guys, Jenn's grandmother is dead.

Later that evening, Celia slipped out the front door, careful not to make a sound. She crossed the porch and took a seat on the front steps next to the boy named Noah. She had sent him on an errand and was eager to hear what he had to tell her.

"Hello, my friend," she said. He nodded in greeting, his features difficult to make out in the moonlight. She had purposely left the porch light off, not wanting to attract any attention. "Any luck?"

"Yes," he said. "I went over to Martha Gregory's home like you asked."

After hearing about the death of Jenn's aunt, Celia had asked him to visit Martha Gregory's house—she had a sneaking suspicion that Malleus Hodge had played a role in the woman's demise. Noah had a unique ability to get into locked places that she sometimes relied upon, so it made sense to send him rather than Corvin.

"What did you find?" she asked.

"Something attacked her. I think you were right. It wasn't a natural death," he said. "Her body wasn't there anymore, but there was blood everywhere."

"I was afraid of that," she said, thoughtfully. She glanced at the boy. "Thanks again for your help, Noah."

"Any time," he said. Without another word, he faded from sight, leaving her alone on the steps.

Celia heard a sound off to her left. A bicycle flew out of the driveway, making a quick turn in the direction of town. It was gone before she had a chance to react. *Nate, where are you going?* she thought, feeling a tightening in her stomach. *I told you not to leave after dark.* Realizing she had no time to lose, she rose and ran back inside for her car keys. She just hoped she would find Nate before someone, or something, else did.

Nate pedaled with all his might down Windsor Avenue until he reached the hill that led toward the center of town where Alex was meeting him. As he coasted down the long sloping road, he thought about their brief conversation on the phone. He was worried about her. She had called him in tears, sounding distraught—a fight with her father had left her at the end of her rope. With no other emotional support in town, there was no choice but for him to go to her right away. He still felt bad about how he'd skipped out on her that morning at the Shad Derby—and he hadn't had the chance to ask how she had felt about that bizarre series of events.

Fortunately, he remembered the old bicycle he had seen in the garage. He knew Aunt Celia would be upset. It probably wasn't the wisest move, but he didn't plan to be out for long. If his luck held, she would never find out—what she didn't know wouldn't hurt her, or him, he hoped.

Pedaling furiously, he soon passed the library and arrived at the green, nearing the bench outside of the town hall. Alex sat by herself on the bench, red curls escaping from beneath a dark hoodie. She stood when she saw him, and he felt his heart swell. He hopped off the bike before coming to a complete stop, letting it fall to the grass in a heap of spinning wheels.

A wave of sadness replaced the elation he'd felt as he got closer and saw the dampness on her cheek. The light from the lamppost reflected off her skin. Nate put his arms around her and held her for some time, reveling in the closeness and warmth, and feeling gratitude that she had chosen him to turn to in her time of need.

"Thank you," she said, once they had broken the embrace. "I feel stupid and embarrassed."

"Don't, really," he replied. "I'm glad you called. Are you OK?"

"I'm much better now that you're here," she forced a smile, wiping her eyes with her sleeve.

"Do you want to talk about what happened?"

Alex sighed.

"Oh, it's the same old thing. My father gets angry when I don't do as I'm told or challenge him on anything."

"Did it have to do with you going to the Shad Derby this morning?"

"It's related to that, yeah."

"I'm sorry," said Nate. He could wait until she was ready to talk, but he had a nagging feeling that something was off. He raised his hands to the hood that shadowed much of Alex's face.

"Nate, wait," she said, grabbing his wrists. Nate slowly pushed the hood back until it fell away, coming to rest against her back.

Even in the dim light cast by the lamppost, it was clear that Alex's left eye was swollen and discolored. Something had struck her—something hard and unforgiving.

"Oh my God, Alex. Did he do this to you?"

"I got him angry. I know better than to push his buttons."

"Alex, this isn't OK at all! I'm not going to let him hurt you anymore. You're coming with me to my house. Aunt Celia will know what to do."

Alex raised her hands in protest. "Look, I don't want to do anything that'll make this worse," she said.

Nate could see she was reluctant to involve anyone else. But she had called him, hadn't she?

"We're going to my house," he insisted. "You can stay there until we figure out what to do."

Alex's shoulders relaxed in resignation. Nate ran over and picked up the bike. He wanted to get back to the house before she changed her mind. He wasn't looking forward to telling Aunt Celia he had left the house, but he knew she could help. She would know exactly what to do.

"Let's go," he said.

Celia tore out of the driveway, heading down the street in the direction of the town center. She didn't know where Nate was headed, but hopefully she would be able to locate him before anything dangerous did. What could have been so important for him to sneak out of the house after dark? It was after midnight—he should have been in bed already, not bicycling around town. She had specifically warned him against doing anything like that.

She was also disturbed by the news Noah had brought her. While she hadn't really known Jennifer's grandmother, she had met her and had some knowledge of her history. They both attended services at First Church, and Celia had always suspected the woman of having the potential for magick. Whether or not Martha Gregory was aware of the possibility, she didn't know—but the unusual circumstances of her death lead her to believe she was correct. In his weakened state, Malleus Hodge would be looking for sources of magick to strengthen his own. There were rituals for stealing magick from others. All of them were dark and unscrupulous and required the death of the victim in order to remain permanent.

She didn't know how Hodge would have known of Martha Gregory's magick. If he had a way to locate such individuals from a distance in the same way he was able to track the bracelet, then other people were in danger. She would have to discreetly test Jennifer to see if she was a potential target—to see if there was a chance that she had inherited some of her grandmother's magick. And while she was at it, she would test Nate and Marc. Although magickal abilities were most frequently passed through the maternal line, there were exceptions to the rule.

Celia's train of thought was broken by the appearance of flashing lights in her rearview mirror. Streaks of red and blue flashed across her field of vision. *Damn*, she thought. *Not now.* In her haste she hadn't noticed the parked police car—and she had been driving pretty fast.

Pulling over to the side of the road, she looked into the rearview mirror. The police cruiser slowed to a stop behind her. The officer got out and made his way to the side of her vehicle. Celia rolled down the window and read the man's name tag: Officer Hendricks.

"License and registration, ma'am," he said. He was a young, muscular man, probably in his midtwenties.

"Something wrong, officer?" she asked, handing over the requested documents.

"Do you know how fast you were going?"

"I'm sorry officer, I'm trying to find my nephew. I think he may be in trouble."

"Stay here please," he said before walking back to the cruiser. As the officer opened the door and the interior light came on, Celia saw another officer sitting in the passenger seat. Of all the times to get pulled over, this was the worst—her chances of finding Nate decreased by the second and they hadn't been great to begin with.

After a couple minutes, the officer left the car and returned to her open window.

"Ma'am, I need you to step out of the vehicle, please."

"What?" she said, surprised. "Why?"

"Ma'am, step out of the vehicle now, please."

Celia had never been pulled over before, even for speeding. She couldn't imagine why she was being asked to leave the car. Had her license or registration expired? She released her seat belt and pushed open the door, stepping into the street.

"Turn around and face the car, ma'am. Hands behind your back."

Celia obeyed, shocked to feel the handcuffs that were suddenly locked around her wrists.

"Officer, what's going on?" she asked.

"You have the right to remain silent . . ." he began. She zoned out as he finished reciting her rights, trying to make sense of what was happening. Could this have something to do with the events at the festival?

"Do you understand these rights?" he finished after several moments.

"Yes," she said. "Am I being arrested?"

"Ma'am, you have a warrant involving an alleged homicide that took place earlier today."

Oh my God, she thought. *They think I killed Hodge.* Had someone recognized her at the festival and reported what they had seen? There could be no actual evidence against her since there had been no actual murder, unless—could Hodge have concocted something incriminating and planted it at the scene? She wouldn't put it past him. He was creative and cunning—and he was certainly out to get her.

Officer Hendricks took her by the arm and walking slightly behind her, led her to the cruiser. As they approached, the second officer came out of the vehicle and stood, turning toward them as he placed a hat on his head. Dread filled Celia—she recognized the hat and knew this was no police officer. The cruiser's flashing lights illuminated the visage of Malleus Hodge, confirming what she already knew.

"Hello, Alice," he said. One moment his face was a demonic crimson, the next a deathly blue. "So nice to see you. Did you enjoy my show this morning?" It was then that she heard the hum, and turning toward Hendricks, saw the flash of electric blue in his eyes. For the first time, she looked at his shoulder and noticed the large chunk of flesh that was missing from the base of his neck. Bone and muscle were visible, as if something large had taken a bite from the officer's shoulder. A dark stain flowed from the wound and down his left side—the side he had kept turned away from her for the entirety of their encounter.

"No comment—none at all?" said Hodge after she failed to respond. He closed the cruiser's door. "You must not be a fan of the theater."

"Did you kill Martha Gregory?" she asked, not willing to participate in his repartee.

"Oh, you heard about that?" he smiled. "Such a lovely old lady. She fed me cookies when I returned her beloved pet to her. She was unwell though—very sick indeed."

"You killed her!"

"Oh, my dear Alice. The poor woman was suffering. Her mind was deteriorating with no hope of recovery. I saved her from the worst of the confusion and pain that was heading her way. Imagine no longer recognizing your family—or wondering where your husband had gone, only to face the horror of learning over and over that he'd passed away. I did her—and her family—a great favor. One that happened to benefit myself as much as it did them."

"That wasn't your call, Hodge," she said. It was just as she had suspected. Hodge had killed Jenn's grandmother, and he showed no sign of regret. This infuriated her. She struggled against Officer Hendrick's grip, but she had no chance of breaking free.

Celia closed her eyes for a moment, sending out a mental call for help, hoping for a response. When she opened them, she saw movement from a nearby hedge. Could something have arrived to help her so quickly? She didn't think so. By this time, Hodge had rounded the car and was now just a few steps away. An animal leaped from behind the hedge to stand by his side—it was the surviving bobcat, its charred fur carrying the scent of smoke and death. Its fur and flesh were gone completely on one side, leaving its ribs and organs visible.

"Do you remember your old friend?" he asked, that horrible grin returning to his face. "He's my friend now, too. It took some time, but we've grown quite close over the last several days. He follows me everywhere now."

"You're definitely an acquired taste." Celia sneered at him.

"I would have brought your bear friend as well, but it would have been difficult walking him down the streets of town without people taking notice. I wouldn't want to scare anyone. Our fine Officer Hendricks has made his acquaintance," he said glancing at the officer's throat. "I have to say, they've gotten along quite famously."

"What do you want, Hodge?"

"I think you know—but first I wanted to tell you I've recovered nicely from our meeting in the woods, in case you were worried. It wasn't nice of you to send your friends to attack me like that. But since things have turned out so well, all is forgiven." He bowed dramatically.

"You're very generous," replied Celia. She was tired of his patronizing, narcissistic blather, and while she would have normally told him to shut up and get to the point, she was still holding out hope for an answer to her call. It would seem that she had run out of time, however. Hodge took a couple steps toward her and pulled something out of his cloak. Officer Hendricks's grip on her arm prevented her from moving away from Hodge as he advanced.

"Do you know what this is?" he asked, showing her the dark crystal in his hand. It was blacker than obsidian and glistened unnaturally in the darkness. "This is a shard of Endora's Ember. The Ember is said to be the final remains of the Witch of Endor."

The witch from the Bible, Celia thought.

"When Saul, the king of Israel, sought wisdom from God for his upcoming battle with the Philistines, God—unsurprisingly—failed to respond," Hodge went on. "Still desperate for advice, Saul sought out a necromancer to summon the ghost of the prophet Samuel. He eventually located the Witch of Endor and with her assistance, spoke to the prophet's spirit—only to be told that he and his whole army would die in battle against the Philistine forces. The next day, of course, this is exactly what came to pass."

"Thanks for the Bible study," said Celia, "but I'm already familiar with the story."

"Fair enough. What you may not know—as this wasn't recorded in the Bible—is that before he died, Saul ordered the death of the Witch of Endor. He'd already driven out all necromancers and sorcerers from Israel, you see, and he wasn't about to let this one run free—especially after the devastating news he received from the shade she'd summoned. The witch was burned alive at the stake. And when the fire died away, all that was left of her withered body was the Ember."

He raised the crystal in the air so that it glinted in the flashing lights.

"I was fortunate to come across a number of these shards in my travels. They have the ability to siphon the magick from a witch—without the messy and time-consuming spells and rituals. The first one I lent to dear Martha's cat. It returned fully charged to me upon her death and her magick is now mine. The second shard is for you, dear Alice."

"I gathered that. So you plan to kill me?" She glared at him.

"Oh no. Not yet anyway. You're more valuable to me alive at the moment. I need my serpent, and you'll do nicely as leverage. Hopefully young Nate will realize that it's in his best interest to return it to me. I will, however, siphon your powers in the meantime. They'll return to you over time, unfortunately, so I'll have to be vigilant in keeping you drained—at least until your death, at which time they'll be bound permanently to me."

Hodge stepped over to the cruiser's rear door and, pulling it open, retrieved his staff from the back seat. He returned to his spot in front of Celia and tapped the heel of the staff on the pavement. A small flame appeared at the top, adding to the illumination provided by the flashing red and blue lights.

"Tell me one thing," said Celia, partly out of curiosity and partly in an attempt to delay whatever it was Hodge was about to do. "I gather you did something to Martha Gregory's cat to make it kill her," she said, glancing at Officer Hendricks and the bobcat. "Why didn't you just kill her yourself if you were so concerned about putting an end to her suffering?"

"I could have," he said, "but where would the fun have been in that? Besides, the cat will spread so much excitement now that it's free to run about the town. I'm looking forward to it. The furor of this morning was only just the beginning. I have many thrilling things planned for the coming days. Life can become so boring and monotonous over time—as I'm sure you're all too aware. The people around here deserve much more than that. There's nothing better than getting the heart beating and the adrenaline pumping to make a person feel alive."

So she had been correct. Hodge intended to stir up things in Windsor, causing panic and hysteria not seen since the early days of Salem Village. And here she was in handcuffs, about to be drained of her magick, with no chance of warning anyone of what was to come. Unless—

From down the street she heard the sounds of barking. Celia glanced past Hodge and into the distance where two dark shapes, both low to the ground, were heading in their direction. *Yes! I knew they'd come!* But that wasn't all—not far behind she saw the figures of two people on either side of a bicycle, climbing the hill from the center of town. Could it be Nate? If so, who was with him? While she welcomed assistance of any kind, she certainly didn't want Nate anywhere near Hodge.

The two shapes resolved into a pair of pit bulls, one of which was dragging a length of chain behind him, its links rattling on the concrete sidewalk. They stopped several feet short of Hodge, their attention focused on him. They stood barking and growling, teeth exposed, spit dripping from the corners of their mouths. They had heard Celia's call and responded, ready for battle. Perhaps all was not lost.

Her hope was short-lived, however. Officer Hendricks pulled the gun from his holster and with two perfect shots dropped the pit bulls where they stood. The bullets tore through the animals' hearts, killing them instantly—along with any chance she had of escape. And things only got worse from there. Before her eyes the dogs rose slowly to their feet, their limp bodies rising from the ground like hideous marionettes. They came alive, refocusing their attention on her. Celia saw the flash of electric blue in their eyes that told her Hodge was now in full control. She had called them here only to die—and if that wasn't bad enough, Hodge was now using their undead corpses against her.

"Aunt Celia?" it was Nate and his friend, Alex, from the Shad Derby— they had arrived at the worst possible moment.

"Nate, just stay back," she said. She didn't want to tell him to run for fear that the undead pit bulls would give chase.

"Hello, Nate," said Hodge, turning to greet the newcomers. "And who do we have here? I don't believe we've met." Nate dropped the bike and moved to stand in front of Alex, saying nothing in response.

"Oh, a shy one—no matter, you two are just in time," Hodge continued. He lifted the black shard and pressed it to Celia's forehead. She felt no pain, just a dreadful feeling of violation as the magick was stripped from her body. Her knees gave out, and she would have fallen to the ground if not for Officer Hendricks's firm grip on her arm. Her surroundings were spinning, and by the time the vertigo subsided, there was nothing left of the magick within her.

"Aunt Celia!" Nate shouted. "What did he do?" He took a step forward, but Alex held him back.

"Nate, don't," she said, grasping his arm.

"I've just removed all traces of magick from your—Aunt Celia, is it?" said Hodge, before she could gather her wits to respond. "Whether she'll be OK is entirely up to you. Due to your impeccable timing, I'll make you this generous one-time offer—hand me my serpent now, and I'll return your aunt to you. The magick will return to her in time. But be warned—if you choose to decline my offer, your aunt will come with me—and her fate will be very unpleasant."

"But it doesn't come off," said Nate as he lifted his sleeve, exposing the snake encircling his forearm. "I've tried to remove it, but it just won't budge."

"Nonsense—you just have to will it off," said Hodge. "It's as simple as that—don't try to lie to me, boy."

"I've tried that," said Nate, still desperately tugging at the metallic viper. "It doesn't work."

"Nate, don't listen to him—" said Celia, once again able to speak. She could hear the fear in Nate's voice. "If you give it to him, we'll all die." She knew there was no way Hodge would let them walk away from this.

"This is your last chance," said Hodge, getting angrier by the moment.

Nate glanced frantically between Hodge and Celia. Celia could tell that her nephew had no idea what to do—and neither did she.

"The serpent doesn't want you, Hodge," she said in an attempt to take the focus off Nate. "It's found someone it likes better—you shouldn't be surprised."

"It won't respond to me—" said Nate, holding his arm out toward the sorcerer. "Here! Just take it!" Celia saw the desperation rising in Nate—the need to save her and protect Alex.

"You know it doesn't work that way. Once it's in place, only the wearer can remove it," said Hodge. "That restriction goes away with the death of the wearer, of course."

Celia knew the threat was intended to scare Nate into turning over the serpent—and she felt he would have done so if he were able to remove it. If killing Nate would allow Hodge to retrieve it, then why wasn't Hodge doing just that? It would be a simple matter to have Hendricks kill him. Then she remembered how the serpent had defended Nate from the imp at their first encounter. It had also warned Nate of danger on at least one occasion—she suddenly knew the answer.

"Nate, he's afraid the bracelet will defend you if he tries to harm you or take it by force—remember the imp?" she said.

Hodge looked at her with pure undisguised hatred. She had guessed correctly and would surely pay for it later—but the important thing was that Nate wasn't in immediate danger. She had no doubt that Hodge would eventually find a way to take the serpent from him, but that wasn't going to happen tonight.

"I'm disappointed in you, Nate," he said. "Listen carefully—this is what we're going to do. You have forty-eight hours to remove the serpent. The next time you see me, you'll hand it over immediately—no whining, no bargaining, no delays. And if you don't do just that, know this—your Aunt Celia won't be the only one who pays the price." He glanced past Nate, his gaze landing on Alex. "Whatever comes next is entirely up to you."

Hodge turned and placed the dark crystal within a shallow depression near the top of the staff. Celia saw it slide perfectly into place and become one with the wood, the orange flame on top turning a deep violet—the staff's response to her stolen magick. Hodge tapped the staff on the ground and this time a circle of purple flame radiated outward from its base, growing to encircle the animals, Hendricks, Hodge, and herself, with Nate and Alex just outside its border. The flame felt cold to the touch. She had never seen anything like it.

Helplessly, Celia glanced at Nate and Alex, seeing the fear and confusion on their faces as she waited for Hodge to finish whatever it was he was doing. Fortunately, she didn't have to wait long. A feeling of weightlessness overtook her as Hodge brought his staff down two more times in rapid succession. Celia felt her consciousness slipping away just as everything around her faded to black.

Chapter 17

MR. FLUFFERTON RETURNS

"Celia is an obvious alias for her to have chosen," said Jenn.

The six friends sat around the table in what Nate now called the "artifact room." Marc had referred to it as "Aunt Celia's witch room" exactly one time in her presence. They had both cringed at her reaction, and it wasn't long after that that the new name had been adopted.

At Nate's insistence, Alex had stayed at the house with the two brothers following the previous night's abduction. Between her father's violence and the threat posed by Hodge, the warded house was the safest place to be. Jenn, Zach, and Douglas had arrived first thing in the morning to join them, Jenn carrying a bag of clothing for Alex, in case she needed to stay a few days. Nate hoped that together they would be able to locate Aunt Celia and find a way to deal with Hodge, even though the odds didn't seem to favor them.

"What do you mean?" asked Nate, unsure what Jenn meant regarding his aunt's choice of alias.

"'Celia' is an anagram of 'Alice,'" she said. "Just switch the letters around."

"Wow, you're right," said Nate. "How could I have missed that?"

"You would notice that," said Zach, shaking his head in amusement before turning to Nate. "So, let me summarize what we've learned this morning. One, your aunt is a witch named Alice, and she's over 350 years old. Two, her mother was the Alse Young we learned about in class. Three, your aunt trapped an ancient witch hunter from Europe in a bottle for several centuries, and by the way, he's now an evil witch himself. Four, you and your brother freed evil witch dude and stole his Satan-powered metal serpent, which you can't get off your arm. Five, he drained the magick from your aunt and kidnapped her to try to make you give the serpent back. Six, he caused all that craziness at the Shad Derby and wants to start Witch Hunt 3000. And, seven, 'Celia' is made up of the same letters as 'Alice.'"

"Don't forget—" began Marc.

"Oh, right," said Zach. "And eight, your aunt talks to fish. Does that about sum it up?"

"Uh, yeah—I think that covers it," said Nate. "And by the way, she doesn't like being called a witch." Nate looked around at his friends' expressions, wondering how well they were processing the information. He really needed them to accept what he was saying, but he hadn't appreciated how ridiculous the whole thing sounded until he heard Zach's summarization.

"Well?" he said after several moments of silence. "Are you—do you believe us?" Everyone began speaking at once.

"Hell, yeah," said Zach, slapping the table with his palm. "We've seen some crazy shit."

"You know *I* do," said Alex, her eyebrows raised.

"I believe you," said Douglas. He leaned forward, looking at the others.

"As insane as it sounds, it explains some of the other unexplainable things that have happened," said Jenn, weighing in after the others. "And then there's all this." She gestured around the room at all the unusual items—the pentacle, the crystals, the dried herbs hanging from the ceiling. "So, what do we do?"

"Thanks guys," said Nate, relieved by their responses. "We need to find and rescue Aunt Celia. I don't think there's much we can do about Hodge without her. Unfortunately, I don't even know where to begin."

"And you said she just vanished?" asked Jenn.

"She and all the others," said Alex.

"Others?" asked Jenn.

"It was quite a crew," said Nate. "She and Hodge along with a police officer, a bobcat, and two pit bulls—and none of them appeared healthy."

Douglas's eyes went wide as he listened.

"I'll say," said Alex. "The cop was covered in blood—he shot the pit bulls in front of us, but they appeared to shake it off pretty quickly. And then there was the cat—I can't explain that one at all—it looked dead, as if it had crawled out of a grave before being set on fire."

"That sounds like your grandmother's cat!" said Zach to Jenn. She started to say something but changed her mind.

"I think it was one of the bobcats Aunt Celia sent after him in Northwest Park," said Nate. "Somehow he'd gained control of it."

"If you were that outnumbered, why didn't he just take the serpent?" Jenn asked.

"He was afraid it would defend me if attacked," said Nate. "That's what Aunt Celia believed—it chose its new owner, and everyone else, including Hodge, was now the enemy. We were basically in a stalemate. I couldn't give it to him, and he couldn't take it. His best hope was that I was telling the truth—that I couldn't remove it—and to give me a couple days to find a way to get it off."

At that moment, Nate heard the doorbell ring. He considered ignoring it for just a moment, but thought better of it—what if it had to do with Aunt Celia? He sent Marc off to answer the door, asking Alex to go along with him for good measure. Zach and Douglas took the opportunity to stand and stretch. They began walking around the room, picking up various objects for inspection.

"Does your aunt have a bird?" asked Douglas, noting the empty birdcage.

"Um, yeah—it kinda comes and goes at will," said Nate. Douglas's eyebrows rose in surprise, to which Nate shrugged his shoulders.

"How's your family doing, Jenn?" Nate asked, changing the subject.

She frowned. "I don't know; feeling mostly numb, I guess. We've all been dealing with the loss of Gran, but we also don't really understand how she died."

"What are the police saying?" asked Nate.

"Nothing that makes sense," she said with a frustrated shake of her head. "The evidence indicates she was attacked by a cat and died from blood loss. But no house cat could do that much damage. And then there were the partially decomposed remains of the cat they found in her bathtub, and their only explanation is that they were already there when she died. Gran was suffering from dementia, but there's no way she was collecting chunks of dead cat."

"Well, there's a hobby," said Zach with a smirk.

Everyone glared at him.

"And her cat—the one that had just returned home—was nowhere to be found. It's insane, but I'm starting to think that Zach could be right. Could Gran's cat have been brought back from the dead? I can't believe I'm even considering it—but is that something he could do? And if so, why her cat?"

"I don't know," said Nate, "but Aunt Celia felt he may very well do things like that—supernatural things—to stir up panic around town."

"I'm going over to her house today. After I leave here, I have to stop there to pick up a dress for her burial."

"Your parents are making you do that?" asked Zach, his mouth agape.

"I offered," Jenn grimaced, "but I'm not looking forward to it. The police sealed off the bathroom where she died, but I'm still nervous about going into the house alone."

"Can we help?" asked Douglas enthusiastically, hoping to be of assistance.

"That would be great," said Jenn. Nate saw her eyes well with tears. If they could help her, they definitely would. She was here helping him, after all.

Just then he heard voices heading in their direction: Marc and Alex, but there was also a third voice he knew, a man's voice, that he couldn't place.

He exchanged eye contact with the others in the room. They too were curious who the newcomer could be.

The visitor turned out to be Mr. Black, their biology teacher from school. What was he doing here? Nate wondered. And why had Marc and Alex brought him right to the artifact room? But then he recalled the exchange that took place at school following the meeting with the principal. Mr. Black and Aunt Celia were definitely acquaintances of some sort.

"Hello all," Mr. Black said, nodding at each one in turn. He wore jeans and a polo shirt rather than his customary teaching attire.

"Mr. Black?" said Nate. "This is, uh, a surprise." He stood awkwardly.

"Please sit," Mr. Black said. Nate retook his seat at the table.

"I know you're surprised to see me here," he continued, "so I'll get right to the point. Your Aunt Celia and I are old friends, and I know something has happened to her. Furthermore, I'm familiar with the circumstances—the whole thing—Matthew Hopkins a.k.a. Malleus Hodge, his current activities, and your aunt's true identity. Your aunt has kept me posted on everything. She asked me to keep an eye on the situation and on you while you were at school. And she asked me to step in should anything happen to her." He walked slowly around the table as he spoke until he stood before the glass cabinet.

"Uh, yes, sir—" Nate said. He was thrown off by Mr. Black's sudden appearance and his knowledge of the situation. Why hadn't Aunt Celia told them about Mr. Black—unless this was another trick of Hodge's? Could Hodge be standing right before them now in disguise? No, that wasn't possible—the wards they had placed within the house wouldn't have allowed anything evil to enter. He started to feel a little better. If Aunt Celia had planned for this eventuality, and Mr. Black could provide them much needed assistance, then their chance of getting Aunt Celia back and dealing with Hodge had just vastly improved.

"As of now, I don't know where the warlock is holding your aunt—but I'm working on that," Mr. Black continued. "For expediency's sake, your aunt had decided to create a witch's bottle to imprison him, similar to the one she had used before. To do so requires a number of ingredients, which

I'll need your assistance in obtaining. One thing that we'll require and don't have at our disposal is a witch—however, I do have some ideas on how to address that. What questions do you have?" He glanced at each of the teenagers.

"Why didn't Aunt Celia tell us about you?" asked Marc.

"She felt the fewer people who knew the better—I was an ace up her sleeve, so to speak. She had to eliminate any chance of Hopkins/Hodge finding out about me just in case a situation like this one arose."

"How long have you known her?" asked Nate.

"I've known her for a while now—I'll share more details with you later," he said, "but first let's deal with the current crisis."

"What do you need us to gather for the witch's bottle?" asked Jenn.

"I have a list," he said, pulling out several copies from a pocket and passing them around the table. "Take a look, and divvy it up among yourselves."

Nate and his friends studied the list of ingredients.

"Hair of the witch?" Jenn frowned. "Does that mean we need to get a sample of Hodge's hair?"

"Yes," said Mr. Black. "Although that actually may be the easiest item on the list." He opened the case and lifted the cracked witch's bottle several inches into the air, firmly bringing it down against the shelf's surface. It immediately shattered into a dozen pieces, causing everyone around the table to jump. He then sifted through the broken remains, retrieving something between two fingers. He turned around and showed them what he had found. It was a clump of hair that looked like something you might fish out of the shower drain.

"Is that his?" asked Nate, slightly repulsed by the ancient snarl of hair. He took note of the fact that Mr. Black knew exactly where to find it. Aunt Celia must have shown him the room at some point.

"Yes, we should be able to reuse this," said Mr. Black.

"Most of these things don't seem too bad," said Zach. He read off a few items. "Sulfur, copper, rosemary, nails or pins, urine—hey wait a minute. We have to get a sample of his urine?" Jenn's mouth dropped open and everyone else's face showed some level of disgust.

"No, any urine will do," said Mr. Black.

"Oh, in that case," said Zach with a grin, "leave that one to me."

Marc snickered.

Once they had divvied up the list among themselves to Mr. Black's satisfaction, he took his leave, saying he would work on locating Aunt Celia. They agreed to meet later that evening in the artifact room to share their progress. Nate was relieved that they now had a plan of action. But before they broke into teams to search for ingredients, they had promised to help Jenn. They were going to go to Martha Gregory's house—the place where Jenn's grandmother had died.

Nate, Zach, and Douglas rode bicycles with Jenn to her grandmother's house. Marc and Alex had remained behind since there were only four bikes between the six of them. As they pulled into the driveway, Nate wondered exactly what they would find there. Jenn had said the police had closed off the bathroom where her grandmother had died, but he assumed that the clothing they needed to collect would be in the bedroom right next to it.

"Are you ready for this?" he asked Jenn as they climbed the front steps.

"Ready as I'll ever be," she said, turning the key in the lock and pushing open the door. They went into the small tidy living room. It seemed ordinary to Nate—nothing disorganized or out of place. He did notice an unusual odor, but it wasn't overpowering by any means.

"Thanks again for coming, guys," said Jenn as they went into the bedroom. "I think I'd be really freaking out about now if you weren't here."

"Of course," said Zach.

"No problem," said Douglas.

Dozens of tiny dark paw prints peppered the floor. *That's blood*, Nate thought. The smell in the bedroom was stronger than it had been in the living room. On the right wall he saw what must have been the door to the bathroom. The police had covered it in a zigzagged pattern of yellow tape that read POLICE LINE DO NOT CROSS.

Jenn made her way to the closet and pulled open the folding doors. She began sliding hangers, flipping through the dozens of dresses, searching for something specific. The others stood nearby, watching.

"Here it is," she said after a moment, holding up a blue dress before laying it on the bed. "I just need to grab a pair of shoes, and we can get outta here." She kneeled and began looking through the footwear that lined the closet floor.

Suddenly she got to her feet, her face showing confusion. "Can one of you give me a hand?"

"Sure thing," said Zach.

With Zach's help, Jenn lifted a large wooden box from the floor and set it on a nearby dresser. It looked old and dusty. From where Nate stood, he could see it was covered in intricate carvings. On its top in flowery script was etched the number ninety-seven.

"This is strange," said Jenn with a frown. "I've never seen this before." She blew a layer of dust off the top of the box as Nate and Douglas walked over to get a closer look.

"Ninety-seven?" asked Nate. "What does that mean?"

"Could it be a year?" asked Zach. "1997?"

"This looks a lot older than that," said Douglas.

"I don't see any way of opening it," said Jenn.

There were no obvious hinges or latches. Jenn ran her fingers across the individual carvings. Various shapes and designs were visible across the top and sides of the box, intricately etched in relief. The box was beautiful and old, and for some reason, Nate felt certain it held something important.

"Help me turn it over," she said, and with Zach's assistance she laid the box on its back, revealing the smooth wooden bottom. It was free of decoration except for the lone symbol carved at its center—a pentacle, similar to the one on the wall in Aunt Celia's artifact room.

"What do you suppose it means?" asked Nate glancing at Jenn. "Did your grandmother have an interest in the occult?"

"Not that I'm aware of," she said, visibly shaken. "Let's get out of here. I can't deal with this right now."

Nate didn't know what to make of the box or the presence of the pen-tacle. He wished Aunt Celia were around to give an opinion. Could the box have had something to do with Martha Gregory's death? Perhaps he could raise the subject after the funeral.

He and Douglas started toward the living room as Jenn turned to retrieve her grandmother's belongings. He glanced at the police-taped door, finding it surreal that someone had died just on the other side.

And so violently, he thought.

He found his eyes drawn to an area of darkness near the floor. Taking a step closer, Nate realized the bottom corner of the door had been torn away, leaving a four- to five-inch hole. Bits of shredded wood littered the carpet that appeared to have been scratched—*or chewed?*—away.

"I'm ready," said Jenn from across the room. "Let's go."

"Uh, guys," Nate called to the others, pointing toward the bathroom door, "take a look at—"

A loud, threatening hiss reached Nate's ears. He spun in time to see a cat-sized creature emerge from beneath the bed. It was greasy and putrid, with moist patches of fur. Immediately, it leaped at him, claws extended. The serpent roared to life, burning away Nate's sleeve in a burst of flame.

"Whoa!" cried Douglas at the sight of the serpent's activation.

By pure reflex, Nate intercepted the beast with a kick to the middle, sending it soaring in the opposite direction. The horrible stench it left behind caused him to gag. With the trouble momentarily averted, the ser-pent's fire flickered out.

"I knew it!" Zach yelled, as the undead animal flew toward him. His triumphant expression changed to one of horror as he realized the impli-cations of having been correct. He dodged in the nick of time. The cat creature sailed past with a hideous screech, landing gracefully on its feet. It turned in a fluid motion and jumped onto the bed, quickly rotating in a circle as if to evaluate each of the four humans that surrounded it.

After a moment the creature stopped, focusing its attention on Jenn. With a loud hiss, it leaped at her. She screamed, raising her arms to protect herself, instinctively shoving it away with her hands. The dress she had been holding dropped over the animal as it fell back to the bed. Tangled in the fabric, the creature began furiously shredding the material—tearing at it with tooth and claw in an attempt to get free.

Before it could escape, Nate picked up a floor lamp and struck the squirming, dress-covered mass. Lightbulbs shattered, strewing glass across the bed, but the creature didn't slow. He struck it again and again with all his strength. Douglas, who had remained frozen until this moment, began picking up knickknacks from Martha Gregory's dresser and lobbing them at the writhing heap. The blows did little to harm the creature, and eventually it freed itself. It leaped off the bed with lightning speed and dove through the hole in the bathroom door, scraping off chunks of flesh in the process.

"Guys, what do we do?" screamed Zach.

"Run!" yelled Nate and Jenn in unison. Everything had happened so fast, that Nate hadn't had time to be afraid. He was running on pure adrenaline and right now his one goal was to make sure everyone got out of the house.

Jenn ran into the living room followed by Zach. Nate held back a moment, allowing Douglas to precede him through the doorway. But before Douglas was able to cross the threshold, the undead creature re-emerged from the hole and with furious speed, sprang past Nate. A wail burst from Douglas as the creature landed on his back, digging claws into flesh and raising bloody welts beneath his shirt. Douglas twirled around, pounding himself repeatedly on the back with his fists in an attempt to dislodge the creature.

"Get it off! Get it off!" Douglas cried.

Zach grabbed the creature's tail with one hand and a leg with the other, pulling with all his might. Fur and flesh slid free of the animal, preventing Zach from securing a firm grip. Quickly shaking the slime from his fingers, he reached once more for the creature, tightly grasping the now-exposed bone.

Douglas screamed in pain as Zach tore the creature from his back. It twisted in Zach's grip, digging its teeth and claws deeply into his skin. He dropped to his knees, the pain visible on his face, and began pounding the creature into the ground with his fists—finally, with a loud crack, the creature went limp and released its hold on Zach, dropping to the floor. As Zach regained his feet, Nate could see the creature's back was bent at an unnatural angle. Its spine was broken.

But Nate's relief was short-lived.

"Guys—" exclaimed Jenn. "What's happening?"

Before their eyes the creature's bones began to reknit. Its spine moved slowly back into place with a pop. Slowly it rose to its feet.

Douglas was the first to react—raising his foot, he brought it down onto the creature, flattening it and pinning it in place with the full weight of his body. Both ends of the deceased cat began to squirm, flopping about in an attempt to wriggle free. Immediately, Douglas began stomping the animal's rear with his free foot, bringing his shoe down repeatedly with all his strength.

"It. Just. Won't. Die!" he cried in frustration, emphasizing each word with a crushing blow.

"The head!" yelled Zach. "Get the head!"

Nate grabbed the floor lamp he had discarded in his haste to flee and turned it around, bringing the heavy base down on the creature's head. The skull gave way immediately and the creature went limp. A flash of blue light was visible from beneath the lamp, and at that same moment, the serpent went still. Filled with relief, Nate knew that this time it was over—the creature was truly and permanently dead.

Chapter 18

THE WITCHFINDER'S LETTER

Hartford, Colony of Connecticut, May 1647

Allie heard someone step into the guard's chamber from outside. She ran to the cell door and stood on tiptoes, struggling to peek through the small, barred window. She wasn't sure how long she had been there, but it had been a while and she knew Hodge would be returning for her. No one else was likely to appear. There were no prisoners to oversee, and she doubted anyone else knew she was there.

Then through the bars, she saw him. He stood with his back to the room as he closed and bolted the exterior door. She watched silently as he removed his hat and cloak, hanging them on a hook by the entrance. Turning, he placed several items on the center table—an apple, a book, and a ring of keys. She knew immediately they were the keys to her prison. He picked up a ceramic cup and poured water from the pitcher that sat there. When he glanced toward her at last, he started visibly. He must not have expected to see her there, only her eyes and forehead visible, peering back at him through the bars.

"Hello, my child," he said, recovering quickly.

The words distressed her. She wasn't his child. She said nothing in return, maintaining eye contact as he picked up the apple and keys and approached. When he was within a couple feet of her, she backed into the room and waited as he unlocked the door and entered. She saw the ring of keys in his hand. They taunted her—a means of escape just out of reach.

Hodge took a step forward, placing the cup and apple on the floor in front of her.

"These are for you," he said before stepping back. "It's been a long day. You must be hungry."

Allie ran to the cup and picked it up, drinking every drop. She set the cup on the floor and grabbed the apple, taking a huge bite. Although she didn't trust him, she didn't think twice about accepting his offerings. She hadn't eaten since the wagon ride and had brought nothing at all from home to drink.

"First of all, I'd like to apologize," said Hodge. "I'm sorry you had to witness that awful event in the square. It must have been difficult seeing your mother like that."

The apology confused Allie. Was he telling the truth? She still felt he was responsible for her mother's fate. Could he possibly care one way or another about her feelings? She didn't think so.

"Why am I here?" she asked, gathering the courage to speak.

"You're here because I have some important things to discuss with you."

"Where's my father?"

"Your father is—gone. He collected your mother's body and went home."

Could that be true? He wouldn't have left for home without her, would he? But then again, he hadn't stopped them from killing her mother. She was so confused—she didn't know what to believe.

"Does he know I'm here?" she asked. Hodge shrugged.

"It would seem you aren't that important to him." The smile that had unnerved Allie on previous occasions flashed briefly across his face. If Hodge was telling the truth, her father had abandoned her just as he had her mother. Considering recent events, she didn't find that difficult to believe. The realization saddened her. In all likelihood she was on her own—if she couldn't find a way to escape, she would remain at the mercy of Hodge.

She took a quick look at the door behind him. If she could distract him for a moment, she just might make it past him and out of the building.

"Don't try it," he said, noticing the glance. "I've locked the outer door, and no one can get in or out without the keys. And in case you were wondering, no one will be by to bother us. Neither Jailor Ruscoe nor his assistant spend time here unless there's a prisoner to watch over. Conveniently for us, the whole place is left unlocked when not in use, the keys kept on a hook in the outer room."

Allie stepped back until she stood in the center of the room. The sun was shining through the high windows, brightening her features. She remained silent for a moment, unsure of what to do or say. She forced herself to finish the apple even though she no longer felt like eating. She would use the time to listen and think.

"Tell me, Alice," he said, taking a step farther into the room. "Do you believe in God?"

The question surprised her, and she found herself answering immediately.

"Of course," she said.

"Alice, how long have you known your mother was a witch?"

"She's no witch!" she shouted, dropping the apple core onto the ground.

"Come, now," he said making a wide gesture with his hand. "She confessed. I know you were aware of her abilities."

Allie was too shocked by his words to respond. Could her mother have confessed? How could that be? She had her special talents. That was true. But she had never called herself a witch. All witches were evil, weren't they?

"You're aware of the Covenant, are you not?" he asked, his voice suddenly softer, more serious. "The agreement God made with us as His children?"

Allie nodded. The Covenant promised God's grace and salvation to those who lived by His laws.

"I'm going to ask you a question," he said, looking her right in the eyes, "and it's important you answer me honestly—your life may depend upon it. Do you yourself share any of your mother's abilities?"

Allie said no by shaking her head, unsure which answer he was hoping for. She couldn't do any of the things her mother did. She wondered if he would believe her. But after seeing what had happened to her mother, she would hardly tell him even if she did.

"When God dictated the first books of the Bible to Moses on Mount Sinai," he said, "the Covenant Code was included in the Book of Exodus, along with the Ten Commandments. Are you familiar with the Code?"

"Yes." Her father had read her that section of the Bible before, but she wasn't sure where Hodge was going with this.

"Then you're familiar with Exodus 22:18?"

She shrugged—she wasn't that familiar with the Code. They were the rules God expected them to live by, but she hadn't memorized them.

"Listen," he said. "I'm trying to make you an offer, one that could one day save your life. If you would help me—"

Just then there was a knock on the outer door. Allie saw that Hodge wasn't surprised by the interruption. He had been expecting this.

"Please excuse me," he said. "There's something I must do. Don't make a sound. I shall return shortly." He turned and went out the door, locking it again as he passed. She heard him open the outer door, which was followed by a quick exchange of words—and then he was gone. She considered crying out but decided against it. Hodge had been expecting the caller. The person was unlikely to provide her assistance.

Allie ran once again to the door and peered through the window, confirming that he had indeed left the building. It was then she noticed the set of keys that hung from the hook on the far wall, high enough that she would need a chair to reach them. They appeared identical to the ones she had seen in Hodge's hand. Were they a spare set? Sadly, with no way to reach them, they may as well have been back home in Windsor for all the good they would do.

She took a seat, resting her back against the hard wall, unsure of what to do next. What did Hodge want? He had started asking for her help with something, but how and why would she help him?

Allie saw movement from the corner of her eye. There was a small brown mouse sitting on its hind legs, eating a crumb it held in its paws. How strange, she thought. Mice were usually so skittish. She was surprised to see it so calmly sitting there.

"Hello," she said. The mouse watched her as it nibbled, unfazed by her presence. Finishing its meal, it surprised her by jumping into her lap. Reflexively, she reached down to touch its soft fur and when she did, the most extraordinary thing happened: she felt the warm embrace of her mother and an incredible feeling of love and hope infused her body. Instantly she knew this small creature had in some way shared an intimate bond with her mother. For several moments she basked in the feeling of her mother's presence and then, before she could make sense of it, both it and the mouse were gone.

She looked around but saw no sign of her visitor. Where had it gone? Her mother must have befriended the animal—most likely in this very place. The mouse probably kept her company during her final days. Allie prayed it would return and along with it, the sensation of her mother's proximity.

Allie heard a loud *thunk* from the outer room. She jumped at the sound. Had Hodge returned? No, the jail was once again silent. She sat still for several moments, listening. Soon, a soft rattling could be heard, like the sound of a chain dragging against stone. Standing, she walked back to the door and peered through the window to identify its source. There was no movement on the other side—but the sound continued, and it was coming from somewhere close by.

Something moved by her feet, and she looked down to see the mouse—or a portion of it, anyway. Its tail and hindquarters were visible and wiggling as if its head had been pinched beneath the door. Never before had she seen anything like it. She watched with fascination as it slowly emerged from the crack—its body and then its head soon appeared, followed shortly by a metallic object. It took Allie several moments to realize it held the ring of spare keys in its mouth.

Full of excitement, she reached down, picking up the mouse in one hand, the keys in the other. Immediately she sensed her mother again. Somehow, through her bond with the animal, her mother had provided her the means to escape. Allie wasted no time in unlocking the door, swinging it open with a creak. As she moved through the guards' chamber, her eyes fell upon the book that Hodge had left on the table. Her curiosity got the better of her, and she stopped for a moment, setting down the mouse and picking up the book. *The Discovery of Witches*, it read.

She opened the cover, sending several sheets of parchment falling to the floor. She retrieved what appeared to be a letter, written in small careful script—three pages in all, the first two filled on both sides. Allie couldn't help herself. She began reading the letter, forgetting for the moment that Hodge was due to return.

To John Stearne, Lawshall near Burie Saint Edmonds, Suffolke, England

My dear John,

I write to you from Hartford in the Connecticut Colony. There is much excitement here, for today the first witch in America was hanged. Men and women came from miles around to witness this latest victory in the war against Satan. It is gratifying to know that the settlers of this land now understand the threat that witches pose to their survival. Although I received no monetary recompense for my involvement, I have begun to rebuild my reputation as an expert in the field, which will serve me greatly in days to come. I take satisfaction in the role that I played in the eradication of the witch—the extent of which I shall share with you in a moment.

Alse Young was her name, a woman of the nearby Windsor settlement. It is there that I have been living since leaving the Massachusetts Bay Colony. I expected the smaller community to serve my purposes perfectly, and that has proven to be the case. Not only was I able to prove my value to Windsor's town leaders in the handling of the witch, but I also made the acquaintance of Reverend Thomas Hooker, founder of both the Hartford settlement and the entire Connecticut Colony—a powerful man and a powerful ally; all the more so since he seems particularly receptive to my influence and persuasion.

The atmosphere here is comparable to East Anglia; the settlers search for Satan behind every tree. It has been a challenging time for them. They are certain that the devil is out to ensure they fail. Many consider the native people to be his vile servants. As a result, it was not difficult to convince them of the need to search for witches in their midst.

Here, I go by the name of Malleus Hodge. I think it best to leave my birth name in England, although I have brought copies of my book to America and there are those here who have actually heard of the great Matthew Hopkins, Witchfinder General! Little do they know we are one and the same! The disparagements on our work and the aspersions cast on our motives by John Gaule and the others have not yet found their way across the sea. I can't guarantee that that will remain the case however, and therefore I intend to start anew.

I trust that you will do as we discussed and arrange for my sudden and unfortunate demise. The courts of assize will not come after a dead man. For some time, I had felt guilt in the fact that I gained most of the fame and glory from our partnership; however, now that the acclaim has turned to notoriety, I am comforted that you are still able to live peacefully in our homeland.

Now—regarding the witch! Upon my arrival, the settlement had just gone through a harsh winter, during which many of its children died. I sensed great sadness as I introduced myself to the townsfolk during those first several days. Many insisted the illness had been Satan's doing, which assured me that they were ready for my assistance. As I asked around, one name was mentioned several times— Alse Young. Using elixirs made from ingredients found in the woods, she had treated many of those who had passed; would they consider the possibility she was a witch? I realized she could be the ideal subject to introduce my services to the community.

"How well do you really know her?" I asked. "Why didn't her child die?" It was far too easy. A couple questions here and a couple comments there and before I knew it the whole town was in an uproar. They questioned her actions and motives, and it wasn't long before someone uttered the word "witch." And of course, there I was, ready and willing to assist. I had arrived in town just in time to help them—an expert on the matter, the great witchfinder's guidebook in hand.

Alse Young had a peculiarity about her that I noticed the moment I met her. She wasn't like everyone else— perhaps that is why they were so quick to accuse her of practicing witchcraft. Was I convinced she was a witch? No—no more so than all those others we tested during our travels. But even if there was a chance of her being a witch, she had to be dealt with. In a war with Satan, there will of course be casualties. The important thing was that her indictment, conviction, and execution, if handled properly, would demonstrate the need for my services and provide a means for gaining celebrity as the prominent authority on the subject.

Now, as a dear friend with whom I've made clear my deepest fascinations, desires, and obsessions, I will share with you something that I intend to tell no other.

Allie had finished reading the first page, front and back. Her eyes were moist with tears. She had been correct all along. Malleus Hodge was an evil man with a history, and he had been directly involved in her mother's fate. Regardless of his intentions to save the world from Satan, she knew her mother deserved none of what she had gotten. Whether she could be considered a witch or not, she was a good person and certainly not under the devil's control.

She continued reading:

For a long time now, I have been tormented by the fact that we have never once witnessed a tangible demonstration of the witchcraft we've worked so hard to eradicate. In our work we have relied on accusations, tests, and confessions—and yet never once have we seen magick firsthand. This has been something that I have dreamed of experiencing; the idea of seeing that magick excites me to no end. I shall admit to you something else that I have shared with no one—the work that we have done has always been for the noblest of reasons and most if not all the people we have condemned have in fact been witches. I have chosen to believe these things true, and yet there have always been the smallest traces of doubt in my mind. What if magick doesn't truly exist? What if these people were innocent of any crime? Could we have let profitability and popularity get in the way of justice?

A part of me worried of such matters, and my long-
ing to witness witchcraft in action grew in time to become
my greatest desire. And then one day, it finally came to
pass! It was the witch, Alse Young, who satisfied this longtime yearning. When I first focused attention on her, it was
largely for convenience. Little did I know that I would soon
see her practicing sorcery before my very eyes!

I had heard from others about her mysterious walks
into the forest. My curiosity got the better of me one day
and when opportunity presented itself, I decided to follow
her on one of her journeys. I had already been talking to
the townsfolk at this point and the gears were already in
motion to have her selected for evaluation.

On the day in question, she had taken her daughter
into the forest with her which I understood to be common
practice. I took great care to maintain distance and remain
out of sight, but she must have sensed my presence, for
she sent one of her familiars to attack me! It wasn't like
the familiars we had told stories about—Jarmara the fat
spaniel, Newes the polecat or any of those others we had
claimed to see—this was a large and ferocious wolf! It came
out of the bushes and leaped for my throat. Fortunately, I
was able to retrieve my dagger and put an end to the beast,
but not before it drew blood. The wound in my shoulder
troubles me still to this day.

I wasn't about to let that or Alse Young get the better of
me however; after dispatching the creature, I pushed forward and soon came upon the witch at the river's edge. She
stood there, arms spread, and I watched with excitement
and fascination as she toppled an oak with her mind. It fell
across the river with a splash, but not of the magnitude one
would expect from a tree that size; it was as if it were laid
down gently across the water. The tree then rotated in place

like a giant waterwheel, and I watched as its branches swept a body up from the depths, the limp form nestled within its greenery. It was the witch's daughter, unconscious and no longer breathing.

The branches then passed the girl down the length of the tree, setting her at the feet of her mother, who dragged her from the water's edge before attempting to clear the water from her lungs. I remained there watching for a time as the girl was revived, hidden safely behind a tree. It wasn't long before Alse Young left the girl and once again raised her arms. Before my eyes, the tree began to rise from the water as she worked to return it to its upright position. It was then that I chose to leave the forest, not wishing to be seen.

The experience was extraordinary, and yet having been the sole person to see it, I chose to say nothing. As I am working toward building trust, I felt doing so would have focused too much attention on me and been counter-productive. I couldn't afford the appearance of spreading falsehoods for the purpose of personal gain. How I wish you had been there to witness it, old friend. What must it feel like to wield such power? It gives me great hope on my prospects. If there are witches here with undeni-able abilities that can be demonstrated to the public, our previous work could regain credibility; one day perhaps I could even restore the good name of Matthew Hopkins, Witchfinder.

The daughter of the witch shares her mother's name; ever since the encounter I have been wondering if she may also share her mother's magick. Could she develop simi-lar abilities as she grows up? Could she already have them? Could she help in finding other witches? Are there other ways I could make use of her skills? Imagine having the means to use Satan's own resources against him! The girl is young; if she has the power and I am able to gain her obedience, I will be a force to be reckoned with. This is another situation where I feel the end justifies the means. My mind marvels at the possibilities.

Allie's heart was beating faster. She had been correct! Hodge had seen her mother pull her from the river that day, and he had killed the wolf! And now he somehow wanted to use her in whatever scheme he had in mind. That was the reason he had imprisoned her. Except she had no abilities. What would he do when he realized that? She doubted he would let her live—he would probably accuse her of practicing witchcraft if he didn't just kill her outright.

Allie picked up the final page, of which only one side had been filled:

Alse Young's daughter is as lovely as her mother, and quite precocious. She made her way to Hartford today on her own, arriving at the hanging just in time to see her mother executed. She was naturally upset and I think I may be able to make use of that. I was able to extract her from the crowd as her father dealt with the body. I have her contained for the time being and will go to her as soon as I've finished writing this. I told her father that she's run away, so he is unaware that I have her. I will talk to her and convince her to submit to me and if she refuses to do as I ask—I will sadly have to find a way to ensure that she cannot interfere in my future ventures.

I must go to her now and so I will close with this—while I earned no coin for my work in eliminating the witch, Alse Young, I have no doubt proven myself to the community and have made a strong ally in Reverend Hooker. I expect to soon enjoy great success in my endeavors; consider this my friend—if things progress as I believe they will, then perhaps I may one day convince you to join me here to continue the hunt? Please reflect upon the possibilities. Until then,

Respectfully,

Matthew Hopkins, now Malleus Hodge

Allie had to find a way to stop him. He was going to continue what he had set in motion, with the help of Reverend Hooker and anyone else who would listen. More innocent people were going to die. She didn't know what she could possibly do about it, but she knew she had to first escape this place. She would take these items with her; the letter was definitely incriminating—she may be able to put it to good use. She picked up the mouse, placing it in a pocket of her skirt—it didn't seem to mind, and she couldn't bear to leave it behind. As she turned toward the door, she folded the letter and opened the book to place it inside.

There on the page in front of her was the passage from the Bible to which Hodge had referred: Exodus 22:18.

Thou shalt not suffer a witch to live.

And just at that moment she realized her luck had run out as she heard the sound of the key being inserted into the door's lock. She watched in horror as the bolt slid aside, the latch was lifted, and the door began to swing slowly open. Malleus Hodge had returned, and she had wasted her only chance to escape.

Chapter 19

CRAFTING THE BOTTLE

Windsor, Connecticut, May 2019

"Are you sure this is a good idea?" asked Douglas as he and Zach approached Windsor High from Capen Street on their bikes. They had come straight from Martha Gregory's house. Jenn had found another dress for her grandmother's burial, and Nate had headed home to meet up with Alex.

"It'll be fine," said Zach. "We need chemicals for the witch's bottle and where better to get them than from Mr. Sullivan's chemistry supply?"

"We'll be trespassing—we aren't supposed to be here when school's out."

"Don't you want to help Nate?" asked Zach.

"Of course." Douglas sighed. He knew what they were doing was important. He had just never considered breaking and entering something he would ever have to do. But Nate had helped him out, and he really wanted to return the favor.

"There's a window in the cafeteria that's never fully shut. We'll just slip in, grab what we need, and get out. No one will ever know."

"OK."

Douglas followed Zach to a corner window. Through the glass he saw the sea of tables. Zach popped the window open with a quick flick of the wrist.

"Man, I don't think I'll fit through that," said Douglas.

"Sure you will. Let's go."

Zach lifted himself over the sill and tumbled inside.

Please don't get stuck, thought Douglas as he slid through the window with a little help from Zach, flopping ungracefully onto the hard floor. *I did it—I'm through!*

Zach helped him to his feet just in time to hear the clang of falling cookware resonating from behind the closed kitchen door.

"What the heck was that?" asked Douglas, feeling a rush of anxiety. He exchanged glances with Zach, who seemed equally concerned. He didn't know if he would be able to do this. He wasn't made for this type of covert activity. He heard another loud clatter as the door to the kitchen began to swing open.

"Get down!" said Zach, ducking under the nearest table and pulling Douglas down after him.

The door opened and they watched silently as Mrs. King, the lunch lady, appeared, carrying a reusable supermarket bag in one hand, a lit cigarette in the other. Her hair was mussed as if she had just pulled off a hairnet. She shuffled her large figure slowly across the cafeteria, moving through the door and down the corridor.

"What's she doing here?" asked Douglas. "It's Sunday—and there's no smoking in this building!"

"Maybe this is where she does her grocery shopping—I don't really want to know. Let's get to the chemistry lab, grab what we need, and get out of here."

They stood and made their way to the doorway Mrs. King had passed through, peering in all directions before heading toward the lab. Mrs. King was nowhere to be seen. Douglas inhaled a whiff of lingering cigarette smoke and something else—something that reminded him of unwashed laundry. Sickened by the smell, he breathed as shallowly as possible for as long as he could. By the time they neared the lab, he was again inhaling normally. Either the smell had dissipated or he had just grown used to it—he wasn't sure which, but he hoped it was the former.

Mr. Sullivan's chemistry lab lay ahead, just around the corner. Douglas thought about the odd little teacher for a moment. In addition to his short stature and ever-present dandruff, he always wore a suit that seemed slightly too big for him. Recently, he began wearing a toothbrush mustache that made him look a bit like Hitler. It had earned him the nickname of Mr. Studly, which a number of students called him behind his back. Douglas felt bad when they made fun of the teacher because he knew what it was like to be teased, and Mr. Sullivan had always been decent to him.

"Do you hear that?" asked Zach, breaking Douglas's train of thought.

"What?" he asked. He had heard nothing.

"Never mind, I must have imagined it."

Just then, the door to the chemistry lab flew open, and Mr. Sullivan came out. He started down the hallway in the opposite direction. Zach grabbed Douglas just in time, yanking him into the adjoining hallway. They peeked around the corner and watched the teacher stroll down the corridor.

"Amazing," said Zach. "He wears that suit even on his day off."

"What's going on?" asked Douglas. "Why's everyone here today?"

"I don't know—listen, he could be back any time now. Let's get in there and grab what we came for."

Douglas questioned the wisdom of going into the lab with Mr. Sullivan nearby, but he held his tongue and followed Zach into the room. The lights were on, and the blinds were closed. A Bunsen burner on Mr. Sullivan's lab table was lit and emitting a bright blue flame.

"What're we looking for again?" he asked as they approached the supply cabinet. He was careful to keep his voice to a whisper. Zach pulled a crumpled piece of paper from his pocket and read.

"Let's see—sulfur, copper, sodium chloride, acetic acid, and—oh yeah, urine." Zach tugged on the cabinet door. It refused to budge. "Damn, it's locked."

"Great," said Douglas. "Now what're we going to do?" The mission was going worse than he had feared, and he was getting close to abandoning the whole thing. With the luck they had been having, it wouldn't surprise him if Mr. Sullivan chose that moment to return.

As if in answer to his thoughts, the door to the lab began to swing open. Zach and Douglas dove behind a nearby lab station just in time to avoid being seen. Zach exchanged glances with Douglas and then peeked briefly around the corner before flattening himself against the lab station.

"It's Mrs. King!" he whispered.

Douglas lifted his eyebrows in surprise.

"What's she doing here?" he asked.

Zach shrugged in response.

Carefully and quietly exchanging places with Zach, Douglas took a look for himself. Peering around the corner, he saw her. She opened the grocery bag that she had set on the table and pulled out a large kitchen knife. Holding it in one hand, she tapped her index finger against its sharp tip as she began moving about the room.

Douglas wondered what she was up to. It couldn't be anything good. Was she waiting for Mr. Sullivan to return? He suddenly feared for the chemistry teacher. Was his life in danger? Was she planning to stab him to death as he walked through the door? What other purpose could she have for the knife? With all the strange stuff that had been happening lately—witches and witch's bottles, satanic serpent bracelets, and unkill-able house cats—Douglas would have believed just about anything. Maybe the strange woman was a witch herself in search of a human sacrifice for some satanic ritual—or *maybe* she wasn't even human at all.

Mrs. King was now heading in their direction, still toying with the knife that she clutched in her hand. He turned and mouthed *she's coming* to Zach as he flattened himself against the lab station.

They sat side by side, not daring to move as the lunch lady approached. Douglas caught a whiff of her cigarette-laden aroma and knew she was close. He closed his eyes and held his breath, certain they were about to be discovered.

And that was when he heard the sound of the door opening.

"Oh," he heard Mr. Sullivan say. "Hello."

Gathering his courage, Douglas peeked around the corner to see Mr. Sullivan standing in the doorway holding a box in his arms. Mrs. King walked slowly toward him, the large blade visible behind her back.

"She—has—a—knife," Douglas whispered frantically to Zach.

Suddenly the lights went out. They heard tussling, followed by a groan and the sound of a body falling to the floor. Douglas began to panic. A low inhuman growling sound could be heard, and he was certain it was emanating from the creature known as Mrs. King.

Gathering his courage, he peeked around the corner once again and was horrified by the sight before him. In the bluish light cast by the Bunsen burner he saw the lunch lady hovering over the still form of Mr. Sullivan. She was grunting and snapping at his face. She grabbed at the flesh of his lip, stretching it with her teeth until it snapped free from her bite. He heard a soft moan in between moist slurping sounds and realized the chemistry teacher was still alive. They had to save him from the creature—and they had to do it now, before it was too late.

"We have to do something!" he whispered, turning back to Zach. Zach took a quick peek and his face contorted in revulsion.

"Let's get out of here," he whispered back. Before Douglas could say anything else, Zach popped up and tiptoed quickly and silently for the door.

Douglas clumsily stood to follow. He took a step farther into the room, glancing at the writhing mass before him, and then he understood. He saw Mrs. King's fleshy backside and the clothing that had been casually tossed to one side. Ahead, Zach reached the door and the sound of it opening was far louder than Douglas would have thought possible.

"Who's there?" Mr. Sullivan's voice rose from beneath the lunch lady's massive bulk.

That was all it took to spur Douglas into motion. He ran—faster than he had ever run before. He ran past the lab table and through the door, throwing it wide in his hurry to escape. He ran past Zach, who had paused to wait for him in the adjoining corridor. He ran to the cafeteria, slowing only long enough to heave himself through the window and retrieve his bike.

"Dude! Wait up!" It was Zach, pedaling after him and laughing hysterically.

After a few more blocks, Douglas was exhausted and stopped. Zach coasted up next to him, still laughing.

"Did you see the cake?"

"What?" Douglas had no idea what he meant.

"The *cake*. It said 'Happy Anniversary, My Darling.'" Zach couldn't stop laughing.

Douglas stood there, mouth open and panting. Two things of which he was now certain: never again would he accept food from Lunch Lady King—and never again would he let Zach drag him into another of his crazy, lamebrained schemes.

"How will these rocks take the place of a witch?" asked Nate, studying the crude-looking crystals that Mr. Black placed in the center of the table. Nate, Alex, and Mr. Black sat in the artifact room.

"These stones have a unique quality," said Mr. Black, retrieving one of the three crystals and rotating it between his fingers. "They can be used to store a quantity of magick to be used later—like a battery for powering spells."

"Like the one Hodge used to drain Aunt Celia's magick?" asked Nate.

"Quite possibly, although these don't have anywhere near the capacity to drain someone as powerful as your aunt." He held the crystal between his index finger and thumb. "I'm not sure what Hodge used, but these are significantly less potent."

"Don't we still have the same problem though?" asked Alex. She leaned forward and eyed the crystal. "No one to charge it?"

He glanced at Nate. "Well, that's where I'm hoping Nate will be able to help."

"Me? What can I do?" he asked, raising his eyebrows. He wondered what Mr. Black expected of him. He had no magick—except—

"The serpent on your arm is extremely powerful," said Mr. Black. "Your aunt believes it to be made of black gold—a rare infernal metal said to be infused with Satan's own power. I think we can make use of it to charge one of the crystals."

"Black gold?" asked Nate. He pulled back his sleeve, revealing the serpent. Its dark body glistened as he rotated his forearm.

"Yes, it's said to be gold that's been chemically altered and tarnished black—by Satan's own hand, if you can believe it. The metal's able to store and enhance blood magick."

"Blood magick?" asked Nate, frowning. Everything Mr. Black said brought forth so many new questions—Nate felt overwhelmed by the amount of stuff he didn't know. How could he possibly help in the fight against Hodge when everything was so new to him?

"Yes, it's a type of magick that draws power from blood. The serpent penetrated your skin, did it not?"

"I'll say," said Nate, remembering those first agonizing hours after the witchfinder's serpent had claimed its new home. He glanced at the metallic fangs still lodged in his skin. By now, he was used to them.

"So, are you willing to try?" asked Mr. Black.

"Sure. What do I do?" Nate was eternally grateful to Mr. Black for showing up when he did. He had been in way over his head with no clear path ahead of him, and he was willing to follow any of the teacher's suggestions.

"It should be quite simple, really. Holding the crystal is usually all that's required if the person has the power." Mr. Black reached out his hand, offering Nate the crystal that lay on his open palm.

"OK then, well here goes," said Nate. He picked up the crystal and as soon as he touched it, he felt the bracelet tighten—it was drawing on his blood to power itself for what was about to occur. The realization made him light-headed. He did his best to focus on the stone in front of him, rather than on the unknown cost to his health.

They all stared at the rock's crystalline surfaces, waiting for something to change. The pressure exerted by the serpent was the only indication to Nate that anything was happening. Alex and Mr. Black exchanged glances. Nate nodded his head to indicate that the process had indeed started. He could feel the serpent reacting to the crystal's presence. Slowly, a soft blue glow became visible at its center.

"Yes! You're doing it, Nate!" cried Mr. Black, with an excited smile. He hopped to his feet.

The crystal grew brighter by the second until it radiated a vibrant blue. Nate could feel the magick flowing through his body and into the stone. It was working! He felt an amazing sense of accomplishment—the crystal was charging, and as soon as the others arrived, they would have the remaining ingredients required to construct the witch's bottle. Malleus Hodge's hours of freedom were numbered!

Then Nate sensed a change in the flow of magick. Something felt wrong. The serpent began to vibrate fiercely, causing his whole arm to shake. Moments later, a sharp whine began to emanate from the crystal itself. The brilliant blue became a bright hot white that grew brighter with every second. He could barely see.

Alarmed, he tried to release the crystal only to find his whole arm had grown numb—as hard as he tried, his hand refused to unwrap itself from the stone.

Mr. Black reached over and yanked the stone from his fingers. The teacher's fist glowed red as the ever-brightening crystal radiated through skin, flesh, and bone. Turning quickly, Mr. Black threw the rock with all his might toward the fireplace. With a loud, shrill pop the rock exploded, showering the inside of the fireplace with dozens of tiny crystal fragments. The ornamental logs that had been arranged inside immediately burst into flames as if doused with gasoline and set ablaze.

Nate slid off his chair and ducked under the table, pulling Alex along with him.

"Are you guys OK?" shouted Mr. Black as he ran to the fireplace to open the flue.

Nate's ears were ringing, and afterimages of the white-hot crystal floated across his vision.

"I think so," he said, peeking over the tabletop. *Other than the messed-up hearing and vision, and the overwhelming sense of failure,* he thought. The serpent had once again quieted itself.

"What the hell just happened?" asked Alex. She and Nate rose to their feet and walked around the table to the fireplace. The fire was already starting to die down.

"It would seem the serpent was just too powerful for the stone," said Mr. Black. "I'm afraid we're back to square one—and down a crystal as well."

"Can we get more of them?" asked Nate.

"I'm afraid not. They're actually quite rare," said Mr. Black. He frowned. "And we have no way to charge them, in any event. This is an unfortunate setback. I'll find a solution, but it'll take time."

Mr. Black turned away from them and gazed at the dying fire, stroking his chin with one hand. Nate and Alex shared a glance. It was clear that the biology teacher was disappointed by the failure.

Just then the doorbell rang. Glancing at his watch, Nate realized it was later than he thought.

"Your visitors have arrived," said Mr. Black. "Let's hope that they've fared better in their tasks than I have."

Several minutes later, Marc came into the room and took a seat, placing an empty jar and a bottle of red liquid on the table before him. He was followed shortly by Jenn, Zach, and Douglas, who looked displeased.

"Hello, my peeps," said Zach. He set the paper grocery bag he carried on the floor next to his chair.

Mr. Black gave his seat to Jenn and waited for the rest of them to settle in. "How are we doing with the ingredients for the witch's bottle?" he asked, glancing around the table.

"I found these," said Marc, eagerly. He slid forward an empty but clean Hellmann's mayonnaise jar and the bottle of red liquid. "We needed a container for the ingredients—and red wine. I hope these'll work?"

"We're going to trap Hodge for all eternity in an old plastic mayonnaise jar?" Zach chuckled. "I love it." He raised his hand to high-five Marc, who responded in kind.

"That's great, Marc—thank you," said Mr. Black. "I'd imagined something fancier, but this'll do. Good thinking on the plastic—it'll be less likely to break than the last bottle. If plastic had been around in the seventeenth century, we probably wouldn't be in this predicament."

"Red wine *vinegar?*" said Jenn, reading the label on Marc's bottle.

Mr. Black frowned.

"Unfortunately," he said, "that won't do for the red wine component— but I do remember seeing vinegar on the list—so, good job, Marc."

Marc beamed as Mr. Black unscrewed the top of the jar and poured in a small amount of vinegar. He then opened the cabinet containing the remains of the original witch's bottle. Retrieving the snarl of hair, he added it to the mix.

"Vinegar?" asked Zach. "I don't remember seeing that on the list."

"I do," said Jenn. "As a matter of fact, it was one of the items *you* volunteered to get."

"It was?" he pulled the crumpled list from his pocket.

"Yes," she said, pointing to the sheet. "Acetic acid—right there."

"That's vinegar?" Zach looked confused. "Why didn't you say so?"

"It's OK, Zach," said Mr. Black. "How did you and Douglas do with your other items?"

"Well . . ."

"We failed miserably," said Douglas, turning to glare at Zach before he could respond further. Nate could hear the irritation in Douglas's voice.

"Yeah," said Zach with a look of embarrassment. "Things didn't go as planned—but I *did* bring *this*." He removed a two-liter bottle of Mountain Dew from the grocery bag and set it on the table.

"Mountain Dew?" asked Mr. Black.

"That's not Dew," he said. "I've been drinking water all afternoon—I wasn't sure how much you'd need."

"Oh," said Mr. Black with a frown. "That should be . . . uh, more than enough." Mr. Black gingerly picked up the bottle. Holding it at arm's length, he set it carefully beside the mayonnaise jar.

"I'll add this to the mixture later. What else was on your list?"

"Let's see," said Zach, scanning the piece of paper. "Sulfur, copper, and sodium chloride. Unfortunately, we weren't able to get any of them."

"Sodium chloride?" asked Jenn. "That's table salt." She opened her bag and pulled out a few leftover salt packets from the school cafeteria and tossed them across the table.

"Table salt?" Douglas gasped, a look of disbelief on his face. He turned and punched Zach in the arm. Zach rolled his eyes in response.

"Excellent," said Mr. Black as he tore open the packets and dumped their contents into the mix. "Now, for the sulfur—do we have any matches in the house? The wooden ones you scratch on the box?"

"Yeah," said Marc. "There're some by the fireplace in the living room."

"Great," he said. "Next we need to gather some copper pennies. The older the better—any dated prior to 1982 would be ideal. Nowadays they're primarily made of zinc."

"Oh my God," Douglas planted his face on the table before him.

"Are you OK, Doug?" asked Nate.

"He's fine," said Zach, snickering. "I'll tell you about it later."

"Aunt Celia has a jar of old pennies," said Marc. "I'll get them and the matches."

"Fantastic," said Mr. Black as Marc headed for the door.

Nate and Alex had collected the remaining items. A quick trip to the grocery store on Nate's bike (Alex on the seat, Nate riding the pedals and wearing a fresh shirt) had procured a bottle of dried rosemary. From there, they had traveled next door to the hardware store to purchase a container of nails and ball of twine, since the spell called for a piece of knotted string. Nate found the spell components truly bizarre: nails, knotted twine, and urine? Who came up with these things? The spell-casting process was mind-boggling, but Nate knew this wasn't the time to question it.

By far, the strangest ingredient they had obtained that afternoon was the small sample of dirt—cemetery dirt, to be exact. They rode to the ancient Palisado Cemetery behind First Church and in the far back corner—where the oldest graves could be found—Alex had kept watch while Nate went to work with a spade. Mr. Black had insisted the dirt be taken from at least a foot below the surface. Nate hadn't had time to ask why. His heart beat faster with each shovelful, until at last, he had excavated twelve inches of earth. After filling a small plastic baggie with soil, Nate refilled the hole, certain that at any moment they would be discovered defiling the historic graveyard. It was with great relief when, mission accomplished, he and Alex were able to mount the bike and flee the cemetery.

Now, back in the artifact room, Nate gave Mr. Black the items they had collected and one by one, the teacher added them to the jar. By the time he finished, Marc had returned with the matches and pennies. Using a pocketknife, Mr. Black scraped the ends off a dozen matches while the group dug through pennies looking for the oldest coins. Aunt Celia had been collecting them for some time, so they had no trouble finding ones suitable for the spell.

After adding the pennies, Mr. Black poured in several drops from the Mountain Dew bottle, carefully recapping it before returning it to Zach. Finally, he stirred the mixture with a feather retrieved from the birdcage, eventually tossing it inside and tightly closing the jar.

"Thank you, everyone," said Mr. Black at last. "Great job—I'm proud of all of you. The only missing ingredient is the red wine, which I'll locate myself. Now, I'd suggest everyone go home and get some rest. It's been a long day and you all have school tomorrow."

Nate agreed—it *had* been a long day. As his friends left the room, he thought once more about the crystal and their failed attempt to charge it. They had obtained most of the components, but they were worthless without magick to perform the spell—and Mr. Black had no clear solution to the problem.

Alex led the others down the stairs toward the front door. She would be staying another night. Nate was worried about her. He wanted her to speak with a guidance counselor at school for help with her father, who was blowing up her phone with texts, apologetically asking her to return home. But for now, at least, he was happy that she had agreed to stay put where Aunt Celia's spell could protect them from Hodge.

"Wow, cool!" exclaimed Marc from behind. "What is this thing?"

As Nate turned, his eyes fell on Mr. Black, and he was immediately shaken by the teacher's alarmed expression. *Oh God*, he thought. *What now?* Nate glanced toward his brother, his anxiety building. What he saw surprised, worried, and terrified him—and yet also solved an immediate problem.

Marc sat at the table holding one of the power crystals between his fingers—and it was glowing a brilliant blue.

Chapter 20

NEVER TRUST A WITCH

Hartford, Colony of Connecticut, May 1647

Allie watched in horror as the heavy door swung inward. In seconds—if she didn't do something immediately—she would again be under the control of Malleus Hodge. She had had enough of the Hartford Gaol and knew that she had to act fast.

He wouldn't expect her to be in the outer guards' chamber. The only thing in her favor was the element of surprise—and so she did the only thing she could think of in the two seconds she had to prepare. By the time the door had opened far enough for her to see her captor, she was already running in his direction. Hodge's eyes widened in astonishment as Allie struck him full force in the stomach, knocking him to the ground. She struggled quickly to her feet, still clutching Hodge's book and letter under her arm, and took off running.

She had only taken two steps when she was yanked backward. Hodge grabbed the hem of her skirt and, from his position on the ground, started dragging her back toward him. In moments he had pulled her far enough to grab hold of her waist—but Allie hadn't gotten this far to give up so easily. With all her might, she struck him in the face with the spine of the book. He howled and his grip relaxed just long enough for her to bolt forward. Hodge grabbed hold of her skirt a second time. Allie struggled for the ties that held it about her waist. She loosened them and slipped free, leaving the garment behind in his grasp.

Wearing only her long shift and waistcoat, she ran for her life—not daring to slow until she had gotten well away from Meetinghouse Square. When she turned at last to see if she had been pursued, she saw no sign of Hodge. With a sigh of relief, she plopped down beneath a tree, out of sight of any pursuers.

The tears started flowing again as she sat there catching her breath. This had been, beyond a doubt, the worst day of her life—and it wasn't over yet. She was alone and being pursued by the evil man who had killed her mother, and she had no idea what to do.

She remembered—her mother! The mouse was in the pocket of the skirt she had left behind with Hodge. She felt her heart break all over again.

Might her father still be looking for her after all? Allie knew after reading the letter that Hodge hadn't been honest with her. If her father hadn't yet left for home and she could get back to the wagon, that would be the best-case solution. And to do so, she would have to avoid Hodge. Those were several big ifs, but she could think of no better solution.

Rising to her feet, she peered around the side of the tree. She carefully scanned the area, seeing no one. The way back to Meetinghouse Square seemed clear. Something nagged at her, however—something didn't seem quite right.

She heard a twig snap from behind, and before she knew what was happening, a powerful arm encircled her waist and she was yanked into the air.

"You're a naughty girl, Alice."

It was Hodge's voice, although she couldn't see his face. He held her suspended beside him, her back against his side so that her arms and legs flailed uselessly in the air. She could reach the arm that circled her waist, but it was far too strong for her to pry away and she soon saw no reason to keep trying. She hung limply at his side as he marched her back toward her prison, completely and utterly defeated. There was nothing she could do—Hodge had won, and she was now his to do with as he pleased.

No! She couldn't let Hodge win. A new resolve rose within her, like a spark lit somewhere deep inside. She couldn't give up. Hodge was evil and she couldn't let evil win.

Her thoughts reached out in a way they never had before—it was an entirely new sensation, and yet it felt familiar. She was aware of other living beings around her, even if she couldn't see them. She knew they were there.

Please, I'm in trouble—can you help me? she pleaded silently. She sensed a feeling, or maybe a complex series of feelings, a response. She didn't understand it. It was new and exciting, and it filled her with hope. The connection she felt reminded her of the connection she had sensed between the mouse and her mother.

The next thing she knew, she was dropped face-first in the dirt. She heard a cry of surprise that soon morphed into anger. She struggled to her knees, crawling several feet before turning to glance behind her.

What she saw shocked her. Hodge stood there, arms flailing in the air, trying to swat away the cloud of birds that swarmed his head. Robins and sparrows took turns diving at his skin, their beaks drawing blood. A hummingbird flitted in front of his face, making it difficult for him to see past its hovering body. These were the creatures that had answered her call. Allie felt a deep gratitude to every one of them.

She could also sense Hodge's fury—no psychic connection was required for that. He shouted in pain and frustration. She watched in horror as he snatched the hummingbird out of the air, squeezing it tightly in his fist until she heard the cracking of its bones. She felt its pain in her mind as it died in its effort to help her. These creatures were willing to sacrifice everything for her—she couldn't let that sacrifice be in vain. She had to get away.

She got to her feet again and ran. She didn't consider the direction. Soon she had cramps in her legs and in her side—but that was nothing compared to the mental anguish she felt from the birds as Hodge harmed them, one by one. Several suffered broken bones from well-timed blows while others died outright in sudden bursts of agony. Allie knew that Hodge still pursued her—the birds somehow made that clear in her mind—and so she continued to run until she could do so no longer.

When the last living birds grew weak with exhaustion, Allie sensed their retreat from Hodge. She couldn't blame them. They had done her a great service at great cost to themselves. By then Allie found herself by the river. The birds had given her a good head start, but she couldn't maintain this pace. She sat by the bank to catch her breath. She still held Hodge's book and letter in hand, knowing she needed to keep them with her.

If she had read the sun's position correctly, her journey had taken her first to the southeast and then northeast to the river. Meetinghouse Square should be off to the west. If she hurried, she should be able to get there before Hodge. She could think of no other option. Her father *had* to be there and she *would* find him. She couldn't bear any other outcome. *Just a brief rest first*, she told herself, *to catch my breath*. She flopped backward in the tall grass and gradually her breathing slowed. She allowed herself to close her eyes for just one short moment—

—and was jolted awake by the intense pain in her arm as Hodge dragged her to her feet. By relaxing her guard for just that instant, she had allowed herself to be captured and had nullified the sacrifices of the birds. Not only would she remain Hodge's prisoner, but he would be able to continue his evil crusade unchecked—and all of it was her fault.

"You nasty little thing," he said, as he held her like a rag doll in his vice-like grip.

Allie looked into his eyes and was terrified by the fury she saw there. The bloody gouges and scratches that covered his face made him all the more frightening, and she knew in that instant he would most likely kill her right then and there. Hodge dragged her the short distance to the riverbank and with a strength fueled by rage, held her dangling by the arm over the quickly flowing water.

"You lied to me, Alice," he said. "You do have your mother's gifts."

Allie didn't tell him that she had only just realized that herself. He wouldn't believe her, and it made little difference. She didn't know the extent of her abilities, but Hodge may not realize that. Maybe she could use that to her advantage . . .

"You'll put me down now, if you know what's good for you," she said as defiantly as she could manage.

"Or what?" he asked. "You'll bring down a tree on my head? No, I don't think so—if you could do something like that, you already would have. I don't think you're as powerful as your mother. In fact, I'm not sure why I'm wasting my time with you. Perhaps it would be best if we parted ways?"

Allie's attempt to gain the upper hand had failed miserably, and Hodge's intentions were clear. He knew she couldn't swim—he had been there the time she fell into the rivulet. If he released his grip now, she would drown in the strong river currents. Her fate was entirely in the hands of Malleus Hodge.

"Or," he said, "we could do something else—and be warned: this is the only time I'll make you this offer. If you promise to behave yourself and agree to become my ward, we can leave this place. You will do as I ask, whenever I ask, and I'll make no mention to anyone of your witchy abilities. I'll protect you, and in return, you'll use your talents to further my cause. I wouldn't advise turning down my offer." The dreaded grin reappeared. "What do you say?"

Allie didn't want to accept Hodge's proposal. He wasn't truly offering her a choice—to decline would be to drown. And yet she couldn't bring herself to say yes. He believed her to be a witch and expected her to behave as such. *Was* she a witch? Just because she shared one of her mother's unusual abilities? She thought of the birds that had sacrificed themselves for her. She could never allow that to happen at Hodge's bidding. For a moment, she considered letting him toss her in the river. What did it matter, anyway?

"I need your response now," he said, his patience at an end.

Allie's mind suddenly touched the consciousness of another—and this new presence felt familiar. It was fast approaching, and it brought with it a feeling of happiness and unconditional love—something she sorely needed at the moment. Could it be the mouse? She didn't think so.

Suddenly, everything became clear, and she knew exactly what she had to do.

"Yes! I'll do as you say," she said.

Hodge was surprised by her sudden acquiescence.

"Good choice," he said, setting her down on the bank but maintaining his firm grip on her arm.

"But there's just one thing," she said, looking him in his eyes.

"What is it?"

A mischievous smile played across her face.

"You really should never trust a witch."

In that moment, Allie brought her shoe down on Hodge's foot with all the force she could muster. She quickly turned and, with her free hand, lifted the sleeve of the arm that held her and buried her teeth into the exposed flesh.

With a cry of pain, Hodge shoved her to the ground—and was struck from behind by a large furry shape. The stray dog Allie had met earlier knocked Hodge off balance, and the two of them went tumbling into the river with a huge splash. Allie watched, waiting for them to surface, and when they did, they were already several yards downstream. The dog went for Hodge with its teeth, and the two of them sank once more beneath the surface.

Thank you, my friend, she thought. The dog had been there for her earlier when she needed consoling, and it had assisted her again in her most recent time of need. She could sense it was a good swimmer and would be just fine. There was still goodness in the world, and she was grateful to her new friend for showing her that. Allie sent off feelings of affection and appreciation as she turned to run back toward Meetinghouse Square. The love that was echoed back at her filled her heart with joy.

Chapter 21

FISH AND LOBSTER

Windsor, Connecticut, May 2019

Jenn walked into the school library at lunchtime. She was relieved to see that Ms. Brooks was away from the checkout station, because she was in no mood to chat. She needed peace and quiet away from the other students and—to be honest—away from the teachers as well. Everyone had heard about the death of her grandmother, and she couldn't bear talking about it anymore.

She saw no students in the library and breathed a sigh of relief. People had also been talking about the series of unusual events that had happened over the weekend, starting with the Shad Derby. Students and teachers alike were excitedly discussing the possibility of there being witches in town, or arguing against it.

If they only knew, thought Jenn. After the visit to her grandmother's house, there was no question in her mind: something supernatural was happening in town.

She made her way to her favorite table in the rear of the room. It was nestled in a nook created by two perpendicular bookcases and out of view of the rest of the library. She sat and pulled out her books to get a head start on her homework. She saw the pentacle she had doodled on her notebook during Mr. Sampson's French class and thought again about the one she had seen on the old box with the number 97 engraved on its top. Was it only a coincidence, or did it mean something? Maybe her grandmother had found the box at an antique shop and simply fallen in love with its intricate carvings. But then why have it hidden away at the bottom of her closet beneath a pair of worn-out slippers? It just didn't make sense. Her parents didn't know anything about the box, either.

Jenn sighed and got to work on her French. No sooner had she cracked the book than she heard a sound from the other side of the nearest bookcase.

"Damn," said a voice. It was Courtney.

Damn, thought Jenn, hoping that just this *one* time, Courtney would turn and walk away, toward the other side of the library . . .

And that was when Courtney rounded the corner. Her arms were crossed over the pile of books she held pressed against her chest, and she had a troubled look on her face. She stopped abruptly when she saw Jenn seated there.

"Uh, hi, Courtney," said Jenn. "What are you doing here?"

Courtney opened her mouth to speak, closed it again and then said, "I, um—had some research I wanted to do."

Jenn would never have imagined Courtney using the words "research" and "wanted to do" in the same sentence. Finding the girl alone in the library at lunchtime was *very* out of character.

"Is everything OK?"

"Do you think there're witches in town?"

Jenn didn't know how to answer.

"Did something happen?" she asked instead. "Do you want to talk?"

Courtney nodded, and Jenn was surprised to see that she looked like she might cry. Something was really troubling her. Seeing her in this state was almost unnerving. She motioned for her to sit, and Courtney dropped her books next to Jenn's.

"What's wrong?" Jenn asked.

"The witches are out to kill me, and I've been trying to find a way to protect myself."

"The witches are out to kill you?"

Courtney nodded and continued, the words flowing from her in a torrent.

"My life's in danger—they're after me," she said. "And my parents are no help. They not only missed my coronation, but they've abandoned me in my time of need. I'm afraid to even go *near* the aquarium in the living room—and the housekeeper? I knew something was wrong with her the moment I saw that big, disgusting mole on her cheek. Kat and Kam are useless, of course—they rarely think for themselves. What could they possibly do to protect me from a witch, anyway? They went to the cafeteria where they're serving fish sticks—do they *think* I have a death wish?!" Courtney's voice was rising in volume. Jenn glanced past her nervously to make sure no one had heard.

"Whoa," said Jenn. "Slow down and start from the beginning."

Courtney took a deep breath and made an effort to calm herself.

"I'm sorry, I forget that most people think more slowly than I do. Try to keep up."

OK, thought Jenn.

"It all started when my parents planned their annual trip to Acapulco. Do you know what they eat there, by the way? It's the *land* of seafood: ceviche, pescado a la talla, vuelve a la vida. Do you know what 'vuelve a la vida' means in that language they speak there? It means 'come back to life.' They're just *begging* for trouble if you ask me."

Come back to life? A wave of anxiety passed through Jenn. She didn't know where this story was headed.

"My parents frequently travel and leave me behind," Courtney continued. "I can't miss school, they say. But when I was elected Shad Derby queen, they refused to change their plans. I worked so hard and finally achieved my life-long dream—but they couldn't be bothered to be here to see me in the parade."

Jenn had no idea about any of this. Maybe it explained some of Courtney's behavior. But what was she trying to say? And why was she telling this to *her*?

"And then on Saturday, while the mayor was introducing me, I was subjected to the first witch attack. That haggy, blond witch dumped slimy fish all over me and my subjects—and for what reason? I can only assume it was jealousy."

Jenn frowned. Apparently, Courtney hadn't realized the witch was Nate's Aunt Celia, and Jenn wasn't about to inform her of that fact. She wouldn't tell Nate that Courtney had called her "haggy," either.

"Fortunately, the mayor came to my rescue. But little did I know that a second attack was to come later that afternoon. I always knew there was something evil about Marta, but I never suspected my life was in danger."

"Marta?" asked Jenn.

"Yes, our housekeeper. She tried to kill me and then yelled at me for breaking the disposal in the kitchen sink—can you believe it?" Courtney's eyes went wide. "She's in league with the other one—I'm sure of it. They probably have a coven or something."

"You think she's a witch?"

"I know she's a witch—I knew it as soon as I read this." To Jenn's enormous surprise, Courtney pulled out a copy of *The Discovery of Witches* from the pile of schoolbooks in front of her. "She's got this hideous mole right in the middle of her cheek." She pointed to her own cheek for emphasis. "If the horrible thing isn't a devil's mark, I don't know what is. It has a disgusting hair growing out of it—I mean, why wouldn't she have the thing removed unless the devil put it there?!" Courtney grimaced.

Jenn sat back in her chair. "You think she's a witch because of a mole?"

"I told you, it's not just any mole," she said indignantly. She held two fingers in the air, several inches apart. "If that hair grows any longer, she'll have to put a bow on it! It's pure evil."

Jenn sat forward again. "Courtney, a lot of people have moles. It doesn't mean they're witches."

"Look," Courtney said, sounding excited. "I have no intention of searching her for a third nipple if that's what you're getting at—I mean, gross! Besides, she's a witch—it's as clear as the mole on her face."

"OK, what happened next?" Jenn knew she wouldn't be able to convince her she was wrong about the housekeeper.

"Well, as a consolation prize, my parents arranged for Marta to cook my favorite dinner and have it waiting for me when I got home from the Derby—fresh boiled lobster with butter and all the fixings. Marta set the table and she served it before running out of the house. She said she had things to do, but I think she just didn't want to be there for the carnage."

"Carnage?"

"Yeah, I was sitting there, you know," Courtney's eyes grew wide as she spoke. "I hadn't even tasted the lobster when suddenly its antenna-things began to wave around in the air. Before I knew it, my beautiful, big, red lobster began crawling toward me, its pincers opening and closing. It was terrifying. I knocked my chair over and the lobster fell off the table. I wanted to stomp on it—its legs were twitching in the air. But it looked so delicious, and I didn't want to get it on my shoes."

Jenn was almost dizzy from trying to follow all of this, but she let Courtney continue.

"Anyway, I waited too long, and it started coming at me again. I grabbed my mother's Louis Vuitton from where she'd left it on the counter and shoved a big ashtray inside. I began beating the thing with it—legs, claws, and antenna things flew everywhere, but the thing wouldn't stop moving. It was horrible."

"You hit it with your mother's Louis Vuitton?"

"Well, of course—I wasn't going to hit it with *mine*. Once the legs had snapped off, it wasn't going anywhere, so I grabbed some tongs from the kitchen to pick it up and shoved it down the garbage disposal. The disposal jammed right away. When Marta arrived this morning and saw the mess, she actually *yelled* at me—can you believe it? She said if I didn't like the meal, I could have just told her. I think she actually expected me to clean it up after *she* sent it to attack *me*. Between the shad and the lobster, I'm never going near seafood again."

Jenn sat there with her mouth open, unsure of what to say. It was quite a story, she thought. But why would Malleus Hodge have singled out Courtney of all people for an attack? It made about as much sense as sending the cat to attack her grandmother.

"I've been looking for ways to protect myself. Unsurprisingly, I've found nothing to assist me in this useless library. But do you know what, Jenn? It doesn't even matter. I refuse to be defenseless. I've been looking into archery classes—there's an intensive practice group that meets every night. I need to protect myself, and I've always wanted to learn. One thing's for sure—if that housekeeper comes near me or tries to cook seafood in my house again, she's going to get an arrow right in her droopy old ass."

And with that, Courtney stood, collected her books, and walked out. Jenn sat in the empty library, speechless and in disbelief of the insane events occurring within the old New England town she called home.

"What happened to Alex?" asked Zach, dipping his fish stick into the large blob of ketchup on his plate. "Wasn't she meeting us for lunch?"

"Something must have come up," replied Nate.

He couldn't say for certain why Alex had missed their lunch date, but he had suggested she use the time to speak to a guidance counselor about her issues with her father. She had been staying at Aunt Celia's house since the run-in with Hodge. Her father was allowing her to stay with friends for the time being, but sooner or later, he would insist she come home, and she needed to be ready.

"Can you believe how many people are talking about Aunt Celia and the Shad Derby?" he asked, changing the subject. "I'm just lucky no one has connected her to me. I've been dealing with enough stuff without being called out as the witch's nephew."

"Yeah, it's crazy," said Zach. "And speaking of crazy, did you notice the Ducks sitting over there? Donald keeps looking in your direction."

Nate nodded. The three bullies sat on the other side of the cafeteria.

With the busy weekend they had had, he had totally forgotten this was his and Douglas's first day of after-school detention. But he no longer felt the slightest bit afraid of Donald. It was funny how your perspective could change after running afoul of a centuries-old evil warlock. He doubted Donald would appreciate the fact that he had been downgraded to the small-potatoes category—but at the moment, he didn't care a whole lot about what Donald thought.

He still couldn't get over the fact that Marc had charged the power crystal the night before by simply picking it up from the table. He had spoken to Mr. Black about it again this morning, and the teacher maintained that the only explanation was that Marc had some amount of magickal energy within him. He must have inherited it from Aunt Celia and her ancestors through their father—but according to Mr. Black, a male inheriting such power was rare, and inheriting it through a male ancestor was even rarer. In over ninety-nine percent of cases, magick was passed down through the maternal line.

Nate had sworn Mr. Black to secrecy. Under no circumstances could any of this be shared with Marc until he had had the chance to talk it over with Aunt Celia. The thing he feared most was for Hodge to do something to harm his brother. If Hodge learned that Marc had magick, he was sure Hodge would drain him of his power and then kill him so he could permanently take the magick as his own.

Nate scanned the room one last time for Alex, inadvertently making eye contact with Donald. Donald sneered at him until Nate finally looked away. Sooner or later, he knew things were going to come to a head between them, but at this moment, he had many more pressing things to worry about.

"So, this is what you're gonna do," said Donald, before cramming half a cheeseburger into his mouth.

Huey sat at the lunch table with Donald and Louie. His brother had been teasing him for days about the incident in the locker room and the embarrassing way in which it had ended. The constant ribbing was more than he could handle—and now, Donald was expecting him to use the detention as an opportunity to take his revenge.

"As soon as the teacher leaves the room for any reason, you need to grab one of those guys and sucker punch him in the gut," continued Donald, jabbing a ketchup-covered finger in his face for emphasis. Bits of hamburger bun fell from his mouth as he talked. "Once you've taken care of one, do the same to the other. Start with Watson first, he'll give you the most trouble otherwise."

"But Don," replied Huey. "I'm already in enough trouble as—"

"They *humiliated* you, bro—or don't you remember that bareback riding lesson?"

Huey wasn't sure what to do. He didn't want to suffer his brother's wrath. Donald was almost as bad as their father, and a good bit stronger.

"And what if I get caught?" asked Huey.

"Just don't," Donald replied. He shoved the last of his fries into his mouth and stood up. He headed out of the cafeteria, leaving his tray behind.

"Great," said Huey. "Now we have to clean up after him, too. Why do we always have to do what he says?"

"What're you gonna do?" asked Louie.

"I don't see I have much of a choice," said Huey.

"No, I don't suppose you do," replied Louie.

The moment Douglas had dreaded all day had arrived. He and Nate went to the classroom to serve their detention sentence—that was how it felt to Douglas. He had never been in trouble before and here he was, about to do prison time.

Mr. Sampson sat at the desk in front of the room, already grading the pile of pages that sat in front of him.

"Hello, gentlemen," he said as Douglas and Nate took seats.

The room was empty. Assuming Huey showed up, Douglas expected it would be just the three of them this afternoon. He hadn't heard of anyone else getting detention and everyone had been too preoccupied today with talk of witches to stir up any significant trouble. Douglas couldn't wait for the hour to be over. He could still hear his mother sobbing after the meeting in the principal's office. The blubbering had continued throughout the weekend.

"Oh, my baby," she had said over and over. Douglas had felt bad for disappointing his parents, especially his mother—but it wasn't like he had really done anything other than get tortured yet again by a bunch of bullies. Truth be told, he was pleased with himself for coming to Nate's aid as he had. It was the first time he had ever done anything to fight back—and in his mind, at least, it had won him a couple of coolness points. Maybe he could use the incident as a turning point. He was tired of being a victim. Could he find the courage to stick up for himself the next time something like this happened? He hoped so.

Huey walked in and took a seat by the door, and in spite of his newfound courage, Douglas felt a rush of panic wash through him. It wasn't as if Huey was going to do anything with Mr. Sampson seated right there. Douglas wondered for a moment if he really could change. Maybe he was just destined to be a coward and a target. He had thought his mission with Zach this past weekend had shown he had some potential for bravery—but then why was he so terrified of just sharing a room with Huey?

A tap on his arm startled him, causing him to jump. He turned and saw Nate take an exaggerated glance toward the windows. Following his gaze, Douglas saw the other two-thirds of the bully trio, Donald and Louie, standing off in the distance, just out of Mr. Sampson's line of sight. *Great*, he thought. *Just what we need.*

The next forty-five minutes or so went by uneventfully. Douglas and Nate spent the time working on homework as Huey sat, elbows on the desk and hands on head, staring down at the desktop. Every time Douglas wondered if maybe he had fallen asleep, he would shift position slightly, but without ever looking up from the desk.

Donald and Louie remained outside during this time, gradually moving closer until they were just a few yards away—all the while unconvincingly pretending to focus on anything but the classroom. Douglas wished Mr. Sampson would look up from his work just once. They were clearly visible now and if the French teacher took just one glance in their direction, maybe he would see they were up to nothing good and put an end to whatever horrible plan they had in mind.

As if hearing Douglas's thoughts, Mr. Sampson put down his pen and got to his feet. But rather than looking out the window, he turned, moving toward the door.

"Gentlemen," he said, "I'll be back shortly. I trust that you'll be here when I return." With that, Mr. Sampson left the room.

No, thought Douglas. *You can't seriously be leaving us alone with him.* Douglas's heart started beating faster.

A clod of dirt hit one of the windows and exploded. Bits of grass and dirt flew in all directions, leaving a brown smear at the point of impact. All three of them, Douglas, Nate, and Huey, jumped at the loud *thunk*. Donald, having seen Mr. Sampson's departure, was approaching the window, Louie close behind.

Huey stood and moved in Douglas's direction. Paralyzed with fear, Douglas watched Huey pull back a meaty fist. He knew what was about to happen and was unable to do anything about it. As Huey made his move, Nate rose to his feet—but it was too late. Douglas felt the jarring impact as the fist made contact. He doubled over instinctively to prevent additional blows to his stomach. The desk was sent sliding a short distance across the floor.

It took Douglas several seconds to realize he felt no pain. Huey had hit the metal frame of his desk instead of his stomach. His hand was red and already starting to swell. *Had he missed?* Huey's large form towered over him.

"Look, I don't want to get into any more trouble today," Huey whispered, a stern look on his face. "Don't say anything. You hear me?"

Douglas was stunned. What had just happened? He glanced out the window to see Donald jumping up and down with a smile on his face, fists in the air. Had he pretended to hit him for his brother's benefit?

With a sudden deep inhalation of air, Douglas gasped, "*You're* afraid of him, too!"

A look of rage crossed Huey's face and Douglas knew he was going to be hit again—but this time, it was *really* going to hurt.

Approaching voices could be heard in the distance. It was Mr. Sampson saying goodbye to someone in the hallway. Huey and Nate quickly retreated to their seats as Douglas straightened his desk.

Mr. Sampson walked into the room and immediately spotted Donald, who was still jumping up and down outside the window. As soon as they realized the teacher had returned, Donald and Louie hit the ground hoping not to be noticed—but it was too late. Mr. Sampson crossed to the window, opening it far enough to be heard.

"Leave—now," he said. "Unless you two would like to join this group for the rest of the week."

The two Ducks took off running. Satisfied they had left, Mr. Sampson returned to his desk. After several more minutes, he said, "All right gentlemen, time's up—you may leave. Same time tomorrow."

Huey stood immediately and darted through the door as Douglas and Nate gathered their things. Douglas would have to think through what had taken place after some of the shock had worn off. For now, he was just relieved that he had survived his first day of detention.

"Well, *that* just happened," said Nate as they left the classroom. "Although I'm not exactly sure what *that* was."

"Yeah," said Douglas, too distracted to come up with anything else.

Chapter 22

UNFAIR EXPECTATIONS

"What the hell's a dipper anyway?" asked Alex. "It looks like a giant soup ladle."

Nate laughed.

"Something like that," he said. "But if you line up those two stars—the ones that make up the right side of the Big Dipper—and follow them northward, you will find the North Star." He moved Alex's outstretched arm a short distance in the indicated direction. The two of them lay side by side on the highest, flattest portion of Aunt Celia's roof, gazing at the night sky. The evening air was cool, the sky clear. They had closed the trap door of the widow's walk to quiet the music Marc was playing in the room below.

"That bright one there?" asked Alex.

"Yep, and the North Star is the final star in the *Little* Dipper's handle."

"Oh, I see it—the Little Dipper looks like it's pouring itself into the Big Dipper."

"That's right—the Big Dipper is part of the Ursa Major constellation—the Great Bear. Although I've always felt you needed to be heavily medicated to see anything remotely resembling a bear. Supposedly Ursa Minor's up there, too." Nate laughed. "Astronomy is not a huge strength of mine."

"Don't be hard on yourself. Your understanding of giant space scoops is impressive."

Nate squeezed her hand. It was a relief to set aside their problems for the moment, even if only briefly.

"The two days Hodge gave you will be up in a few hours," said Alex.

Nate groaned.

"Don't remind me," he said. It was true—the warlock could show up at any time, and he didn't feel the slightest bit prepared.

"Are you worried?"

"Yeah, but mostly about what he'll do when I don't give him the serpent. You and Marc may be his next targets. I don't think he'll ever give up trying to get it back."

"You should figure out how to remove it. Then you can just get rid of it—hide it or give it to someone else to get the target off you."

"I'm sure the person I gave it to would really appreciate that," he laughed. "Besides, I've already tried everything to get it off—do you remember the band saw? I was actually trying to cut it off at the time."

"Oh my God, seriously?!" Alex grinned.

"And even if I could remove it, I could never let him get his hands on it. He's already far too powerful." Nate turned his head to look at her. In the distance he could make out the tops of several trees, their leaves ruffling in the breeze.

"Maybe you should stay here at the house where it's safe," Alex said.

Nate considered this. "I can't hide indefinitely. Besides, the serpent will probably protect me. I'd feel better if you and Marc stayed inside the house, though."

"And leave you out there on your own? No way. Besides, they'll send people out searching for us if we don't show up at school. It's not like your aunt or my father will be calling either of us out sick. I'm lucky my father hasn't sent out a search party as it is—if he hears from the school that I never showed up for class . . ."

"I suppose." Nate looked skyward once more, studying the stars. He didn't like it. There were no good options. Alex was right—he and Marc were living alone with no legal guardian at the moment, and he didn't want to draw attention to that. Hopefully, Mr. Black would determine where Hodge was holding Aunt Celia soon, and they would be able to put an end to this nightmare once and for all.

"Speaking of your father, how'd it go with the school counselor?" he asked.

There was a long pause before Alex responded.

"Don't kill me," she said, "but I chickened out."

Nate sat partway up and turned toward her, resting his weight on one arm. He turned on his phone's flashlight, pointing it upward so there was enough light to see her face.

"Alex—" he said.

"I know, I know," she interrupted. "I'd planned to talk to someone—but I'm not ready. If I tell them what happened, then what?"

"Maybe it would be for the best if someone knew," Nate said.

"Maybe," she sighed. "Anyway, just as I reached the office, he called."

"And you answered? What made you pick up this time?"

"Yeah, I did." Alex shrugged. "I don't know why. Part of me felt guilty, I guess, for what I was about to do. He apologized. He said it wouldn't happen again, and he asked me to come back home."

"You didn't say yes, did you?"

"Of course not—I'm here, aren't I?" She smiled.

"And he's cool with that?"

Alex suddenly looked sad. "For now, I guess. It's hard, you know. It's just been the two of us for so long."

"I know," he said, giving her a gentle kiss on the cheek. Alex's eyes began to tear up. Her emotions seemed to be all over the place. Several seconds passed before she said anything.

"Who are you people, and why are you so nice?" Alex laughed. A tear rolled down her cheek. "I mean it—your family, your friends, and especially you. I've never met anyone like you."

He squeezed her hand, and it struck him how pretty she looked—even with her face all splotchy and damp from crying. He felt the same—he had never met anyone like her.

It was then that he felt the small line of roughness as his thumb brushed the skin of her wrist. It felt like a scab—had she hurt herself? Concerned, he sat upright and pulled back her sleeve. What he saw both horrified him and broke his heart. There in the soft light cast by his phone, he saw the crisscross of scars that marked her forearm—some of the lines were fresh and raw, others were old and faded. It looked like someone had carved a hideous game of tic-tac-toe into her flesh.

Alex bolted upright and pulled her sleeve down, fear and shame transforming her features.

"Alex—" Nate wasn't sure what to say, but he realized the anguish she had been experiencing went far deeper than he had ever imagined. Was her father responsible for all her suffering? Was there more that she hadn't shared?

"You weren't supposed to see that," said Alex, pulling herself into a fetal position, head down, arms crossed between chest and knees. Nate could tell from her voice that the tears had started flowing again. "I'm sorry—I'm a freak." She began rocking slightly back and forth. A cool breeze chose that moment to toss her hair and Nate's heart went out to her. He realized her usually tough demeanor hid a frightened young woman who felt alone in the world.

He put his arm around her shoulders.

"You're not a freak. It's all right. We have a lot of problems." His eyebrows rose for a moment as he paused to consider everything going on in their lives. The tone of his voice rose slightly as he continued. "Some pretty amazing problems, really—but we'll figure them out."

She looked at him and laughed, in spite of the tears, in spite of the sadness.

"How do you do that?" she asked.

"Do what?"

"Stay so positive—and make me laugh even when I'm feeling like shit."

Nate just smiled and shrugged.

They sat in silence for some time, gazing at the twinkling night sky.

"Did you do that because of your father?" Nate asked, indicating her forearm.

Alex glanced at him and after a moment, looked down and nodded.

"I'm sorry," he said. "I didn't know it was that bad."

"He changed after my mother died," Alex explained. "He wasn't always that way. He loved her. I think it broke him somehow."

"How old were you when she died?"

"It was on my sixth birthday."

"On your birthday?" Nate frowned.

Alex nodded.

"Sheesh," Nate said. In comparison, he had been lucky. His father had never turned bitter on them.

"Can I ask how she died?"

Alex nodded slowly again and began to speak.

"We were living in Groton at the time. There was a fire in the house. My father was able to save me, but my mother didn't make it. He went into a deep depression after that. I think he still blames me on some level."

"Blames you?"

"He chose to save me over my mother. My mother died so that I could live."

"That's not fair—you were only six. Do they know how the fire started?"

Alex shrugged her shoulders.

"I keep trying to make it up to him. I do what he asks, but it's never enough. He hasn't remarried, and we've moved around a lot, so it's tough to make friends. We have no family. It's been just the two of us. I've tried really hard not to let him down, but it seems I always do."

"Has he told you he blames you for your mother's death?" asked Nate. "'Cause that's just crazy."

"No," Alex shook her head, "he hasn't used those words, but I believe it's true."

"I think you're being too hard on yourself," he said, touching her hand with his own. "It wasn't your fault. You don't owe him anything." He paused a moment before continuing. "I know what it feels like to let your father down, though."

"What're you talking about?" asked Alex.

Nate didn't particularly want to discuss the incident with his father, but Alex had just shared a *lot* of painful private stuff. Maybe his story would help in some way.

He took a deep breath, exhaling as he stretched out flat on his back and stared once more toward the stars. Alex lay beside him and grabbed hold of his hand. As the two of them lay there, the expansive night sky before them, Nate told Alex about the last conversation he had with his father.

"You win again!" said Nate as he set down the Wii remote. "I don't know how you do it." The brothers had been playing *Mario Kart* for a couple hours at this point, and the smile on Marc's face was jubilant. In Nate's opinion, it made his efforts at *not* winning entirely worthwhile. The old game console provided the boys with hours of distraction from the lung cancer eating its way through their father in the next room.

Nate had been told that his death could come any day now—or it could be as much as a month away. A steady stream of hospice workers and helpful neighbors had been flowing through the apartment for days as Nate struggled between wishing for his father to live forever—and wishing, with guilt, for an end to come.

He had been doing his best to be positive for Marc's sake, but it felt now as if they were all in a holding pattern. It was unclear what would happen when his father did die—where would he and Marc go? Would they be separated? The prospects were terrifying, and no one had talked to them about it.

"Nate, honey," said Nurse O'Hara as she left his father's room, yanking off a rubber glove with a snap. "I'm all set for today. Will you guys be OK until the night nurse arrives?"

The doctor had inserted a catheter to drain the fluid collecting around his father's lungs. It had noticeably improved his breathing. The goal at this point was to ease his suffering during these final days—palliative care, they called it. Nate knew the catheter was the last thing Nurse O'Hara examined before leaving for the day.

"Yes, ma'am," he said. "Thank you."

"Are you holding up OK?" she asked. "I know this must be tough."

"Yeah," he said. He appreciated the nurse's concern. He liked Nurse O'Hara, but he was looking forward to a time when people stopped asking that question—he felt like he was lying every time he answered.

"OK, you let me know if you need anything," she said. "Goodbye, Marc. I'll see you boys tomorrow."

She turned to go and then turned back.

"Nate, by the way—your father asked to speak with you," she said. She mouthed the word *alone*.

Nate nodded. His father frequently wanted to speak to him after the nurses had left to see how he and his brother were faring. He followed the nurse to the front door and closed and locked it behind her before heading in to see his father.

His father's bedroom had been turned into a hospital room. Many of his personal items had been removed to make way for the hospital bed, IV pole, and all the other pieces of equipment. Nurse O'Hara had opened the curtains to let in the afternoon sun. His father sat propped up in bed, beneath the freshly changed sheets. He had lost a lot of weight and was looking much older than his forty-five years.

"Come in for a moment," his father said. His voice was weak, and his breathing strained. "And please lock the door."

His father had never asked him to lock the door before—this was something new and it frightened Nate. Marc was the only other person home. For some reason, his father must not want his brother to walk in on their conversation.

Nate did as instructed and approached his father's bedside. He pulled up a chair and sat.

"Nate, I know the past several months have been difficult for you. I wanted to thank you for everything you've done to help your brother through them."

"You're welcome," said Nate. "I do what I can."

"I know you do. I'm proud of you and the man you're becoming. You're kind and caring—you get that from your mother." He laughed, the laugh turning into a coughing fit that seemed to last an eternity.

"You're also strong and responsible. You'll make a fine leader one day— I'd like to take credit for that, but I know there's some of your mother in there, too." He smiled.

Nate felt his eyes well with tears. Despite his father's self-deprecation, Nate knew he'd learned most of those things from the man lying in the bed before him. He loved his mother dearly, but she had been around for such a relatively short portion of his life.

"I love you, son."

He knew his father loved him, but he had never been one to use those words. Why was his father telling him these things now? It felt as if—it felt as if his father was saying goodbye.

"I love you, too. Dad—" He didn't know what else to say.

"Nate. I asked you in here to make me a promise—and to do me a tremendous favor."

"What is it?" Nate glanced nervously about the room as his father spoke. A vase of flowers sat on the bedside table. Its pink and yellow flow-ers were wilting, and their petals were beginning to drop. He didn't know who had sent them, but it had been a while since anyone other than his nurses had been by to visit.

"First of all, I want you to promise me that after I'm gone, you'll look after Marc—that you'll stay with him and protect him until he's ready to be on his own. I've made arrangements for you two after my death, but promise me you'll continue to be there for him."

"Of course I will," said Nate. The tears were flowing freely now. His father's eyes looked wet, too.

"Thank you. You have no idea how much that puts me at ease. I know it's a big responsibility." His father smiled through the sadness and pain.

"And another favor. An even bigger one."

"What?" Nate asked. He felt a pinprick of dread.

His father took a deep breath. "The nurse has just replaced my morphine drip. I'd like you to open the flow clamp."

"What do you mean?" Nate asked. He glanced at the IV stand and followed the transparent tube to his father's arm.

"I'd do it myself if I could," his father went on. "It should allow me to fall peacefully asleep. I'm tired—I'm so tired and I'd like to see your mother again."

So that's *what he meant*, Nate thought. He jumped up and threw his arms around his father, laying his head against his chest. He felt his father return the embrace and as the tears flowed from both of them, Nate considered what he had to do. This was his father's final wish—to put an end to his suffering. How could he say no? Could he live with himself if he helped? Could he live with himself if he didn't? He was terrified, but he wanted to do what his father asked.

"OK," he said, swallowing hard.

He picked himself up and looked at the IV stand. There was a bag filled with saline and another containing the morphine. He saw the clamp that restricted the flow of the morphine into the IV tube.

"I love you, Dad," he said as he turned back to his father to give him another brief hug.

"I love you, Nate. Thank you."

Nate held the clamp in his hand and turned the roller, opening the flow.

All the fear and anxiety he had been struggling so hard to suppress forced its way to the surface, overwhelming him. How could they live without him? What would they do? His father hadn't even told him where they would be going. He wasn't ready to be fully responsible for himself, much less his brother. He couldn't do this. They still needed him. There was just no way.

Rubbing the tears from his eyes, Nate closed the clamp and turned toward his father.

"I'm sorry Dad—please don't hate me. I can't do it. I just can't."

"Nate—"

Nate turned toward the door, unlocked it, and ran through, closing it quickly behind himself.

That night, their father passed away peacefully in his sleep.

"I let him down when he needed me most," said Nate. He squeezed her hand as he stared up at the sky. "That was the last time I ever spoke to him."

"But he died that night anyway," said Alex. "His suffering came to an end."

"I know, but he died knowing that I'd let him down. It's something I can never fix."

"Oh Nate, your father was a desperate man in a desperate situation—but he should never have put that responsibility on you. I mean we're just . . . kids."

"I can't let Hodge harm my brother—I'd die first. I can't let my father down again."

"I know—and you won't, Nate Watson. I'm sure of that." Alex snuggled closer to him, propping herself up so she could look him in the eyes. "Your father was right about you—you're the nicest, most caring person I've ever met. You always put the needs of others above your own. And you're a leader—your friends will rally around you in an instant, just because of the person you are. You'll get us through this—we'll all get through this—together. Malleus Hodge doesn't stand a chance."

She kissed him. It was a long and exciting kiss, and Nate felt his body react. Did people really feel this way about him? Could he really lead them through this? Could he keep his brother and Alex and the others safe? He didn't know—but he didn't have much choice in the matter—he had to try.

There was one thing he did realize that night as he and Alex lay on that platform under the stars—for the first time in his life he, Nate Watson, was truly, hopelessly, and completely in love.

Chapter 23

THE FUNERAL

"She doesn't look real," said Jenn to herself as she stood in front of her grandmother's casket. She wondered why her parents had gone ahead with the open-casket viewing. Her grandmother's chin and neck looked as if they had been molded from clay and coated in the same thick makeup that covered the rest of her face. The whole thing seemed a bit barbaric.

The wake had gone well, all things considered. She was surprised at the number of her grandmother's friends who had been there. Jenn hadn't known most of them. Her parents had greeted and spoken with them while she had remained mostly silent, unable to focus.

Zach, Douglas, Alex, and Nate had all come, as had Mr. Black, Ms. Brooks, and Mr. Foster from school. She was surprised they had all made it, since it was a school day. Mr. Foster had brought his wife, Samantha. They hadn't had a chance to talk at any length, but Jenn hoped she would get the opportunity at the cemetery. She knew Samantha Foster was the police officer who had found her grandmother, and she wondered what else she may have seen.

The viewing room was clear of people now, and only she and her parents remained.

"We're waiting for them to bring the hearse around to take her to the cemetery," said her father. "How're you holding up?"

"I don't know," said Jenn. "OK, I guess."

They said their final goodbyes, and then her father closed the lid of the casket. Despite the unnatural look of the makeup, her grandmother appeared peaceful.

Her parents left the room to check on the arrangements, leaving Jenn to her thoughts.

Goodbye, Gran. I'll miss you. Fond memories flooded her mind. It saddened her to know there would never be new ones.

Then she became aware of a faint scratching sound. It seemed to be coming from the direction of the casket. She thought of the creature that had been Mr. Flufferton and a sudden wave of anxiety washed through her. Was the sound getting louder? Where was it coming from? Could it be . . . ?

She thought of the story Courtney had told her and wondered if she was just letting paranoia get the better of her—but she just had to know for certain. Jenn got closer to the casket and with some effort, lifted the lid.

Her grandmother rested as peacefully as before.

She closed the lid, feeling a bit irritated with herself.

"*No*," she said. "Just—*no*." And turning away from the casket, Jenn strode out of the room.

Nate stood in the cemetery. It was a lovely day for a funeral, if there could be such a thing. The sun was shining, and there was a soft breeze moving through the trees. Fluffy clouds drifted across the bright, blue sky. The reverend from First Church was presiding. Behind him stretched gravestones of all shapes and sizes.

"We are gathered here today to say farewell to Martha Gregory and to commit her into the hands of God," said Reverend Reed, standing beside the casket. The casket rested on the device that would later be used to lower it into the ground.

"As many of you know, Martha was a beloved mother, grandmother, and friend," continued the reverend. "She loved visitors. She'd always have fresh treats ready on the chance that someone would stop by."

There were a couple dozen people standing around the gravesite, most of them dressed in black. Only a small portion of the people who had appeared at the viewing had made it to the cemetery for the burial. Mr. Black had given Nate a ride, along with Douglas, Zach, and Alex. Jenn had seemed relieved to see them, but the events of the past several days were obviously weighing heavily on her mind.

"Would anyone like to share any of their experiences with Martha?" asked Reverend Reed.

Several people supplied anecdotes, sharing warm or funny stories. Nate was sorry he had never gotten to meet her. He soon found his mind wandering. He scanned the crowd and saw Mr. Foster, his history teacher, standing with a woman he assumed to be his wife. The school librarian was also there, as were several other familiar faces. Nate recognized Noah, the neighbor boy he had met on the day they had moved into town. Nate waved at him and received a smile and nod in response.

At that moment, Nate heard a collective "Amen" from the gathering.

"We should not fear death," said Reverend Reed. "It's but another step in our journey with God. And with that, ladies and gentlemen, I thank you for coming, and for sharing your love and support with Martha's family."

The casket was lowered into the ground, after which the gathering began to disperse. Jenn, who had been talking to her parents, turned and headed in his direction. Zach, Douglas, and Alex stood beside him.

"Hey," said Jenn. "Thanks, guys. I mean it." Jenn hugged each of them in turn.

Nate saw Mr. Black and Ms. Brooks approaching, the Fosters a few steps behind.

"Hon, I just wanted to say goodbye," said Ms. Brooks as she arrived, giving Jenn a quick hug. "Please let me know if there's anything I can do for you or your family."

"Thanks, Ms. Brooks," said Jenn.

Mr. Foster joined the group and said, "I'd like to introduce you to my wife, Samantha."

They exchanged hellos and chatted for a few minutes before Ms. Brooks walked off toward the parking lot. Mr. Black and the Fosters had broken off from the students and were conversing nearby.

"I'm going to do it," Jenn whispered to her friends. "I'm going to talk to Ms. Foster."

"Go for it," whispered Zach. Nate and Douglas nodded their agreement.

Jenn paused a moment to build up her courage. "Ms. Foster—" Jenn called, at last. The three adults stopped talking and turned back to the students. "I understand you were the person who found my grandmother?"

Samantha Foster's smile disappeared and was replaced with a look of concern.

"Yes, that's true," she replied. "I'm really sorry for your loss."

Jenn glanced at Zach and Nate in quick succession. Each nodded in turn, encouraging her to continue. *Well, here goes*, she thought.

"Thanks. I—I'm not really sure how to—" started Jenn. "I'm just going to ask—did you see anything unusual at my grandmother's house that morning?"

"Unusual?" Ms. Foster looked at her husband with a frown. Jenn could tell immediately that *something* strange had taken place and that she had already shared the experience with Mr. Foster.

"Yeah," said Zach, stepping forward, "like a living, breathing, rotting cat with a stench and an attitude?"

"And sharp claws," added Douglas, eagerly.

"Hard to kill," said Nate, quickly.

Ms. Foster's eyes widened. She looked at Jenn.

"Yeah," Jenn said, uncomfortably, as she made eye contact with Ms. Foster. "Something . . . unusual like *that* . . ."

She watched the uneasiness leave Ms. Foster's features. It was replaced with relief.

"You all saw that, too?" said Ms. Foster, glancing at each of them.

They nodded. Jenn caught a wink from Mr. Black who had been standing by quietly during the exchange.

"I didn't think anyone else witnessed it," the police officer said, excitedly. "It ran out the back door and no one believed me. Except my husband of course." She looked at Mr. Foster, who smiled. "And I'm not *fully* sure even he believed."

"The cat came back," said Zach.

"Back to your grandmother's?" asked Mr. Foster.

Jenn nodded.

"Nate killed it with a lamp," added Douglas.

Everyone started talking at once. Ms. Foster shared her experience with the cat creature, and the students shared theirs, along with everything they had learned about Hodge and his plans. For the first time in days, Jenn felt as though a weight had been lifted off her shoulders. The Fosters were two more adults who could help them, should they need it—adults who understood who and what they were up against. And Jenn knew that in the fight against Malleus Hodge, they would need all the help they could get.

Chapter 24

GOODBYE

Hartford, Colony of Connecticut, May 1647

As Allie ran from the riverbank, she realized the letter was missing, and she started to panic. Where was it? Had Hodge taken it? If so, it was likely at the bottom of the river by now. She hurried back to the spot where he had yanked her roughly awake—and to her tremendous relief, she saw it nestled there in the grass. The book was where it had fallen, a portion of the letter visible along one edge.

She snatched it up and started running toward Meetinghouse Square. She realized that by this time, it was unlikely her father would still be there, but she had something more important to do at the moment than worry about getting home. She had to get the letter to someone who could do something with it—someone with the power to stop Malleus Hodge and put an end to his evil agenda. That was the only way for her to remain safe—her and many other innocent people. She had to get the letter to Reverend Thomas Hooker.

As founder of the Connecticut Colony, he more than anyone would be able to put an end to Hodge's plan and banish him from the area.

Reverend Hooker gave visiting sermons at the Windsor Meetinghouse and her mother had said he was a fair man. Whether or not he would believe her she didn't know, but she had to take the chance.

She thought of her mother. Her mother was the Windsor Witch—she couldn't get over that. It was a horrible thing to call a person. But if her mother *was* a witch, she was a good witch—a witch that loved God and his creatures—and somehow Allie was now one as well.

Evening was approaching as Allie neared Meetinghouse Square. The families and other attendees of the day's events had long since returned home. As she passed the Hartford Gaol, she saw the lone figure of Goody Davies sitting by the fence where she had spoken with her earlier. Oddly, the old woman was looking in her direction.

"There you are, my dear," said Goody Davies as Allie approached, traces of tomato still visible on her dress. The old woman was as clear minded as when they had spoken earlier in the day. "We haven't much time, so let's speak quickly."

"Excuse me, ma'am?"

"He'll be here shortly, and we have much to discuss." Goody Davies turned her head to the side. "The letters? Of course, I remember—do you think I'm daft?" she said to no one in particular.

Allie wasn't sure what to think of the exchange. Who was she talking to? Could she possibly know about Malleus Hodge? And who did she expect would be arriving soon? Before she had a chance to put her questions into words, Goody Davies spoke.

"Hand it over, my child," she said holding out her weathered palm. "Come now, we haven't got all day."

"Ma'am?"

"The letter, give it to me please—I'll get it to Reverend Hooker—never you fear."

"You know about the letter?" asked Allie. Somehow, she knew it to be true—there was more to this woman than people realized—and in that moment she decided to trust her.

"Of course, dear," she said, impatiently wiggling her wrinkled fingers.

Allie handed her the book with the letter inside—and then, almost as an afterthought, yanked it back. Goody Davies nodded, seeming to understand what Allie had in mind. She pulled the letter from the book, removing the second page that detailed her mother's use of magick. There was no need to share that information with anyone—the remaining pages provided enough evidence against Hodge. She placed those in the book and handed it to the old woman.

Goody Davies hid the book beneath her skirts. As she pulled back her hand, Allie saw it contained a folded piece of parchment. The old woman extended her arm.

"Here you go, child," she said.

Allie took the parchment, her curiosity growing as she opened each fold. She had lost track of how many times she had cried that day, but the tears began flowing once more as she realized what she held in her hand.

"Momma?" She glanced at Goody Davies. "But how?"

"A friend gave it to me for safekeeping," she said, glancing at the ground by Allie's feet.

Allie looked down, overjoyed to see the small brown mouse she'd left behind as she had fled from Malleus Hodge. She scooped it up and was once again flooded with feelings of her mother. Comforted by love and warmth, she read her mother's final messages to her.

She savored every word as she consumed the letter, knowing they were the last words she would receive. Questions were answered, and by the time she finished reading it, she knew what to do in the days to come. When she was finished, she threw her arms around the old woman, sobbing gratefully into her shoulder for several long moments.

"There, there, dear," Goody Davies said at last. "There's one more thing I must say before he arrives."

Breaking the embrace, Allie looked at the old woman, waiting for her to speak. The old woman's vacant eyes stared straight ahead for several seconds before her mouth fell open to reveal decaying, yellowed teeth. She swiveled her wrinkled neck toward Allie and with a newly returned clarity, spoke to her again.

"You handled yourself well today," she said, "but be warned—although many winters pass, the hunter *will* return. And when he does, he'll have great evil on his side."

"Great evil?" Allie asked.

"We're out of time, child," she said. "Do what you feel is right, and you'll be just fine." Goody Davies turned her head and began whispering to her imaginary friend.

"Ma'am?"

The old woman didn't respond. As she turned to go, she heard a call from across the square.

"Allie? *Allie!*"

It was her father—so he had come looking for her after all! She ran toward him and then stopped, turning back to glance at Goody Davies. The old woman turned to meet her gaze, her wrinkled face contorting into a wink.

"Allie, my sweet girl," said her father, grabbing her up when she reached his side. Goody Davies turned away. "I've been looking everywhere for you. That old woman said you would be back—but I never truly believed it."

He carried her toward the wagon, now located on the other side of the meetinghouse—near the spot where the gallows stood.

"Allie, I'm sorry I didn't tell you about your mother," he said. "I'm sorry you found out the way you did, and I'm sorry there was nothing I could do to stop what happened. Please, please forgive me."

Allie remained quiet as he spoke, enjoying the familiar sound of his voice and feeling safe for the first time in hours. She had many questions—but those could wait. She didn't have energy for any of that right now. She kept an eye out for Hodge as her father carried her across the square, but he was nowhere to be found. It occurred to her that Hodge must be the hunter of whom Goody Davies had spoken. The old woman had said he would be back some day, but not for a long while—so for the moment, at least, she put him out of her thoughts.

Her father placed her in the back of the wagon, where she curled up in a corner for the journey home. The rough, wooden casket, which now contained her mother's body, was beside her, along with the burial tools that Reverend Thomas and her father had placed there that morning. She knew her father would be stopping along the way and that her mother wouldn't make the full journey home.

The sun sank low in the sky as the wagon set off for Windsor, and soon it grew dark. Allie turned toward the casket. Setting down the pieces of parchment and the mouse she had held protectively against her chest, she shoved the lid partway to the side.

Her father heard the sound. "Allie?" he called back to her.

"Yes," she replied. Satisfied, he focused once again on the road.

She gazed at her mother inside the casket. After all the woman had been through, she looked peaceful, and Allie wasn't afraid.

"I love you, Momma," she said. "I'll do as you've asked."

Allie then retrieved her mother's letter and placed it carefully within her waistcoat. She picked up the page she had pulled from Hodge's correspondence and tore it into tiny pieces, which she scattered gently into the evening wind.

"Stay there, little one," she said to the mouse sitting on the bed of the wagon. She somehow knew the mouse wouldn't run away.

Allie slid gingerly over the side of the casket and nestled herself against her mother's cool breast. She lay there thinking about the events of the day and how they had changed her world. Suddenly, she felt that familiar loving warmth that had filled her with joy. Opening her eyes, she saw that the mouse had followed her inside and settled in the crook of her arm against her mother's chest. From that moment until Allie fell fast asleep, the two of them stayed there in the dark, relishing their final moments with Alse Young.

Chapter 25

TIME IS UP

Windsor, Connecticut, May 2019

Nate went to detention on Tuesday afternoon expecting a repeat of the day before—a tense and uncomfortable truce between Huey, Douglas, and himself, supervised by a disinterested teacher who ignored them. To his surprise and delight, what he experienced was something quite different—thanks primarily to two unexpected attendees.

"What're you doing here?!" he asked Alex as she came into the room and took the seat next to his.

"Detention—same as you," she smiled. "Ms. Wright sentenced me to a day of detention as a reward for soaking Courtney the other day. She said she was letting me off lightly because I'm new—but I think it was because she knows Courtney."

Douglas arrived a moment later, followed by Huey. Douglas sat behind Nate. Huey took a seat by the door. To Nate's surprise, Mr. Black came in behind them carrying a small pile of paperwork in his arms.

"Hello, folks," he said. "I'll be covering for Mr. Sampson this afternoon." He glanced at Alex. "Miss Bradley? I wasn't expecting to see you here."

"She soaked Courtney with a bottle of water," offered Douglas with a grin.

"Oh, my," said Mr. Black, as he sat behind the teacher's desk.

"Well, she deserved it," said Alex. "After Ms. Wright left us that afternoon, she called me a Princess Merida wannabe." She frowned. "Not cool!"

Nate banged a palm on his desk and started laughing.

"The girl with the bow and arrows?" asked Douglas with a grin. "From that Disney movie?"

Alex nodded with a frown. "Yeah. I know." She smirked. "The wide, goofy eyes and the big, crazy, red hair. Go on, get your laughs out."

By this time Nate's face was red, and he was short of breath from laughing so hard.

Mr. Black glanced up at them with a smile before returning to his paperwork. Huey remained silent and motionless, staring at the floor.

"One time," said Douglas, changing the subject, "I heard Courtney, Kat, and Kam talking in the cafeteria. Courtney asked, 'What does IDK stand for?' and Kat answered, 'I don't care?'"

"Seriously?" Nate sat up in his chair, a smile on his face.

"Courtney got mad and called her rude," said Douglas.

"No way," said Alex, with a laugh.

"Then Kam said, 'IDK stands for I don't know,' and Courtney yelled 'OMG! *Nobody* does!'" Douglas beamed. His face revealed that the whole exchange had been a joke.

Alex covered her mouth with a hand to stifle her laughter.

Mr. Black looked up. He grinned again and went back to work, shuffling papers.

"Douglas," said Nate with a smirk, "you made that up!"

"Yep, but it made you laugh." Douglas made a silly face, and they laughed some more.

The hour went by in this manner, the three friends and, occasionally, Mr. Black sharing stories and jokes. Huey sat quietly by the door and kept to himself. On at least one occasion however—after the rest of the room had dissolved into laughter—Nate glimpsed a smile as it flashed across Huey's face.

Toward the end of the hour, Alex told Nate she would be stopping at home before returning to the house.

"I'm getting tired of wearing Jenn's clothes," she said. "I want to grab some of my own."

"Are you sure that's safe?" he asked.

"It'll be fine," she said. "My father's probably not even home, and if he is—I'm good at coming and going without being seen."

"At least let me come with you." Marc was supposed to meet him at the high school after detention. It was a short distance from the middle school, and Marc had promised to have a friend walk him over. If they could take Marc home before heading to Alex's house—

"No, I'll be fine," she said. "Just get your brother home, and I'll be along shortly."

Nate wasn't thrilled with the idea, but he knew Alex was unlikely to change her mind.

When the period ended, Huey left quickly, followed by Alex and Douglas. "Nate, can I talk to you for a moment?" asked Mr. Black. His expression was serious.

"What's up?" asked Nate.

"I have some great news I'd like to keep between the two of us for the moment."

"Is it Aunt Celia?" he asked excitedly. "Did you find her?"

"Yes, as a matter of fact. I know where she is—Hodge has been keeping her at the abandoned movie theater in the center of town. I'd like to meet later at the house to discuss our options."

"What're we waiting for? Let's go now!" Nate started moving toward the door.

"Hold on—" said Mr. Black, grabbing his shoulder. "We have to prepare. Hodge has magick at his disposal, we don't—at least not magick we know how to control." It was clear that Mr. Black referred to the serpent.

Of course, he's right, thought Nate. There were things to be done before they could risk confronting the warlock. And, anyway, he needed to get Marc home.

"I understand," said Nate.

"Let's meet at the house in two hours—just you and me," said Mr. Black.

"It's a plan. I'll see you there."

Huey set off across the schoolyard in a fury. Donald had promised to pick him up after detention and had been a no-show. His brother was as reliable as wet toilet paper, and Huey was fed up. He had gotten him into this trouble to begin with—the least he could do was be there to give him a lift home. He wasn't even answering his cell.

Now he would have to make his way to Windsor Avenue and take a bus across town—assuming he could convince one of the passengers to give him the fare—or spend the next forty minutes or so walking the distance on foot. He didn't want to bother his mother at work. She had enough to deal with, trying to keep a roof over their heads, without having to cut her hours short. His father? Forget it.

He wondered what other people's families and houses were like. As he had stood by the curb, he had seen Douglas come out of the building and hop into a waiting car. Did Douglas's mother and father get along? Did they go home and eat dinner each night around the dining room table and share the events of their day? Huey wondered what that was like.

He envied Nate and his friends. The easy conversation they had shared during detention was quite different from the overbearing lectures he and Louie often received from Donald. Even if Huey wasn't a participant—clearly the other kids hated him, and he couldn't blame them—he had enjoyed listening to their interactions and had found himself wondering what it would be like to have friends of that sort.

Huey paused for a moment, remembering the weed he had stashed in his cigarette pack. *I could use some of that right now*, he thought as he probed his jacket's inner breast pocket. He took a joint from the pack of cigarettes, placing it in his mouth as he searched for a light. By pure chance, he glanced toward the tree line and saw a creature bearing down on him from across the grassy field. His mouth fell open in surprise as his mind tried to grasp what he was seeing. It was something out of *The Wizard of Oz*, but worse—a winged monkey on crack. Its wings were leathery like a bat's, and the face—the face was the most frightening of all. It looked almost human, wrinkled and ugly, with two small horns protruding from the forehead.

What the hell? he thought. He hadn't even smoked the dope yet.

In a panic, he turned to run—and stumbled over his own feet, falling forward onto the grass. With a quick motion, he flipped onto his back and sat up, supporting himself with his arms. The monkey-bat thing was fast, and it was closing in on him. He would never be able to outrun it. With his heart racing, Huey looked around frantically for a weapon—a stick or a rock, anything. There was nothing within reach. When he glanced back toward the monster, it was only a few feet away. As the creature descended upon him, its hideous chittering filled his ears, making his skin crawl.

Huey was certain that it was the last sound he would ever hear.

Mr. Black peered around the corner as Marc and Nate Watson walked away from the high school's main doors. As soon as they were gone, the teacher glanced around to be certain no one had seen him. Moving quickly and silently, he retreated to the privacy of his classroom. The elements of his plan were falling into place. The boys trusted him and were doing everything he had asked—and no one had discovered his deception. It wouldn't be long now, but he had to remain vigilant. Nothing could be allowed to interfere with this evening's objectives and the next few minutes were critical to his success. There was something he needed to accomplish, and he had no time to waste.

As he and Marc began walking home, Nate reflected on the conversation he had just had with Mr. Black. He was dying to share with Marc the news that Aunt Celia had been found, but he refrained for several reasons. He didn't want to get his brother's hopes up in case something didn't pan out. He also didn't want Marc trying to come along for the rescue. And Mr. Black had insisted on keeping the information between the two of them.

He wondered how quickly Mr. Black would be ready to act. He didn't want to wait any longer than necessary—who knew what kind of conditions Aunt Celia had been enduring for the last two days. Malleus Hodge didn't seem the type to provide his captives with luxury accommodations.

Nate had kept his eye out for Hodge all day. He hadn't really expected the warlock to show up in the middle of the school day, but now they had a fifteen-minute walk home and they were out in the open. With any luck—

"Nate, look!" Marc cried, pointing his finger into the distance.

Instantly on the defensive, Nate focused his attention on the direction indicated by his brother. What he saw shocked him. Huey stood across the grassy schoolyard—with Hodge's imp loping toward him at full speed. Nate felt the serpent suddenly come to life. It began constricting his arm as it pumped the blood required to power itself.

He didn't know why the imp had chosen to target Huey Jones of all people, but he knew he had to act immediately—or Huey would die a painful, fiery death.

He turned to Marc, placing a hand on his shoulder.

"Listen to me carefully. Stay here and don't follow until I say otherwise. Find some place to hide."

Marc didn't argue. He hurried off toward some parked cars that he could use for cover. Nate ran toward Huey at full speed. Huey turned to flee from the creature—and promptly fell to the ground.

The hell beast was only a few yards from its target. Nate had closed much of the distance, but there was no way he would make it in time. His only hope of saving Huey was to get the bracelet between him and the imp and pray it reacted to the beast's presence—but Huey was too far away.

At the last second, the creature leaped into the air.

"*No!*" shouted Nate.

Nate's sleeve burst into flame as the serpent roared to life, releasing a torrent of fire that shot forward and engulfed the demon beast in midair. The creature emitted an ear-splitting shriek as it was knocked off course by the steady flow of burning energy.

The imp hit the ground, rolling to a stop, its motionless body charred and smoking. Nate glanced down to see that his sleeve had burned away past the elbow, revealing the serpent in all its glory—and as had been the case last time, the skin beneath it remained cool and undamaged.

"What the fuck?" said a voice.

It was Huey. He was sprawled on the grass, his arms propping him up from behind. Nate recognized the look of confused horror on his face—the same one he had worn that day in the forest.

"You OK?" asked Nate, as he reached down a hand to help Huey to his feet.

"Are you one of those witches they're talking about?" Huey sounded uncharacteristically calm. He maintained eye contact with Nate as he brushed off his clothing.

"No, but one of them is after me. We have to get out of here—"

"Nate?" said a third voice. It was Marc—and there was something in his brother's tone that frightened him immensely.

"Marc?" he said, spinning around.

Nate's worst fear and biggest nightmare became one as he took in the sight before him.

Marc's body floated in the air before him, his head cocked to the side as if suspended from an invisible noose. His whole body trembled with fear as tears flowed freely down his cheeks.

Malleus Hodge stood behind him, one hand resting on his staff.

"What's it going to be, Nate?" he asked, raising his free hand to take possession of the serpent. Marc whimpered in fear.

"Please, don't—not him," Nate pleaded, utterly defeated. He remembered his final promise to his father. He couldn't fail again. "I'll do anything—please, take me instead."

"The serpent—*now*," was all that Hodge said.

"But I told you—I can't—"

"My patience is at an end, Nate Watson—but here's the thing. I believe you. You can't remove it, or you would have—especially now that I have your brother's life in my hands. You're in over your head. You have no idea what you're doing. You can't remove the serpent, and as you've gathered, I can't take it from you by force—at least, not yet."

What did the warlock mean? Nate wondered.

"I've already drained the magick from your aunt," continued Hodge. "Tonight, she dies—and her magick will permanently be added to my own. You can do nothing to stop that. With each witch I drain, my power grows significantly—and it won't be long before I'll be able to take the bracelet from you myself."

"Who is this jackass? And how is he doing that?" asked Huey, approaching from behind. "He looks like he escaped from a Thanksgiving Day parade."

Hodge ignored him and continued his monologue.

"And fortunately for me, an opportunity has arisen that I'd never anticipated." Hodge grinned maliciously as he removed a familiar-looking crystal from his pocket.

"Why did no one tell me this young man was a witch?" he asked, looking up at Marc, hanging suspended in the air before him.

No! Nate thought. Things had gone from bad to worse.

Marc seemed to be in shock. He hung suspended from the invisible noose, staring straight ahead and trembling, seemingly unaware of what was going on around him.

Hodge stepped forward and raised the stone to Marc's forehead. In desperation, Nate willed the bracelet to come to his aid—and to his astonishment, it did. A torrent of flame burst forth, Hodge directly in its path. The wizard tapped his staff on the ground, and the familiar circle of purple flame radiated out from its base, encircling Marc and his captor. The serpent's fury bounced harmlessly around the circle as if an invisible force field had been erected along its circumference.

Nate was actually relieved that Hodge had intervened, unsure what the bracelet's flame would have done to his brother—but the knowledge that he had no way to stop Hodge was devastating. What could he do?

"Nice try, Nate, but I'll tell you, this would be so much easier on everyone if you'd just stop fighting me," said the warlock.

Hodge placed the dark shard against Marc's forehead. It shone brightly for a moment before reverting to black. Marc's body went limp. He dangled from the invisible rope, head cocked to the side—but Nate was relieved to see the slight rise and fall of his chest. His brother was still breathing.

"Please don't hurt him," said Nate, offering one final, desperate plea.

Hodge said nothing, instead making a clicking sound with his tongue.

The still-smoldering imp rose to its feet and limped into the burning purple circle. With a double rap of the staff, Hodge, the imp, and his brother vanished from sight, leaving Nate and a stunned Huey staring at the now-empty area of grass.

"What the hell was *that*?" asked Huey, coming to Nate's side.

Dozens of thoughts passed through Nate's mind. Hodge had said Aunt Celia would die tonight. He had already taken his brother's newly discovered magick and had no reason to keep Marc alive—after all, he had only kept Aunt Celia around to use as leverage, and that hadn't helped him in obtaining the serpent. And yet there must have been a reason Hodge had kidnapped his brother rather than killing him on the spot.

He didn't know what he was going to do, but he knew he had to act now. He had to get to the old movie theater on the green.

"I have to go," Nate said, turning to Huey. "I have to help him. I have to help both of them."

Without another word, Nate took off running across the schoolyard toward the center of town.

Chapter 26

CORVIN AND MR. BLACK

It's not easy being a familiar, thought Corvin the crow, as he soared through the sky in search of the Watson brothers. He had a duty to watch over them. He owed it to his mistress to keep them safe until she returned. He knew that Allie, or Celia as she was calling herself these days, was alive—at least for the moment. As her familiar, his longevity was tied to hers. The moment she died, their tie would be severed, and he would most likely turn to dust. Crows weren't designed to live for three-and-a-half centuries. He wasn't afraid of dying—but neither of them was ready for that just yet. They still had important things to do.

Celia had promised the boys' father that she would look out for his sons. She and Ken had been close when Ken was a boy, but the difficulty in explaining her eternal youth to people outside the family made it necessary for them to maintain a distance as he grew older. They met occasionally over the years, but that changed when Ken married and had children. He felt it would be easier on the members of his new family if they remained ignorant of his extraordinary ancestry.

Corvin remembered how difficult it had been for Celia, but she had accepted it. She had outlived and moved on from so many of her descendants over the years that it was routine. Living forever wasn't all it was cracked up to be. The enchanted life-sustaining amulet around her neck had grown heavy with time. If not for her duties as warlock warden, Corvin suspected she would have removed it ages ago.

He thought of the last time he had seen Ken Watson, when Celia had sent him into the city to check on his declining health. Landing on the ledge outside his sickroom, Corvin saw him lying there on his deathbed, deep in conversation with a boy Corvin would learn to be Nate. Father and son had been profoundly distraught—and by the end of that day Kenneth Watson would be dead.

A gust of wind tossed Corvin higher into the air, breaking his train of thought. He looked down to see two figures in the grassy area below him. One of them was Nate. He stood over a second boy, a large gout of flame dying from the serpent bracelet he knew to be around Nate's wrist.

Corvin circled above the field, attempting to identify the threat that had triggered the bracelet. A bright circle of violet appeared behind Nate, only to vanish a moment later, leaving in its spot none other than Malleus Hodge. Marc hung suspended in the air before him.

Corvin immediately changed course, heading for the tree line. If Hodge saw him now, all would be lost. He came to rest on a high branch at the edge of the field. There was little he could do in a confrontation with Hodge now—his best bet was to remain hidden and wait until the odds were more favorable.

From his vantage, he watched the scene play out before him. A chill ruffled his feathers, but not from the cold. As long as Nate held the bracelet, he would be safe from the warlock—but the same couldn't be said of Marc. The boy was in danger and there was nothing Corvin could do about it.

The violet flames returned, and Hodge vanished, taking Marc with him. For the time being, at least, it meant Hodge planned to keep the younger boy alive. But Corvin was worried about Nate's reaction. He decided to follow him.

Nate turned and fled—but not in the direction of the house, as Corvin had expected. Instead, he ran in the opposite direction—straight toward the center of town.

Oh, Nate, no—what are you doing, foolish boy? Corvin was dismayed.

He knew instantly where Nate was going and what he had in mind. The boy was headed for disaster. He would have to act fast. He hopped off the branch and flew at full speed back in the direction from which he had come. Crows were smart birds, and as a familiar, Corvin was smarter than most—but for the life of him, he couldn't fathom why Mr. Black had chosen to inform the boy of Celia's location before it was time to act.

Corvin soared around the side of the building and dove through the open window into the classroom beyond, for once not even noticing the aquarium of tasty mice that sat on the nearby table. Before his claws even hit the floor, he felt the transformation begin. Agony spread through every part of his body as his bones grew longer and thicker, twisting into new and painful configurations. Muscle and fat reworked itself into new shapes as his feathers retracted into his skin to be replaced in places by the growth of new hair. Hair was one thing he would never get used to— humans had clumps of hair in the strangest of places.

As the pain subsided, the final part of the transformation began. He could feel his brain growing to fill the now-larger skull cavity. Feelings and emotions grew stronger and deeper, layers of knowledge and memories returned, and levels of reasoning and comprehension expanded as the pathways of his mind reconstructed themselves into the patterns familiar to the man known as Mr. Black.

Relieved that all his human parts were present and that the painful transformation was complete, Corvin Black reached for the pile of clothing he had left by the window and quickly began to dress. He didn't have a lot of time. He had to collect the completed witch's bottle and get to the abandoned movie theater to deal with Hodge before Nate ruined whatever chance they had of rescuing Celia and Marc.

Fully dressed, he hurried to the desk and opened the side drawer, retrieving the mayonnaise jar full of spell components. He had added the red wine and sealed the jar with wax. All that remained was to perform the incantation with the use of the power crystal Marc had unknowingly charged. This had to be done at the theater, in proximity to Malleus Hodge.

He grabbed his car keys and ran out of the classroom toward the parking lot. It would be faster to fly, of course, but he needed his hands to carry the witch's bottle and his human mind to perform the incantation.

Truth be told, he preferred his human form and its greater capacity for thought. He spent most of his time these days as Mr. Black, but when the need arose, he embraced his crow form. There were times when his avian skills proved useful, and there was nothing more exhilarating than flight.

At the moment, he too questioned the wisdom of having shared Celia's location with Nate. What his crow mind couldn't comprehend was that the boy needed something to boost his spirits—some good news in the midst of everything else he was dealing with. Especially with Celia gone, a lot of responsibility had been placed on the boy's shoulders, and a touch of hope could go a long way.

He had to hurry, but as he hopped into the car and pulled out of the parking lot toward the center of town, he thought about the other day when he and Celia discussed telling the boys about his dual identity.

"If we tell them the truth, then I can just live here as Mr. Black," Corvin said to Celia in the artifact room, "and I won't have to hide changes of clothes wherever I go." He smiled, unashamed of his nakedness. He had just shifted out of crow form as she entered the room.

"I know it's difficult," she said, "but they've just lost their father—I don't think we should lay this on them right now."

"Won't they be upset when they eventually learn the truth?"

"Perhaps—but they're still getting used to their new lives—a new home, new schools, new friends—"

"A new aunt who isn't their aunt and a biology teacher who can fly?"

"I'm serious," she said, suppressing a smile. "We'll tell them—I promise. I just want to give them more time to adjust. They'll have to keep our secret, and I'm not ready to burden them with that."

Celia had a point, and her instincts were usually on-target.

"I trust your judgment, but are you sure I can't change your mind?"

"No, I've managed to keep them in the dark this long," she said as she headed for the door. "We must stay the course."

Corvin nodded in response, shifting back into crow form as Celia left the room. He hopped onto the sill and soared out of the window, turning gracefully in the air toward the high school. He had papers to grade before meeting Celia for dinner, followed by a showing of their favorite movie. They had seen the film three times already—but he had a soft spot for Natasha Romanoff and who could resist an epic clash of heroes and villains?

It was later that night, as he dozed in his cage, that Malleus Hodge escaped.

WINDSOR'S OWN
PLAZA THEATRE
Corner Broad & Elm Streets

Gala Opening Tonight, 8 P.M.
December 2nd 1939

Laurence Olivier and Valerie Hobson in
"Clouds Over Europe"

Edith Fellows in
"Five Little Peppers"

Allie Young Beamon strode down the aisle of the brand-new Plaza Theatre, impressed by the number of well-dressed couples there for the cinema's opening gala. The women wore beautiful gowns and hats, the men, their best suits. Allie, likewise, was dressed to the nines, eager for a rare and exciting evening on the town.

She found a seat in the front row and removed her hat, placing it on the cushion beside her. That was the problem with fancy hats: it was bad form to wear them during the show and yet there was nowhere to place them once you took them off. She chuckled to herself as she scanned the audience, wondering how many of the husbands present would be watching this evening's picture with stylish hats on their laps.

The five-hundred-seat auditorium was nearly filled to capacity. She sat, finding the seat quite comfortable. It was plush with wooden trim, covered in a rich, red fabric that matched the floor-to-ceiling draperies that lined the room.

"Popcorn, my lady?" said a voice.

She glanced up to see Corvin, his crisp black suit standing in sharp contrast against the red walls.

"Thank you, kind sir," she said as her companion sat beside her, picking up her hat and placing it gently on his lap. She couldn't help but smile at the image.

Both she and Corvin had been looking forward to the theater's opening and seeing the film *Clouds Over Europe*. The British spy drama, featuring Laurence Olivier, was supposed to be exciting with elements of comedy. It was hard to believe how far motion pictures had come in the last decade. Only ten years ago, talkies made their first appearance. It seemed like only yesterday that they had seen Al Jolson in 1927's *The Jazz Singer*—how exciting it had been to see moving pictures with singing and spoken dialogue, perfectly in sync with the actors.

Motion pictures filmed in color were gaining popularity. Although the film they would see this evening was black and white, Allie was intrigued by the advancements being made in that area. The much-talked-about *Gone with the Wind* would debut in two weeks in brilliant color. She had heard, too, of the recently released *The Wizard of Oz* starring Judy Garland, where the picture's Kansas scenes were filmed in black and white, while those in Oz were in vibrant Technicolor.

As if witches needed any further bad press! She hadn't seen it yet, but she already had mixed feelings. Margaret Hamilton's Wicked Witch was supposed to be quite frightening—and she was *green* of all things! On the other hand, the beautiful Billie Burke's portrayal of Glinda, the story's good witch, would hopefully provide a good counterbalance. One could only hope.

Soon the lights dimmed, signaling the start of the show, and a hush fell over the auditorium as the crowd settled into their seats. The curtains slowly parted to reveal the magnificent two-story screen before them. Filled with excitement, Allie waited for the picture to begin. Long moments passed in dark silence.

As her eyes grew accustomed to the dark, it occurred to her that the room was *too* silent. She heard no whispered conversations, no clearing of throats, no munching of popcorn, no hand-muffled coughs. Something suddenly felt very wrong.

She turned her head to look at the audience behind her. She could make out figures in the dark—staring straight ahead at the blank screen before them. No one seemed upset that the film hadn't started. In fact, they showed no reaction or movement at all. A sudden sharp pain blossomed at the base of her neck.

She turned to her companion, placing her hand on top of his.

"Corvin?" she whispered, her anxiety building.

He turned his head slowly in her direction but said nothing. She felt movement beneath her hand. She gasped as Corvin began to change shape. His body seemed to melt, his suit folding in on itself as he shifted to bird form. *No*, she thought—they had worked so hard to fit in, to appear normal, and he had just transformed here, in public, in front of all these people! What was he thinking?

She heard a ruffle of wings and felt a draft brush past her face just moments before the light snapped on.

It wasn't the light of the film projector or even the overhead lights—it was a spotlight aimed at the floor in front of the big screen, and the scene it illuminated was something out of a different era.

A woman stood just yards away locked in a pillory, her neck through the center hole, her wrists trapped within the holes on either side of her head. Stringy blond hair hung down, covering her face. A crow—*her* crow—stood perched on one end of the device.

This can't be happening, Allie thought, as she tried to rise from her seat. But her body refused to obey. The pain in her neck throbbed. Unable to move, she watched the woman begin to stir.

A low moan emanated from the woman's throat, unusually loud in the silent room.

"Alice, you've dropped your hat," said a voice beside her.

She struggled to turn her neck against the worsening pain. Seated beside her was Malleus Hodge, grinning as he extended his arm, her forgotten hat in his hand.

This is a nightmare. I'm having a nightmare, Allie thought.

The woman's moaning grew louder and then she lifted her head. When Allie saw the woman's face, she was not entirely surprised to see it was her own.

Suddenly her perspective shifted, and she *was* the woman in the pillory, looking out at the audience before her, the faces now illuminated. The well-dressed men and women looked back at her in disgust. A boy resembling her young friend Noah watched from an aisle between the rows of seats. Malleus Hodge smiled at her from his spot in the front row.

"Witch!" cried a girl with braids, her sparkling red slippers shining in the darkness. A small dog jumped from her basket to nip viciously at Allie's ankles, tearing relentlessly at her flesh until she could feel the blood flowing into her shoes.

Wake up! Wake up now! her mind screamed as the jeering audience began pelting her with eggs and tomatoes and rotten pieces of fruit. Unimaginable pain radiated from the base of her neck and down her spine. She felt a sudden electric jolt as a thrown rock struck her temple causing her vision to flash a brilliant white—only to fade moments later into complete and utter darkness.

Celia Watson, a.k.a. Allie Young Beamon, woke from her nightmare to find she was still inside the Plaza Theatre—not the new and beautiful art deco–style movie house where she had seen *Clouds Over Europe* so many decades ago, but rather its run-down and abandoned twenty-first-century corpse. But like the dream, she was locked in a pillory that had been erected in front of the ruined screen.

When Hodge teleported them from the street and materialized them moments later inside the old theater, she recognized the place immediately even though it was just a shadow of its former self. It had fallen into disrepair over the years before closing for good in the late 1990s. Many of the cloth-covered seats were broken or missing entirely, and a thick layer of dust coated everything. Old crates and boxes were stacked randomly around the auditorium and what was left of the once-magnificent screen was now stained and in tatters.

Hodge came and went regularly since that night, using the Endora shard to redrain her magick each time to ensure she remained powerless. Celia didn't know where he went or why. Was he stirring up more trouble in town, somehow furthering new beliefs in witches and witchcraft? She hoped rational heads would prevail—it was the twenty-first century, after all—but she had seen firsthand how easily a group of people could be moved to hysteria under the right circumstances.

Celia's neck throbbed. The restraint was made of two parallel boards with opposing half-circle cutouts, hinged together on one end and mounted on a frame. When locked together around the neck and wrists, there was little a person could do to escape. It had been close to two hundred years since Celia had seen such a device used in America—leave it to Malleus Hodge to revive such a barbaric instrument of confinement and torture.

"Are you comfortable, Alice?" Hodge asked, clearly relishing the reversal in their roles as captive and captor.

"It's quite lovely, thank you. You always were a marvelous host," she replied, thinking of the time he imprisoned her in the Hartford Gaol.

Hodge's taunting smile was instantly replaced with a look of fury.

"*You imprisoned me for centuries* in a bottle filled with God only knows what—don't talk to me about hospitality."

Fair enough, she thought.

He walked toward her, stepping over a torn section of movie screen.

"You try spending three hundred years in an incorporeal state," he continued, "aware of everything going on around you but unable to do anything about it—forever growing more and more restless and angry over the injustice of it all."

"Injustice? If you think—" she began indignantly, stopping herself from completing the sentence. *Maybe this isn't the best time to anger him even more*, she thought. She had no idea the warlock had been conscious during his captivity. The spell mentioned nothing about that. She couldn't imagine being trapped like that for so long—years' worth of boredom and helplessness fueling a hatred focused on one person.

"You had no intention of letting me go—even if Nate *had* turned over the serpent," she said at last.

"Alice, you've caused me more trouble than anyone else I've known—although your nephew is quickly gaining ground on you. There's nothing I look forward to more in this life than making sure you're repaid for everything you've done."

Celia said nothing in response.

"You set me on an unalterable course that day in Hartford—one that I can never forgive you for. You forced me to cross a line which affected many of my choices later on."

"What are you talking about?" she asked.

"While I'd participated in the conviction and execution of many a witch, never had I been placed in a situation where I had to take a life myself—never had I been forced to kill an innocent with my own hands."

"I don't understand—what are you saying?"

"You have no idea, do you? When you turned my letter over to the authorities, you exposed my past dealings in England and made it clear that I'd orchestrated the case against your mother for my own benefit—but that wasn't all. You removed the portion of the letter that revealed the truth about your mother—information that would have gone a long way in mitigating the damage to my reputation. But even that wasn't the worst of it. Did you reread the letter after removing that page?"

"No," she said, unsure where he was going with this. She had torn up the middle page and given the rest to Goody Davies.

"The portion of the letter where I confessed to abducting you remained—but none of my purposes for doing so. It read—quite clearly in fact—as though I had an unusual obsession with . . . young girls. That was *not* something that went over well with *Reverend* Thomas Hooker.

"He threatened to spread word of my 'perverse inclinations' throughout the colonies. I tried to explain the truth of it to him—to explain the missing content of the letter. He finally told me to leave—to give him time to consider my words. It was only because we'd become friendly prior to the incident that he'd even allowed me that much. I left for the Bay Colony for a time, hoping that he'd come to his senses. When I returned, I learned he planned to follow through on his threat. I'd been unable to change his mind. I suspect he'd started to regret his participation in your mother's hanging. I didn't know what to do. I was desperate—I couldn't return to England, or risk word of my escape to America getting out. I also couldn't allow my reputation—personal or professional—to be ruined in the New World. I really had no choice in the matter—I had to stop him."

Celia was surprised to sense regret in his voice. She was hit by a stunning realization. She remembered that Thomas Hooker, founder of the Connecticut Colony, died just weeks after her mother's hanging—six weeks to the day, in fact. There were rumors at the time—whispered suggestions that his death was caused by the Windsor Witch, that she sought revenge from beyond the grave for his part in her execution. Celia knew those charges to be ridiculous, of course. But was Hodge now telling her *he* played a role in the reverend's death? She was told Reverend Hooker died of a sudden illness—possibly even of the same flu that had ravaged Windsor that winter—but could Hodge have murdered him to keep him quiet?

"Are you saying you killed—" Celia began.

"What I'm saying, Alice," said Hodge, the anger returning to his voice, "is that you better make the most of the time you have left—as soon as I've retrieved my serpent from your nephew, I'll see to it that you can never make trouble for me again."

Chapter 27

THE ABANDONED THEATER

C elia woke with a start. She dozed occasionally when exhaustion over-rode the pain of standing hunched over, her neck and wrists bent at uncomfortable angles through the holes of the pillory. True sleep rarely came—and when it did, the relaxing of her knees soon brought agony as the weight of her body exerted stress on the bones of her neck.

Celia lifted her head, straining to look around the room, the hard wood rubbing against her already raw skin. The room was dark and quiet. Malleus Hodge was nowhere to be seen. She tried once more to reach out with her mind, to make contact with any living being in her proximity—but without her magick, it was pointless.

It was then she saw the wooden structure off to her right—another pillory, similar to her own, had appeared in front of the ruined movie screen. Had Hodge carried it in after she fell asleep? Had he somehow magicked it up out of thin air? She still didn't know the extent of the warlock's abilities—with that staff of his, he was capable of far more than she was.

More important than how it got there, however, was its intended purpose. The time that Hodge had given Nate to remove the serpent had surely passed. Could his intention be to abduct Nate and lock him in the pillory until he could find a way to remove the bracelet himself? Would it even allow Hodge to do that? The serpent seemed to favor its new owner, a fact her abductor no doubt despised.

She wondered how the boys were faring without her. She felt great guilt at abandoning them, even though she had had little choice in the matter. She prayed that Corvin would be able to provide them with guidance. He would have to gain their trust first, of course, but she knew he would do his best to help them. Her familiar had been correct—the two of them should have shared their secrets with the boys sooner.

Celia heard the distinct electric crackle that usually preceded Hodge's return. A flickering violet light illuminated the room, only to burn away seconds later—but before it vanished, she saw that the warlock brought company. With him was the imp—and someone else. In front of Malleus Hodge hung the limp form of a human being, suspended vertically in the air. *Oh no*, Celia thought in despair. Hodge had abducted Nate after all.

The warlock brought down the heel of his staff, igniting a fireball that bathed the lower portion of the auditorium in bright light. It took a moment for her eyes to adjust after so many hours spent in darkness.

"Alice, we have a visitor," said Hodge in an annoyingly cheerful voice.

"Marc!" she said, recognizing the warlock's latest captive. To her relief the boy chose that moment to let out a moan, demonstrating he was still alive. "What have you done to him?" she asked. Marc appeared unconscious and totally under Hodge's control.

"He'll be fine—for the time being at least. But more importantly—I bring news! Tell me, would you like to hear the good news first? Or the bad news?"

Celia frowned as Hodge approached, Marc gliding through the air beside him.

"Good for whom?"

"You're right—my good news will probably be your bad news, and vice versa. It's all a matter of perspective, isn't it? Funny how that works."

As he secured Marc within the empty pillory, Hodge described the events that had unfolded after school. Celia was shocked to hear about

Marc's magick. She wished she had tested him earlier, but the odds had been very much against it. And now it appeared that he would pay the price of her oversight.

"So you see—with your magick and your nephew's magick added to mine, I should be close to having what I need to take the serpent by force. If I can locate just one more witch—well, I'll be unstoppable. Unfortunately for you, I promised young Nate that you'd die this evening and there really is no sense in postponing it any longer. I'll keep his brother around for a while in case I need some leverage, but you really are worth more to me dead at this point. It's sad really—I don't think you've suffered nearly enough."

With Marc secure, Hodge began to pace the floor in front of the pillories, the rows of broken seats stretching out behind him.

So this is it, she thought. *He's going to kill me right here and now.* A deep sadness overtook her—not for herself, but for Nate and Marc. She let them down, and while her suffering would end, theirs would continue. Hodge would strip them of everything worth taking, their lives included—and there was nothing she could do to stop it.

"I was thinking a good old-fashioned witch burning would be appropriate. I attended one once in Suffolk—the old bird went up like kindling," he chuckled. "It's a shame they never caught on in America." The ball of flame shot from the tip of the staff to land at her feet, where it blazed for a moment before burning out and reforming atop the staff. "Or perhaps a hanging? It was good enough for your mother."

Celia said nothing, refusing to take the bait.

The chirp of a cell phone broke the silence. Celia was surprised to see Hodge pull the device out of a jacket pocket. *He certainly wasted no time in catching up with modern technology*, she thought.

"Lucky you," he said with a look of disappointment. "You've gained a temporary reprieve." And, without further comment, Malleus Hodge returned the phone to his pocket, rapped his staff twice on the ground and vanished from sight.

Nate was winded. He had run straight from the high school to the center of town and as he reached the block of storefronts containing the abandoned theater, he began to regret his lack of preparation.

What am I doing? he thought. *I'm on my own, I have no plan of attack, and I'm gasping for breath.*

Time was of the essence, but there was no wisdom in rushing into the theater alone like this. He needed to come up with a plan.

He turned left between two storefronts where a small alley led away from the street. The path appeared rarely used. Grass sprouted undisturbed from the pavement's numerous cracks, and as Nate passed deeper down the corridor, his face brushed the remnants of a spider's web strung between the opposing brick walls.

"Great," he muttered as he paused to rub sticky strands from his eyelashes. *At least I can rest here a moment without being seen.* He sat on the pavement, his back against the wall. As his breathing slowed, he tried desperately to come up with a plan. What was he going to do? He was no superhero. What chance did he have against Malleus Hodge? So far only the serpent had saved him, but he had no idea how to control it.

For a moment he considered calling Jenn and Zach, but even if his friends could arrive in time, they had less of a chance against the powerful warlock than he did. There was only one thing he could think of to do—get ahold of Mr. Black. If anyone could help him, it was the biology teacher. Nate should have consulted with him back at the school—but better late than never.

He pulled out his phone and saw that Mr. Black had already tried to reach him. He read the text:

What do you think you're doing? Call me—ASAP!

Did the teacher know what he was up to? How could he? Had he witnessed the altercation with Hodge at the school? His phone had been on silent mode. He checked the time. It was 4:20, nearly ten minutes after Mr. Black had sent the text. Nate rose to his feet and called the biology teacher.

The call rolled over to voicemail. He disconnected and tried again. The second call rolled over as well. He shot off a text and waited a few moments for a response, but none came.

Nate returned the phone to his pocket. Now anxious and unsure of what to do, he began to pace. Should he wait here until he reached Mr. Black? Should he proceed alone and hope for the best?

Up ahead, the alley dead-ended at a plain metal door. Weeds sprouted from the ground, rising well above its threshold. The door seemed oddly out of place. Did it belong to one of the businesses on the block? If so, wouldn't there be some amount of foot traffic either to it or from it? Most businesses with back entrances used them for deliveries and such and yet this door— the whole alley in fact—seemed untouched. Why would that be?

The door must belong to the old Plaza Theatre, Nate realized. The movie house had a large auditorium with hundreds of seats—the only place it *could* be located was at the rear of the building complex, running behind the other stores. A venue of that size would also have to have emergency exits—and this door, in all likelihood, was one such exit. His heart beat faster as the realization hit him. He approached the door cautiously, placing his ear against the old metal surface.

From within came the sounds of conversation—the words themselves were unintelligible, but he heard two voices and even though they were muffled, Nate knew immediately they belonged to Malleus Hodge and Aunt Celia.

She's still alive!

He tried the old doorknob, but it refused to turn. The door was locked from the other side.

Backtracking down the alley, he made a left toward the theater's main entrance. As he passed beneath the empty marquee, he realized that he had no plan for getting inside. The front doors were surely locked, too—but he had to give them a try.

He pushed gently on the doors with both hands—and to his amazement, they swung gently inward. Nate couldn't believe his luck. He stepped into the dark and dusty foyer, letting the doors swing closed behind him.

Now that he was safely off the street and out of sight, he paused to consider his next move. He decided to try reaching Mr. Black one final time before moving farther into the theater. Hodge and his captives were deep inside the auditorium—far enough away that he shouldn't be overheard. If the biology teacher failed to answer this time, he would proceed on his own. He couldn't afford to wait any longer.

Nate suddenly felt a hand clamp tightly over his nose and mouth, cutting off his ability to breathe. Before he could register what was happening, he was yanked roughly backward into the darkness, his phone falling to the floor.

Corvin Black slowed the car as he approached the main entrance to the theater. He glanced at the clock on the dash. It was 4:15. He hadn't been able to reach Nate, and he had seen no sign of him along the way. The route from the high school to the Plaza was fairly direct—either Nate had already made it inside the building or he had suffered some mishap along the way.

He drove past the theater and turned onto Elm Street. The road was quiet. He made a quick U-turn and pulled up alongside the large brick building where he knew Malleus Hodge had set up shop. As he exited the car, he grabbed the plastic shopping bag containing the jar of spell components. The best way out of their current predicament was to complete the entrapment spell before Hodge was any the wiser—any other course would likely end in disaster. He hoped it wasn't already too late. If Nate's actions had in any way tipped off the warlock to their presence, their chance of success would be close to zero.

At the theater's main entrance, Corvin tried the doors, but as expected, they were locked. Fortunately, he came prepared. Removing the leather pouch from his pocket, he extracted two metal rods and inserted them into the old lock. After several moments of manipulation, the lock's tumblers shifted into place, and he was inside, the doors swinging shut behind him.

One doesn't live for over three hundred and fifty years without picking up a few useful tricks, he thought.

He glanced at his cell—still nothing from Nate. He silenced the phone so it wouldn't give him away. He slipped deeper into the theater, past the remains of the ticket counter and the concession stand, watching his surroundings carefully. He was familiar with the layout. The projection room upstairs and the auditorium beyond were the only places Hodge and his minions could be.

Corvin had enlisted Noah's help in the search for Celia, and as usual, he had come through. As a ghost, Noah could get into places that others could not. The warlock had been holding her in the auditorium, and most likely that's where he would find Marc as well. As he approached the doors, he saw a sliver of light shining between them. He gazed through the gap at the scene on the other side.

To his relief, down in front were Celia and Marc—and although they were yards away, he could see they were alive. Both were locked in matching wooden pillories. Celia looked terrible, her hair hanging in limp strands— but she was moving her head in response to Hodge. The warlock, true to form, was pacing back and forth and lecturing her on some topic or other. *The pompous fool likes to hear himself talk*, Corvin thought.

Marc, on the other hand, hung limply. He appeared unconscious. There was no sign of Nate. And fortunately, so far, Hodge seemed unaware of Corvin's presence. Hopefully he could perform the spell and be rid of the warlock within minutes. But where was Nate? The last thing he needed was for him to show up at the wrong moment, putting Hodge on alert or even worse—getting captured himself.

A bright flash of violet illuminated the crack between the doors, followed by darkness, and Corvin realized that it was Hodge teleporting away. This would put a wrench in his plans—or would it? He would no doubt be back, but Corvin could use the time to prepare the spell for his return. He didn't dare enter the auditorium just yet. Hodge could reappear at any moment, and he had seen the imp wandering about inside.

Before he did anything else, however, he had to try to find Nate. He quickly retraced his steps to the entrance. Just as he went into the foyer, the front doors began to part, letting in light from the outside. Reflexively, he dove behind one of the widening doors, just barely vacating the spot before light from outside brightened the floor. It was Nate. As soon as the doors swung closed behind him and the room returned to darkness, Corvin leaped forward, clamping his hand over Nate's mouth to prevent him from crying out.

"Shhh, it's me," he whispered as Nate struggled. He immediately relaxed, and Corvin removed his hand from the boy's mouth.

"Oh, thank God!" Nate whispered back. "*They're in there*—I heard Aunt Celia speaking to Hodge—*I heard them!*"

"Shhh—you heard them?" Corvin asked. "Never mind. Listen, Hodge just vanished. I need to prepare the spell before he returns. Your aunt and your brother are all right, but we need to act quickly."

He led Nate back to the doors of the auditorium. The best place to perform the spell would be the projection room—it would have a good view of the area below and less of a chance for interruption. But first he had to verify that it was empty.

"Stay here," he said to Nate. "I have to go check something. Stay out of sight and keep quiet. I'll be right back."

Corvin climbed the stairs to the projection room. It was dark and appeared empty. He pulled out his phone and turned on the flashlight, taking care not to let it shine on anything that could be seen from below. He was taking a chance, but he needed to understand the lay of the room.

Much like the rest of the place, it was dusty and full of old clutter. The two-reel movie projector still sat by its window, but slightly off to the side—an antique in its own right since the adoption of digital media. Corvin shut off the flashlight and made his way to the window. He removed the mayonnaise jar from the plastic bag and placed it on the sill. He would perform the spell from here. From a pocket he removed a small wooden box and opened it a crack. He saw the soft blue glow of the magick crystal. He had everything he needed. He could start the spell at any time—as long as he completed it *after* Hodge's return. But first, he needed to retrieve Nate.

Just as he was about to turn from the window, a light appeared in the room below. Corvin flattened himself against the wall and peered into the auditorium. Hodge had returned. The violet glow of his teleportation spell quickly faded and was replaced with the crimson light cast by his staff and the fireball floating above it.

But Hodge hadn't returned alone. This time, a girl was with him. His large hand was wrapped tightly about her upper arm. Unceremoniously, he dragged her to the auditorium's front row and shoved her into one of the seats. It was the bounce of red curls that revealed to Corvin who she was.

Dread filled him a moment later when he spotted the figure slowly making its way along the back row of seats. It was Nate, heading toward one of the aisles that led to the front.

Damn, thought Corvin, feeling his last grasp of the situation begin to give way. Like a train wreck in progress, he saw Nate, hunched low so as not to be seen, turn the corner and move down the aisle. Hodge argued with Alex as Celia watched, all of them unaware of Nate's approach. Disaster was imminent and Corvin had no way to intervene—so he did the only thing he could do.

Removing the glowing blue stone from the wooden box and holding it tightly in one fist, he began reciting the words to the entrapment spell—desperately hoping he wasn't already too late.

Nate stood in the darkness, waiting for the biology teacher to return. From somewhere deep within the auditorium, he heard the brief chittering of Hodge's imp—but that was the only indication of life within the darkened building. He pressed his eye to the slit between the auditorium doors, but without light, there wasn't much to be seen—just open areas of darkness and shadow. Somewhere within that blackness, he knew, were Marc and Aunt Celia.

Tentatively, he pushed on one of the doors. It moved slightly without making a sound, and so he pushed a little further until the gap widened enough to slip his head through. Nate leaned in and listened. The room was silent. He squinted his eyes and scanned the room—unfortunately, even with both eyes, it was just too dark to see.

His brother and aunt were in there, mere yards away—and yet he couldn't go to them or even let them know he was here to help. What was taking Mr. Black so long? What if something had happened to him? What if he wasn't coming back?

The serpent clamped down around his arm. Nate gasped and fell forward into the auditorium, fighting the urge to cry out at the pain. He landed on his hands and knees as gently as possible, praying the noise he made was nowhere near as loud as it seemed. He froze in that position for several seconds, holding his breath, certain the imp would leap out at him from the darkness at any moment.

Fortunately, the attack never came—and yet the serpent continued to contract, drawing on his blood to power itself. Why had it come awake? Did it sense danger? Was it just reacting to the presence of the imp?

Then a familiar purple illumination cut through the darkness.

Oh shit, thought Nate, as he pulled his foot from between the doors, allowing them to swing shut. Quickly, on hands and knees, he crawled forward, taking cover behind the nearest row of seats. He was unsure of what to do next. The sound of raised voices reached his ears and curiosity got the better of him. Slowly, he raised his head to get a glimpse of the speakers—just in time to be blinded by the huge fireball that appeared above Hodge's staff.

Nate's eyes slowly adjusted to the light bathing the front of the auditorium.

Down in front, before the remains of the giant screen, were Marc and Aunt Celia, locked in wooden torture devices that were straight out of seventeenth-century Salem. And there was Hodge with his hands on Alex, roughly shoving her into a front row seat. Nate's blood boiled, and the serpent pumped faster. Its eyes glowed brightly in the dim light.

But Nate was determined. Stealthily, he crawled to the farthest aisle leading down toward the front, aiming for a spot opposite Hodge. From that vantage, he would be able to size up the situation and look for an opening without being seen. Ahead he saw his brother, hanging unconscious in the warlock's barbaric device.

As he drew closer, Hodge's conversation became clearer.

"You're not listening, Alexandra," he said. "And I'm getting angry."

"Do what you want to me," she said. "I won't do it. I won't help you."

"You'd rather watch your friends die, one by one? Because that's what'll happen."

"If you think I'm stupid enough to believe you won't harm them anyway, you're mad."

Nate wondered what it was Hodge wanted Alex to do. It probably had something to do with obtaining the serpent. She wasn't letting the warlock intimidate her, no matter how frightened she must be. But surely she knew how dangerous he was.

As he listened, Nate looked around the auditorium. To the left of Marc, he saw a door with an unlit exit sign hanging above it—he realized it was the door to the alleyway he found earlier. To the right of his brother was Aunt Celia, awake and silently listening to the conversation happening before her. Hodge's imp lay off to the right by a stack of dusty boxes.

"You have no future with that boy," said Hodge. "Surely you see that—where is this unwarranted loyalty coming from?"

"You have no idea what you're talking about," said Alex. "You've forgotten what it's like to care for someone—or what it's like to have someone care for you." She pushed herself angrily out of the seat with two hands and stood to face the warlock.

From his position, Nate caught a glimpse of Hodge's face and was surprised to see he looked hurt.

"You certainly have a way with women," said Aunt Celia, breaking her silence.

"*You*—stay out of this," he said, pointing a furious finger in her direction. "Fine, Alexandra—we'll finish this discussion later. I promised young Nate that his *faux* aunt would die this evening, and I see no reason to wait any longer. She's been particularly irritating today."

Oh my God, thought Nate. *What do I do?*

He glanced at Aunt Celia in time to see her eyes go wide. Then she quickly refocused her gaze toward the ground. It was clear she saw something—something she didn't want anyone else to notice. Turning his head toward the back of the theater, he immediately saw what had caught her eye.

There in the darkness, on the sill of the projection room window, sat a Hellmann's mayonnaise jar, visible to anyone who might glance in its direction—and it was glowing a brilliant eye-catching blue.

Chapter 28

CONFRONTATION

*W**hy did this spell have to be so long?* Corvin thought desperately as he continued the incantation.

> *Semper anticus,*
> *Semper apertus,*
> *Semper fortis*

He was starting to sweat. As soon as he began reciting the words, the crystal grew dim, its magick flowing into the witch's bottle, causing it to glow vibrantly in the darkness. He hadn't remembered that, or he wouldn't have placed the bottle in such a visible location. But he didn't dare stop now. He just hoped he could finish the spell before anyone could reach him.

> *Semper liber,*
> *Bono malum superate,*
> *Capax infiniti*

He was only halfway through. He was relieved that Nate had, so far, remained unseen and that Hodge was wasting his final free moments chatting rather than causing real damage. But things would change the moment someone noticed the jar.

Dona nobis pacem . . .

Corvin continued to chant.

It was clear to Celia that something was happening. Someone was casting a spell, and she was fairly certain it wasn't team Hodge. Corvin must have located her and made his way into the building—but if he were casting the entrapment spell, why do it in such a visible location?

Hodge and Alex continued arguing in front of her. The girl was trying to convince him to keep her alive. Celia's eyes scanned the auditorium, landing eventually on Nate. They *had* come to rescue her! Her heart filled with pride as their eyes met. *Be careful,* she thought. Nate was resourceful and stronger than even he realized. For the first time in days, she felt hopeful this nightmare would end.

But it wasn't over yet. She glanced back at Alex and wondered what Nate was planning to do. Had he heard the full exchange between the girl and the warlock? Had he learned the dark secret she had been keeping from him? She found the girl's intentions and motivations a mystery. She had suspicions concerning them—but what if she was wrong? Well—the truth would become clear soon enough.

In the meantime, she must keep Hodge's attention focused away from Nate, Corvin, and the spell. She had to buy them time in any way possible.

"Do you think Nate will give you the serpent if you kill his aunt?" asked Alex.

"We've moved past that, Alexandra," said Hodge. "We all know he can't remove it. The only option remaining is for me to take it—and to do so I'll need her magick."

Nate listened to the conversation between Alex and Hodge as he considered the best course of action. As much as he felt the need to act quickly, the safest solution—for everyone—would be for Mr. Black to complete the entrapment spell. Of course, if anyone saw the glowing witch's bottle, that plan could change in an instant. Fortunately, it was up high, and Hodge was too busy arguing with Alex to notice it.

He was glad Aunt Celia had spotted him. She didn't look in his direction again, no doubt to avoid calling attention to his location. Hopefully, she recognized the spell and would help draw Hodge's attention from it. At least she was now on alert and ready for whatever was about to follow.

"Why do you have to kill her if you can just drain and use her magick?" Alex asked. She gestured in Celia's direction.

"There are limits to that approach," Hodge said, shaking his head. "And even without magick, she's dangerous—do you propose I drag her around for all eternity, milking her like a cow? And what about the others? In addition to her, I'll need to absorb the magick of two other witches to become powerful enough to retrieve the serpent—and that's if I take their magick in its entirety, which requires death. I don't have the shards—not to mention the witches—to obtain enough power in any other way."

"Even if you kill Aunt Celia and Marc, you're still short one witch."

"Watch yourself, Alexandra—we both know where we can find a third."

A third witch? What was Hodge talking about? Nate was stunned.

"I won't let you hurt her. And stop calling me Alexandra!"

"Alex, it's OK," said Aunt Celia from her wooden prison. "He's going to do it—there's nothing you can do to stop him. He's a power-hungry coward. He's always preferred to target the defenseless—pulling strings behind the scenes to get others to do his dirty work. The hundreds of innocents he's condemned for his own personal gain . . . I was one of the few to ever stand up to him, and now that he has me in a vulnerable position, he'll never let me live. He's afraid of me."

"Shut up, Alice," said Hodge, glaring at her, his anger rising.

"You know it's true, Alex," said Aunt Celia, shifting her head in Alex's direction. "It's only a matter of time until he comes after you."

"Shut up. Shut up. Shut up!" Hodge slammed his staff on the ground, and the fireball doubled in size. His face was a mask of fury.

Aunt Celia was obviously going out of her way to piss off Hodge. Nate assumed it was to keep him preoccupied, to keep his attention focused away from the witch's bottle—but he hoped it didn't backfire. She was pushing his buttons, and he was growing more irate by the moment.

"Alex, what *did* happen to your mother?" Aunt Celia asked.

In a frenzy of rage, Hodge turned and aimed the tip of his staff toward Aunt Celia. The fireball shot out, exploding at her feet. Immediately, the base of the old wooden pillory began to burn.

Alex ran toward Hodge just as another fireball appeared atop his staff. She struggled to grab it, locking both hands on either side of his large fist. Hodge struck her across the face with his free hand, knocking her to the ground like a rag doll.

"Alex, no!" cried Nate as he leaped to his feet. Hodge and Alex were both clearly surprised by his sudden appearance. The serpent roared to life, sending a gout of flame at the warlock, hitting him in the chest and knocking him to the ground. The imp jumped to its feet, chittering as it hopped about its fallen master.

Nate ran to Aunt Celia's pillory. He could feel the heat of the rising flames as he reached for the pin that held the latch in place. The serpent's eyes glowed a demonic red as he lifted the upper plank, releasing her. His aunt tumbled free of the burning device, her lower pant legs ablaze. She began beating at them with a nearby scrap of fabric from the ruined movie screen, smothering the fire.

"Alex—are you OK?" Nate turned to her, his brows furrowed in concern. She lay on the floor where Hodge had left her, but she wasn't looking at him. She was looking at—

"Oh, my God . . ." she said, her eyes focused on the glowing witch's bottle at the rear of the auditorium.

"Alex?" He started toward her but stopped abruptly as she leaped to her feet.

Alex pulled back her sleeve, revealing the angry pattern of scars on her forearm. Nate watched in confusion as she raised her hand above her head. Her fist closed upon empty air, and yet as she pulled it back toward her torso, he saw it contained a large metal ring, the size of a Frisbee—and as black as the serpent.

With a quick dragging motion, the ring's sharp edge parted the flesh of her forearm, adding to the horrible collection of marks there—and as the dark metal made contact with her blood, it burst into flames.

Stunned, Nate watched Alex send the ring flying with a flick of the wrist. With a sharp clang, it ricocheted off a wall and changed direction. Alex's fiery disk was on a collision course with the glowing witch's bottle.

Almost there . . . thought Corvin.

> *Bona fide,*
> *Concilio et labore*

Something was going on in the auditorium below, but the spell was so close to completion that he didn't dare concentrate on anything else.

> *Coniunctis viribus,*
> *Consummatum—*

Suddenly the glowing mayonnaise jar before him split in two, spraying him with urine, vinegar, and the other ingredients. The magick dissipated as the flaming metallic object ricocheted around the room behind him. After several loud clangs it soared past him again, flying back through the window and into the auditorium beyond.

Corvin ran to the window in time to see the metal circlet return to

Alex's open hand. He recognized the weapon as a war quoit—and this one seemed made of black gold, like the witchfinder's serpent. He didn't understand what was happening. Was Alex a witch? Why would she have disrupted their spell? Was she somehow in league with Hodge?

He saw that Celia was free. She was dragging remnants of the old movie screen toward the burning pillory to snuff the flames. Nate had revealed himself and was standing there staring in shock at Alex, who stared back at him, her eyes wide, her mouth open.

He had failed. The spell had been unsuccessful, and they had no backup plan. Whatever happened next was going to be disastrous.

He saw Hodge slowly rising to his feet, the imp hopping about beside him. The warlock bent to retrieve his staff and suddenly, Corvin knew what he had to do. Hodge's magick was tied to that staff and as long as Hodge had it, Celia, Nate, and Marc didn't stand a chance. He had to get it away from the warlock—and he had to do it now before it was too late . . .

"Alex, what have you done?" cried Nate.

"Nate—I'm sorry," she said. She stepped slowly away from him. "I didn't mean for this to happen this way."

"Now you've done it, Alexandra," said Hodge, his face twisted in a sadistic grin. "Your boyfriend's upset."

"Who are you? *What* are you?" asked Nate, heartbroken and confused. He took a step toward her. "Are you a witch? Do you know this monster?" Nate glanced in Hodge's direction.

Alex said nothing. She stood there, the flaming circlet in her hand, looking ready to burst into tears. Nate wasn't sure what was happening, much less how he should feel about it.

"Are you working for him?" asked Nate. "Please say something—tell me what's going on. I trusted you. I welcomed you into our family. I—I loved you."

Alex continued backing slowly away, frowning and shaking her head, as though she had nothing to say. And the farther away she got from Nate, the closer she was getting to Hodge.

"Alex, come away from him," he said. "He's—"

A dark shape appeared out of the corner of his eye. He glanced up to see a large black bird flying in a graceful arc across the auditorium. Before his eyes, it changed course and dove directly toward Hodge and Alex.

As if by pure reflex, Alex let the flaming circlet fly. It intercepted the bird in midair, slicing through its wing like butter.

"Corvin!" Aunt Celia screamed. Nate was so preoccupied with Alex and Hodge, he had forgotten she was there.

The bird changed shape as it fell, enlarging and shifting, lightening in color, feathers disappearing into pink flesh. It struck the ground with a meaty thud. Horrified, Nate realized he was looking at the nude form of Mr. Black. Blood flowed from the biology teacher's upper arm where it had been severed, the amputated limb laying nearby.

Nate felt his senses closing in on him. Things were happening around him, but he felt somehow distant—not really there.

He saw Marc, free of his restraint, standing upright and confused next to the biology teacher's body.

He saw the smoldering wooden pillory, its flames now smothered, large remnants of the screen's fabric wadded around its base.

He saw Aunt Celia retrieving Mr. Black's severed arm, blood dripping from its end.

He saw Alex, sobbing on hands and knees, looking more anguished and despondent than he had ever seen her.

He saw Malleus Hodge reaching for Alex, grabbing her roughly by the arm, and dragging her backward toward the imp.

Nate forced his mind to clear—he didn't have the option of checking out. He had to focus, to act. It didn't matter what Alex had done. It was up to him to help them all.

"Alex, get away from him!" he yelled.

"I didn't know that was Mr. Black!" she said through her sobs. "I didn't know!"

"Let her go!" Nate yelled at the warlock.

"Congratulations, Nate," said Hodge with a smirk, maintaining his hold on Alex. "I think you've just surpassed your aunt as my biggest pain in the ass. I can't take the serpent from you—but I can stop you from taking *them* from me." Hodge nodded toward Aunt Celia and Marc, both of whom were attempting to help Mr. Black.

Hodge struck the ground with the heel of his staff, summoning the violet circle around himself, Alex, and the imp.

"I'm afraid they're just too troublesome to keep alive," he added.

Hodge brought his staff down a second time, and twin beams of electricity shot from the staff directly toward Aunt Celia and Marc. They began shaking involuntarily as soon as the magickal lightning reached them. Their bodies rose into the air and began floating toward the protective circle.

"Stop!" Nate cried. "You're killing them!"

"Yes, Nate—that's kind of the point," said Hodge.

Fueled by a sudden burst of rage, Nate willed the serpent to strike out at the warlock—and it responded. Torrents of flame shot toward Hodge, only to be deflected by the protective energies of the warlock's magick circle. Nate extinguished the flame with a thought, not wishing to set the theater ablaze. Once again, he was amazed by the serpent's sudden obedience.

"You're wasting your time, Nate," said Hodge. "No magick—not even the serpent's—can penetrate this field."

Nate glanced frantically toward Marc and Aunt Celia. They floated, suspended in midair, now just outside of the circle, the warlock's glowing beams of electricity surrounding their bodies. *They can't survive much more of this*, he thought, refusing to believe that it was already too late. Hodge must be stopped. But how? The serpent was unable to penetrate the field.

And yet . . . Hodge's magick was passing right through it!

Nate called on the serpent's power, this time targeting the crackling blue stream of energy that ran between the warlock's staff and his brother. The serpent responded immediately. Its magickal flame made contact, mingling with the staff's electric beam. With his mind, he guided the bracelet's fire toward the protective barrier, and again it obeyed. The serpent's fire rode the electric conduit, traveling with ease against the current, through the magickal shield and back to the witchfinder's staff.

As soon as the serpent's flame reached it, the staff overloaded in a blinding flash of light. The protective circle instantly fizzled out, and the beams vanished, releasing Nate's brother and aunt, dropping their trembling bodies limply to the floor. The staff's excess power shot skyward, punching through the ceiling in a shower of debris.

The warlock fell backward, his hand scorched and blistered from the power surge. His head struck the brick wall, knocking him unconscious, as the staff tumbled from his grasp. Alex, her eyes wide in fear, dodged the falling rubble in the nick of time. A heavy spike of jagged wood from the ceiling sliced through the air and embedded itself into the warlock's shoulder.

With a hideous shriek, the imp ran to its master and began hopping around Hodge's unconscious form. Then it started lapping at the blood seeping from the ugly wound. Alex stood nearby, looking stunned and horrified, her face damp with tears.

Nate ran to the unconscious forms of Marc and Aunt Celia, reassured to find pulses. He wasn't sure what kind of permanent damage Hodge's attack might have done to them, but at least they were alive. He ran over to Mr. Black. He too had a pulse. Aunt Celia had managed to slow the bleeding with a tourniquet made, apparently, from his brother's belt.

He turned to see Alex standing over the warlock's body, the staff grasped in both of her hands.

"Alex? Are you OK? What are you—" He stopped when he saw the expression on her face.

"Nate, I'm sorry. I can't do this anymore. He's right—there's no hope for us. Not after everything I've done. Not after everything *he's* done . . ."

"Alex, I don't understand." Nate longed to comfort her, wishing she would do the same. "What are you talking about?"

Alex glanced at the warlock.

"For as long as I can remember, I've longed to find my place in this world. I've tried to be my own person—a good person. I actually thought I might succeed this time. I made friends. I met you. And for the first time in my life, I actually stood up to him in a meaningful way. But when the time came—when it truly mattered, I just couldn't bear the idea of being permanently separated from him."

"From who? *Him?*" Nate asked in astonishment. He glanced at the unconscious warlock.

Alex nodded.

"That's why I stopped the spell. Malleus Hodge, former Witchfinder General and current public menace, is my father—and there is nothing I'll ever be able to do to escape that. I—I'm sorry."

Nate's mouth fell open in stunned silence. Before he could find the words to respond, Alex hefted the staff in her hands, bringing it down twice on the floor in front of her. She vanished in a circle of light, taking her wounded father and her father's hell beast along with her. Nate stood silent and unmoving as darkness returned to the auditorium of the old Plaza Theatre.

"Nate?" Marc said groggily from somewhere nearby.

Nate pulled out his phone and turned on the flashlight. Marc was sitting up, rubbing his eyes. Nate breathed a sigh of relief. His brother had survived.

"Where are we?" he asked.

Nate ran to him and placed a hand on his shoulder. "How do you feel?"

"Like my head is about to explode," said Marc with a frown. "What happened? Did I see Alex? Where's Hodge?"

"Shhh," he replied, reassuringly. "They're gone. Everything is fine. Everything is going to be fine." Nate saw that Aunt Celia, too, was stirring. He helped her into a sitting position.

"Thanks, Nate," she said, massaging her temples. "You did it. You saved us. Your father would be proud."

The words brought comfort to Nate, and a sense of joy. They *had* survived, and *he* had saved them.

"Hey, what about me?" said a voice. It was Mr. Black.

They stood and made their way to the biology teacher, still lying where he had fallen, the makeshift tourniquet around his severed stump. Aunt Celia crouched beside him, pressing her hand to his forehead.

"We have to get you home," she said. "But you'll be OK."

"What about his arm?" asked Nate, nodding toward the limb resting on the floor beside the biology teacher's body.

"Did Hodge do that?" asked Marc. His face made it clear he was grossed out at the sight.

Nate just nodded. When he was ready, he would tell his brother the full story, including Alex's involvement.

"Don't worry," said Aunt Celia. "We can fix that—but first we need to get back to the house."

Nate collected Mr. Black's clothing from the projection room, and then he and Aunt Celia prepared him for travel. She wrapped the severed arm in a scrap of movie screen. It wasn't the most sanitary way to transport it, but they couldn't risk anyone seeing it.

Supporting the biology teacher on either side, Nate and Marc helped him to his feet. They guided him through the old theater and out to his car. Aunt Celia carried the arm, placing it gently in the trunk. In moments, Mr. Black was buckled safely in the front passenger seat, and they were ready to go.

As Aunt Celia drove them home, Marc leaned over to his brother in the back seat.

"Hey," he whispered, his eyes wide. "I was wondering . . . why was Mr. Black . . . naked?!"

Nate responded in the only way he could in that moment.

He laughed.

Chapter 29

HOPE

"Alex is a witch?" asked Zach. His dark hair hung loose about his shoulders. "That's crazy, dude."

"Yeah," Nate nodded. He, Zach, Jenn, and Douglas stood straddling their bicycles on the town green. Across the street from them stood the abandoned theater where he and Mr. Black had rescued Aunt Celia and Marc earlier that afternoon. A young couple sat in front of the fountain on the green, holding hands. The street was quiet. Nate was wearing a fresh, unblemished shirt.

"But where did Alex *come* from?" asked Jenn, her brows furrowed. She brushed an unruly strand of brown curls behind her ear. "And where did they go?"

Nate shrugged. They were both good questions that he wasn't able to answer. "I don't know. But I'm sure we haven't seen the last of them."

"You beat them once," said Zach matter-of-factly. "And if they come back, you'll do it again. But next time, call us. We'll help." He gestured toward himself and the others as he spoke.

Jenn and Douglas nodded their agreement.

"Definitely," said Jenn. She smiled reassuringly.

"We'll be your Scooby gang," said Douglas, enthusiastically. "I'll be Shaggy, and Zach can be Velma."

"I'm definitely more of a Daphne," Zach responded with a straight face.

They all laughed. Nate was grateful for their support.

"Thanks, guys," said Nate. They were right. He had beaten Hodge this time, and he would do so again. And he had family and friends to help him do it.

A police car rounded the corner and pulled up along the curb beside them. The window was open. It was Officer Sam Foster. She waved at them as the vehicle rolled to a stop. Nate hadn't seen her since the funeral.

"Hey guys," she said. She looked at Nate. "Any word on your aunt?"

"As a matter of fact, she's home." He filled her in on the rescue, leaving out the parts about Mr. Black's avian history and Marc's magick. He hadn't told the others about those things yet, either.

"I'm glad she's safe," said Officer Foster. "There is still a lot of talk of witches around town, but maybe this is a sign that things are about to change."

"I sure hope so," he said.

After a moment, they said their goodbyes, and Officer Foster drove off down the street. They waved after her.

No sooner had the police cruiser disappeared than a trio of bicycles appeared, coming toward them in the opposite direction. They rode on the sidewalk, and Nate recognized the riders. It was Courtney and her crew, Kat and Kam. The blond and her two black-haired companions wore similar, expensive-looking sporting outfits with matching sneakers.

"What's *this* now?" Zach nodded toward the quickly approaching group.

"Coming through," Courtney called. She glanced at Jenn as they rode past, and Nate thought he saw Jenn wink in response. This was forgotten a moment later, however, when he saw the identical pink compound bows strapped to the girls' backs.

"Where are they off to dressed like *that*?" wondered Douglas. His gaze followed them as they continued down the sidewalk.

"Archery practice, of course," said Jenn.

They all turned and looked at her quizzically. She shrugged her shoulders.

"Archery practice?" asked Nate. "What for?" As far as he knew, Courtney was more of the indoor, sweat-will-ruin-my-makeup type of girl.

Jenn sighed. "You don't want to know," she said enigmatically, shaking her head. "Trust me—you really don't."

Nate resisted the urge to ask for an explanation. He wanted to get back home to check on Marc and Mr. Black. No one else pressed the issue, either.

The four friends said their goodbyes and each of them rode off in a different direction. As Nate headed down the road for home, he looked at the trees, which were full of new spring leaves. Colorful flowers bloomed and the lawns were green and healthy. He hadn't had the time to really consider it before, but he liked this town. Alex's betrayal was devastating, yet he felt at peace. *I'm lucky*, he thought. He had great friends, and his family was safe. Mr. Black was already on the mend thanks to Aunt Celia's herbal concoctions, and for the time being at least, they could relax.

But Malleus Hodge was still out there somewhere—and so was Alex. Nate knew the time would come when he would have to face them again, but when he did, he would have the support of family and friends.

Not to mention the witchfinder's serpent, he thought. He removed his left hand from the handlebar long enough to lift his sleeve. He glanced at his arm. The bracelet's eyes were dark and its body still, as it had remained since the rescue. When he had called on it at the theater, it had responded and obeyed. He was used to it now, and it seemed to be used to him.

The serpent's eyes chose that moment to burn a fiery red.

It agrees with me, thought Nate. He was not afraid, but rather amused by the bracelet's response.

Much had changed since that evening when the serpent had first attached itself to his arm. He still hoped someday to find a way to remove it. But in the meantime, he thought, for better or for worse, it was part of him.

And he was OK with that.

AUTHOR'S NOTE

Between the years 1644 and 1647, during a time of civil war, a witch hunter by the name of Matthew Hopkins traveled the English countryside with his partner, John Stearne. Proclaiming himself Witchfinder General—a title never bestowed upon him by Parliament—Hopkins took on the role of the country's "unofficial official" witch expert. Using questionable methods and means, he was responsible for the identification and execution of as many as 230 innocent men and women until his sudden forced retirement in 1647. Later that year, Matthew Hopkins died of an unspecified illness; he was only in his twenties.

In that same year, across the Atlantic, Alse Young of Windsor, Connecticut, became the first person in the American colonies to be hanged as a witch. Her execution on May 26, 1647, marked the beginning of a witch hysteria that would spread across Connecticut and into other colonies, culminating in the tragic events that took place in Salem, Massachusetts, some forty five years later. A second woman from Windsor, Lydia Gilbert, was convicted of practicing witchcraft on November 28, 1654, and was likely executed shortly thereafter.

The majority of the seventeenth-century characters in this novel were actual living people. This includes Matthew Hopkins and the residents of ancient Windsor, including Alse Young, her daughter, Alice Young Beamon, and Lydia Gilbert. The facts and backstories of the people portrayed in this novel draw on my research, but obviously other elements have been added for the sake of this fictional story. While most of the locations represented in modern-day Windsor exist, the town's inhabitants are 100 percent fictitious.

Did Matthew Hopkins really die in 1647? Could there have been real witches in colonial America? Those questions are for you to decide.

—Rande Goodwin, December 22, 2022

ACKNOWLEDGMENTS

The year 2020 was difficult for all of us. COVID-19 turned the world on its head, with most of us having to isolate in our homes for what seemed like an eternity. With office buildings closed, my wife Beth and I found ourselves working out of our basement full time. My daughter Sarah spent her sophomore year of college in her bedroom, staring at a computer screen. My daughter Emily, like her sister before her, finished twelfth grade at the top of her class—without ever stepping foot into the high school.

It was a frightening time with case counts on the rise and no end in sight. As we waited for the world's scientists to develop a vaccine, American politics reached a low point. Facts became fantasy and vice versa, depending upon which news channel you watched or whose social media you followed.

I wrote the first two books in this series during the COVID isolation period; the project provided an escape for me, a way to leave the house without leaving the house. I purposely set the modern-day story elements in 2019, figuring Nate and his friends had enough to deal with without the added burden of masks and social distancing.

The town of Windsor, Connecticut, where I grew up, provided a fascinating locale for my story. As an early New England settlement and the home of America's first witch-hanging victim, the setting was ripe with possibilities. When writing the historical passages, it was important to me to treat Alse Young and her family with the utmost respect. They were innocent victims of the times and should be remembered as such.

I'd like to thank Steve Alten, best-selling author of the Meg series, for acting as my writing coach during this project. Thanks to Peter David, best-selling author and self-proclaimed Writer of Stuff, for reviewing my work. Thanks as well to David Endris, Tyler LeBleu, Morgan Robinson, Anne Sanow, Brian Welch, Mimi Bark, Trish Lockard, Danielle Green, and the other people at Greenleaf Book Group who made the publishing process interesting and stress-free. Love and appreciation to my family for all their support and encouragement.

If you are interested in the story of Alse Young, I'd recommend reading Beth M. Caruso's well-researched historical novel, *One of Windsor: The Untold Story of America's First Witch Hanging*.

About the Author

RANDE GOODWIN is a full-time IT professional and part-time raptor trainer (the prehistoric kind). In his free time, he enjoys reading and travel, restoring vintage Borg drones, dusting vamps in Sunnydale, and being one with the Force. Oh, and writing is fun, too. He lives in New England with his wife, two daughters, and four dogs. *The Witchfinder's Serpent* is his first novel. See what he's up to at www.randegoodwin.com.